DRUID DREAMS

THE CHRONICLES OF SLOANE KING

1

Copyright © 2020 M.F. Adele

All rights reserved. No part of this book may be reproduced in any form or any electronic or mechanical means, including information storage and retrieval systems, without written permission from the author, except for the use of brief quotations in a book review.

This is a work of fiction. All names, characters, places, businesses, incidents, and events are either used in a fictitious manner or stem from the author's imagination. Any resemblance to real events or real people, living or dead, is entirely coincidental.

Cover design by:
Claire at Luminescence Covers

Editing by:
Kaye Kemp Book Polishing

Published by:
Langston Press, LLC

Latest Content Update:
February 14, 2023

CONTENTS

Disclaimer	v
Prologue	1
1. Sloane	11
2. Vaughn	27
3. Sloane	39
4. Sloane	57
5. Vaughn	71
6. Vaughn	85
7. Novak	99
8. Sloane	123
9. Palmer	147
10. Briggs	161
11. Sloane	175
12. Novak	191
13. York	205
14. Sloane	221
15. Sloane	237
16. Sloane	249
17. Stone	267
18. Sloane	287
19. Briggs	301
20. York	315
21. Palmer	327
22. Sloane	343
23. Stone	359
24. Sloane	375
25. York	393
26. Sloane	413

27. Sloane	427
28. Sloane	443
Epilogue	461
Character Information	471
More PNR by MF Adele	475
Contemporary by MF Adele	476
Co-writes with MF Adele	477
About the Author	479
Author's Note	481

DISCLAIMER

<u>This paranormal reverse harem romance is intended for mature audiences only.</u>

Druid Dreams is the first book in the seven-book series, **The Chronicles of Sloane King**.

<u>This is a *series-wide disclaimer* for **The Chronicles of Sloane King**.</u>

Current books include: explicit language, murder, blood, graphic violence, controversial religious beliefs, BDSM scenes, and MM scenes.

Current books include *mentions* of: child abuse, rape, drugs, domestic violence, suicide, and open relationships.

Disclaimer

If any of the scenarios listed above trigger or offend you, please do not read this series. If you have any questions about content, please contact me for clarification.

AuthorMFAdele@gmail.com

To all the closet badasses out there...
Girl, I see you, and I fucking love it.
This is for you.

I hope you always have the courage to be true to yourself.
No matter what day it is, what obstacles you face, or how many of those pesky emotions you battle, always be yourself.
Unapologetically and wholeheartedly.

MATE MARKS

Sloane
York
Novak
Stone

MATE MARKS

Briggs

Palmer

Vaughn

THE DEVIL'S SEAL

PROLOGUE

York

Five Years Ago

I ambled down the path from the river after washing off, and I thought about how much I hated this place. *I've been here for years.* It was time to go... but they'd never just let me leave.

"It's time for my disappearance," I whispered to the trees.

The branches swayed in answer, telling me they'd help however they could. They weren't the same trees from my kingdom, but they knew a druid when they felt one standing among them. They sensed my power and my connection to nature.

I headed to my tent to load up my backpack. I wanted

everything ready for when I made my escape tonight. I didn't care about the clothes or other nonsense I'd collected—those things were replaceable—but I did care about a few precious items that I kept buried in the earth under my tent.

Things I'd need when I found a companion. Things needed to reclaim my kingdom. Things that would prove my birthright.

I heard Kelvin roar my name in the distance. That meant he was heading this way. That also meant packing would have to wait a couple hours.

That's probably for the best. I don't want them to catch on.

I snatched a ratty t-shirt from the pile in the corner of my tent and walked out to meet him. He was in charge. It would be best to keep him happy.

"We have a new prisoner. They just brought her in. I think she's the one, York. This is the hybrid bitch I've been looking for." He was joyous with his latest catch.

His mood had me despising him even more. I didn't sign up for this shit, but I'd go along with it until I could get away.

This is my last night here. I can make it through this.

"That's awesome news, Kelvin." I faked an exuberance that I definitely didn't feel as I spoke with him. "What are we gonna do with her?"

"Toss her down in the dungeon with the Fae King, my boy. They can find company with each other until we kill him. We have no need for him anymore, not after finding her. The power she holds in her bones is more than you can even imagine. She's got a greater amount of power in her pinkie finger than that ungrateful fucking Fae had in his whole body. We'll use the rest of him, though, and then start draining her."

He was so giddy that I grew physically ill. My stomach rolled with sour distaste. My mind revolted against his plans, urging me to run.

I hustled off to grab her before one of the other guys came around and spotted an unconscious woman facedown in the dirt. When I rounded the corner, they were already scoping her out. Their comments sickened me more than Kelvin's.

"Think Ol' Kev will let us get a piece of the action, or keep her all to himself?"

"Nah, man, I plan on fucking her either way."

"She's soft right now, but after a couple weeks here she'll be too hard to get a reaction from. It won't be as fun to knock her around."

"What's wrong, bitch? Don't you want to play with us?"

When I got close enough to see her, I noticed that her eyes were open. She had fury written all over her face.

The moment her raging multi-colored irises locked on mine, my steps faltered. Her eyes widened the tiniest bit, giving nothing away to the men surrounding her. I knew she sensed it too.

But surely not...
It can't be.
I'd heard about this feeling, but druids did not have mates. My race procreated for power and status.

There was no mistaking that feeling, though. My heart raced, my vision tunneling until I could see nothing except her. I wanted to murder every one of those guys drooling over her while she was vulnerable, but I had to reel in my emotions so I didn't give anything away.

I memorized all their faces, for I knew I'd kill them before I tried to leave this place. I wasn't leaving without her, though. I'd have to push my plans back.

Just one more day.

Then we were both getting out.

I pushed my way through the pigs and gently scooped her up. I didn't want to aggravate any injuries she may have had, but I needed to get her away from them.

Away. Space. Privacy.

All I could think about was plotting their murder as I made my way to the dungeon. The steps went on and on. It seemed like it took forever before I finally had her shielded from prying eyes.

I refused to stop, not until I managed to get her behind closed doors. There were only a few of us permitted to be down here, so she'd be safer in a cell than anywhere in the camp. I just had to find a way to keep Kelvin from coming near her.

I strode into the one room that was not a cell and sat her gently on the medical table within. She was seething mad. I could feel the heat of her anger. I knew if I removed those cuffs on her wrists, I'd be dead before I pulled the key out.

I couldn't chance it.

Prologue

I needed to talk to her.

"Did you feel it?" I questioned, and it sounded so fucking stupid when I said it aloud.

I should've thought of a better way to ask, but I couldn't think straight so close to her. She nodded her head, and I waited for her to speak.

"Are you going to talk?" I finally inquired after minutes of silence.

She eyeballed me like I was as stupid as I felt before arching a delicate brow and looking down with crossed eyes towards her mouth.

"Right." *Right, her mouth was taped.*

I needed to get a grip. I had to get us both out of this death sentence. I knew without really knowing her that I'd die before I let them harm her.

"I don't want to hurt you," I proclaimed.

She rolled her gold and green eyes at me. *Okay.*

"I'll just snatch it off like a Band-Aid. Are you ready?"

She nodded once in answer. I reached up to peel the corner back before snatching the tape as quickly as I could.

"Fuck," she quietly snarled. "I'm going to kill those bastards. Make sure you stay the fuck out of my way."

Wow. My eyebrows nearly hit my hairline.

"I know you're angry, Sweetheart, but we gotta play this smart. Okay?" I prodded around her pride as gently as I could. She glared at me, never breaking eye contact as she breathed deeply to calm herself.

"Put me in the cell. I'll hang out for two days, then

I'm gone. I have a few guys to kill on my way out, so if you have anyone you want to add to my list, tell me now. Then stay the fuck away from me until you want to get out. I don't have time to be coddled," she warned.

Oh, she's feisty. This should be fun.

"Where are you hurt?" I changed the subject in hopes that it would calm her.

I needed to know. I couldn't leave her down here if she was hurt, and I knew she was. There was blood on the side of her head. It had soaked right through her shirt, making the fabric stick to her skin. The blood wasn't hard to see on the black cloth under the bright overhead lights. Her shirt shone, giving the appearance that the surface was metallic.

"No." Her response was clipped. She didn't trust me, but I could work with that.

When I extended my hand towards her, she didn't flinch. She stared uncaring at me.

"York Briar, it's nice to finally meet you..." I trailed off, hoping for her name. As soon as I got her out of this place and we were safe, she would be gone.

I needed to know how to find her after she disappeared. I wanted to know her and make a life with her. It was a strange feeling for me.

She was gorgeous, even covered in blood and dirt, and... was that skin? *I don't know if I wanted to know what it was. I just wanted to know her name.*

"Sloane," she replied, finally accepting my hand.

She wasn't as fragile as she appeared. Her handshake was strong and almost professional. She didn't add a last name, and I wouldn't push her for one either.

Not yet.

"Right this way then, Sweetheart," I announced as I turned and made my way to the door.

I didn't feel threatened with her at my back. *She wouldn't hurt me.* I couldn't say that about the rest of the guys in the camp, though.

She hopped off the table and strolled leisurely behind me, like she was being escorted to a hotel room rather than a cell.

She didn't say a word as I opened the door and closed it after she walked through. I led the way down the hall to the cells, and I opened the metal door for her, closing it softly when she spun around to face me. She nodded her head reassuringly at me but didn't utter another sound.

"The Fae King is on his deathbed. You may want to plan your escape sooner than two days. The full moon will happen then and they'll want to drain you both," I whispered the warning to her.

My words were so quiet I wasn't sure she heard me until she bobbed her head the slightest bit. She was composed and eerily confident.

I found it to be a little worrisome. *If I was being honest. Why wasn't she scared?*

That's my mate. I thought about Sloane one last time and shut down the raging river of questions I had about her.

I built my mental shield tighter and went searching for Kelvin. I'd let him know she was in the cell, but still unconscious. It should buy her a couple of hours before he came down to assess the king and interrogate her.

I wanted to keep her safe, and I only knew one way to do that.

As I walked across the hall to the Fae King's cell, I knew it was time to strike a deal. I couldn't save his life, but I could give him something that would ensure he erased the last couple hours of her memory.

And that he kept it wiped clean until he died.

I'd let him call his son one last time before they came to drain what was left of his power. It was all I could do for him in this situation. Even if it *was* risky, the benefits were worth it.

Kelvin would try to invade her mind. He'd know that she knew I was her mate and he would use it against her.

I couldn't be her weakness, but I could give her this to strengthen her while she was captive.

I would find her again. I wouldn't lose her.

It felt like there was a thread in my chest that would lead me straight to her now that I'd found her. I planned to follow it, wherever it led.

I'd follow her to the depths of hell. It seemed like an irrational thought, but I knew it to be true.

I must keep her safe.

CHAPTER 1
Sloane

Thursday, May 14th
Late Night

"Cheers, bitch!" The handsome male to my right slammed his beer bottle against the top of mine, making it foam and spill from the top. I watched as the cold liquid ran over my left hand.

I wasn't really in a celebratory mood, but Jack dragged me out of my house tonight to be his wing woman.

I would usually call Jack my best friend. *Tonight, I hated him.* He pulled me from my cluttered study to bring me to a grimy bar so he could hit on some straight guys while his boyfriend was working.

They had a thing. An agreement of sorts. It was what he did on his nights off. *I didn't have time for nights off.* I had shit to do, an inch thick contract to read through and about a dozen new reports of missing supes.

The hole-in-the-wall bar wasn't really my style either. The sticky floor made me want to toss my boots in the trash before I put my feet back in my car.

The music was terrible. The bartender couldn't make a drink with more than two ingredients. The patrons were loud, angry, and obnoxious.

I sighed audibly as I thought about how badly I loathed this place. Jack directed his glare at me with so much ire I honestly thought he might tell me to go home. *I had my fingers crossed. Literally.*

"Lo," he groaned. "If you didn't want to come, then you should've said no."

"I did. You told me no wasn't an option. Then, you slung me over your shoulder and tossed me in my own car." I cut my eyes at him in a hard stare. He huffed before he snatched my hand, dragging me to the bathroom.

Oh gods. The bathroom. The place was a breeding ground for infections.

Again, the sticky floor followed me all the way through the bar into the stall Jack had us crammed in.

I was pretty sure the toilets didn't work. It didn't matter. We weren't in here to use them. We were here so Jack could chew me out over my bad attitude.

Attitude adjustment in 3... 2....

"Sloane," he snapped at me, gaining my attention as I

tried real fucking hard not to touch a single thing in this three foot wide space. *Gross.*

"Just one night. One fucking night. Stop thinking about work. Any of it! Drink a fucking beer with me and then go hustle some assholes over poker in the back room or something. Why don't you flirt a little? Find a one-night stand? Your dry spell is killing us both. You need to get laid, bitch. That's why you're so stressed all the time."

I gawked at him for a solid minute. *It hadn't been that long since I'd had sex.* He was being ridiculous. I'd let him throw his little tantrum. Then I was going home in exactly one hour. *For real, I was going to time this shit.*

"It has been that long," he called me out incredulously. "You've had a few flings and one short relationship, if you can even call it that, since that asshole druid left you. That was two fucking years ago!" His voice rose a little at the end.

I knew he hated throwing that in my face, but it was his last resort. *And... Well, it was true. Godsdammit.*

"Fine. I'll stay for an hour. Then I'm going home to finish my work, Jack. I have a meeting in the morning and I need to be prepared." I rolled my eyes at myself. *I'd become really lame, I know.*

"Okay," Jack conceded. "One hour then you can go home and be boring all by yourself. But drink with me while you're here, at least," he whined and tugged on my hand.

"Fine," I conceded as he led me back out of the bathroom.

Thank the Devil. That stall was making me itch. He

was right, though. He happened to always be right when it came to me.

I did need to loosen up a little and have some fun.

I walked up to the bar and ordered four shots of chilled, top-shelf tequila with salt and limes. *Dressed, I wanted dressed shots.* Surely the bartender could handle that.

Everything else I'd ordered since we'd been here had been way too sweet. Basically pure sugar poured over liquor, and it was fucking disgusting.

As I waited for my shots, I gave the filthy bar a good look. There were a few pool tables spaced sporadically around the open area. The thought of hustling some alphas out of their money made me happy. Maybe the night wouldn't be a total waste.

When I looked back to the bar-top, there were four shots of cool, *yes cool*, tequila sitting in front of me. *Not chilled.* He didn't shake them. He'd just pulled the bottle from the cooler and poured them straight into the filmy shot glasses. I supposed a clean glass would be too much to ask for in this shit hole. *Whatever.*

I tossed them all back. Back to back. The bartender raised a bushy eyebrow at me and I smiled innocently as I ordered four more. *I'll share these with Jack.*

When I got to our table and hoisted myself up on the high stool, Jack looked at me with a mischievous grin on his face. *Drunk Jack was fun, but also the worst.*

"See that hunky, tattooed, lumberjack guy over there?" He described almost every male in the bar to me with a tilt of his head. "I'm taking him home tonight. I bet he likes bottom."

"Gods, Jack, don't even try! He's been hitting on that tiny she-wolf all night." I had no idea who he was talking about, but call it a hunch.

"Biiiiitch," he slurred, "that she-wolf has nothing on my big, horse d—" I slapped my hand over his mouth.

I did not want any *more* images swimming around my head and ruining the tipsy state that I'd spent so much money on tonight. *I needed like six more shots before I might be able to forget what he was about to say.*

Jack and I weaved our way back to the bar, abandoning our table so we could really get the night going. I downed a couple more shots while searching for the bartender again.

When he popped back in from his smoke break, I requested tequila in a clean glass, with ice that was—hopefully—from a clean ice machine.

Okay, let's get real. It was all dirty. I knew it was. I'd just have to suck it up and take some antibiotics when I got home.

Problem solved.
Just kidding.
Kinda.

"You have fun with that. I'm going to go play darts with those guys over there. They look pretty good, but I wonder if they like to gamble." I smirked at him as I eased away from the bar with my drink.

They saw me coming from across the room. With

eyes locked on me, they stalked me like the predators they were, not sensing that I was the bigger predator. *Yet.*

That's cute. They didn't know they were my prey.

I threw a few hundred-dollar bills on the table where they had their drinks and began flirting in my most sultry voice. "You boys up for a little fun? I've got a bill for each male who can beat me."

Take the bait, boys. Take the bait.

I made eye contact with each one, smirk still held firmly in place, and waited for them to make a decision. They all bobbed their heads and the leader of their little pack stepped up.

"Do you know how to play, or are we just gonna be taking your daddy's money? Not that I mind. This bar is no place for a prissy little rich cunt or that faggot you came in with."

Ha. Ha. Jack would eat them alive.

I smiled brightly and let my canines elongate. They'd underestimate me if they thought I was just a shifter female.

Without missing a beat, the condescending reply slipped beyond my full lips in a velvety voice, "Oh, Daddy, show me how to lose, and then maybe you can teach me to submit."

I pouted a little for that *extra* effect. They didn't notice my attitude at all.

I wanted to pat myself on the back for hustling them so effortlessly. I lost the first game on purpose, then dominated the next five before they seemed to figure out I was hustling them.

When they couldn't pay me anymore, I decided to make them strip in the middle of the bar.

"Strip boys. You owe this rich cunt money so I'll be taking your shit. Have fun covering your tab."

I gave them a sweet finger wave and strutted to the bar to pay my own tab with the money I had just won off them.

Fuuuuck them. I would have paid their tabs too. If they hadn't called Jack a faggot.

All in all... it was a good night. I did a fuck load of flirting with those burly shifters during the games we played. I left the bar and went home alone, which wasn't anything unusual for me.

Jack went home with that male I was sure wasn't into other males, even though I had no idea which one he was talking about. That was his favorite drinking game, though. So again, not that crazy for a night out with Jack.

When I roused the next morning, it was 10 a.m. and my alarm clock was screaming at me. I had a headache from hell and someone was banging on my bedroom door.

Lovely. Just fucking lovely.

Whoever it was could wait. I needed to get dressed. I

was in a foul mood and missing coffee. I had *not* rested well after coming home a few hours ago.

I didn't need a ton of sleep, or really any at all, but resting my body was normally a good refresher.

It wasn't this morning. I had the same nightmare of a memory that I got whenever I drank too much. It wasn't some made up shit in my head like a regular nightmare, either. It was the past, and it liked to come back to bite me in the ass when I least expected it.

I just wished I could remember everything instead of that one scene. There were some things missing, but after years of the same dreamlike situation, nothing new ever appeared.

*C**old, damp stone floor touches my cheek as my eyes crack open. My head is killing me and I know there's a large gash behind my right ear. I feel the wound throbbing and my blood still leaking into my hair.*

Why hasn't it healed yet? It should've healed by now. Is it new?

I slowly sit up to look around, trying to get my bearings to see where I am or if anyone is nearby, but all I see are stone walls dripping with water. A mossy looking substance covers parts of the walls where the water drips down.

Algae*?*

It smells like dirty water, not the ocean. That sort of helps me narrow down the location. Not by much, though.

I close my eyes and try to focus more on my heightened sense of smell.

I can smell that people have been down here every couple of hours. Wherever here is. The scents meld together, but I can pick out four different people. Maybe five. One is familiar, but I can't place it. It's too faint.

I know I'm under the ground near water or under the water, but I can't catch much of anything else. No trees, no grass, no dirt. No exhaust from the city factories or cars.

Well, there is one more thing I become aware of as I sniff the rancid, moldy air around me.

Death*. New and close by.*

I pop my eyes back open and scan the cell I'm in. No one else is here with me. Then I walk to the bars and scan the cell across from me.

There*.*

In the back left corner of the cell across from me is a body. His arms and legs lay in odd angles while his back rests in a pool of blood on the stone floor.

His face is looking in my direction, but he's looking past me. Long, dark gray hair is matted together with the blood around his body. It's still draining down his face from his nose and eyes.

His ice blue irises are cloudy and lifeless. He died

terrified, but for himself or for someone else? **I don't know.**

I argue with myself, but ultimately decide I need to take a closer look.

As I fade through the bars in front of me, I hear a door open to my right. Heavy boots pound on the stairs, taking them two at a time.

I twist and back myself through the dead guy's cell bars while keeping my eyes focused in the direction of the incoming male. I don't fade back into sight. I stay hidden from the threat.

The male with the loud footsteps comes into view, peeking into my cell. He's the familiar smell I noticed a moment ago, but who is he?

"I know you're in here somewhere, Sweetheart. Come out, come out, wherever you are....." *he calls quietly to me.*

Why is he looking for me?

I silently pad over to the dead male and look him over. I find nothing. Nothing except his eyes. They look familiar, too. Have I seen this man before? Or maybe I'll meet him soon. How did he get here and how did he die?

"Damn it, Sloane," *the man with the familiar scent whispers frantically.* "Where did you go? I need to get you out of here while they still trust me. We talked about this last night. It's time to go."

Yeah, maybe we did, but that last blow to my head won't let me remember anything before waking up. I don't know who this man is or what he wants with me.

My heart aches a little when I decide it's time for me

to leave. They may have caught me, but they'll never keep me in that cell. It's time to run.

I'll come back to fight another day.

As I was saying, I didn't *need* to sleep, but I did like to rest my body and meditate for a couple of hours every night or morning.

Or whenever I got the chance.

It helped me in honing my Sight ability and let me relax after, uhm, stressful nights. Jack would say masturbation worked the same as meditation, but it didn't.

Definitely was not the fucking same.

When I hadn't been drinking, the premonitions were typically helpful. I could see the future of people, and sometimes the past. I only needed to touch them once to get more than a glimpse into their lives. I saw too much sometimes, but it was why I was so good at my job.

Or jobsss. Plural. Two out of three, anyway.

During the regular waking hours, I helped run a billion dollar holdings company. A company owned by my Dad.

Well, one of my dads. I had three of those, too.

They were all exceptional males. They'd raised me well and spoiled me rotten since I was the only child they got to have together before my mother disappeared.

My life got a little complicated when explaining that I had three male parents. Usually people thought I was joking. *But I wasn't.*

My mother was a powerful mage of royal descent, and she had three mates. Together they united kingdoms. Blah, blah, blah... It was a really romantic story, the way they met and fell in love with the same woman.

Honestly, it made me a little queasy every time I heard it. *They were my parents!! Gross.*

Basically, I was a hybrid. The best qualities from all their genes, all thanks to my mother's mage magic. *Yeah, thanks, Mom.*

People flocked away from me because they thought I was an abomination. I shouldn't have been created, let alone born... You know, the same old shit people said and did when something was different and they couldn't understand or explain it.

Another knock at my door had me pausing on the pity party of my life. Franklin—the chauffeur my father, Charles, hired—was standing on the other side of my bedroom door. He was a wiry vampire with a kind smile and a gentle voice. He looked more like a grandfather than a vampire, but looks could be deceiving.

"Madam, I've been trying to reach you for an hour. You have a meeting in thirty minutes and we have a twenty minute drive." He kept eye contact with me while he spoke.

Normally I loved it because so few people could maintain eye contact with me. Most glanced at my eyes for a moment before averting their gaze, either looking at my chest or anywhere else.

Something about the way Franklin was looking around had me wondering if he was alright, though.

"I'll be down in a moment!" I shouted as I scanned my desk for the contract I needed today.

Got it. I rushed downstairs in a flash of movement, but couldn't quite shake the feeling that I had forgotten something.

Where was my purse?

"We need to go," Franklin called from the doorway.

"Okay, let me grab my purse," I agreed as I rummaged around the foyer for it. I didn't see it. There was no telling where it went since I stumbled in at 6:30 this morning, still drunk from my first night off in a month.

I was still a little buzzed, if I was being honest. I needed to eat something so I could sober up before I went into this meeting.

Franklin cleared his throat, making it clear that he was uncomfortable. "Maybe you should put on some clothes and skip the purse for today?"

He looked towards the ceiling to avoid me, and a faint smile touched his lips. "I seem to have found your bag, Madam."

I peered up, and sure enough, there was my purse. Hanging from the chandelier. I rubbed my hand down my face, feeling a smidgen of embarrassment. It must have been a hell of a night since I didn't remember all of it.

Franklin cleared his throat again and bowed his head as he informed me he was leaving the room. "I'll bring the car around. We need to leave in five minutes or you're going to be late to your meeting with Mr. Rigid and his son."

Right. Fuck.

Mr. Rigid, as Franklin and I liked to call him, was really Ronald Caplin. He happened to be one of the owners of Caplin Bowers Pharmaceuticals. Today I was supposed to be meeting him to finish the negotiations for buying his company.

I slapped myself on the forehead while I scrutinized myself in the mirror to my right. That's when I saw it, and Franklin's words finally clicked.

Holy... what the fuck!? I AM naked. Shit, shit, shit.

With a quick snap of my fingers, and a silent thanks to my mom for giving me the magic I so often cursed, I took another quick glance in the mirror before rushing out the door to the waiting car.

The sooner I could get this meeting over with, the quicker my day would end and my night would begin. *One of my other jobs.*

CHAPTER 2
VAUGHN

Friday, May 15th
Midday

I stood facing the mirror and scowled at myself while I straightened my tie. *I hated wearing ties.*

"This is ridiculously absurd," I muttered to myself.

Today the company that I worked for was being sold. Sold for an obscene amount of money. I rolled my icy blue eyes in disgust. I couldn't believe I had to parade around for a new owner instead of catching up on all the bullshit paperwork I had sitting on my desk.

I heard what the previous owner of the company was asking for. We'd all heard. We'd also heard that the woman who came in to do the negotiations was a stickler and didn't give them the over-priced amount they were asking for.

It was hard to put a price on a pharmaceutical company; I got it, but the man was asking for billions. Literally. I mean, the company just wasn't that big yet. Maybe in the hundred millions, but billions? No way.

I knew the son of one of the owners had screwed up the negotiations somehow. That thought made the side of my lip curl up a bit. He was always a dick.

I'm sure he thought he could hit on her and get what he wanted.

That was Taylor's usual MO. He'd throw a few lines out and expect to reel a woman in with his daddy's money making his pockets look fat.

Let's be honest. He liked THOTs. You know? That ho over there. The easier they were, the more he liked them. *Whatever floats his boat.* I was sure this woman wouldn't fall for his shit, though.

I was slightly apprehensive about meeting the new owner, or the new owner's daughter, I should say. She'd be coming in today to do a walkthrough after their meeting wrapped up. Which meant there would probably be budget cuts and firing sprees in the near future. I had worked too hard to get to my position, and I was not ready to give that up.

I stood by the window and sighed as I looked out over the floor that I managed. *Five years in this company, five years kissing ass and moving up the ladder.* It could all come crumbling down after the buyout. I didn't need the actual job so much as I needed the intel from within the walls.

As I scanned the floor, I noticed some frenzied movement near the sixth aisle. *Fuck*. I'd bet Susan came in drunk again today. Of all the days to have visible fuck ups, today was definitely not the one.

Sighing again, I opened my office door and trotted down the stairs. My paperwork and inventory checks would have to wait until later. I needed to send this lady home, or to a rehab facility.

The latter would be the best option. I couldn't fire her today, but I also couldn't have her on the line messing up the sorting rotation or dropping the pills. So that would have to wait until Monday.

I'd have to make sure to ask the new boss before I did it. I didn't know if I'd still have that authority in my job description after today.

I approached the red-headed woman in question and her neighboring coworker, John. He gave me an apologetic smile. He knew today was the worst kind of day for her mistakes.

I tapped her on the shoulder as politely as I could and said in the most gentle voice I could muster, "Susan, I think you should go home."

She reeked of alcohol so strongly that I wondered if she'd been bathing in it. The smell flared through my nostrils, making me nearly gag. It was cheap whiskey and cigarette smoke.

She was probably wearing the same clothes that she wore last night under her white lab coat. If her strappy silver heels were anything to go by, I'd say she was wearing a short, glittery dress she'd found in the prom section of a local thrift shop. It was just an educated guess based on past experiences with her, though.

She glanced up at me with dark, bloodshot eyes and batted her eyelashes. What was left of her makeup was smudged across her face. Mascara flaked off her sparse eyelashes onto her sunken cheeks. Lipstick smeared on the edges of her thin lips.

She was a fucking mess. I had to fight not to roll my eyes.

"Sir, I'll be fine. I just lost my balance and needed a hand," she slurred in what I thought was meant to be a flirtatious tone. Her voice came out thick and rough from years of smoking.

Right. Sure she did.

From over her shoulder, John shook his head. He was done with her antics too. She still had a buzz from her night out.

"Susan," I addressed her a little more sternly to take her attention off my covered body and bring it back to my face. "I need you to get off the floor. You have to go home. We're expecting visitors today and I cannot afford you causing any sort of commotion. Please leave. We'll talk about this on Monday morning."

I didn't give her a chance to say anything else. I needed no more excuses from her.

Turning, I exhaustedly muttered to John, "Would you mind walking her to the back to gather her things? I'll call a cab to pick her up at the back exit." I was already fishing my cell phone from my pocket as I spoke.

Today would've been easier if she'd have skipped work. *Great.* Now I'd be meeting the new owner *and* covering Susan's shift. *What a fan-fucking-tastic Friday.* I thought through all the times I should have fired Susan as I mindlessly started sifting through pills.

John came back a few minutes later and thanked me as he took his position back on the line. He was a wise older gentleman who should be doing my job but said he didn't want the added stress. I hadn't quite understood what he'd meant at the time, but I damn sure did now.

I was twenty minutes in on the line work when I heard the creaking of the large double doors on the other side of the factory floor open. We never opened both doors, so I hadn't felt the need to request for maintenance to fix the hinges on the unused door. I'd add that to my to-do list after hearing the heinous noise, though.

It was showtime, I guess.

Sort of....

Taylor Caplin, the previous owner's son, was escorting a woman in, standing a little too close to her for propriety's sake. He was the definition of a scumbag. He had nearly black hair that was gelled back, a patchy goatee, and a greasy grin.

The guy had always rubbed me the wrong way. *And not just because of the way he looked.*

Last June I came nose to nose with him in a bar downtown. I wanted to beat his ass but didn't want to lose my job. He took my date home that night, but not before I ran his tab up.

Petty, I know... but that's what happened when you were friends with the bartenders.

Free drinks for everyone all night, courtesy of dicks-for-brains. That shit still made me grin.

I couldn't see her well, though I could hear her edgy tone politely telling Taylor off. "You can let go of my elbow now. I can walk unassisted on concrete flooring. Thanks."

I ground my teeth together after hearing the revulsion in her rasping, musical voice. "I just didn't want you to slip in those heels you're wearing. Sometimes it happens." Taylor's tone grated on every nerve in my body.

Have I mentioned how much I disliked him?

The sound of his slimy voice made me want to crawl out of my skin for a moment. I couldn't imagine how she felt with him touching her.

He didn't want to let her go, and she didn't sound too happy about it. With my sensitive hearing, I picked up on the growl she gave him as she snatched her arm away, making him stumble forward.

"I see what you mean. Must be hard to maneuver over these slick concrete floors wearing your heels." She said it so sarcastically that I had to fight to keep the grin off my face.

His dress shoes did have a bit of a heel on them. It still didn't make him tall enough to look me in the eyes, but I bet he wished he could. It's the only reason why he leaned over my desk when he spoke to me. He wanted to feel superior.

He wasn't. But... whatever helped him sleep at night.

She was getting closer. I heard each footstep she took, even though her steps were near silent. There was no clicking of her heels on the concrete. It seemed like she was gliding as she slowly made her way to the end of the aisles.

I counted every stop she made to greet the workers, listening to their heartbeats speed up in her presence. It was easy to pick up on the smile in her voice as she acknowledged them, like they were *real people* and not beneath her. Maybe she wouldn't be so bad.

And then she was close enough to see. I had to swallow hard when my throat suddenly dried. She turned a sharp eye to me and headed in my direction like she already knew who I was.

When her eyes locked on mine, I felt an insane pull. I'd never experienced anything like it before.

She stood at 6'2" or so, easily matching my exact height. I knew those killer "fuck me" pumps she walked so effortlessly in were giving her a good five inch boost. They helped her radiate that professional "don't fuck with me" attitude. She'd need it around the assholes in this company.

She extended a hand to me with her introduction. I couldn't help but watch her lips move as she spoke. My lack of attention nearly made me miss her hand completely.

Her lips, though. They were blood red and designed

with perfection in mind. The V shape of her jawline made me wonder if she was a demon, but the creamy honey color of her skin looked all shifter to me. It was a bit of an anomaly.

"Hi. You must be Vaughn Winter. My name is Sloane King. It's a pleasure to meet you, sir."

S*ir*. I almost scoffed. Palmer would jizz his pants right here if she said "Sir" to him with those full, pouty lips.

Thankfully, I didn't have the same kinks as my roommate, and *excuse me,* but I wasn't that much older than her. Maybe four or five years, if I was judging it based on her looks. But I guess formalities and all that bullshit.

"It's a pleasure to meet you as well, Ms. King. Please enjoy your tour around the factory floor. If you have any questions, I'll be happy to answer them for you."

Yeah, I was so fucking formal.

I smiled brightly at her and she exchanged a genuine smile back. Her gesture made the dipshit beside her sneer and try to call me out on bullshit that had nothing to do with him. He'd never worked a day in his life and he knew nothing about this company, except the inside of his daddy's secretary.

"Vaughn, why are you on the floor when you should be finishing your paperwork. Are you slacking again?" Taylor gave me a shit-eating grin as he spoke, like he'd just made me look bad.

He tried to hide it, but he wasn't successful. Taylor didn't realize the woman standing beside him was a predator. She saw his grin slide away and his fidgeting fingers tuck into his pants pockets as he waited for me to snap.

He was baiting me. I knew it. She knew it. I wasn't the kind of male to deal with his bullshit line of questioning. Especially with him being someone who knew not a godsdamn thing about what I did for this company.

Constructive criticism? Yeah, absolutely. Being a dick and trying to make me look like I didn't do my job? Big, fat fucking nope.

Before I could say anything to defend myself, Ms. King interjected on my behalf. She seemed to be more done with his shit than I was. I'd wager a bet and say I wasn't the first person he'd done that to today. I bet her tour had been quite insightful.

He's such a hard worker. I barely managed to not roll my eyes at my own wayward thoughts.

"If you're trying to make him look bad, that won't work with me, Mr. Caplin. Just like none of your other shit has worked today. You seem to be under the assumption that your opinion matters to me and that you're needed to show me around a company that is now under my control. Why don't you run along and start cleaning that wasted space of an office out before I have you thrown from the building on your ass?"

I stood there gaping. Like mouth slack, jaw unhinged, wide-eyed, gaping. *It wasn't a good look on me. That I was sure of.* I snapped my mouth shut real quick and bit the inside of my lips together to help me hide the smile that wanted to break loose. I thought she may be my new favorite person after that.

Taylor opened his mouth, then closed his mouth and opened it again, like a fish gasping for breath. When she arched a delicate brow at him, he turned tail and bolted from the factory floor.

It was the best thing I'd seen in months. He'd be pissed about that shutdown. We'd both have to watch him or he'd become an issue for one of us. *No telling who, yet. Both, if we're unlucky.*

She turned her head back to me and I suddenly saw how truly otherworldly she looked. Her hair was a light silvery blue color that shone like the stars from my home.

Her eyes were the most mesmerizing pools of liquid color that I'd ever peered into. The tie-dyed effect of gold and deep forest green, with a slim red ring around the outside of her irises that blazed like fire, sucked me right in. I had never seen anything like them before.

"I apologize for his shitty behavior. He's going to be removed from the property immediately. Between you and me, he gives me the creeps." She laughed lightly, like she couldn't believe she'd just said that aloud.

"Would you mind showing me around for the rest of my tour? I'm afraid this place is quite a labyrinth." Her smile returned to the genuine gesture she'd given me earlier. It was such a glorious sight that it took me a moment to get my tongue to work again.

I nodded my head to her as I cleared my throat to get some sort of words to come out. "John, would you please call in a replacement for Susan? I'm going to show Ms. King around."

I twisted my head slightly to see him and he nodded his own reply. I knew he'd have the task covered, so I didn't waste another second of time. I stripped off my gloves and lab coat and escorted Sloane King off the factory floor.

We headed up the stairs, where I dropped my coat and gloves off at my office as we passed by. I walked beside her down the hallway to the next destination on her agenda.

Ms. King was brimming with questions. Some I could answer and the rest I was able to, at least, point her in the direction of the right people to ask. She listened attentively, almost like she was taking notes with no pen or paper. It felt as though she was just memorizing every detailed answer I gave her.

I didn't know if that was a good thing or not. I did *not* need someone else to get in the way of my investigation.

I also didn't know if spending this much time with her was good or bad. That strange pulling sensation never went away. I had to fight with myself to not walk too close to her.

I wanted to grab her hand, snatch her to me, and wrap my arms around her. I really wanted to fuck her against the wall, right here in the middle of the corridor, in nothing but her blood red heels. Fuck.

Fuck.

FUCK!

What was wrong with me?

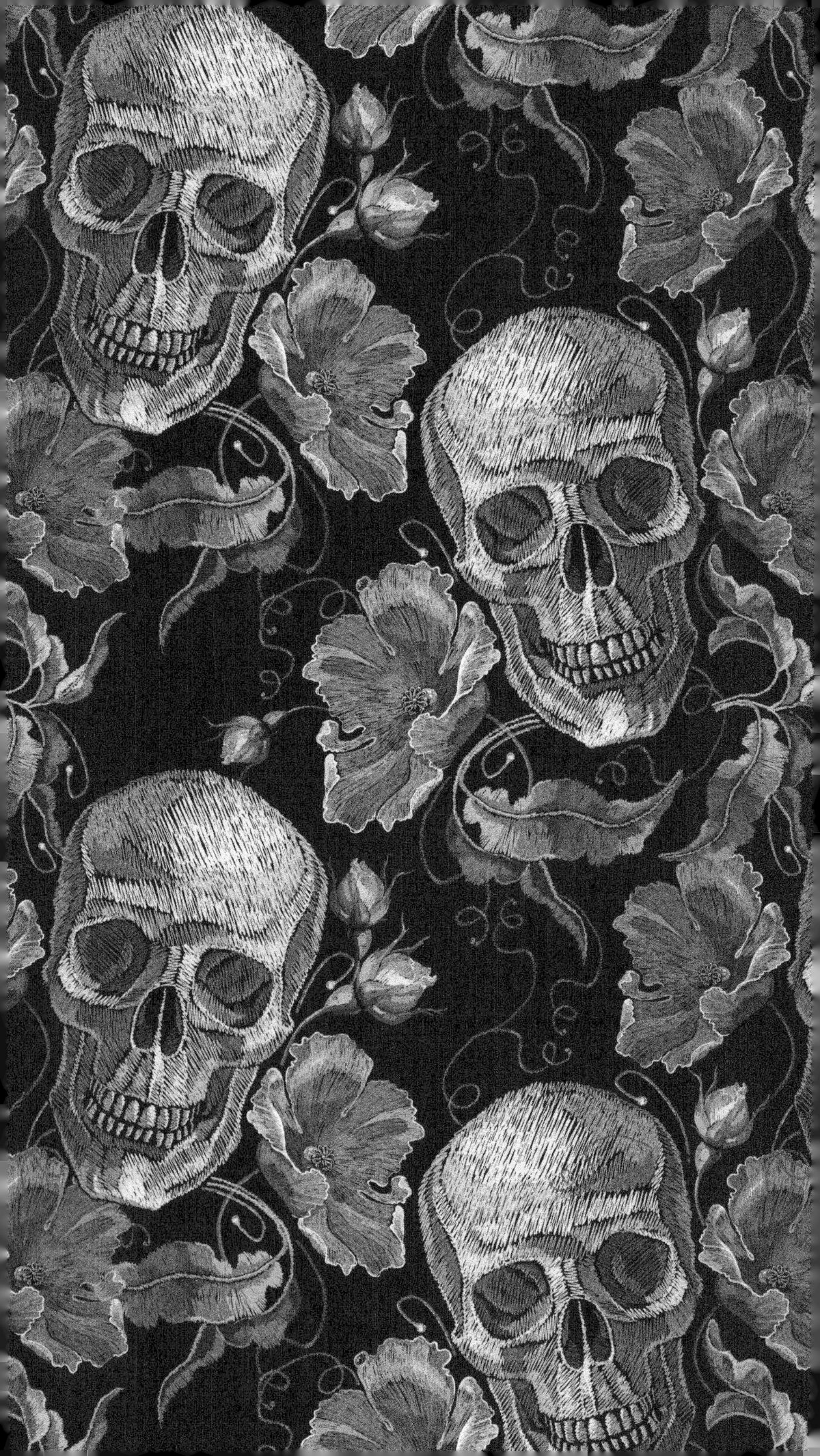

CHAPTER 3
Sloane

Friday, May 15th
Mid Afternoon

Today was exhausting. As I thanked Mr. Winter for walking me through the rest of the tour—and highlighting the areas that Caplin asshat decided to skip—I couldn't keep the smile off my face.

A real smile.

It felt ridiculous to be so happy. I hadn't felt this feeling in a long time, and I was honestly trying not to freak out.

You just met the male. I told myself that over and over again, but it didn't seem to matter.

I couldn't stop thinking about him. The strange pull

that I noticed when I first locked eyes with him hadn't stopped either. I almost wanted to ask Franklin to turn the car around so I could go back in there and jump his bones.

Bone? Just one bone... Godsdamnit. I needed to figure my shit out.

Really, though... When was the last time I enjoyed a conversation? I couldn't even remember.

Vaughn spoke animatedly about all the things going on in the company, and it put my restless mind at ease. That company was purchased for one reason, but it might not be such a drag to keep around.

We'd have to do some work, but I didn't think it would be anything major. I'd have to do some research on other pharmaceutical companies. Then I would find a few people from within to promote into the higher positions that were vacated today.

I had to make myself memorize basically every word he was saying because I couldn't stop my spiraling, gutter-bound thoughts.

While we were in one of the research labs, I kept thinking about what it would feel like to have him bend me over the gleaming metal countertop and slam into me with all his fae strength. Lifting me onto my toes with every thrust. My tits bouncing so hard they popped right out of the top of my dress, leaving both of us exposed to anyone who might walk in.

I had to clear my throat before I could speak to him while we were in that room. The thoughts kept coming, just like I was in them. I had to ask him to continue

Sloane

with the rest of my tour. I needed to get out of that room.

Anyway...

He thanked me for my time as I eased into the back seat of the Audi SUV Franklin was driving today. He closed the door with a small wave and a sexy tilt to his god-like lips.

He was basically walking sin for a part demon like myself. I had to mentally fight with my inner self to get my thoughts off him.

This was godsdamn ridiculous. Why was I acting like a love-struck teenager?

Nope. Can't be. Not going there.

I'd shove those awful, emotional thoughts away for later. Maybe never. I didn't know. I'd pencil it in my schedule. A solid three and a half minutes titled *"Figure your shit out, Sloane"* and then a solid twenty minutes to revisit those filthy thoughts.

FUCK!

Begone, dirty thoughts! Stay focused, Sloane.

Alone with my business thoughts once more, I was finally able to think clearly again. I worked through all the things that I could do to boost profits without making any budget cuts or firing anyone else.

I had already fired everyone who was getting paid to do nothing. Six people were let go from the company today. I emptied out four offices, too. Two Caplins and two Bowers, and I fired one very slutty secretary and a horribly under-qualified head of security.

I'd promote as many people from within the company

as I could and hire a new secretary next week. I needed to put out a job listing, but first, I needed to know what I'd *need* from a secretary.

It was going to be fun. *Just fucking kidding.* None of it was fun. Hiring people sucked. Firing people sucked more. I was good at my job, but my job was not always good to me.

Sighing, I quickly called my dad, Charles, and left him a short voicemail asking him to call me back once he'd reviewed my notes. They were all in his email, but I didn't know when he'd actually have the time to read it all.

He called me back almost immediately, and it was so relaxing to hear his voice. I hadn't seen him in a week and our usual Sunday dinner was fast approaching.

I looked forward to the weekly dinners with my parents. We laughed and bickered, and the conversations were always effortless and fun.

When Jack joined, I wasn't the only one they teased and told Dad jokes to. Maybe I could get him to come with me this weekend. They'd always treated Jack like their son, and he hadn't been to dinner with us in two months. *I knew they'd love to see him.*

"Hi, Dad," I called out cheerfully before I went into the details of the negotiations and tour.

He sounded genuinely excited, and that made me feel joyful. This was going to be a good purchase to add to the family portfolio. I wouldn't let it be anything else.

As I ended the call with my dad, Franklin pulled the car up to the door of my home. I knew he'd wait for me while I got ready, so I didn't say a word as I rushed out of the car and into the house. I had to change clothes and get prepared to be the nightclub princess, which was my second job.

There was really no need to rush. Honestly, I was just anxious about my encounter with Mr. Winter. *Vaughn*. My insides were all knotted up and that strange pull in my chest still wouldn't leave.

I'd felt the feeling before. Only once before. It was a feeling I'd never forget. It was also a feeling that ended up breaking my cold, black heart.

Two years I wasted with that fucking druid, and he just vanished. No text. No phone call. No tracks. He disappeared. Like my mother. Except, when he went missing, so did the pull in my chest. Almost like he was—nope. *Not fucking going there.*

I was spiraling again, and there was nothing fun or dirty about the tangled web of emotions I'd found myself in.

White knuckling the counter in my kitchen, I shoved all those thoughts away. I locked them back in the box they belonged in. I could handle so much, but those emotions? The sad ones? The ones that made my hurt surface and led me to be bitter? Nope. Not my thing.

I hated them. I didn't have time to deal with that shit show. I'd simply close my eyes to it all. I would will them away with sheer determination.

Pencil it in, Sloane. You've got a metric fuck load of shit to do. You cannot afford a mental breakdown right now.

Breathe in. Breathe out.

Breathe in. Breathe out.

Right. Now that I had my head back on straight, I needed to get ready. Maybe I'd primp a little more tonight and try to look like I wasn't balancing on the cliff's edge in a downward tailspin of emotional trauma.

With a nod to myself, I headed to my bathroom and jumped in the shower. I really didn't want to wash my hair, so just a quick scrub to get the feeling of that slimy man's hands off me would do. If I stood under the hot water for too long, I'd get lost in my thoughts again.

I couldn't let that happen.

An hour and a half later and I was feeling much better.

Who was I kidding?

What I meant to say was two-and-a-half hours and I wanted to drink for the second night in a row, but it was fine. I was fine. *Totally fine.*

I'd go to the club and get tonight started and over with. I had more work to do when I got home, but after today, I may skip it and watch a gory movie or read some book porn.

Fuck. Jack was right. I did need to get laid. I had a hunch that it might make me feel better.

Get back to work, Sloane.

Right.

Work.

Club.

My father, Nathaniel, owned one of the most exclusive nightclubs on the eastern coast. The entry list was booked eight months in advance and never held cancellations.

The crowd outside wrapped around the entire block every night that we were open, with the hope that they'd get in.

There was red carpet on the shallow stairs, covered by a long black awning. Red velvet ropes blocked the door, attached to golden posts, manned by what most people called breathing steel.

Almost literally. The bouncers outside were some of the largest males I'd ever seen, and they stood stoic in tailor made, solid black suits.

That's where I was headed tonight. To work. *Insert sarcastic finger air quotes.*

I jumped back in the SUV thirty minutes later.

I'd tried on seven different outfits, but none of them matched my mood until I found a dress that I hadn't worn yet in the back of my closet.

Now, I was in a tight black minidress with blood red stilettos that matched my lips. I could already tell that this dress was going to be one of my favorites.

It had an upside-down triangle-shaped cut out under my breasts that was about four inches long and six inches wide, showing off some extra skin. It felt so comfortable that it seemed nearly as good as being naked in a warm room.

It made me feel sexy and alluring, and that was all I really needed to get this job done.

I tried to ease my mind on the drive to the club.

Closing my eyes, I inhaled deeply and released the breath slowly. I peeked into my future.

I didn't much care for surprises, but I also knew better than to look too far, or too often, into my own future. It never ended well.

Maybe one little peek would simply show me that it was going to be a boring and uneventful night. Then I could go home early and get back to all that important shit I had left to do.

What I Saw wasn't what I was hoping for, though.

It never worked like I wanted it to. I spotted a muscular man sitting next to me in my VIP booth. He had his head turned, and I couldn't see his face, but his build seemed familiar to me.

I'd seen him somewhere before. I knew I had.

His shoulders and arm muscles were tense, his hand squeezed so tightly into a fist that his knuckles were changing colors. His jaw was clenched, and as I followed the direction that held his attention, I *saw* a familiar face.

Taylor Caplin would be in the club tonight, and he would be watching me. *Us.*

Maybe tonight wouldn't be the same boring routine of ignoring the people who wanted to sit with me in my permanently reserved booth just to say they'd been there.

Maybe the mysterious male was someone who was genuinely interested in a conversation with me. And maybe Taylor would leave me the fuck alone.

It was a long shot, I know. A bitch could dream, though.

We pulled up outside the club while I was still lost in

my Sight. Franklin patiently waited for me to tell him when I was ready to exit the SUV.

The people waiting in line all stared and gossiped in hushed tones. They knew who I was, or so they thought.

I could hear their whispers like they were speaking directly in front of me, not from fifteen feet away and through bullet proof, steel lined doors.

I heard their thoughts too, and that happened to be what jerked me from my Sight. Every dark and dirty thing that crossed their minds was on display for me.

It took me years to learn how to block other people's thoughts, and even more time to learn how to select which thoughts to hear. Tonight I didn't want to hear any of their thoughts, so I locked my mind down tighter than my dress.

I tapped the shoulder of Franklin's seat to get his attention. He hopped out of the driver's side door and opened mine with haste. I gave him a polite "thank you" and strutted towards the bouncers.

Sarge was working tonight.

He was one of my favorite brooding beasts. He was smaller than the other bouncers, but twice as deadly. He never cracked a smile, and he absolutely hated when I joked at his expense.

He was good at his job, though. He kept a tight leash on the security team. The patrons very rarely stepped out of line with him here.

He moved away from the ropes, handing the clipboard to the male I'd nicknamed Hulk, and extended his hand to help me up the stairs.

"Are you always such a gentleman, or do you just really like me?" I teased him with a saccharine smile while mentally reprimanding myself.

Or maybe it was in his job description, you thirsty bitch.

He grunted his reply as he ushered me through the ropes and glared at the people who dared to complain about me walking straight in.

He tugged me through the club, the crowd parting as he neared. He didn't stop until he escorted me right up to the VIP section where he passed me off to Jack, my personal VIP security, and also my very gay best friend.

The inside of the club was filled with warm light and comfortable white leather sofas, but I didn't pay any attention to it. I was ready to sit down and attempt to crack some jokes to ease my tension while Jack tried to keep a straight face at his post near my table.

He handed me a wine list and winked at me before saying, "Wine or tequila tonight, you filthy skank, or maybe some water to rehydrate yourself after all the shots you had last night?"

Then he really looked at me, you know, the way someone does when they know you too well.

"You look like you've had a long fucking day," he acknowledged.

"You have no idea, Jack," I admitted to him. "Tell Courtney to bring me a bottle of the best tequila they've got in-house tonight, on ice, with a shot glass and a plate of sliced pineapple, please."

I didn't need to look at the menu. I already knew

Sloane

what I wanted. It was *not* going to be found on a list of expensive wines that I'd never been able to enjoy, much less taste the "smokey grapes" they claimed to use when making it.

I wanted to forget.

And enough tequila would do that for anyone.

Jack reached along his collar to hit a button attached to his ear piece while he whispered quietly into it.

Normally I'd tell him to stop ignoring me while he flipped through his porn playlist, because porn wasn't fun to listen to. He'd shoot back with "No, it's only fun to participate in." We'd giggle about it, though in reality, Jack wasn't joking. He wouldn't watch porn. He only enjoyed making it.

But all I could think about was the short premonition I had on the way here. I wondered, briefly, if I should tell Jack about Taylor Caplin potentially being a new stalker.

He had sat outside of CBP property until I'd left, and then he'd followed us halfway home before Franklin decided it was a good time to lose him.

Franklin knew better than to mention the issue while I was on the phone with my Dad. Charles would've sent for Taylor's head.

Jack saw me staring off into space and raised a perfectly shaped eyebrow at me. He was waiting for me to be snarky, and he knew his eyebrows really pissed me off. They were always so fucking perfect.

I rolled my eyes at myself, or him. *I wasn't even sure which of us was annoying me more.* We could both see that I wasn't in the mood tonight.

I decided to gloss over the Caplin issue for now, but I did have to tell him that I was expecting a visitor at some point tonight.

Jack was a horse shifter, sort of. Well, kind of. We called him a horse shifter, anyway.

He looked every bit of it by his size too. He was bulky in his human form. All tanned muscle and dark hair with nearly black irises that always looked like he was whispering "fuck me" to anyone he was looking at.

His shifted form was a beautiful, solid black steed, darker than pitch. His flame colored eyes and the hellfire trailing in his wake let everyone know that he was all demon if they ever saw him. Most didn't live to tell anyone what they'd witnessed. He was a demon myth, and we liked to keep it that way.

I'd ridden Jack bareback a few times. He refused to let me put a saddle on him. I pouted every single time. Riding bareback made my thighs sweaty, and I hated it.

Uhm, not ridden in a dirty way. Though I suppose that point is moot.

I guess I should have revised the way I talked about trying to get over my phobia of horses. The animals were beautiful, but they used to terrify me.

Jack stood at a brag-worthy twenty hands or so and thought he could help. Whatever that meant. He didn't help. I didn't enjoy lessons with Jack, but I did enjoy Jack's company when he was *not* an ass, err, horse.

You know what I meant. When he wasn't an ass or a horse.

"Jack," I quietly called for him.

He immediately strode to me, bending over so I could speak to him without the other people in the VIP section hearing us.

"I'm expecting company tonight, a well-built man, but I couldn't get a glimpse of his face."

There was no need to explain anything else, because Jack knew me and the gifts I possessed. Most of them, anyway. I didn't even know them all. My powers were constantly evolving and growing.

He raised both of those perfectly arched eyebrows and replied with a whispered "hit me", which meant he wanted me to show him what I saw.

I slid the vision in his mind carefully. If I sent images too fast to someone I didn't have a connection with, it could cause a great deal of pain.

Even though Jack and I had maintained a mental connection since we were kids, I still liked to be cautious.

He nodded his head in a way that told me he'd keep his eyes open for the mystery man. He turned his back to me while reclaiming his original position at the far edge of my half-circle booth.

The white leather seating in the VIP section matched the rest of the sitting areas and barstools in the club. The tabletops were all glossy and black and so shiny you could almost see your reflection in them. The flooring throughout the club was a Brazilian cherry with an ebony stain on top, and in the dim overhead lighting it looked black.

There was a red carpet runner that led down the aisle of the VIP section. It began at the bottom stair and ran all the way to the opening of the booth I always occupied.

I was far enough back to be left alone, but close enough that the people who didn't have VIP access could see who was up here.

There were several sets of large, rectangular booths on the left-hand side against the wall. They were all occupied tonight, but one look at Jack as they tried to approach me had them scurrying the opposite way.

Courtney appeared a few moments after Jack and I ended our chat with the things I had requested and a sealed envelope from my father, Nathaniel.

She popped the top on the chilled liquor and poured me the first shot with a smile on her baby-like face.

"Slooooane," she practically slurred at me, "That dress looks fucking amazing on you! Everyone in the club stopped what they were doing to watch you walk by."

"Thanks." My reply was clipped, though I didn't mean for it to sound that way.

She had no idea what those people thought about as they stared at me. She was human and full of pure thoughts. Pure-ish thoughts.

The woman's mind was actually pretty perverted for a human. She didn't constantly think of power, control, or murder, though, so the word "pure" worked well enough.

I spent the next two hours drinking and being eye-fucked by the people brave enough to look my way. I was trying not to get drunk, even though I'd need more than the one bottle I had ordered to achieve true inebriation.

Or the blackout level that I really sought tonight.

I still caught a good buzz off the bottle I made myself slowly finish. I asked Jack for a glass of water, and the male looked worriedly at me. I rolled my eyes at him and he raised that fucking eyebrow at me again.

That. Perfect. Fucking. Eyebrow.

Throwing his shouted thoughts straight into my head while his back remained turned to me, he asked, *"Are you feeling okay? It's 1am and you want water? Fucking water, Lo! Are you sick? Or just trying to stay sober to meet the mystery man."*

He snickered at me as he continued his lecture. *"And I heard that. I'll do your eyebrows next time instead of you going to see that raggedy, old bitch who's been doing them. Oh, wait. That's you!"*

He twisted his head to wink at me. That asshole.

"I'm fine," I stated aloud. "I think I want to go upstairs and play a game of pool in Dad's office. I'm going home before we close."

I stood as Jack offered his hand to me.

With my hand tucked securely in the crook of his arm, we made our way down the red carpet, getting gawked at like we were celebrities. I hated the attention.

Just seven more steps. Nearly there.

Instead of turning right to head down the VIP stairs, we turned left to go to the door that led upstairs to the offices.

That weird pull that never stopped was so strong that I stopped dead in my tracks three steps from the door. Urging myself to turn around, I stole a small breath and angled my head to peek over my shoulder.

Staring at me with a smirk on his face was the male I met at CBP earlier today. *It wasn't the man I saw in my premonition at all.*

He looked completely different than he did at work. His dark brown hair was pushed back to the right, and I didn't think I'd ever seen softer looking waves.

I wanted to run my hands through those fat curls and pull his hair while he... yeah.

His eyes were a tantalizing icy blue color, so light that they were almost white, and they danced with amusement.

I'd really like to see them lit up with desire as I dropped to my knees an—Focus!

His cheeks were a little flushed, like he'd been drinking for about as long as I had. In his hands were two shot glasses and a bottle of my favorite tequila.

My eyes tracked over him like he was a gift from the gods, but I knew he wasn't. This male was trouble. The good kind, but trouble nonetheless.

Jack stood in front of me, and I had to put my hand on his shoulder and squeeze to get his attention. He side-eyed me, nodded sharply, and opened the velvet rope at the top of the stairs.

"Mr. Winter, please come in." Jack welcomed him with a sly smile.

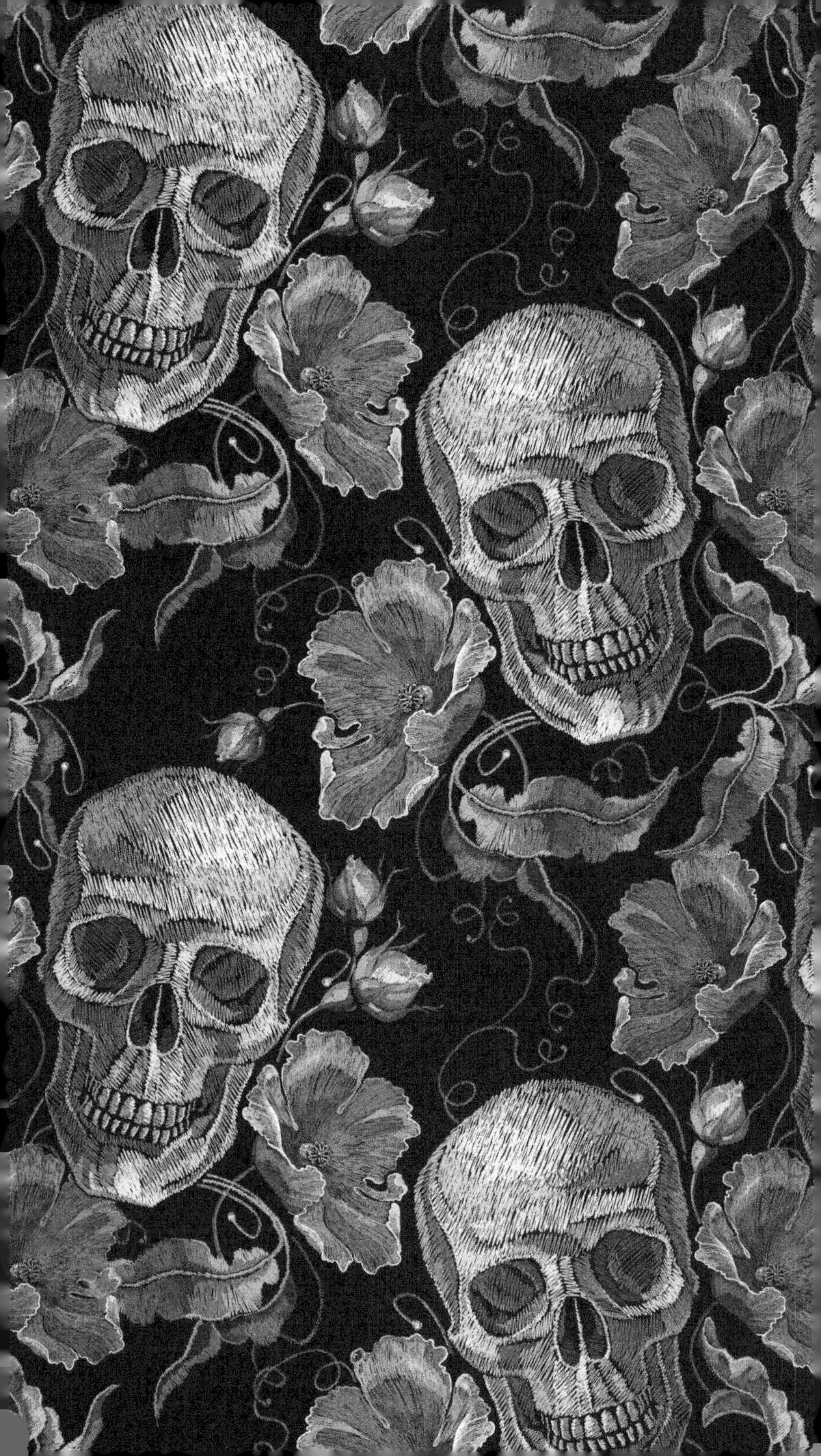

CHAPTER 4
Sloane

Friday, May 15th
Late Night

I guess he got my text about the handsome male Fae I met this afternoon.

"Thanks for replying to my text." I snarked at him in my head.

That motherfucker just winked at me again and tossed back, *"I saw all those naughty thoughts roll across your mind while you were looking at him with your hand on my shoulder. You really are a filthy bitch. I fucking love you, but I'm semi hard right now and it's all your fault."*

"I'm going to kick your ass tomorrow and I hope you know it!" I shouted at him while also trying to keep my

facial expressions from looking like I was screaming in my head.

It was hard work.

"Ms. King." Vaughn's low rumble was so delicious it had me thanking the gods that I decided to wear panties tonight. "You looked rather bored."

He shrugged a muscled shoulder and smiled at me with a coyness that had those panties melting right off my overheated body.

I had to open my mind to see what he was thinking. I didn't want pity. I got paid to sit there and look pretty... and bored, apparently.

I tilted my head to the left in confusion, though. I couldn't hear this male's thoughts. I thought that might be a first for me.

Or second, but again, I was not fucking going there.

Intrigued, I motioned the male to my booth. Seating himself across from me, we eyed each other for a moment before he popped the bottle open and poured two shots.

I offered him my plate of pineapple, watching the confusion cross his chiseled features as he raised a questioning eyebrow at me.

"It's better than lime as a chaser," I explained simply.

He passed me a shot. We clinked the glasses together and threw them back at the same time. He made a disgusted face before biting into his pineapple slice.

"That's not bad," he agreed after swallowing. His comment made me chuckle.

"Did I interrupt you leaving when I walked up?" he asked a little shyly after our shot.

Maybe it had just occurred to him that I was on my way out and might not want any company.

I definitely wanted the company if it was him, though.

Jack groaned in my head, and I forced our connection closed so fast that it felt like slamming a car door shut.

Fuck my life right now.

Jack was going to snoop around in what was left of my love life after hearing everything I just thought.

Uhm, loveless life? Whatever, you know what I meant.

He happened to be a nosy jackass.

"Actually, I was bored," I replied with a small smile of my own. "I was going to go upstairs for a game of pool. Do you play?"

"There are pool tables in such an upscale nightclub?" he inquired, drawing his brows down, a little bewildered and a little sarcastic.

That made me laugh, a real, genuine laugh. He had no idea what secrets this club held.

"Come on," I encouraged him.

Standing and grabbing his hand, I began to pull him along with me.

Jack quirked his stupid eyebrow at me again as we walked towards him hand in hand. He opened the door that led to the stairs and mouthed *"yes, bitch"* when I passed him. He followed quietly behind us, up the stairs and to the large game room across from my father's office.

Once we were inside, Jack closed the door but remained on the outside. I heard him in my mind the moment the door clicked closed, *"If you don't fuck him on that pool table then I totally will, bitch. Grim would be all over him too. He's got a thing for fae. He says they're pretty."*

He made a humming noise and shoved filthy images in my mind. The first image was Vaughn and me, one I pictured myself, and then they quickly morphed into scenes of Jack, Grim, and Vaughn.

I shut him out completely, locking that connection up like Fort Knox. *He was such an ass sometimes!*

Vaughn was standing at the rack that held the cue sticks. He twisted them and ran his dexterous fingers along them all before he went back and selected the sixth cue.

He kneeled at the end of the table and started racking the balls while I opened a cabinet on the wall and pulled out my own personal favorite.

Jack's dirty images flickered in the back of my mind when I saw him start shuffling the balls around. I almost groaned out loud.

Fucking Jack. I hated him so hard right now.

"There were more?" he questioned, looking around like he missed a rack somewhere.

"Nope, this one is mine," I assured him as I started twisting together the black cue. "I play my father when he's in town. He always wins, but I'll beat him, eventually."

"Your father owns this club?" He lifted a curious eyebrow at me.

For fuck's sake. If another male quirked an eyebrow at me tonight...

"Yes, I run it for him while he's out of town." I

needed to get out of my head before I said something I couldn't take back.

"He owns a club and a pharmaceutical company?" He thought his questions aloud. Then he quickly recovered with, "Those don't necessarily go together, but I see how a businessman, or woman, can run both."

He motioned for me to break. I leaned low over the table. *A little lower than necessary, if I was being honest.*

I lined up my shot as I mentally scolded myself. The male was hot, and I needed to get my hormones under control before I did something stupid.

Did something stupid! Okay, now I was just arguing with myself, which was insane. Focus, bitch!

I hit the cue ball effortlessly, and as all the balls scattered, the ten ball hit the top right corner pocket.

"Big balls," I called out as I circled the table once more.

"I'm sorry?" He sounded bemused, and I suddenly remembered his earlier question.

I hoped that he didn't think *that* was my response. Though, I guess it could be. *Takes big lady balls to do some of the shit I did.*

"Stripes. I meant I had stripes. You've never heard anyone say that before? Little balls for solids and big balls for stripes?" I continued circling as I rambled to him.

I knocked three more in before I finally missed my mark. "Damn, that was the easiest shot I had."

I couldn't help the small pout that graced my lips. I was doing so well until I looked up to see him worrying that plump lower lip between his teeth.

I really wanted to be the one biting that lip.

"Yeah, but you left me with nothing." He grinned and shook his head, taking his time to circle the table counterclockwise. "And, no, I've never heard that before. The guys always say solids or stripes, but the next time we play I'm definitely calling someone little balls."

He chuckled to himself and my mind flew off in a tangent of ball sizes. *Shit. There I go again.*

"I'm sure the face of little balls is going to love it," I sassed back with a smirk.

It did sound kind of funny. Jack and Grim always argued over their balls when I said it. It always made me laugh, until they needed a judge, and then I was gone.

"To answer your previous question; my Dad, Charles, bought CBP. My Father, Nathaniel, owns a few nightclubs, bars, and dungeons along the eastern seaboard. And my Papi, Samuel, is the headmaster at a boarding school for demons." I spilled all that before I caught myself.

Small talk with Vaughn was easy. Too easy. It would be best to keep to the lighter subjects. My life was confusing and complicated. I didn't want to talk about deep shit with someone I'd just met.

I also didn't want to talk about work. Thankfully, he seemed to be on the same page as me.

The next three hours passed us by in a blur of good-natured banter, jokes, and laughing.

I honestly thought he let me win the game of pool we played, but not at darts. He had perfect aim. I watched his muscles bunch across his shoulder and upper arm through his thin t-shirt with each dart he released, mesmerized by the fluid movement.

We ran through topics like we'd known each other for years. The longer I was near him, the stronger I felt that odd pull. I almost asked him if he felt it too.

Three times. I almost worked up the nerve to ask him three different times.

Lighter subjects. Stick to the lighter subjects.

"What's your favorite color?" I asked as we sat down to take a break on the oversized black leather couch in the game room.

"Mmm, blue. Like the color of the sky on a cloudless day. You?"

"Black," I grinned. "Like... black."

"What's your favorite type of candy?" He returned my question with another.

I tapped my lips with my index finger as I thought about candy for a moment. I didn't eat much of it, but when I did it was always the same thing. "Cherry Jolly Ranchers or Skittles, but only the red and purple ones."

"Sour Patch Kids. All the flavors."

"Favorite season?"

Vaughn flashed that coy, melt-your-panties-off smile again. "Winter."

The low quality of his voice had been doing a number on my hormones. I could die a happy woman if he whispered in my ear while bending me over the arm of this couch.

"I like them all for one reason or another, but I think

spring is my favorite," I blurted out before I let my imagination run rampant. *Again.*

He tilted his head to the side and watched me while he thought of his next question. His heavy-lidded eyes skimmed my body in a trail that I wished his hands would follow through with. The slight curl of the right side of his mouth exposed a dimple that I'd love to brush my lips over.

"Tell me a drunk story."

His request made me chortle, because I had a few good ones. I rubbed my fingers along the edges of my jaw and looked down at the floor with squinted eyes while I thought it through.

I could tell him about last night. It still made me smile to think about the looks on those shifters' faces when I told them to strip.

"Last night, Jack and I went to this small shifter bar. It was gross." I shuddered as I spoke, and he laughed under his breath.

"Anyway, after getting a little tipsy, I decided I was in a bit of a betting mood. So, I picked out a group of the biggest males I could find and bet them a hundred dollars each that I could beat them in darts. I let them win the first round, and then I won the next few rounds.

"By the time they figured out that I was hustling them, they couldn't pay up on their debt, so I made them strip down naked in the middle of the bar and I took their clothes. I left their shoes, though. I'm not an awful person. Then I threw the clothes out the window on the way home." I ended my short story with a sly smile and a nod of my head.

Vaughn stared at me for a few seconds in disbelief and then laughed. The sound of his laughter brought a bigger smile to my face and made me squeeze my thighs together.

That pull in my chest grew a little stronger too. I didn't know how I felt about it, other than not hating it. I still wasn't quite sure what it was exactly. *And I was not going there tonight either*.

"I have a few friends that I'd love to see you hustle," he told me after he calmed down.

"We can arrange that. Just tell me where and when to be there." I winked at him.

We'd been flirting all night. It was a dangerous little dance between my mind and my body. I had originally tried to keep distance between us, but every time we passed by each other, we touched.

We were sitting so close that I could feel his body heat. My legs were tucked under me. My knees brushed against his right leg while he sat with his back against the arm of the couch to face me better.

I was like three accidental brushes away from lunging at him.

Jack knocked on the door moments after the thought of lunging at Vaughn crossed my mind. It was 5:30am, and he came to tell us the club employees were ready to go home.

Perfect timing. I really didn't want to do something

stupid and regret it next week when I had to see him at work.

I sighed and put the darts away. Grabbing my long ago ditched shoes after shoving the envelope from my father into my purse, I headed to the door with Vaughn.

Jack escorted us downstairs, and I gave my thanks to the bartender, Simon, and Courtney for staying late.

I slid into Simon's mind and told him to put Vaughn's tab on mine. That bottle of tequila was expensive. I didn't know what Simon was thinking when he handed it over, but I was happy that he did.

Once we made it outside, Vaughn walked me to the SUV waiting for me at the curb. He lifted my left hand to his mouth and placed a soft kiss across my palm before saying, "Until another night, Ms. King," in that sexy, low whispered voice that'd had me needing new panties for hours.

Then he stepped away like a proper fucking gentleman. That pull snapped tighter the further he went. I rubbed at the center of my chest, right above the junction of my breasts, like that might ease the ache.

It didn't, though. I had a feeling that sensation would be too hard to avoid. *I didn't think I wanted to avoid it either.*

Jack was glaring at me from the doorway. He was so disappointed that my morning didn't include a naked fae in my bed, and I almost agreed.

Almost.

I didn't want Vaughn to be a one-night stand. That

was *not* something I liked to admit. I didn't like to feel those feelings.

That was why I didn't get close to people. My life was complicated, and having feelings just brought in more complications than I was ready for.

I'd experienced those feelings before.

They led to something stronger than I was ready for at the time. They nearly broke me when it all came crashing down, too.

Would it be any different this time? *Could* it be any different?

I wanted to ponder the situation more, but I also wanted to get to know him better. It seemed counterproductive to turn new feelings into something more than they were.

Was it a chance encounter or an accidental first date?

I didn't know what he saw it as either, since I couldn't read his mind. I didn't want to be the person catching lopsided feelings for someone when they had no intentions of reciprocating them.

I could add "commitments" to the short list of things that terrified me.

Everything always circled back to what happened when I was dating the druid.

I'd fallen in love with him, hard and fast, without a care or reservation in sight.

It had all felt right with him. He'd taught me so much about who I was as a person, both when we were together and when he'd left.

Heartbreak was a numb depression that left me

feeling like I was in a dark cave on my own. It swallowed me whole and spat me out in nothing but fragments of who I once was.

I had to learn how to breathe again. I had to learn how to laugh and smile again.

I found myself in those fragments and pulled my life back together bit by microscopic bit until the tiny pieces were big enough to glue back together.

My heart looked like a shattered vase, missing small details that I'd never get back. All because I trusted the wrong male to keep a slice of my soul for himself.

After all that I'd put myself through in the past, how could I sacrifice any more of my soul to someone who wasn't my mate? How could I have faith in myself to make the right decision?

How did I keep these feelings at bay until I could sort out my problems? Would it be fair to consider a relationship with Vaughn, knowing that my heart still ached for another?

Mate. That was a word I hadn't thought about in many years.

The thoughts whirled around in my head. Coaxing me further and further down that dreary path. The path that led to the inviting darkness of the cave that allowed me to be secluded from trivial things like feelings and uncertainty.

One thought kept whizzing by, the speed of it bringing light to the oppression of my mind.

Why didn't he kiss me?

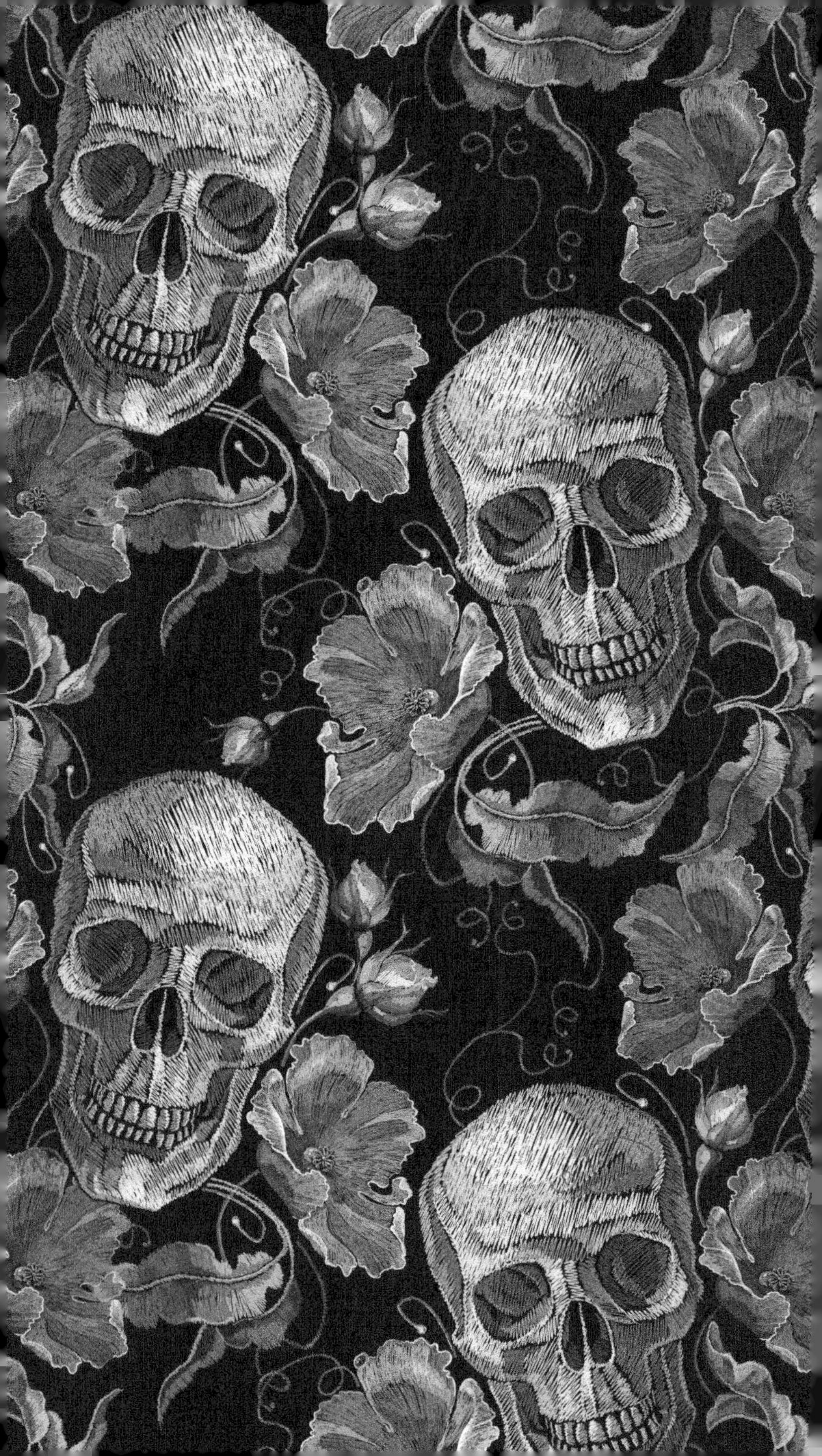

CHAPTER 5
VAUGHN

Saturday, May 16th
Early Morning

What was I thinking!?

I should have kissed her. I wanted to kiss her so fucking bad.

No. I wanted to devour her mouth and skim my hands along her thighs, over her hips, and up her sides.

Then, I wanted to shove my hand in her hair to hold her where I wanted her while I deepened that kiss and rocked her world in a clash of tongues and teeth.

I wanted to taste her until we were both breathless, and then I wanted to stretch her over the edge of that pool table and fuck her until her knees were too weak to hold her body up.

I didn't do any of it, though. I should have. *Fuck. I just* wanted *when she was around. Plain and simple.*

Would it have been too soon? I just met her today. Yesterday.

"Fuck." I groaned as I rubbed my hand up my face and pulled at my hair.

Man, I was so confused. I'd never felt this way about anyone before.

"What the fuck is going on?" And what was this gods-fucking-awful pulling sensation, and when was it going to stop?

Spending time with Sloane was amazing, but I didn't miss Taylor Caplin lurking in the nightclub. He'd obsessed over her every move like the problem I knew he'd become.

I hoped that it didn't escalate from creeping to flat out stalking. He was the reason why I'd decided to put her favorite bottle of tequila on my tab and approach her.

The way Taylor had watched Sloane had made me uncomfortable. I felt an overbearing need to protect her from him.

There was something off about him. I couldn't quite put my finger on it, but he'd always rubbed me the wrong way. I could call it male intuition, or blame it on the fact that I had three younger sisters at home.

This wouldn't be the first time that I'd had to run off a nutter. I was thankful when she took me upstairs so we could get away from his prying eyes.

Vaughn

I spotted him lurking again outside of the club when we left. It was 5:30 in the morning, and he was still there waiting for her, which made my anger surface.

If he touched her, I would kill him. Those thoughts temporarily spun out of control. I had to wrangle them in to focus on my last few moments with her.

After I bid her goodnight, I quickly brought it to her driver's attention before he got in the car. The old Vampire could hear every whispered word that left my lips without me making a show of acknowledging him.

I didn't want Taylor to know I was worried about her safety.

When the car pulled away from the curb he was gone. I also mentioned it to Jack, the security guard who'd been following us around all night.

I didn't miss the fact that they had a telepathic bond. I tried not to look too deep into that observation because I knew he could warn her better than I could. That was the important takeaway.

He seemed like a stand-up kind of guy until he looked at me in irritation and inquired, "Why didn't you kiss her? Are you fucking stupid?"

He threw his hands up and started pacing. "She never brings anyone into her VIP booth, let alone spends hours with them talking and playing stupid fucking games. Do you know how private she is? She. Never. Fucking. Does. That."

The longer he ranted, the more his voice rose, until the last few words were a yelled sort of growl.

I could only stare at him with my jaw slack. *Was he reprimanding me?*

I hadn't felt like I was in trouble in years. Not since I'd left the royal court of the Winter Realm, anyway. He clearly didn't know who I was.

No. No one did.

"Seriously, man, are you listening to me? I've known Sloane for years!"

He visibly tried to calm himself, meticulously running his hands over his suit jacket and resting them on his hips as he stared at me like I was the biggest problem on hand. Not the creep waiting for her, but me. I was the problem.

"You should've kissed her, asked her to breakfast, and then taken her home and fucked her senseless." He was so matter-of-fact about his plan, until he screamed, "Maybe not even in that order. Fucking moron!"

Still, I said nothing. I honestly wasn't sure what to say.

This shifter had balls of steel. I could kill him with a well-placed ice shard, but I wouldn't. I did have self-control. Instead, I smiled at him.

"Why don't you send her my number?" I asked, and the question only served to piss him off more. I chuckled darkly when he glared at me open-mouthed.

"Send her your number?" he growled deeply. "Oh my gods, you are stupid." His sudden change from growl to squeal had me fighting not to flinch. How could one jump so many octaves within seconds?

"I'll give you her number, but don't call or text her

until Sunday evening." He stopped my nonexistent protest with a raised index finger.

"No, no. That's for me. That will give her time to calm the hell down because she's going to be so fucking mad that I butted my ass in this. We'll have brunch in a few hours and I'll tell her what I've done. She has dinner with her parents every Sunday evening and she'll be in a great mood, so text her at like 8 that night. Okay? Do you understand me?"

He uttered the last sentence very slowly, in a way that showed that he really thought I was stupid.

Shit. Maybe I was. I knew I should've kissed her.

"Okay," I replied slowly, mostly to piss him off, and only partially because I was running through the entire night trying to decide if I missed more than that one opportunity.

I did. It was blatantly clear that I'd overlooked quite a few chances.

He snatched a piece of paper off a clipboard at the door, aggressively grabbed at a pen, and then quickly scrawled something down before holding the paper out for me to take. In the neatest handwriting I think I'd ever seen from a male was her phone number.

"Thanks," I replied, still speaking slowly as I folded the paper and tucked it into my pocket.

He grunted a "you're welcome" and walked away, shaking his head.

Casually strolling back to my car with my hands sunk in my pockets, I fingered the paper as I replayed the night's conversations in my head.

She had three dads. That was a little strange. I couldn't really understand how that worked, but okay.

One of them was a demon. I guess that was where the fire in her eyes came from. I wondered what the other two men were. I suspected she may have been a shifter or a vampire, but I didn't have anything solid to go on.

What was her mother? She couldn't be a full-blooded demon. I'd have scented that right away. Every demon I'd ever encountered had a spicy, cinnamon sort of scent to them.

She smelled like safety and home and power. A strange combination of pine trees, crisp snow, and charcoal. I'd never met a hybrid before, so again, I didn't have enough information to go on there either.

I could call Palmer. He would know. The male knew everything, but he was in Northern Ireland and wouldn't be back until Wednesday.

Damn it.

I didn't want to call him while he was busy. I had no idea what he was actually doing there. This could just be a lust thing. Something told me that was wrong, though.

I could call Briggs, but the insufferable asshole had been camping—as he called it—for weeks now. Ever since that she-wolf had broken his fucking heart.

He could probably tell me what this pulling in my chest was. Then he'd probably rant about how women were terrible and he was swearing off love. If he didn't wear his heart on his sleeve, then maybe he wouldn't get it broken so much.

I wouldn't tell him that. The last time I did, we ended

up with a broken dinner table and both of us had black eyes. Lesson learned.

Still lost in my thoughts, I finally made my way to my car.

The sun hadn't started to rise yet, but the night was light. The street lamps on the sidewalks illuminated the area, but didn't quite make it to where I had parked. I could just make out the silhouette of a man standing on the passenger side of my classic car.

My pride and joy, my white 1976 Stingray.

As I got closer, I realized that it was none other than Taylor Caplin.

You have got to be kidding me right now. It was almost 6am.

"Vaughn," he acknowledged like he'd just noticed me for the first time in his entire fucking life, while he was leaning his greasy ass against MY car.

I needed to stay calm, or I was going to kill him. I had to find out what he wanted first.

"Taylor," I responded, laying the sarcasm on thick.

I really wasn't in the mood for his bullshit, and seeing as how he was *not* my boss anymore, I was sure I could solve this quickly.

Not with murder, Vaughn, chill out.

I'd have to continue to talk myself down if he didn't leave soon. He'd pissed me off too many times and talking to myself would only work for so long.

"What do you want?" I questioned him with hostility.

"Oh, nothing much." He side-eyed me while turning

his head to inspect my car. "I was just wondering what you were doing with Sloane."

"Ms. King," I bit out with anger in my voice before I could take a deep breath to calm myself, "and I are none of your business."

"I see," he sneered at me. "So there's nothing going on between you two."

He nodded his hollow skull at me as he pretended to think about his next words. "It sure seemed like you were gone for an awfully long time, but nothing happened. What a pity. A fine woman like that needs someone who can seal the deal, if you know what I mean."

His leering grin set me off. *This dirty dick fucking bastard.*

Oh, I knew what he meant, and I was seeing red.

My jaw muscle ticked as I rolled my neck to the right and then the left to stretch my tense muscles. I let loose an inhuman growl, fully intending on knocking his ass into next week, but not killing him yet.

It was swallowed by a guttural whinny sort of sound just as a big ass black horse came out of *literally* nowhere and kicked him square in the chest.

Taylor sailed through the air and slammed into a light post. What was that? Twenty? Thirty feet away?

Where the fuck did the horse come from? The shadows? I must have been seeing things.

I looked over at the horse, wide-eyed, but didn't dare move another muscle.

Yep, it was a huge godsdamn horse.

I heard Taylor moan painfully, sadly confirming he

was still alive despite how badly I wanted to kill him with my bare hands.

Thick, black smoke began to morph around the horse until Jack stood before me, in his dress pants and nothing else. If I thought it was funny when he was pissed earlier, then maybe he was right and I was a bit dim-witted.

Jack was livid now. He was breathing heavily through his anger and walking barefoot across the gravel lot towards Taylor, with what I could only call a determined gait.

"Jack," I softly called out, trying to steady the raging beast.

He didn't stop or say a word until he made it to Taylor. With all the menace pouring from the male, I started to think this motherfucker might die today.

I hated the man, but Jack looked like he was ready to tear his spleen out through his throat. It truly wouldn't have surprised me if he did. It certainly wouldn't hurt my feelings, and I'd definitely help him hide the body.

He dragged Taylor up off the ground by the collar of his thousand dollar dress shirt and brought him to eye level. Taylor's feet dangled nearly a foot off the ground as Jack held him so close their noses almost touched.

Jack stared at him for a solid minute. I could hear Taylor swallow from where I stood. He was terrified.

I was so fucking ecstatic about it that I wanted to cheer Jack on. I was also a little jealous that it wasn't me doing the terrorizing. I still had to lie low around the people who thought I was human.

That meant not scaring the dipshit with my powers.

Slowly and calmly, oh so fucking calmly, Jack whispered, "If you value your life, you will keep Sloane King's name out of your mouth. You will not come near her or her friends again. The next time I see you, or hear that you have uttered her name, I will personally hunt you down. When I find you, I will rip your still beating heart from your chest so quickly that your last vision will be of me taking a bite out of it. Do you understand me?"

Holy fuck.

I was quite frightened myself, but I almost laughed as Taylor's face went completely white and he started to piss himself.

Jack's nostrils flared as he gave Taylor a good once-over, and then he tossed the man twenty feet in the opposite direction.

He took a visible breath, trying to even his anger out, before turning to me. "So, that's the creep you were talking about, yeah? If Sloane catches him stalking her, she'll kill him herself."

His grin was a little too large for comfort as his long strides ate up the distance between us. "No need to worry about that bitch. She's way more bite than bark. You'd be surprised to know how many ways she can kill a man with something as simple as a spoon."

I was going to save that information for later. *Right now, though,* "Are you okay, mate? Do you need a ride to your car or something?"

"Nah, man, I'm good. Sloane sent me. Apparently she saw him and didn't think it was important to tell me until someone other than herself was in danger. I know you're a high winter fae, but iron bullets are iron bullets and that guy's got a gun."

He casually tossed his head in the direction of an unconscious Taylor Caplin. "Uhm, had a gun," he corrected himself.

I nodded my head while I processed what he'd just told me. Sliding some more information away for later, I looked over and noticed a gun lying a few feet from where Taylor landed. Huh, he wasn't bullshitting. I never saw the gun.

"I think I can fix that gun for him," I offered.

As I made my way over to Taylor, I fought the urge to kick him in his face. I took the gun and bent the barrel up, then removed the bullets and encased them in ice before I crushed them in my hand.

The iron burned the surface of my skin, but a little ice would heal it right up. I'd be left with nothing but a raw area on my palm from the minor iron burns by the time I got home.

I didn't know if Taylor would understand what transpired here tonight. No one would believe his story either.

Not that I gave any flying fucks about him, since it would appear that he was going to try to shoot me. With iron bullets, no less. Did he know I was fae, or was it just a guess?

That would be more information to think about later. I was going to need to get Novak and Stone to help me do some digging. I already dreaded that conversation.

"Maybe we should call an ambulance for him...." I trailed off as I heard the sirens growing closer.

Guess Jack called them before he came from, uhm, wherever the hell he came from.

I had so many questions about tonight.

"Time to go, Vaughn. I'll take that ride around the block to my chariot now," Jack replied with a wink.

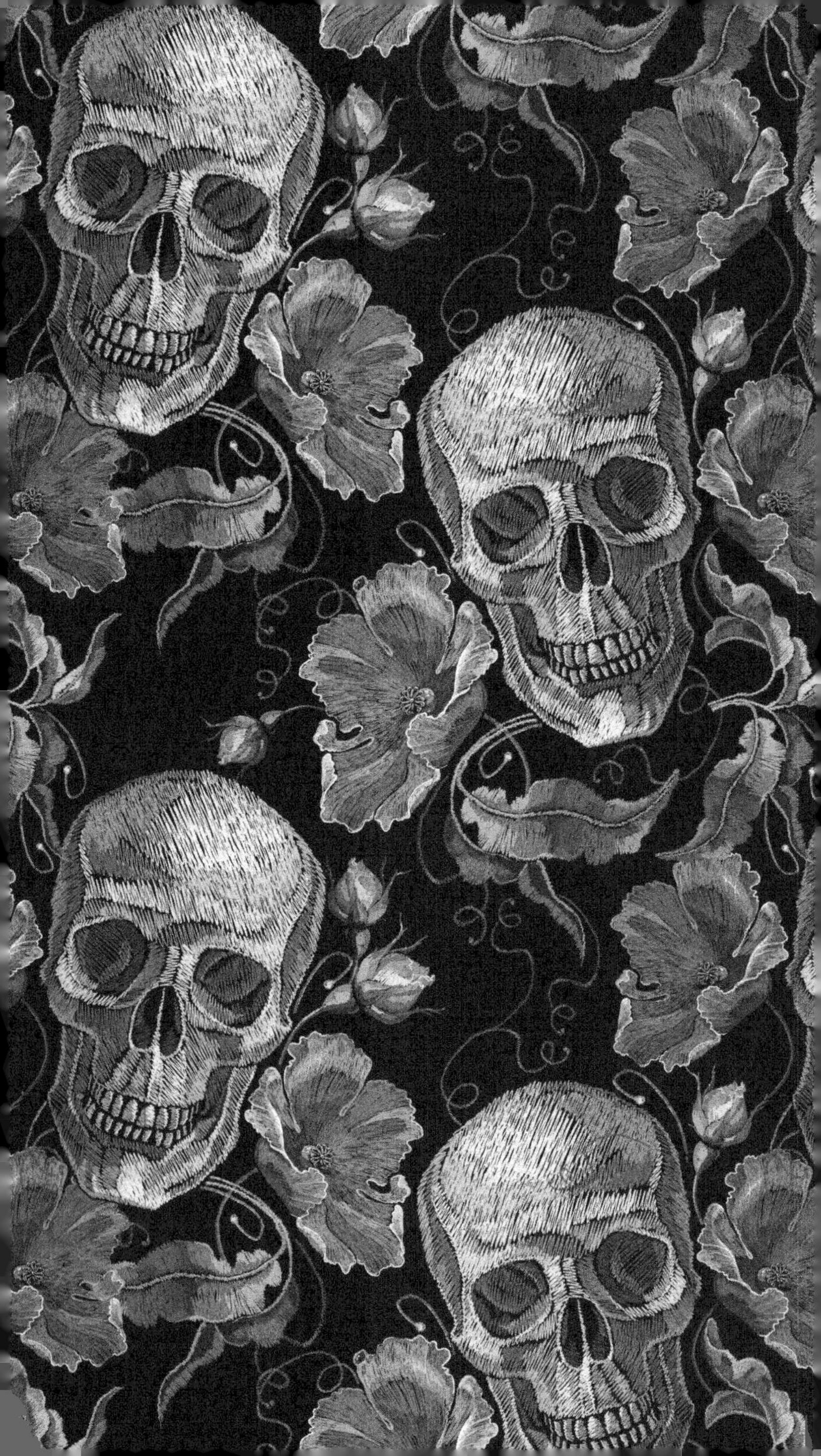

CHAPTER 6
VAUGHN

Saturday, May 16th
Morning

By the time I made it home, it was after 6am. I was exhausted from all the shit that had happened in the last 24 hours.

I really looked forward to falling face first in my bed so I could take a long nap. Maybe I'd dream of Sloane. Her arms wrapped around my neck as she leaned back, leaving her bare breasts on display. Her nipples brushing my chest with each movement we made, long legs locked behind my back as I...

FUCK! Get. A. Fucking. Grip. Vaughn.

On second thought, maybe I didn't want to dream about her. That seemed like a sure way to wake up with a raging boner, or have a wet dream.

As I opened the front door of the flat I shared with my friends, a few smells assaulted me at once. New smells that weren't here last night when I'd come home to change out of my work clothes.

One: It smelled like the gas from the stove mixed with bacon and eggs and orange juice.

Breakfast was being cooked, which meant Palmer came home early from seeing his family. He must have decided Novak and I had enjoyed enough takeout and protein bars in his two-week absence.

Thank the gods.

Novak was a terrible cook, and I wasn't much better. Palmer was a step up from Stone in the kitchen, but none of us compared to Briggs.

Two: The fresh, earthy smell of mud and grass invaded my nostrils as I silently shut the front door and tiptoed through the entryway.

That meant Briggs was home, too. He'd be cleaning all this fucking mud up, because I wasn't the one who tracked it all the way from the front door of our building to our door.

It led from our front door to the couch, and from there it trailed underneath his bedroom door. He was so sloppy sometimes. It wouldn't have been hard to take his shoes off at the door.

He did this shit to aggravate me.

Three: The smell of ash and burning wood like something was on fire. That could only mean—

Fuck! Something was on fire!!

I darted through the flat, following the scent, and found... Stone.

He was squatting in front of the living room fireplace, poker in one hand and a small flame in the other, teasing the fire bigger like the Devil-damned demon he was.

"Fuck! You ballbag. I thought the flat was on fire."

I had to take a deep breath to calm my rapid heartbeat. He wasn't supposed to be home from his convention until the end of the week. The fires never caught me off guard when I knew he was home.

"We told you, Fae, it's an apartment, not a flat. I don't know why that's so hard for you to understand." He rolled his bluish black eyes at me like I was the dumbest fae to walk the earth.

"You're the second person who has acted like I'm stupid in the past three hours," I muttered under my breath.

I knew I wasn't a genius like Palmer, but I wasn't not smart, you know?

"Make that three in as many hours," Palmer slid in, "Where've ya been?"

He gave me a sly look that made me want to roll my eyes. Of course they were going to grill me.

"It's not like ye to come strollin' in at this hour. Busy night, was it?"

I thought about ignoring his questions. I wasn't ready to talk about her with them yet.

Palmer let his accent out when he was at home. When he was working, he acted as American as I did. He didn't have a heavy accent, but you could hear it lightly when he spoke.

He'd been in the States longer than I had. I thought that helped him lose the edge of his accent. It was funny when he bounced back and forth between accents while talking to us.

He hated the questions people asked him about his time in Ireland. My favorite one that he got was, *"Are you Irish or Scottish?"*

It was one of the few times I'd ever see Palmer lose his cool, because he wasn't from either. He was from Norn Iron. That was what he called his homeland.

It was Northern Ireland. Somewhere near Belfast. Please don't get him fucking started. We'd never hear the end of it.

He wasn't the only one that hid it, though. All of the paperwork and information that could be found on me stated that I grew up in Seattle, Washington.

It was a complete lie. I'd grown up in the Fae realm. The portal was hidden in Oxford, England.

If you don't know where that is, then grab a map, because I was shite with directions.

"I thought the flat was on fire," I emphasized again.

"Apartment."

I ignored Stone's interruption and kept talking.

"I didn't know everyone came back last night. You could've called. I do have a cell phone."

I waved my phone around at them and saw that they were both looking at me with blank faces. I glanced down at my phone and touched the screen to wake it up.

"Oh." That was all I could say.

I had sixteen missed calls and twelve text messages. All the calls were from Palmer, Stone, and Briggs. Ten messages were from Novak, because he was a serial texter. One was never good enough for him. Two were from a number I didn't recognize.

"So," Palmer slowly began his interrogation once more, "Are ya gonna tell us what you were doin'? Or should we start guessin'?"

"I went to that red carpet club downtown to see someone," I stated dismissively with a wave of my hand, already halfway down the hall on my way to my bedroom.

I really didn't want to talk to them about Sloane right now. If I stayed in there, they'd keep badgering me. I couldn't believe I was ready to call them a little over an hour ago to figure this shit out. Now that I was face to face with them, I just wasn't ready.

I liked Sloane so far and I knew as soon as they saw her they would too. It would be nice to have my friends like my girlfriend for once.

Fuck. She wasn't my girlfriend. I just met her yesterday. I would like to see her again, though.

Palmer was saying something to me, but I tuned him out. I didn't care what he had to say. All my attention was on the text from an unknown number. The snippet of the first message had my undivided attention as I opened the tab.

"Taylor Caplin will be waiting for you by your car. Please be careful. He's angry that you were with me and his thoughts are dark tonight."

And

"You should've kissed me. (Shoulder shrug emoji.)"

"Who the…" I breathed out before it hit me. "Oh. Ohhhh. Shit. Maybe I am stupid."

Fuck. My. Life.

I knew I should have kissed her. No. I should've done exactly what Jack said.

Godsdamnit. I was a fool.

"We've been telling you that for years," Novak piped up from my bed. *MY bed*. Where he was sprawled diagonally, in nothing but boxers, on his stomach with his face buried under my pillows.

Why was he always in my fucking room? I just wanted to go to sleep.

"Why are you in my bed?" I hissed instead. "You have your own room. A room that has very similar furniture to mine."

He could go lie in his own damn bed.

He moved the pillow from over his head and leaned up just a little, turning his neck at an odd angle.

"There's a naked girl in my bed," he whined. "And she. Just. Won't. Leave. Make her go away, please."

His last words were muffled as he slammed my pillow over his head again, like if he could smother himself then she might magically disappear.

Vaughn

I huffed a laugh at him. *He was so fucking dramatic.*

"If I make her leave, will you get out of my room?" I bartered. I *really* wanted to sleep. I was almost as dead on my feet as he was.

I know. That was a corny vampire joke, but it was true.

"Yes." He dragged the word out. "I asked her to leave hours ago, but she wouldn't take the hint. I mean, she's cute, but not cute enough to stay for breakfast." He rolled his eyes.

"I guess Palmer will be the white knight that he is and feed her. Then she'll never want to leave." He sniffled and wiped imaginary tears from his exposed cheek.

"I'll have to move into your room so I can permanently avoid her." He sighed. He was such an asshole.

"Make her leave, Vaughn," he whined again.

"You could've just compelled her…" I let my sentence hang, waiting for him to figure it out. Maybe he'd be smart today.

Nope. I knew exactly what he was about to say. I mouthed the words as he spoke them, having them memorized long ago.

"Yeah, but then I'd have to look into her eyes again and I just can't do it, Vaughn," he mumbled like it was a new confession.

It was not new. *He was a dog.*

"Bad sex, huh? You let her down?" I couldn't help but tease him.

He was terrified of commitment. Stone and Palmer avoided relationships because they were waiting on their mates, but Novak? He was a one-and-done kind of guy, most of the time.

Occasionally he was a 24-hour kind of guy. Those girls never got brought to our home, though.

Briggs was wary after his last heart break, and wouldn't be looking for a companion anytime soon.

I didn't do relationships because I was too busy. I was leaning towards a change, though.

Fuck. Was I? Did I want to be with Sloane?

I'd have to think about that later. When I was by my godsdamn self.

"Fuck you, Vaughn." There was no heat behind his words. He sounded truly exhausted. He still had his head covered with my pillow.

He thrashed his legs violently, almost like he was throwing a silent tantrum, before rolling over and removing the pillow to continue, "She said she wants a relationship with me." He pointed to himself for clarification.

"After one good fuck. I'm not interested, and I told her straight up. She didn't listen. She's waiting for me to come back in there with my mind changed. It's *not* happening. She doesn't understand that she means absolutely nothing to me. Last night, today, just showed me that I'm fucking sick of this. I'm ready to find my mate. I'm tired of all these bullshit one-night stands."

He heaved a heavy sigh of relief, and if I had to guess, he needed to get that off his chest.

He sounded so serious that I almost wanted to believe him, but Novak was.... well, Novak. *I'd believe it when I saw it.*

We all wondered sometimes if he'd already met his mate and just didn't notice. He'd been binge drinking for the past couple of months, so it wouldn't surprise me.

I'd asked him to talk to me about it, but he always shot me down. He'd talk when he was ready, though, and he knew I was here to listen when he was. I could tell he wasn't going to say anything more, so I decided to reroute the conversation.

"Do fae have mates like vampires do? Because if they do, then I think I found my mate yesterday, Novak. I'm a mixture of confused, terrified, and excited," I whispered.

It was an admission I wasn't quite ready to say out loud, but I'd known Novak longer than anyone in this realm. He was always the first person I told things to. He was what I needed to work my feelings out.

A vampire therapist.

I needed someone to tell me what I felt wasn't my imagination. It was real.

I really hoped it was real.

He looked up at me with wide eyes and then looked around the room like someone else might be in here.

"She's not here," I scoffed. "But, that's where I was last night. I didn't know you guys were all coming back at the same time. I thought you'd be out until later today. The others weren't due back for days. Briggs came home, too? What's going on?" I questioned him, hoping he'd have answers.

"Neither did we." He shrugged his shoulders. "I just had this feeling that I needed to be home. Like something big was gonna happen, but I didn't know what."

He had his brows drawn down and his eyes squinted like he was trying to piece together a puzzle while talking to me. With what pieces, I didn't know, but he never failed to figure it out.

Sometimes he was a dumbass, but other times he made me wonder if he was more of a genius than Palmer.

"What are you thinking?" I inquired.

What did he know that I didn't? The feeling that I was missing something huge was weighing on my shoulders. I still felt that strange pull on my chest, too.

I distractedly rubbed at the center of my chest, and Novak's attention snapped to my hand. His eyes widened, eyebrows flying up in the process, and his mouth gaped open before he could compose himself.

He cleared his throat and then carefully asked, "Vaughn, does your chest hurt like you've been punched?" He paused for a beat, but I knew he wasn't done. "Or does it feel like someone threaded invisible strings through your heart that they're pulling on right now?"

He made a motion with his hand like he was stringing two objects together. I felt the blood rush from my face. My heartbeat was rapidly increasing. My hands were clammy. He saw it all, and he kept talking.

"I've only heard stories about fae having mates, but I suppose it could happen. We'd have to talk with Palmer to be sure. I'm gonna go out on a limb here and say you're not ready to bring that up to the others yet."

He raised a skeptical eyebrow at me, and I nodded my head silently. He slowly nodded his head back at me and dropped his voice.

He sounded like he was speaking to himself when he continued, "Surely we didn't all get the same feeling that we needed to be here solely because you found *your* mate." The way he said "your" didn't go unnoticed.

"What are you talking about, Novak?" I needed to know.

It was going to drive me crazy.

He was onto something. He had that distant look on his face that he got when he was focusing on putting all those invisible puzzle pieces together. I just didn't know what all the pieces he had were. *Clearly more than me.*

He didn't answer. I wasn't even sure that he'd heard me.

I sat on the edge of my bed and gave him a few more minutes of silence before I repeated my question.

This time he looked at me and shook his head. His hair flopped down into his eyes. He pushed it back before he shook his head again.

"It doesn't make sense yet, Vaughn," he admitted to me, but I didn't think he was trying to answer my question.

He was talking about whatever he was working through. *He was answering his own question.* I didn't know what the question was, though, so I couldn't help him.

He shook his head a few more times and then groaned. "Naked chick. In my bed."

He brought me back to the task at hand and I sighed dramatically. I didn't like doing his dirty work, but sometimes it was fun.

"Did you give her a fake name?"

That was what he usually did. He said it was to distance himself from them, but I honestly didn't understand.

It was his thing, though, not mine.

He just flashed me a big smile in answer.

I honestly thought he enjoyed making me do this shit.

That was why he always hid out in my room.

Briggs would let her cry on his shoulder as he told her the truth. Palmer would make her breakfast and send her on her way after calling a cab to come get her. Stone would carry Novak out of his room and throw him back on his own bed with his naked issue.

Me? Well, I had my own way of dealing with his shit.

I wasn't fast enough to catch Novak and use Stone's method. I also wasn't nice enough to handle it the way Briggs and Palmer would.

Which, in a nutshell, was why he came to me. Every. Fucking. Time.

"Let me get the naked girl out of your bed so you can at least put some fucking clothes on. Later, after I've slept for a few hours, we can make some plans to go out tonight. Sounds like we all need a good night out."

I strode out of my room as Novak started muttering to

himself. Probably talking to his dick. That was my educated guess.

I swear, we needed to buy that vampire a chastity cage.

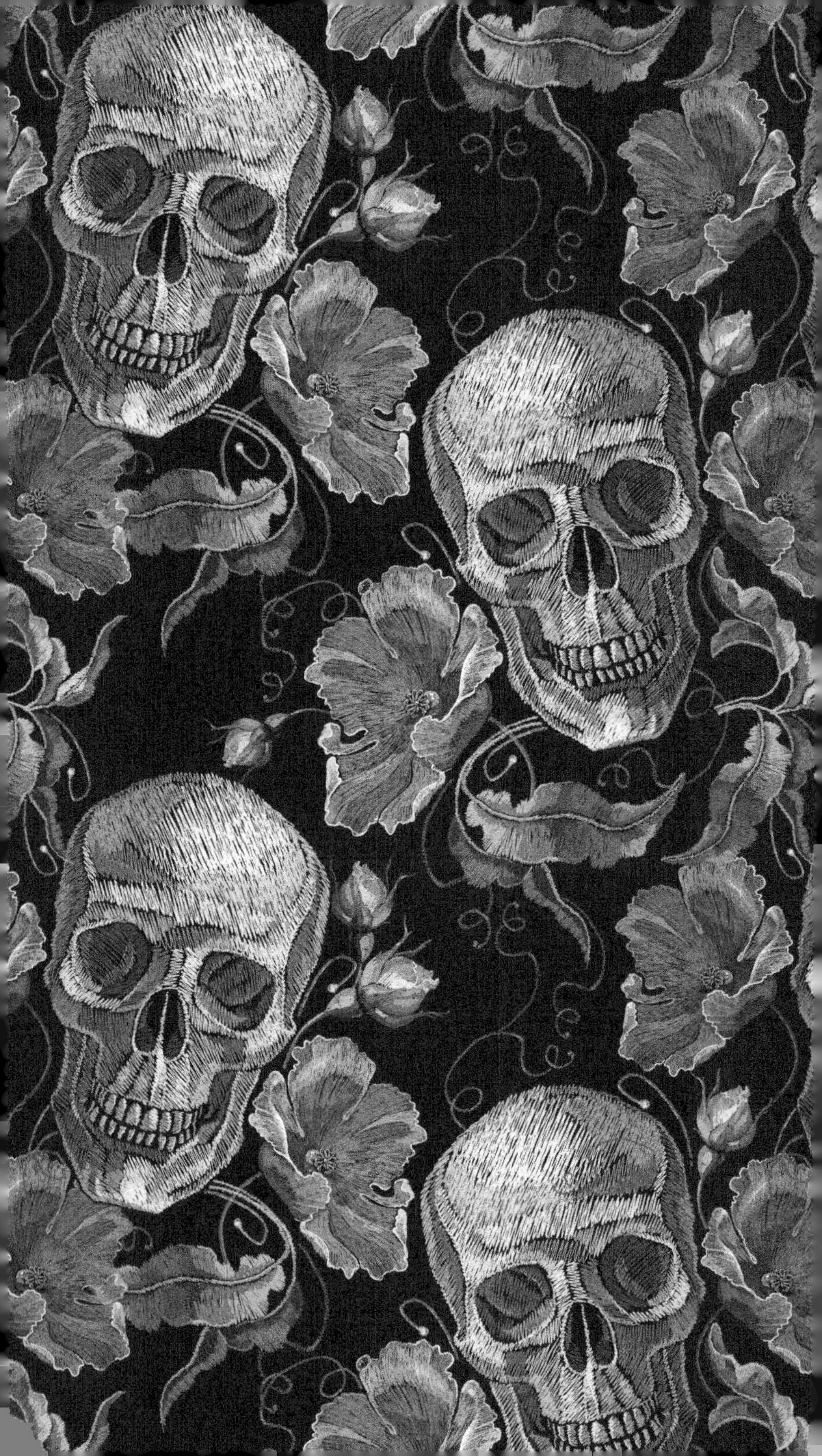

CHAPTER 7
Novak

Saturday, May 16th
Morning

I listened to Vaughn through the bedroom walls while I scolded myself. I'd probably already met my mate and was just too drunk to notice.

We'd all said it before.

I seriously needed to slow down on the drinking before I really fucked my life up.

We'd all said that, too.

What if I had already met my mate? No. I would've known if I had. I hadn't met her yet, but I thought I may know who she was. If I was right, though... Man, it was gonna get a little weird around here. Total mindfuck of the interesting variety.

Vaughn's room was on the other side of mine, so it wasn't too hard to hear him while he put on another one of his best performances.

Academy Awards, here comes Vaughn Winter.

He happened to be great at running them out. It was one of the reasons why I always came to his room when it didn't work my way. I mean, that and he made it so funny to listen to. I almost felt bad for the chick in my room, but then I remembered that I asked her to leave and she refused.

"What are you doing in my bedroom?" he demanded in a voice that reminded me of a war general ending a tirade.

I could picture him with his eyebrows drawn over his cold blue eyes, looking totally offended while staring at the naked human woman in my bed.

He wouldn't even glance at her fake tits, or notice that she used lip fillers, or that she had gray contacts to hide her naturally brown eyes. He didn't give a shit about her or her feelings.

That was the other reason why I hid in his room when I couldn't get the bitch to leave. I didn't use that word lightly when describing a woman. It was just... she refused to leave.

Slapping my forehead, I dragged my hand down my face in a rare moment of self-flagellation. I was such an idiot. I knew better than to sleep with humans. That shit *always* fucking happened, and it blew up in my face every time.

Fuck me. I had to stop thinking with my dick.

A human woman. I scoffed at myself.

That was where I fucked up. They couldn't tell that I wasn't like them, unless I was hungry or showed my powers to get a fright out of someone. I didn't even feed off of them.

I was a bit of a blood snob.

The chick in my bed, especially, had no self preservation. I bet if she knew that I was a vampire, she'd beg me to turn her.

No fucking thanks.

"I didn't... I didn't know this was your room. Where is Noah? He's the reason I'm here," she simpered, probably batting her fake eyelashes at Vaughn.

She was as fake as the nut I busted last night. I should've left her at that shitty wanna-be vampire bar instead of bringing her home. *To our actual home.* I knew better.

"I don't know who the fuck Noah is. I'm gonna be nice and give you five minutes to collect your shit and get out of my apartment before I call the police and ask them to come pick you up for breaking and entering."

I couldn't help the snort that came out. He was so full of shit. I used a fake name *every single time* I brought someone home. He kicked them out with the exact same act when I couldn't get them to leave. He had the routine perfected at this point.

This happened more often than I'd care to admit.

"Okay, okay. No need for the cops. He had a key, I think. He said it was his place. I didn't know! Just... just let me grab my clothes and I'll be gone." Oh, she was frantic now.

Vaughn could be a dick when he needed to be. I bet he was standing in the doorway with his arms crossed over his chest, glaring at her with those icy, emotionless eyes.

He should've kicked that she-wolf, Anna, out when Briggs brought her home. We'd all told him to leave her alone and look at what happened. Eight months wasted on her when he could've been looking for his mate.

She was cheating on him for six of those months. Until Stone caught her shacking up with some businessman in Atlanta, when she was supposed to be on a girls' trip with her sister.

That was a long story for another day.

Stone had a lovely interrogation with the guy after he video-called Briggs so he could see her with him.

Briggs had been camping for the last six weeks. It was his code for running through the woods and killing whatever was in his path. He had more shit to sort out before finding his mate than I did.

I had a feeling we'd be meeting her soon, though; so he needed to pull his head out of his ass. *He was a good guy, don't get me wrong.* He just picked the shittiest women to fall for.

After a few moments I heard the front door slam, and then I knew Nikki, or Jasmine... or was it Kara? Whichever. It didn't matter... *The bitch was finally gone.*

Thank the Devil. I mean the fae. Yes, thank the fae. *Just don't say "thank you" to the fae.*

Vaughn opened his bedroom door and sighed. "Your room is yours again. Now get out so I can take a nap."

He was grouchy, but he had a fuck load of shit on his plate. *AND* he'd found his mate? *Nahhh, that's crazy.*

I believed him, though. I knew all about that pulling in his chest. I wouldn't tell him. *Not yet.* He needed to know that his feelings were his own.

The mate bond pulled you together. It would drive you insane with the need to protect. It wouldn't make you lust after or fall in love with your mate. Those feelings were all your own.

The instant attraction was the same that you'd feel if you had seen a hot chick at the bar; however, the potential mate bond did intensify the feelings that are already there. Or so I'd been told.

"With pleasure." I mock-saluted him. "I'm going to head out for a bit. Do you need anything?"

I wasn't going anywhere except straight to Palmer to sort all this shit out. I wondered if he thought the same thing I did.

"No, but be back by ten tonight so we can go out. I was thinking about seeing if I could get us all into the club I went to last night, but I don't know if that would be wise. The woman I think is my mate is the part owner with her dad or something," he declared while shaking his head.

He took off his shoes and then threw himself onto his

bed. I slid the curtains closed on his window and tossed his shoes in his closet while I waited for him.

I was such a good friend.

He would hate that I didn't line them up properly, but whatever.

I wasn't the OCD one.

"And..." I finally pushed.

I knew he wanted to say more. He'd either tell me now or he'd tell me later, but he always told me.

"And," he sighed again. Uh-oh. "Her dad just bought CBP from Caplin. And," he sighed louder, like he just couldn't deal with all the bullshit that was his life, "Taylor Caplin is stalking her. I don't know if I want to kill him or watch her kill him.

"You know I hate that guy. He was waiting by my car this morning when I left the club and he had a gun with iron bullets. Why did he have iron bullets? It's not like he knows what I am."

He shrugged before powering through his rant. "If it wasn't for her horse-shifter friend, I might be dead right now. And, well, I don't like the idea of that guy being anywhere near her, if I'm being honest."

"Well now, that is intriguing. I've never met a horse shifter, but that's not important. What's her name?" I inquired.

I was bubbling over with curiosity. I wanted to know everything. *Also, horse shifter? What the fuck?*

"Sloane. Sloane King."

"Oh. I know her." He raised his eyebrows, skepticism clear on his face.

I bet he thought I'd fucked her too. I hadn't, but I definitely would. *For sure.*

"I mean, not her, but I know two of her dads, Nathaniel and Charles King. You know that job I had a few weeks ago? When I took out the rogue tiger shifter while I was in Asia? Yeah, Charles hired me. He's head Alpha, big shit."

I nodded my head energetically before continuing. "He controls the shifter factions across the world. All the faction alphas are under him. I bet Briggs knows who he is."

I knew for a fact that he did.

I waited for Vaughn's reply for a moment. I thought he'd fallen asleep with his eyes open. He was just lying there staring at the ceiling.

It looked like he was holding his breath. If I couldn't hear his frantic heartbeat, I might have mistaken him as being dead.

Just as I stepped out of the door to his bedroom, he bolted upright in his bed. Confused. Frantic. About sixty-four other emotions passed over his face, never settling on one for more than a second.

"What?" he demanded loudly. "Her dad is a shifter? But... but... I would have noticed that. Surely. She seemed to be part demon."

He scrubbed his hand up and down his face in quick succession. "I'm sure she was part demon. I mean, she even told me her dad runs a demon boarding school."

"You really don't know, do you?" I asked him with a small smile playing at my lips. "We need to have a talk, my man. Come to the living room before you fall asleep. I'll gather the troops."

Oh, this was definitely going to be a mindfuck.
Why? *Well, I'll tell you.*

I was pretty sure that Nathaniel King's daughter was *my mate,* and that was why he'd been training me to take over his position as High Coven Master.

Though, now that I happened to think about it like that, maybe it wasn't to be the head but to help the head. *With head.* Yeah. I could totally handle that.

I walked out of Vaughn's room, down the hallway, and headed to the living area.

The coffee table was littered with Palmer's books, and he had a coffee cup in his left hand as he turned the pages of a book with his right. I'd bet my left nut that there was whiskey in that cup, not fucking coffee.

Stone was sitting on the floor by the fireplace. When he came through the door of the apartment, it was instantly filled with the sound of crackling wood and the smell of burning pine.

He was a pyromaniac, but I guess that was okay since he was a demon and regular fire wouldn't burn him. It would sure as hell burn the rest of us, though.

Stone and Palmer were sitting there like they knew I was going to call them in. I heard Briggs in the kitchen rifling through the fridge. He was always cooking, but Palmer beat him to breakfast this morning.

I sampled their food, but I didn't need it for sustenance, so it was just more of a curiosity for me.

Briggs was a great cook, though. Better than Palmer.

When they were home, there was something different to eat for every meal.

The cabinets were filled with spices and dried herbs. Nearly everything we ate was home-cooked if Briggs was here, but he didn't cook desserts, although he loved chocolate chip cookies.

Our neighbor, Mrs. Annette, made us a fresh batch each week. Since everyone was out of town this week, we didn't get any, but I was sure we'd get a nice big box of them on Monday.

Palmer was a baker, so kitchen duty worked well between him and Briggs, and then we got left with cleaning up their messes.

Vaughn stormed into the living room, grumpy and still looking skeptical. It was an odd look on him. I felt a smidge evil for finding joy in the situation.

He was always so confident and collected. He really didn't know, and I knew it was killing him. He hated not knowing every little step or detail. Between him and Palmer, we were never short on control freaks.

Today was one of those rare times where we all knew something that he didn't. Granted, we weren't sure if he knew or not, and the subject never came up.

We were probably going to end up telling him information that we weren't supposed to tell anyone. I didn't want to be the one to tell him, but I would if I had to.

Had he really never heard the stories?

I rubbed my hands together excitedly. It was going to

be fun watching him flounder around trying to fit the pieces together.

Palmer and I'd had several conversations in the past few years, since we all moved in together, about what had brought all of us to one place.

Most of us had known each other since we were teenagers, but we didn't start hanging out until a little over six years ago.

Now the puzzle pieces were starting to click. I wondered if Palmer saw it yet.

If my math was correct, six years ago Sloane King had turned eighteen. *Old enough for her to find a mate.* All of that information made me think about the druid we used to be friends with.

"Hey, Briggs? Come in here for a minute." *Or twenty.* I hoped he wasn't cooking anything. "Turn the stove off, it might take more than a minute," I yelled across the apartment.

He growled softly in response and stomped into the room, wiping his hands on a dish towel.

At least he was clean and groomed now.

When he'd come home last night, he'd looked like a caveman. He'd nearly made me jump out of my skin when he'd banged open the door and dropped his bags on the floor.

"Guys, tell Vaughn the story of the King family," I instructed no one in particular, or whoever wanted to answer.

Not me, though. I wanted to watch Vaughn's face.

"No, wait." I held my hand up and closed my eyes,

fighting a smile. "Tell Vaughn about the Kings' daughter. We can save the rest for later. It's not important right now."

The three of them looked from me to Vaughn and back again, probably wondering if I was joking.

"Ye don't know?" Palmer asked incredulously. Eyes narrowed, he shook his head a few times and turned to Vaughn for an answer.

"Uhm, no, but I met her last night." He shrugged his shoulders and looked around. All three of them were staring wide-eyed at him, just like I did.

"We drank a rather expensive bottle of tequila, and I kicked her ass in darts." He rubbed the back of his neck like he was a little embarrassed to admit that last part. I would be, too.

I was surprised she didn't kill him. Rumors, though, you know?

"And she didn't kill you?" Briggs piped up, reading my mind.

Not really, but close enough.

He was awake, not grumbling, and focused completely on Vaughn.

I let myself wonder. Maybe they *were* just rumors and she was actually nice, or maybe she was a crazy bitch. Either way, I knew she was hot as hell. I'd seen pictures of her in her father's office.

"Uhm, no," Vaughn replied, utterly confused by Briggs' reaction. "She was really sweet and funny. Beat my ass at a game of pool, though, and drank me under the table. We left the club at 5:30 this morning and I noticed

Taylor fucking Caplin stalking her. He was waiting outside when we walked out."

He spat Taylor's name with more venom than I'd ever heard come from his mouth. I understood why if he thought she was his mate. I didn't like Taylor either.

I think maybe we should pay him a visit soon.

I'd love to scare him senseless and then compel him to forget so we could do it all over again. For a whole month straight.

Just terrify him until he has a heart attack. Death by scare. It was fucking perfect.

"Wow." That was all Briggs had left to say as he nodded his head. Dumbfounded. Yeah, that was what I would call him right now.

"Well, I dinnea know where ta begin, exactly," Palmer chimed in real fucking helpfully, but at least he was pulling us back to the task at hand.

"She has four parents," Stone was the first to give up real information, "and I know a little about her, but I'm not sure if it's just rumors or not. I've never met her."

He shrugged his shoulders with his hands out to the side. He looked like the demon version of my sister's favorite emoji.

"It's said that her mother was such a powerful mage that she was able to magic herself pregnant from all three of her mates at once. Together they had one child. A daughter.

"She's part mage, demon, vampire, and shifter. The best qualities from each with none of the weaknesses. A dangerous mixed breed hybrid. She is *the* elite predator. There's no one else like her.

"Shortly after she was born, her mother went missing. Her mates are still searching for her." Stone looked genuinely saddened by that last statement. He hung his head a little before he took a deep breath to continue.

"You said her name was Sloane?" he asked Vaughn. "She must be about twenty-four. The Devil himself gifted her with three hellhounds when she graduated high school, but I'm sure that's just another rumor floating around. I've never seen hellhounds when I've visited Hell, only read about them.

"It's said that he's her grandfather, though he could possibly be her demon father. I never worked up the guts to ask Headmaster King when I was sent to the Devil's Academy, but I apprenticed under him enough to hear him talk about her. I still visit him a few times a year. His name is Samuel King."

"Whoa, Stone. I think that's the most I've ever heard you talk at once." I couldn't help it. He was usually so quiet.

I knew all this information, but I still had a slack jaw as he spoke. He never talked that much. Even when he had something to say, it wasn't quite that many words at once.

"Guess you won't speak for the rest of the week," I teased.

He grunted at me and rolled his eyes, but I saw the side of his mouth lift a little, like he was fighting a smile.

I'd count that as a small victory. He liked my sense of humor. He just didn't want me to know.

"Her vampire da's name is Nathaniel King. He rules the Vampire covens," Palmer started.

"Yeah, with an iron fist," I huffed out my interruption.

We had so many rules to follow. *Don't even get me started.*

We couldn't kill humans. We couldn't drink from unwilling participants. We couldn't let them remember we drank from them. The rules went on and on and on.

I followed those big "main" rules, but the smaller ones? No fucking way. I'd just use common sense, thank you very fucking much.

"And he also acts as the Regent to the Guild Leaders in 'er ma's absence," he continued on like I didn't interrupt him.

"Sloane should've taken over when she came of age, but she asked for more time. She'll take over when she mates with a mage. Or so Nathaniel says."

Palmer had wanted to read the contract between the guild leaders and Nathaniel, but he was told it wasn't his business.

He was a salty mage until that sweet talking vampire had told him if Sloane didn't have a mage mate, then Nathaniel would turn the guilds over to Palmer. Something about a treaty after that.

I fell asleep while Palmer was explaining it to me. That's how boring it was. I didn't sleep, but Palmer talked me to boredom so quickly that I was near death.

"Charles King is Supreme Alpha. I've had the honor of meeting him more than a few times before," Briggs finally spoke.

"We have annual meetings with the alpha's apprentices. There are six of us from around the world. Should something happen to him before his daughter takes her place, then we're supposed to meet up and either vote a regent alpha in or fight to the death, unless she steps in. In more or less words."

He growled and covered his face with one hand. "Also, I was not supposed to tell you guys that," he added as an afterthought.

Explained the growl, I guess.

Vaughn looked a little paler than he did earlier. Pale was his normal skin tone, but he was fading from a shimmery cream to a dingy white. It had a real sickly effect on him.

Next he would turn green. I really wanted to make a joke about his changing skin tone.

Not the time, Novak.

I knew what he'd say. He said the same thing every time. *"Fae don't change their skin color, Novak. That's a myth. I could glamor myself, but it doesn't actually change anything. It's just an illusion."*

What was that word Palmer called him again? Something shite. I'd ask him later.

"Fuck," he breathed out and slumped down in his seat. "Jack wasn't lying when he said she'd kill Taylor with a spoon if she caught him stalking her."

Ahhh, now I remembered. A dry shite. Vaughn was a dry shite.

Back to the point.

I arched a brow at him. "Who is Jack?" And why did I feel so jealous?

I was not the jealous type. I'd never even met her.

Never mind, I know. From the look on Palmer's face, I could tell he was figuring it out, too. I'd give him a minute more.

"He's... I don't know. Her bodyguard? Her best friend? Maybe both? Or neither. I don't know!" He threw his hands up, exasperated with the whole situation.

"He saved my ass last night, though. Said she sent him because she "saw" Taylor waiting for me at my car. How? She left in the opposite direction of where I parked."

He jumped up to pace. His air quotes were super cute.

"I mean, he's a big ass horse shifter, and he kicked Taylor right in the chest. Then he threatened him. Jack said he'd rip his heart through his chest and eat it if he caught Taylor ever speaking her name again. It was honestly panic-inducing. I'm kind of glad he likes me. He—"

"We don't have horse shifters," Briggs cut in, sounding very offended. "Shifters are predators, Vaughn. Wolves, large felines, bears, occasionally a snake... you know? Carnivores. Not fucking horses."

"We do," Stone announced so quietly that I thought I was hearing things, and he looked a little pasty too.

I'd never seen Stone any color except that pretty, light caramel color that made him pass as Asian, or the pitch black color of his demon skin.

His demon skin was so black that most of the time I couldn't see him in the dark, even with my night vision. It was like his demon form sucked up all the light around him.

He didn't change forms very often. He did when he went to Hell, though.

Sorry, the Underworld, or whatever. Hell was the capital. They could call it Cincinnati, and I still wouldn't give a fuck.

Before Briggs could dispute him, Stone rolled on.

Ha. I killed myself with puns sometimes.

"We have one, and he *is* a predator. He's a massive steed. Darker than even me. He leaves a trail of smoke when he moves, and he can travel through shadows. His eyes reflect hellfire. He had a son, but no one has seen either of them in decades. Some people say they're both dead, some say he ran after plotting to overthrow the Devil. Others say he went missing just like Samuel's mate. No one knows."

Stone was killing me with all the talking today.

At this rate, he wouldn't say another word for two weeks.

It didn't surprise me that the demon had that kind of information, though. He was a quiet, sneaky fucker, and people never knew when he was listening to them. I thought he'd make a great spy.

That was what they did, right?

Palmer, though, he'd been oddly quiet. I bet he was taking notes in his mind about what was being said, all while planning out the fae's burial before the biggest predator in all the realms could kill him. It was kind of funny, kind of not.

I think I wanted to meet her.

"Okay," Vaughn interjected slowly and nodded his head. "That sounds like Jack. He's also very... nice."

He shrugged his shoulders. I could tell that he didn't know what to think. We were blowing his godsdamn mind.

He got up yesterday morning to go to work, met his mate, met a mythological demon, had a lunatic try to kill him, and then found out we all knew shit we had been keeping from him. He was going to need a stiff drink and a long nap after all that shit.

Stone just laughed. It started out low and then grew louder until it was a deep, hysterical belly laugh. It caught us all off guard.

All four of us were staring at him. I didn't think I'd ever heard him laugh quite like that. It was as if he thought Vaughn was going mad.

And it was also a little scary, if I may say so.

I could understand why he was laughing, though. He'd told Vaughn tales of two creatures: one an unheard of supernatural cocktail and the second a possible myth. Vaughn's like, "Yeah, they're nice."

Anyway. I wanted to fucking meet her.

"You should call her," I advised Vaughn as I sat in the

chair to the left of him. I watched him for a moment before waggling my eyebrows. "She sounds like fun."

"Jack said to wait until Sunday night." He shrugged a shoulder again, and I rolled my eyes.

When did he ever listen to anyone? He barely even listened to what we said. If we told him not to call her, he'd already have the phone to his ear, whispering sweet nothings to her.

Fucking Fae.

"Call 'er. Text 'er. Send 'er a fuckin note with the wind. Whatever ya do." Palmer waved his hand at Vaughn. "I want ta meet 'er."

Palmer surprised the shit out of me sometimes with his eager, scholarly mind. *Like right now.* He started connecting the dots. He didn't want to meet her, he wanted to examine her. With her clothes on.

He was such a bore.

Fucking hell. There went my dick, thinking for my brain again. It wasn't wrong this time, though. This time my dick was very, very right.

Think away, good sir, think away. We would be meeting our mate soon.

Right. I needed to stop talking to my dick before I meet her. Probably.

Vaughn sighed for the thirty-fifth time this morning. He looked to Briggs and Stone for answers, and they nodded their heads in agreement with Palmer and me. He *should* call her.

If she was part vampire, then I doubted she slept. It

wasn't like he'd be waking her up. *He was just stalling. The puss.*

"Do it and stop being a bag of dicks!" I barely contained the shouted words, but I wasn't mad. Quite the opposite, actually.

I grinned extra big at him, flashing my teeth, fangs, and dimples. He glared at me.

"Fine." The word was clipped and dripping in sarcasm. It was like we'd twisted his arm or something.

If he didn't want to call her, then I would.

He grumbled under his breath all the way to his room and came back with his cell.

"I'll text her first. Then, maybe, I'll send a note with the wind." He rolled his ice-blue eyes at Palmer, who just smirked back at him.

Palmer was a legit genius, but he was also a smart ass. He knew how to push each one of our buttons. I loved him for it, but I hated him when he pushed my own.

I got up from my chair to stand behind Vaughn, reading the texts from the number *we* assumed was hers.

I liked the elegant way her texts read and the fact that she didn't misspell her words or shorten them. She said he should've kissed her this morning, and I damn well agreed. Even though I wasn't there. I'd have kissed her. Probably done more.

Forget probably. I definitely would have.

"Sloane?"

By the Devil. Why had no one ever taught him how to pick up a woman? That's just ridiculous. That single text nearly brought saddened tears to my eyes.

She texted back almost immediately, and I couldn't decide if she knew it was coming or just had her phone in her hand.

I scratched my chin while I debated with myself about it. That was an interesting thought to unpack later. I wouldn't point it out yet.

Sloane: *"Jack said you guys took care of Caplin. They took him to the drunk tank to sit for the day. I hope he didn't get any shots off. I'm sorry I didn't warn you before. I thought he was coming after me, not you."*

Vaughn: *"Are you busy today? We need to talk about Caplin. I can meet you somewhere, but I'd rather not wait until Monday to talk about it. The offices at CBP are bugged."*

Oh gods. I groaned as I bit my knuckles. Why didn't he thank her? *Acknowledge her help. Make her feel useful.*

Oh right. He was fae. He didn't thank anyone. I wondered if she knew that.

Sloane: *"Not anymore. I had the whole facility swept last night. And no, I'm not busy today. Jack and I are having brunch, then training. You guys can head over. Tell the nosey vampire not to look through my phone, though. And let the shifter know that I won't kill him unless I have to. (Winking emoji)"*

Sloane: *"13648 Reignwood Drive"*

Vaughn: *"(laughing emoji) I'll let them know. See you in an hour?"*

Sloane: *"Sure. Hit the intercom when you get to the gate. Franklin will let you in. Park in the front by Jack's car and follow the right side path to the back. The hounds will be waiting to escort you. They're big, but very sweet."*

"Well, that's troublesome." I smirked to myself. "How would she know I was reading your texts?"

That made me curious. Also, I was now wondering what was in her phone.

Probably nudes. Godsdamnit. I hoped so.

"I don't know, but she said guys, so she knows that we're all sitting here. And she said to stay away from her phone. So stay away from it, Novak."

He gave me a pointed look, and I raised my hands in surrender. I didn't want to piss her off, but I did want to see her nudes.

Or maybe just her nude. Actually, that would work best for me.

"Also, Briggs, she said she won't kill you unless she

has to. I haven't the slightest clue what that means, but I think that was her way of trying to ease your nerves. Maybe leave the alpha posturing for another day."

Vaughn handed his phone to the guys to let them read the conversation, and another text came in. They bounced their gazes between each other and passed it back for Vaughn and me to read.

Sloane: *"So nosey, boys. Do you share everything?"*

Oh, I fucking liked her.

I was a shameless flirt. Some would even call me a player… but I definitely knew when a female was hitting on a male. *Uhm, a group of males?*

I scratched the back of my neck and chuckled. "I think we've met our match, guys."

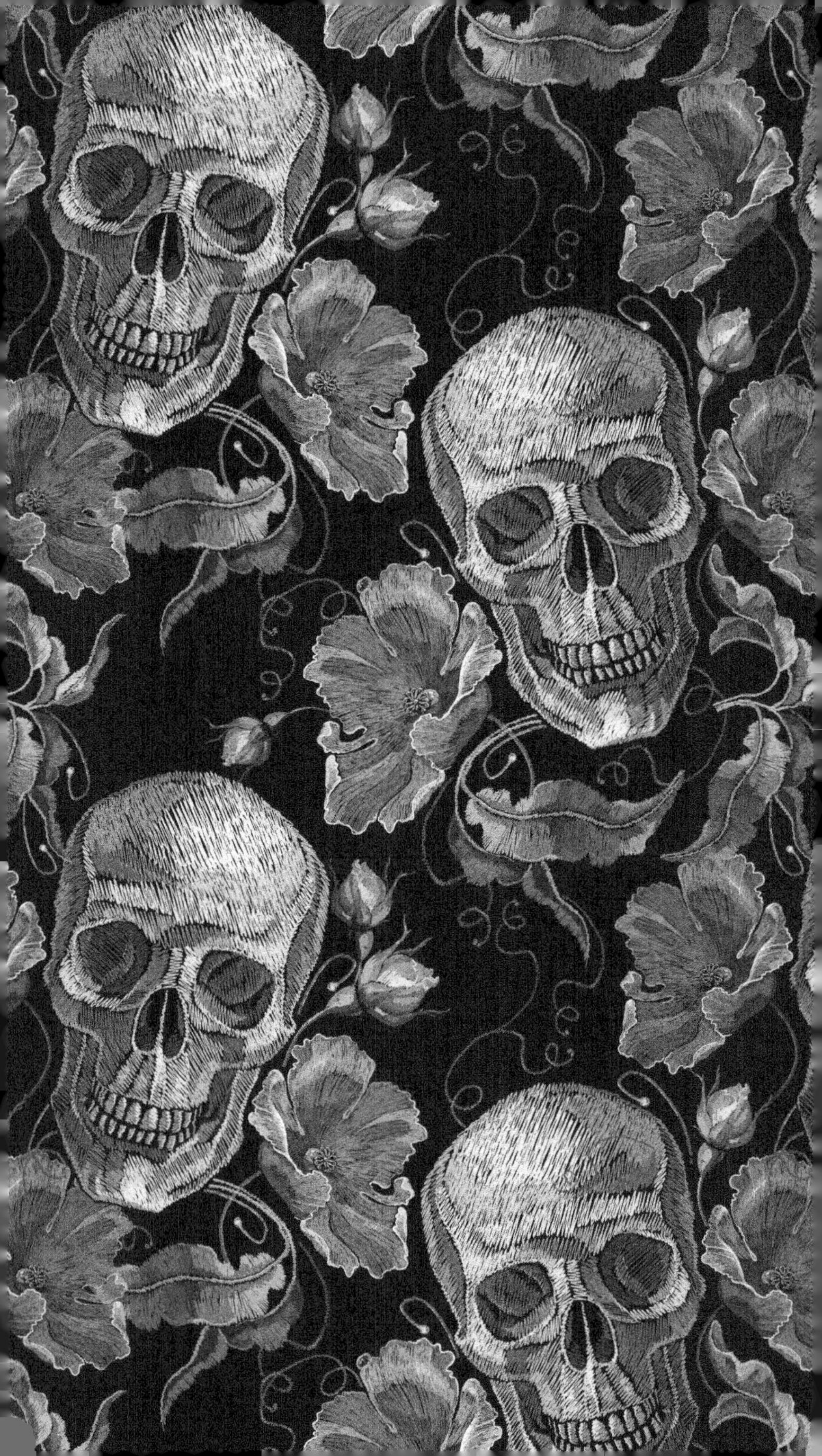

CHAPTER 8
Sloane

Saturday, May 16th
Mid Morning

"Jack," I called out as I maneuvered through the chairs on my patio, "I want to be mad at you for giving him my number, but honestly, I'm not."

Jack laughed low as he sat down. "Can you repeat that?"

"Seriously, Jack." I glared at him. "I like him. His friends seem nice. Nosey, but nice. They're on their way over."

Which freaked me out a bit. Jack and Grim were the only people who ever came to my house. I'd never invited other guests over. Except one.

The fucking druid.

Franklin arrived outside with food and beverages, seemingly ignoring us as we talked.

He had a way of being so silent that sometimes I didn't even notice him. Not in a "you're my staff" sort of way, but more like he projected an "I didn't want you to notice me so you won't" sort of vibe.

I often wondered if he'd been an assassin before my parents had assigned him to me. I'd never asked him, but it would make sense. When I was thirteen, he'd started teaching Jack and me how to use an array of weapons.

He still corrected us when we practiced with them.

"Franklin, I have visitors coming over. They should be here within the hour. They'll park out front and join us on the patio. Please send the hounds to me if you see them. I'd like to warn them of our guests too."

He stared at me for a solid minute with his eyebrows raised to his salt and pepper hairline. Then he grinned down at me and patted my shoulder, like he knew something I didn't, and hustled away to bring more plates.

Sometimes I thought the old male was more than just a vampire. Other times, I was pretty sure my parents told him things they didn't want me to know yet.

Atlas, Cronus, and Helios came bounding up the path a few minutes later. They held the appearance of English Mastiffs, except maybe a hundred pounds heavier.

Father always said they resembled the breed from

hundreds of years ago, like they were ready for the front lines of war or lion hunting.

I may or may not have had special armor made for them in the case of... an emergency. Really, I bought it because I knew they would look badass covered in it when they were on fire.

The armor was made specifically for them by a friend in Stars, and it stayed on their true forms. It couldn't be seen when they looked like *regular-ish* dogs.

They barked, nipped, and bumped into each other as they made their way to me. I found myself smiling at their playfulness.

I mean, they were cute *and* deadly, but still so super cute. It was my favorite mix of adjectives when describing them. *Cute and deadly.*

Just like me.

They really did look like regular dogs from a distance. The remarks were pretty easy to say whenever someone was nearby and didn't understand what they truly were. They usually stayed far enough back that people didn't have a chance to notice their true size.

They weren't regular dogs by any means, though. Not at all. They were hellhounds, gifted to me by my Papi as pups. I'd had them for a little over six years, but they didn't age like dogs.

They'd be with me until I died. That was their level of devotion. I loved them dearly too, but I loathed their diet.

The woodland creatures around my home probably didn't care for them either. I hadn't seen any deer, squirrels, or rabbits here in... ever. Just the half-chewed bones when I ran the wooden paths around my property.

Atlas trotted over and laid his head on my left shoulder, leaning his body weight into me. He was the sweetest of the three and was always laid back unless he sensed a threat.

I rested my head against the right side of his face and rubbed my left hand down his neck. He loved affection.

When he was done with my attention, he headed to Jack. Jack never gave him more than a few strokes to the head. He didn't care for my hounds after being my roommate for several years.

Jack and Cronus had a sticky relationship.

Cronus was extremely overprotective and liked to herd me from my car to the front door. It was annoyingly adorable.

He waited by the gate when it was time for me to get home. He patrolled the grounds like a good watchdog.

If he and Atlas would stop chasing bees, I thought I might love them even more. When they got stung, it fucked with the glamor that was layered on top of their true forms. The swelling distorted the illusion that disguised them, making them look very displeasing to the eye.

Fun fact: giving hellhounds antihistamine was like feeding them cocaine. They went nuts and tore everything apart.

Helios had a fiery personality, hence his name. He was an irritable, growly beast who watched over everything but still loved a good ear scratch. He was a tiny bit temperamental with everyone, except me.

Okay, a large bit.

I was the head bitch of our pack, so he didn't do more than simply test my patience. He wouldn't dare bite the hand that scratched his ears.

I touched each one of them in the center of their heads and sent them blurry images of my visitors so they knew not to attack.

I couldn't see all the males clearly yet, but the idea was that they shouldn't defend against the group of five.

I swear Cronus lifted an eyebrow at me when he understood what I was implying. Rotten hound.

I'd been getting too many of those curious looks lately.

"Cronus," I warned slowly, "Don't look at me like that. These are my guests, and I want you three to escort them to me when they arrive. Please be nice."

I turned hard eyes to my troublemaker. "Helios, don't growl at them. I told them you were sweet. We won't be letting them know that you guys are hellhounds, is that understood?"

Helios huffed smoke from his nostrils but inclined his nose to let me know he comprehended my request.

He was the only one I ever worried about not following instructions. Cronus and Atlas would follow them exactly.

Atlas licked my cheek as the three trotted off to wait by the gate, appearing to anyone else like well-trained dogs. I had a feeling Helios was going to be a dick, though.

It was just his personality.

I was sure before my guests left I'd have to explain why my "dog" had a fire-tipped tail or why smoke was pouring from his nose. Should be a fun conversation. *Insert heavy sarcasm here.*

"I can't believe you: A) trained hellhounds and B) let them lick you. That's gross, Lo. Do you know what they eat?" Jack constantly gave me shit about my boys.

Always had, always would.

"They are my babies, Jack," I told him for the millionth time. "Those hellhounds don't run around looking for ass, and they feed themselves. They even have a bedroom."

I raised my hand before he could interrupt me. "I know, I know. I spoil them."

I rolled my eyes. "But I don't regret it. They are loyal to no one except me. They'll protect me with their lives. Literally. No questions asked, and they expect nothing in return except a good belly scratch."

Who needed a man when I had a thousand pounds of extra warm, cuddly hellhounds in disguise?

Me. I needed company that talked. Preferably of the sexy male variety. Please and thanks.

I felt like I'd rolled my eyes more in the last few days than I had in my entire life. That shit was getting out of hand.

Papi used to tell me they were going to get stuck in the back of my head one day, and that terrified me. Still did. Then Dad laughed at me for that being the one thing that would scare me.

Sloane

I was a little vain, sue me.

I would not look sexy with my eyes permanently viewing the front of my brain.

Also, I got that that wasn't how it worked, but it was what I imagined.

Jack and I chatted about training while we ate... or rather, he ate. I wasn't really hungry for food. I drank a mimosa with a shot of blood added to it.

It sounded nasty, I know.

Orange juice and blood? It wasn't that bad. The champagne made it better. It had been a few days since I'd fed.

The ounce of blood in my glass would hold me for a week. I didn't need nearly as much blood as a pure vampire. I still had to eat regular food, too.

You know, to keep the rest of my body running.

If I was being honest with myself, I just wasn't hungry because I was a little nervous about Vaughn and his friends coming over.

I knew they were heading this way. I felt that thread pulling tighter and tighter with every minute that ticked by.

Fuck me.

I needed to do something active before I started thinking about all the nasty shit that had been floating around in the back of my mind. That feeling had basically reduced me back to a horny teenager with nothing better to do than think about sex.

It was time to fight.

Jack planned today's workout routine while finishing our brunch and headed to the grass for a swift stretch.

We were about twenty minutes into our match when I heard the gates open. My nerves began to ramp up when I spotted a vehicle coming down the drive. I caught a glimpse of a sleek, black SUV before it was out of sight again.

Five new people were in my territory. It made me feel both giddy and uneasy. I was being ridiculous, but I never invited people to my house. Especially people I hadn't met before. It was a big space to occupy by myself, but I was a private sort of person and I liked it that way.

Jack was in his shifted form and took my distraction as the choice opportunity to ambush me. The large horse came barreling in, long legs eating the distance I had put between us moments ago.

Just as he was about to use his head to knock me across the yard, I stepped to the side and gave his ass a hard slap.

He turned to huff smoke in my face. It was an unfair advantage against me, but most fights were like that.

I crouched to make myself a smaller target. I couldn't see through the thick, sooty smoke. I could feel him moving, though.

I heard his light steps flatten the blades of grass as I focused solely on him. His heartbeat was slow and even, his breaths deep and steady.

When I knew he was close enough, I jumped up to wrap my arms and legs around the underside of his neck.

He let out what should be considered a whinny — if

it weren't so deep and guttural — and threw his massive head around to dislodge me.

Flames shot from his nostrils in his frustration, but I wouldn't let go. He should know that by now. He never did account for my stubbornness.

He swung his head from right to left, trying to sling me off. I anticipated the next swing to the right and then used the momentum to launch myself onto the top side of his neck.

I grabbed a fistful of his mane in the process and waited for him to throw his head again.

The pitch black smoke surrounded us more with each step he took as he fought against my hold. I knew he could see through it, so I had to play smart.

I loosened my hold to let him think I was slipping. *He always fell for it.*

When he tossed his head a final time, I launched myself from the smoke cloud around him and laughed as I hit the ground in a crouch.

"I won this round, Jack. You're gonna need to try a new trick with me to even the score," I yelled to him while I straightened my body and dusted my hands off.

He stood in his smoke cloud, huffing.

"Stop burning my grass! Between you and Helios, it's getting hard to explain to the gardener why my grass is always singed!" I shouted at him in mock anger, trying to smother my glee.

I heard the jackass laughing at me as he shifted back, sucking in the hellish smoke surrounding him. He appeared unfazed in his tight jeans and black t-shirt.

"You're supposed to use your demon side to fight me, bitch, not your vampire side. I think we'll call it a draw until you can force my big ass to the ground."

He was still laughing inaudibly as the guys arrived, escorted by my hounds.

They made a triangle formation. Cronus and Atlas were a few feet in front on either side of the group, with Helios walking about ten feet behind them.

I'd trained them so well. I gloated to myself a little and Jack groaned.

"Next time, I'm going to flip your big ass on your back and watch you struggle to get up," I deadpanned.

With my demon form. Uhg. It was so hard to call it forward outside of the Underworld.

"Welcome," I called out to my guests. "We were just finishing up."

I let my hair down now that I wasn't training with Jack and snapped my fingers to change my clothes. I was *not* entertaining guests in a sports bra and barely-there booty shorts.

Not yet, anyway.

I felt more casual and covered in my faded black jeans and my ripped up t-shirt. It read "Killin it" on the front.

I smirked to myself. *Seemed fitting, right?*

I left my feet bare and leaned over to roll the bottom of my jeans up. Not quick enough for Helios, though, who walked over and burned the ends until they were nearly halfway up my calves.

Little embers of hellfire danced across my skin, and I

had to pat my legs to put them out. They didn't burn me, but they did burn my pants. Thanks to Helios, they were now too short.

"Seriously?" I glared at him as I whisper-yelled. "We talked about this, Helios. Like, just today. Not even forty-five minutes ago."

He stared at me, unimpressed. *The fucking asshole.*

When he was done staring, he stomped towards the group of guys standing on my patio. They all seemed a little uneasy and took a step back.

I almost wanted to pick at them a bit, but I didn't. *That wouldn't be very welcoming of me, now would it?*

Father had drilled etiquette into my head for years. It helped with business meetings, and that was exactly what this was about to be.

I'd *seen* what they had been up to while I was meditating on the way home this morning. It should be fun to see the surprise on their faces when I told them what I knew.

I may not have been able to read the fae's thoughts, but I had *seen* some of his past and present. Maybe I'd look into his future later.

"Introduce yourselves to them and they'll leave. They want to know that you're not a threat to me." I needed to explain the hostility my hounds were emanating.

They were trained to separate me from any potential threat. With a one-word command, they'd ruthlessly attack.

"Sit," I instructed them.

"Uhm, us or them?" Vaughn asked as he looked from me to the hounds to the chairs.

His confusion about whether he should follow my instructions or not made me smirk. For future reference, he should, but that command wasn't for him.

I answered with a laugh, "Them."

I straightened my face, adding, "This is Atlas, Cronus, and Helios. My guard dogs."

Helios cut his eyes at me. I shrugged my shoulders slightly in response.

"Now that they're behaving," I cut my eyes back to Helios, "you can shake their paws and introduce yourselves, then they'll scamper off to go hunting or whatever they want to do today."

I half smiled at them, trying to fight my own dry humor while simultaneously waiting to see what they would do.

"Are you being serious? I can't tell," the vampire spoke up in a playful tone. He shook his head and tried hard not to smile at me.

"Ya named yer dogs after Titans?" the mage questioned, completely unconcerned with my request.

"Of course. Who else would I name them after? Angels? Archbishops? Kings?" I shot back at him as I rolled my eyes.

"Yes, I named them after Titans, and yes, I am serious."

I then tilted my head left and right while scrunching my face up in a noncommittal sort of way. "About everything except the paw shaking. You don't want to shake Helios' paw. He has a temper."

I shook my head vigorously and smiled as sweetly as I could at the group as they exchanged looks.

"I know it sounds insane," I waved off their hesitation, "but I have a feeling this won't be your only visit here. I don't want the hounds trying to eat you if you come back and I'm not around. Also, I don't know your names either, and it'd be nice to get that out of the way.

"The hounds don't actually give a fuck about what you call each other. They just need a scent to store and a voice sample to hear. You could literally all say 'shit' and the hounds would remember you. So, you're introducing yourselves to me and also making sure you don't end up as supper in the same breath. Make sense?"

The hounds sat beside me as I stood in the grass at the edge of the patio. Helios was between Jack and me on my right, while Atlas and Cronus perched on my left.

Jack took a seat and popped a grape in his mouth, like he was watching the show.

The mage of the group shrugged his shoulders, then stepped up to me. "I'm Palmer."

He extended his hand with an amused expression playing across his features.

As we shook, that odd pull doubled in my fucking chest. *This was a joke, right?*

I noticed he had a slight Irish accent to his singsong voice. I could listen to him talk all day.

He stepped back after releasing my hand, and immediately I missed the minuscule warmth his grasp exuded. He raised his eyebrows at the vampire and gave his other friends an indifferent look. I couldn't quite decipher either expression.

The vampire came next. He was a little antsy, maybe excited.

After he introduced himself as Novak, Helios swung his head to me again like he just couldn't handle this anymore. He wasn't the one who sniffed out lies, though, so I paid him no attention.

What I did pay attention to was that vexing fucking pull. It was so strong that I had to fight the urge to rub on my chest.

What. The. Fuck. Was going on with my body?

I waited patiently as the shifter stepped up. That godsdamn pull grew even stronger with his proximity.

He was the largest of the group, and I bet his wolf would be even bigger than mine. It didn't happen often. Something told me he was massive when he shifted.

"Briggs," he rasped and tilted his head in acknowledgment, one beast to another.

I didn't mind. I wasn't expecting them to be formal. He moved his eyes over my hounds, and I knew he sensed that they weren't dogs. Not that Helios did a good job of hiding it.

"I'm Stone." The Demon was gruff.

He'd know more about hellhounds than his friends did. It didn't surprise me that he looked like he was ready for them to leave.

I was almost positive he could see right through the bit of glamour they wore. The magic-infused collars might not work on a demon. They didn't work for Jack.

Stone wasn't scared of them, though. I found that I liked that about him.

The wrenching feeling in my chest was so strong after meeting those four that it was becoming a nuisance. I finally reached up to rub once at my chest and then flip my hair over my shoulder to hide it.

Jack was eyeing me strangely. That bastard knew something.

"And you already know who I am," the fae stated.

Atlas growled low in warning. Vaughn peeked at me with a questioning look. I couldn't help but roll my eyes at him.

"Drop the fake accent. He sees through your lies." That was all I needed to say.

I'd read his file. I knew he wasn't from Washington. *He was a fae.*

He should've known better than to try to hide that from me. I wouldn't hold it against him, though. He didn't owe me an explanation, but I did expect honesty.

Last night was a different situation.

"Fine, I'm Vaughn," he announced to the hellhound on my left in his *almost* English accent.

He raised his eyebrows at me, and I gave him a sincere smile.

"Why didn't you call me out on my fake American accent last night?" he inquired.

"We were in public. As fae, I understand that you must sometimes hide your appearance. Humans wouldn't notice that you're not from Oxford, though you don't sound exactly... English. But other fae would, and you never know who lurks in the shadows." I canted my head and lifted my shoulders.

Jack gave us all a sardonic grin. He knew who lurked in the shadows.

Usually him.

He may look like a horse when he was in his demon form, but he was a predator down to his bones.

Have you ever seen a horse eat a person? It was fucking nasty.

Satisfied, the hellhounds turned to leave, but not before Atlas nudged my hip bone. I ran my hand across his head and down his back, all the way to the tip of his tail as he strutted away.

He liked a reward for sniffing out lies, and I was happy to oblige him.

"They're very protective, but they won't bother you now. You can sit if you'd like..." I motioned my hand towards the table on the patio.

"We do need to talk about Caplin, though. I've gone through a quarter of the records this morning, and I'll hopefully have the rest finished by tomorrow. I know you were investigating CBP, Vaughn, and I hate that the buyout put a damper on that, but I'll be happy to help in any way I can. Also, you need not worry about budget cuts or firing sprees. I want the drunk lady on the factory floor fired, but that's it, mostly."

"What do you mean when you say mostly?" he asked dubiously.

"Mmm." I lifted my eyes to the sky in thought before answering. "Well, there's been some experimental things happening there, as you well know. I'll be putting a stop to those and firing everyone involved. I won't be releasing injections that stunt our abilities, and that's what I found before you picked up the tour of the factory.

"Taylor and his father were very pleased with their progress, and they were happy to hear that we'd continue. But it was a lie. We bought the company to put a stop to it. I made sure to negotiate that we kept all the research and notes when we had our meeting.

"They had no patents with the FDA, and nothing submitted to the CDC. If Mr. Caplin and his son could have stopped eye fucking me for thirty minutes, and actually read the contract, then they may have realized what I was doing."

I shrugged one smug shoulder. I felt no shame for lying to them or cheating them out of the harmful drugs. Or slashing their price in half.

It was no sweat on my tits, or however that saying went.

Vaughn nodded his head as he digested what I'd said, and Palmer, the mage, furrowed his brows and leaned his head to the side as he thought through it.

"It was not approved?" he asked me.

"Correct."

"But, it's not what ya were expectin' when ya looked over the research. It does not add up," he surmised.

"Correct again." I sighed. "It appears that a mage is influencing it, but I can't track whoever it is yet. I can only assume that I'll be accumulating pharmaceutical companies to stop it until I can find the magic source that fuels the drug."

"Why are you telling us all of this?" Stone faced me and all eyes turned to him.

He must not talk often.

I saw that when he did, it would be intelligent, though. He asked the best question.

He was suspicious of me, not that I blamed him. They had no reason to trust me, and what I was about to tell them probably wouldn't help my case.

I didn't like starting friendships with lies. I needed their help. They had been digging into this for longer than I'd known about it. They just didn't have the access and tools that they needed, but I did.

"Because, my demon friend, you and the vampire have been hired to hunt the fiends who've used the drug. They're being lied to, told it will make them stronger. And it does for a few weeks, before it turns their instincts against them. It urges them to seek and hunt other non-humans.

"The mage has been spilling over the research, but it's only half of the equation. The half that the fae is able to steal from CBP. And, well, I'm not sure what the shifter has been doing other than camping in the woods and visiting the closest local dive bar."

I waved my hand in Briggs' direction and Palmer covered his lips with the back of his hand.

I cut my eyes quickly to Jack sitting beside me and slid into his mind. *"Am I being rude?"*

Sloane

Jack grinned at me mischievously and answered, *"I mean, you could use their names. It's not like they don't have titles in front of them. You are looking at four apprentices and the Prince of the Winter Realm."*

I tensed and slowly turned the top half of my body towards Jack, squeezing my hands together on the tabletop to keep myself from making a fist.

"Are you serious?" I asked aloud, wide eyed and utterly confused.

I wanted to punch him right now! There was no fucking way. All together? And friends?

"Serious as a heart attack, bitch." Jack chuckled.

"Well, fuck me. I wondered, but I had no way to really know for sure unless I dug deeper or flat out asked, which seems really rude. Were you going to tell me or just wait for me to figure it out?"

I narrowed my eyes on him. *This motherfucker.* I bet he wasn't going to tell me.

All five guys were staring at us.

I realized that I just went from calling them out and insulting the shifter, Briggs, to asking Jack a question that possibly made no sense out of the context of our telepathic conversation.

That they couldn't have heard.

"Oh, sweetheart. Let me blow your mind, please!" Jack begged and stuck his lips out at me in a pout.

He was excited now, and he never called me sweetheart. I didn't like it. Only one other person had ever called me that.

I really hated this. Him. I really hated him right now.

"Tell me," I demanded.

He turned a pompous smile to me and took a deep breath. His chest expanded with his inhale, and he slowly stood up from his chair. He had always been one for theatrics.

"Jack," I ground out through clenched teeth.

"I guess you still haven't read that letter, the one Nathaniel left for you?" He cut his eyes at me and I nodded my head in silent agreement.

Shit, I hadn't read the letter yet.

When my facial expression changed, he raised a perfectly arched eyebrow at me and quickly returned that self-important look to his face.

"So, Sloane King, may I present to you..." he paused dramatically, "drum roll please..." he slapped his hands on his thighs, "your mates."

Jack flourished his left hand towards the table full of guys and bowed at the waist.

Yep. I hated him right now.

"Franklin," I shouted. "Can we get some liquor, please?"

I was trying to process the news as fast as I could, really I was. *I think I needed some whiskey.* It was made for shitshows like today. *That should help, right?*

Fuck!

All I could do was blink as my eyes scanned around the table. I was stunned speechless, but then that fucking pull in my chest made so much godsdamned sense that I felt like a fucking idiot.

Gods-fucking-damnit, this popsicle licking, son of a Devil-loving whore!! He'd fucking known!?

"Jack, I'm going to fucking kill you," I told him with certainty.

They weren't a bad bunch to look at, but seriously? He could've shared the news with me sooner. Like, as soon as he'd found out.

"I'm sorry, what did you just say? I don't think I heard you properly." Vaughn had both eyebrows raised nearly to his hairline, shaking his head as he addressed Jack.

Novak had a knowing grin on his face, like he was privy to some joke that had gone over everyone else's head. Briggs was just blinking.

Stone looked over at Briggs like he was worried.

"Are you okay, mate?" He stopped abruptly before adding, "Uhm, man. Fuck," he stumbled eloquently, suddenly uncomfortable with the male term of endearment.

I got it. I really fucking did.

Briggs stood from the table. "I, uhm, I'm fine. I think I just need some fresh air."

He was still blinking every two seconds, as if that could erase his memory of the last four minutes. *I wish it worked like that.*

"We're outside." Novak laughed and moved his arm around like he was showcasing my yard to the shocked shifter.

"This makes more sense now. Ya knew, didn't ye, Novak? I'd been wonderin' myself..." Palmer trailed off, nodding his head until he saw that we were all looking at him but NOT understanding.

"Wondering what?" I asked warily.

I couldn't fucking help it. I needed to know what in Hell's name was going on right now. I didn't want to know, but I needed to know, damn it. I thought I might be officially freaking out on the inside.

Where the fuck was the liquor, Franklin!?

"Sooooo," Jack sang, "Four apprentices, two Princes, and the future Queen of Supes walk into a bar..." His joke trailed off as he wiggled his hips. "Now, you're just missing one more, bitch, and then you can really get this party started."

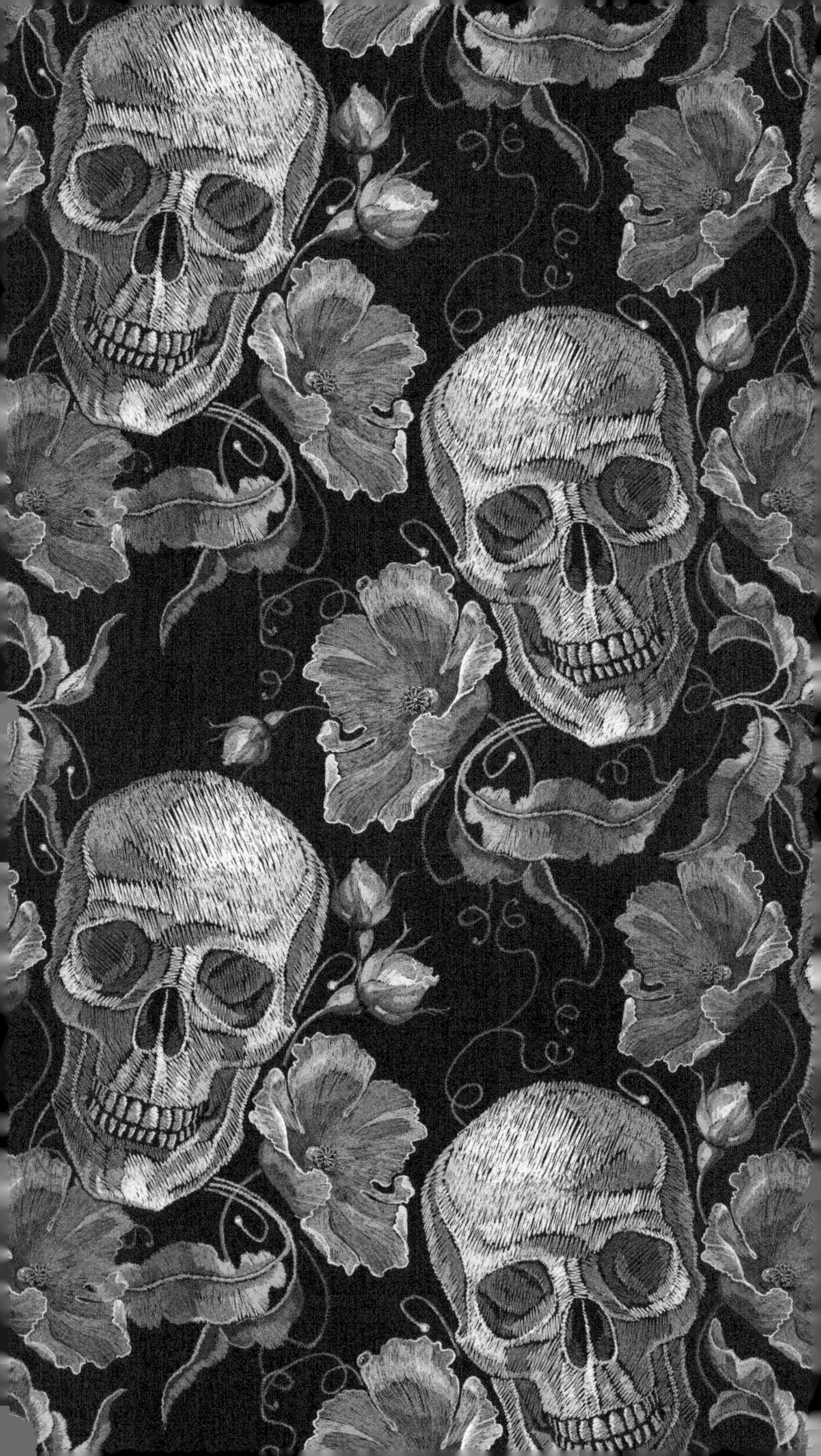

CHAPTER 9
Palmer

Saturday, May 16th
Late Morning

"You're just missing one more..." Jack said eagerly.

That sentence played on repeat in my head. Over and over and over again.

One more.

One more what? Mate? Surely not. That would make six of us.

I thought back over his ill-mannered joke. Four apprentices, check. Two princes? Nope, just the one.

I'd never heard of any supernatural creatures having more than two mates, except Amelia King. She had three.

But, Sloane? She had six? Was that what Novak figured out earlier?

That feckin' eejit. I can't believe he didn't tell me.

"Missing one more what?" Vaughn inquired quietly.

He was never one for red tape. Also, I had it on good authority he was shite at math.

"A sixth mate, what else would I be talking about?" Jack looked around at all of us and paused for a second. "You look like you've just seen a ghost. Did I miss it?" He sounded a little sad, like he'd be really fucking happy if he had seen a ghost.

"Holy shit, where is Franklin?" Sloane murmured as she got up from the table to walk inside.

We all stayed silent and still. No one seemed to know what we should think about the situation. Those dots that were floating around my head started to hasten their efforts in connecting.

I was lost in thought, but I vaguely heard Jack yell, "Read that letter while you're in there, bitch."

"Who is the sixth?" Stone was the first to get to the point.

I was curious too, but I couldn't seem to find my voice just yet. I only knew one other prince. A ball of dread appeared in my stomach at that realization. I hope he didn't say...

Jack answered Stone, confirming my musings. "Name's York, but I can't find him anywhere. I know enough about him to put in a good godsdamn search, but he hasn't surfaced for abo—"

"Two years? Give or take a couple months," Briggs interrupted.

Yeah, we knew York. That fucking druid. He ducked out one evening and never came back. No calls, no letters, no notes with the wind. Nothing. The elemental jackass up and vanished.

The fucking druid? Really?

"You're joking, right?" Novak peered over at Jack. "Just, tell me you're joking. Even if it's a lie."

"No, I'm not. He's the sixth, and we need to find him. The sooner the better. Sloane is in danger and once she amasses all her power..." he let out a deep sigh and ran his hands through his hair. "Let's just say she's gonna have an even bigger target on her back than she already does."

All those leftover dots still floating about my brain finally connected in one huge "holy fuck, how did I not see that" grand slam of a headache.

That was why all six of us were so close. It had to be some kind of secondary bond. We couldn't find her, so we stuck to each other.

I looked around the table at all my friends, and I couldn't help but see a pattern. If we were all mates to Sloane, then the seven of us were going to make one overpowered team.

It wouldn't just be a target on her back. Oh no, we'd all have targets on our backs.

This was a fucking disaster. What the fuck were we gonna do?

I'd read about mate bonds. I knew, theoretically, what happened when the bond snapped into place. Now that I was thinking about it, I could actually feel the pull that drew me to her.

We would share some of our powers. Our bond would be unbreakable, except in death, but with a bond shared between so many, we could potentially keep each other alive.

Our weaknesses could become strengths, but our love would become a weakness to be exploited.

Love? Right. Okay, Palmer, you're getting a wee bit ahead here, mate. Fuck. Mate?

I stood to pace the patio. Pacing helped me work through all my thoughts. It was a nervous reaction for some, but it grounded me.

I ran through all the things we were each good at, thinking about training schedules and what we could teach each other.

I knew I was getting ahead of myself, but for once in my life, I felt like I couldn't do this without a solid plan. I liked to stick to facts, but I was also pretty good at winging shit. Not this, though.

Nuh-uh.

"We need ta train," I stated firmly, drawing everyone's attention. "We need ta start workin' on any weaknesses we may have and figure out some sorta schedule. Someone needs ta be near Sloane every hour. I know she can handle herself, but two, or more, is always gonna be harder to fight than just one."

I slowed my pacing and watched the guys all nod their heads.

Jack chimed in. "I'll call Grim. He can help too, when

he's not working. He loves Sloane. We should also start looking for the druid. You guys seem like you may have had a falling out or something, but she's going to need him."

He reached for his phone and began typing. I was assuming it was a text to Grim. *Whoever that was.*

Sloane came out of the house a few minutes later, pushing a small black cart full of liquor. I thought she had brought way too much, but then, she didn't know what we drank. I knew how her father was all about being proper and sticking to those fancy etiquette lessons.

She sat down at the table and stayed quiet for a moment before turning to Jack. "You know who the sixth is."

It wasn't a question. She was furious with him for keeping that information from her.

The red ring around her pupil looked like it was glowing against the green and gold mix of her irises. Her jaw was clenched and her hands were fisted in her lap.

She radiated power. How could we miss just how powerful she was until now? She kept it so well hidden.

"Lo," Jack slowly approached her, covering her knee with his large hand, "did you read the letter?"

After she gave a sharp nod, he continued, "The druid has been *missing* for over two years. I've looked for him and so have your parents. We need to find him."

I didn't miss the way he said "missing" to her. I wondered what that was about.

"You all know him?" She directed her words to the rest of us. We all nodded.

"He was a, ehh, friend of ours before he disappeared. We were all pretty mad at him for it, but I'm startin' ta think that maybe he's been in trouble this whole time."

I could admit I was a little chagrined. It never occurred to us that he could've been taken against his will.

"Okay." Sloane took a deep breath as she popped open a bottle of whiskey and poured three fingers into a glass.

"This is a lot of shit that's just been dumped on all of our plates." She paused to take a drink. She set her glass down, then picked it right back up to down the rest of it.

"This is what we're going to do."

She bounced her head around a few times and then ran her slim fingers through her long silver hair. She was beautiful with that determined look on her face.

"I don't know if you guys are going to like this, but here goes." One more deep breath. Her chest expanded and her shoulders straightened.

I had no doubts that being in charge came naturally to her. I side-eyed Briggs and Vaughn. If anyone had issues with authority, it was those two. They butted heads constantly.

Vaughn seemed curious, but Briggs was on edge. *This should get interesting soon.*

I wasn't the only one watching Briggs. The alpha male was dangerously close to throwing out a challenge.

Novak was stalking him with his eyes. His predatory glint told me he was more than happy to intervene if a fight started.

If Sloane thought Briggs was going to listen to her without a display of power, then she was sorely mistaken. I didn't think she was that naïve, though.

She grew up under the hand of the Supreme Alpha. I'd bet she knew her way around an alpha fight, *and* I'd bet this wouldn't be her first one either.

Novak saw me watching everyone and leaned over to whisper in my ear, "My money is on the she-wolf. What about you?"

He was a fucking eejit, but I couldn't resist the bet.

I couldn't help the secretive smile that slipped over my lips. Novak and I were always making bets. Some were worth it, others not so much. She was going to "mop the floor" with Briggs, though.

I nodded my head swiftly at Novak.

"If we're all mates, then you now have a huge target on your backs too. I don't expect you to agree, but I have enough empty bedrooms in this house for you guys to stay here while we figure this out.

"The property is patrolled, and the house is spelled. None of us should go anywhere alone. Jack, that includes you. Grim would take what's left of my soul if something happened to you."

She looked at Jack, and we were all amused, watching his bronze cheeks tint a rosy pink.

"Who's Grim?" I'd really like to know.

"Me."

Everyone except Sloane and Jack jumped.

Standing behind Jack, with his very human-looking hand on the demon's shoulder, was a Grim Reaper.

A Grim fucking Reaper. I thought my heart might explode.

At least his trip wouldn't be wasted. He would be taking me or Briggs.

I tried to calm down from the sudden scare, but all I could think was that I wasn't going anywhere until I knew more about Sloane. He could take Briggs with him after Sloane killed him.

"Guys, this is Grim. Grim, these are the guys."

She introduced us one at a time, working her way around the table. She ended with Stone, and he leaned over to shake the reaper's hand.

"Nice to see you again, Grim." Stone nodded to the reaper. Of course the demon knew him.

"You as well, Stone," the reaper replied in a casual tone.

"So," Sloane started, bringing our attention back to her with an authoritative voice, "getting back on track. We need to start looking for the druid. Tomorrow. Tonight, I have to go to the club to keep up my appearances.

"We should have time to go over some of the research from CBP. Franklin is getting the flash drive I prepared for you, Palmer. Vaughn, I'd like you to go to CBP, and take Novak with you. This is my keycard."

She slid over what looked like a credit card with holes punched through it and kept talking. "You'll need it to get into the offices. All the locks and codes have been changed.

"I need you to look in David Preston's office. Search

his files and computer for anything personal. We need to get his banking information, personal email addresses, anything that we can use to look into his involvement with this drug and any supes. He's the only one on personnel that doesn't check out, except you."

She narrowed her eyes at Vaughn. "But I know why, so we can breeze past that.

"Palmer, while you're looking at the stuff Franklin is bringing, please stay on the property. All the electronics here are secure and no one can see what we're doing or hack into our servers."

She paused to pour more whiskey into her glass. She didn't ask us if we wanted any, but I knew she meant to. I grabbed the bottle of expensive whiskey she'd been drinking and poured myself a glass.

It was celebratory. I normally wouldn't drink until after supper, but noon seemed fine with all the information overload.

Stop lying. You had whiskey in your coffee mug this morning.

After she drank some of her whiskey, she turned to Grim and Jack.

"I need you two to look at the club, specifically upstairs and in the VIP section, for bugs or cameras. Jack, do you have your keys?"

He nodded his head, but she never stopped.

"Simon may be there when you arrive, but let's keep him out of the loop for now. We can fill him in if you find anything."

Who the fuck was Simon?

"What about us? Are we just supposed to lounge around all day?" Stone cut a look at her that said he wasn't on board with hanging out, and she smiled darkly at him.

It was a wee bit scary on her delicate face.

I bet that sadistic bastard really fucking loved that look.

I did too. I wouldn't lie. It was in that particular moment that I saw her for the predator I knew her to be. It was so damn hot.

My cock stirred to life at that smile. I could see her strapped down, cane in my hand, with red marks across her ass and thighs. Fuck. I needed to calm down.

That image was gonna haunt my fucking dreams until it happened.

She snapped her eyes to me, and I held her gaze with a different kind of challenge than what Briggs was giving. I had a feeling that she just saw what I was thinking, but I wasn't the least bit embarrassed.

She smirked after my stare melted to desire and hummed delightfully. *"Hmm, maybe later."*

She slid into my mind so fucking easily that it almost startled me. I wasn't a jumpy person, but fuck if that didn't scare me. She was entertained, though. My thoughts were a naughty little treat for her.

Oh, she was a filthy one if she liked what went on in my head.

Fuck. Fuck, fuck, fuck. I was going to end up falling in love with her.

She was gonna flip my whole fucking world upside

down in the best way possible. I could already tell that we were all in deep trouble.

"I'm leaving. I have shit to do this evening," Briggs growled out between clenched teeth.

He turned his back to the group of us and started to walk away. He didn't get more than four steps before Sloane stood and called to him.

Novak laughed under his breath beside me, and I was fighting an elated grin of my own.

It was about time someone put him in his place and showed him he wasn't the biggest wolf in the yard anymore. We had all tried, but Stone was the only one who could beat Briggs.

His human form didn't look exceptionally powerful, but the wolf was no match for the demon that lingered under his skin.

"No, you're not," Sloane stated simply, not even blinking as she stared down the angry alpha wolf.

"We're going to fight. Wolf to wolf or skin to skin, however you want. I'm going to show you that I'm the dominant alpha here, and then Stone, you, and I are going to go handle a pack of rogues an hour south.

"I'd normally take the job on by myself, but I'm curious about watching you work. There are only about fourteen of them, so it'll take us longer to drive there than it will to actually take them out."

She tilted her head left as she stepped away from the table. I realized that she did that head tilt thing when she was thinking.

"That is, if you can. Otherwise you can have the

room on the right, third floor, you know… to lick your wounds."

She shrugged her shoulders like she didn't just insult Briggs. I saw her power play, though.

I was living for this fight right now.

I was almost as worked up as Novak, who was bouncing in his chair with unrestrained glee.

She glided effortlessly towards the open expanse of the yard. When she put a good forty yards between them, she turned back and shouted to Briggs, "Are you coming or are you going to drop the alpha posturing bullshit?"

She stood with her hands on her hips, waiting patiently for him. It was fucking amazing.

Briggs looked at all of us, one by one, as he grumbled under his breath. We were all in various states of amusement. Novak was outright laughing.

It had been awhile since anyone had tested Briggs. I was excited. I couldn't wait to watch him get his ass kicked.

"I don't want to hurt her…" he trailed off as we all watched her toss her shirt into the grass.

The lacy black bra that she was wearing played so hard into my fantasy from moments ago. I groaned and looked towards the sky, wondering what kind of panties she was hiding under those jeans.

A lacy black thong to match? Boy shorts that make her cheeks look edible? Or-

"*None.*" The word flashed into my mind like a strobe light. I sensed the cheeky grin she was wearing on her face without seeing her.

"Stay outta my head," I hoarsely yelled at her.

I knew everyone at the table was staring at me after my outburst. They had no idea about the short exchange between the two of us.

She laughed at me before sassing back, "Stop projecting and I will."

I risked a peek around the table, and judging by their looks, everyone was definitely wondering what we were talking about.

I didn't even care.

I threw my hands over my face as she slid images into my mind. It was my new favorite kind of foreplay.

It made me wonder how she could possibly be everything that we all desired. She had a brilliant mind with a sarcastic mouth, an athletic body with a spontaneous streak, and a grounded nature with elegance that rivaled a queen.

That last thought just sealed the declaration I made shortly after we arrived. I wasn't letting go of this one. Briggs could be a dick and push her away if he wanted to, but I was making this one mine.

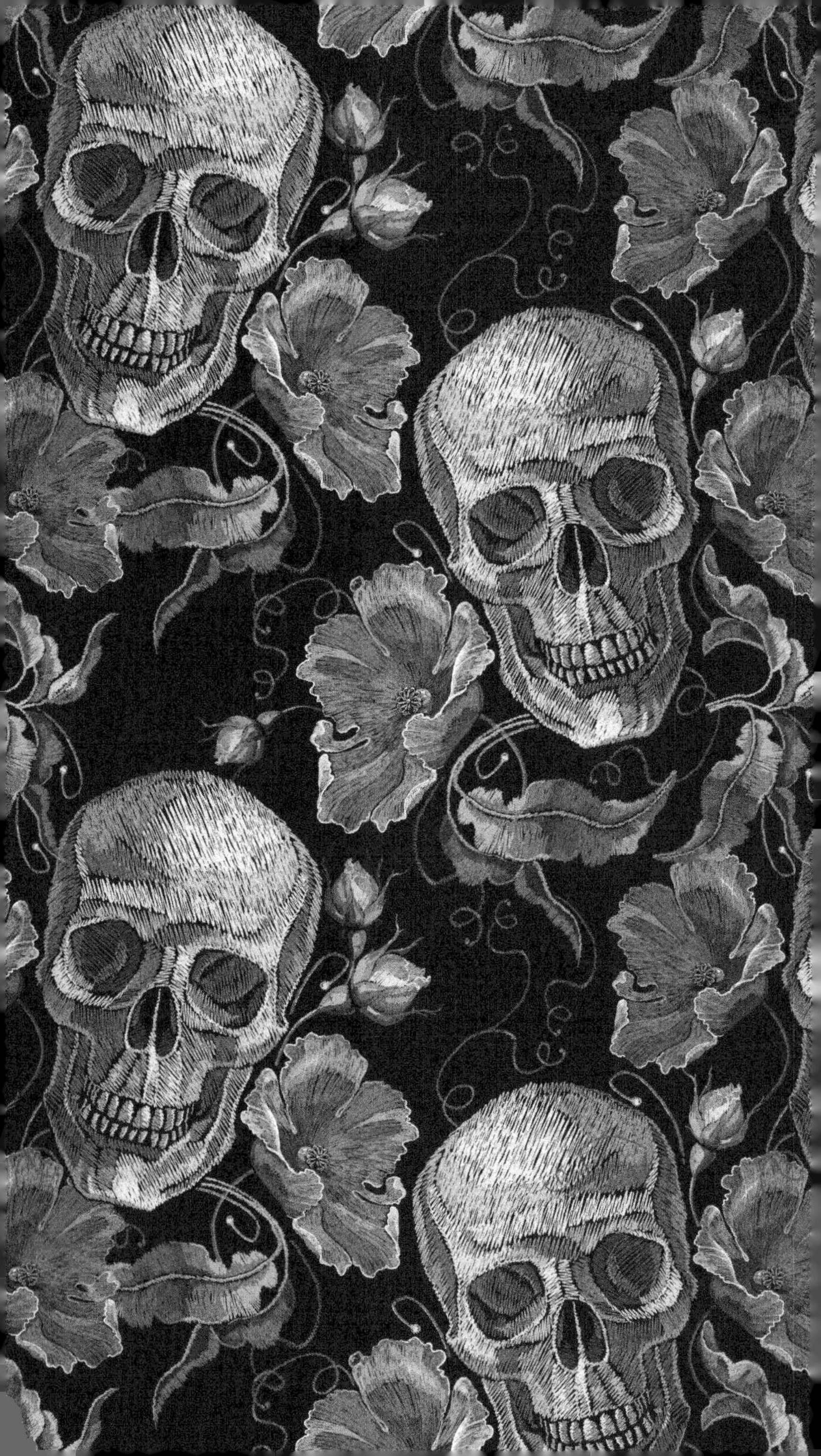

CHAPTER 10
Briggs

Saturday, May 16th
Late Morning

"I don't want to hurt her..." I left the statement hanging, hoping someone could talk her out of it.

They were all gawking at her, except for Jack and Grim. They kept whispering back and forth while looking between the two of us.

She was grinning like the cat who caught the canary.

I didn't know if I was excited for a challenge or horrified about walking into a fight that I knew I could possibly lose. *Because, yeah, I'd never fought in an alpha fight where my opponent smiled at me like she was.*

I'd also never fought in an alpha fight against a female, or a hybrid. I was stubborn, not stupid. I was also getting a little nauseous about what was fixing to happen.

Jack looked me up and down before he scoffed.

"Please." He disagreed with thick condescension, like I'd offended him somehow.

"If you go easy on her, she'll know. You better give it all you've got. I mean, she's gonna win either way, but," he stopped dramatically before bobbing his head, "I'd go man to man if I were you. That way you have height and weight as an advantage.

"Sloane as a wolf is beautiful, but frightening. The bitch that's standing there now? She's still gonna give you a run for your money, man. She won't kill you, but you will submit." He clicked his tongue at me.

What the fuck?

I did *not* want to hurt her. I couldn't even think about swinging at her, much less actually landing a punch. That felt like the opposite of what the mate bond was begging for. I needed to protect her, not harm her.

I could shed my skin and fight as a wolf, though. The bond would be stronger with my animalistic side, but so would the challenge she'd just thrown me.

A wolf didn't back out of an alpha challenge. They fought until they submitted or were killed.

I had to have a hundred pounds on her in my skin. I would guess I had even more weight on her as a wolf. I knew she-wolves were small, quick, and agile. I'd have to be smart about my movements and keep some distance between us.

Hope my wolf didn't go bat shit and hump her in front of everyone. That'd be embarrassing.

"I bet she ends the fight in her skin either way. I'd even bet money on it. She'll fight you skin to skin if she's given the option to choose." Jack's matter-of-fact tone piqued my interest.

I stared at her from across the yard, trying to figure out what she was hiding. There was no way she could beat my wolf in her skin. Was he insane? Had he never seen wolves fight before?

"Any time now," she sassed at me while tapping the imaginary watch on her wrist. "I have a couple jobs to do. I can't wait all day for you to make up your mind."

Fucking brat.
This was stupid.

Why did I feel like I was going to lose? I was always confident when it came to fighting. I'd never been taken down by a she-wolf in practice, and I wasn't about to let it happen in a real fight. But I had also never fought the Supreme Alpha's daughter either.

This is a hard fight to walk away from. Damn it.

I sighed and ran my hand over the back of my neck, thinking about my options.

"I'll take that bet," Novak perked up more at the prospect. "I bet she starts the fight as a wolf and finishes as a woman. You won't catch me challenging her. I know when there's a bigger predator around."

He coughed, trying to cover up the laughter in his voice. It didn't work, so he just gave me a jovial smile and slapped a hundred-dollar bill on the table. Jack matched him.

Grim was looking worried. For me? For her? Or for the betting? *Probably for me. Did I mention this was stupid?*

I may be an alpha by nature, but it wasn't my smartest move to show even the slightest signs of a challenge to her. I should've known better the moment I'd found out who she was.

"So what'll it be, mutt?" she taunted me.

The dig was just what I needed to accept, and damn if she didn't know it. *She really is a brat.*

"Alright, she-wolf. What form are we fighting in?" I'd leave that up to her.

"Whatever you want."

She snapped her fingers and was back in those amazing booty shorts she was wearing when we walked up the path to the back patio.

Damn it. Why was she so distracting?

"You won't get mad when I win, right?" I questioned myself as much as her.

Would I be mad if she won? I wanted to think about that, but mostly I stared at her for longer than necessary.

I didn't think about strategy at all. I thought about throwing her over my shoulder and trotting off into the trees surrounding her house. Finding a nice wide trunk to fuck her against until she was so hoarse from screaming she couldn't talk back.

Fuck me. It would be difficult to fight her with my dick hard.

Briggs

Head in the game, Briggs. Head in the game.

"My dad may have trained you, but my wolf is one of a kind," she jeered at me and shrugged a bare shoulder.

I bit my cheek so hard I tasted blood. My wolf wanted to bite *her*, mark her as his own. His feelings of lust were fueling my own.

What should I do?

Stop thinking about sex for starters, you fucking horndog.

"Both," I drawled confidently. "We'll fight as both."

I grabbed the back of my t-shirt and jerked it over my head in one smooth motion. I unbuttoned my jeans but left them hanging on my hips.

I kept an extra pair in everyone's vehicles, just in case. So when I shredded these, it wouldn't be a big deal.

"Okay," she conceded. "Whatever you want."

Wait, what? Why did she agree to that?

Fuck.

Shit.

That was when I knew I'd clearly fucked up.

Stand tall and take your beating, Briggs. There was a first time for everything.

In a split second flash of bright light, she shifted and stood across the yard as a wolf.

She was the same height as my wolf but thinner, all lean muscle to my bulk. It was the difference between an MMA fighter and a bodybuilder.

It was also crystal clear that I was going to lose before we even began.

A smart wolf would have submitted before they got injured. I wasn't a smart wolf, though. I was stubborn.

She gave me the wolf equivalent of a grin. She charged me with a speed I had never seen any wolf move in before. Her attack gave me no more time to look her over.

I rushed forward to meet her and shifted mid-jump. We both lunged for the other and slammed together in the air.

The momentum pushed us back, allowing me distance once again. She snarled at me, and I returned the favor with a low, warning growl.

We were all teeth, claws, and tangled limbs on display for the watching audience seated safely on the patio.

Her shiny silver-blue coat reflected the sunlight.

I took a second to notice that her fur was the same color as her hair. She almost looked like a powdery-blue wolf.

Her body was hard and her muscles are long, lean, and coiled for her next attack. She was ready to pounce on me, but she played cat and mouse as she circled my bulky body.

I'd never been a mouse in this game before.

I had to twist to keep her in my line of vision. I did *not* want her at my back.

Jack was right. Her wolf was beautiful, terrifying, and deadly. She stalked me gracefully on her paws as she continued to move counterclockwise. It was a sight I wanted to memorize, but she didn't give me another second.

She dove for me. I barely missed her as I adjusted to my left, out of her circle. Her claws tore up the grass when she came to a stop where I was just standing.

She glared down at the grass with her large, cold eyes and huffed her distaste. She didn't like messing up her yard.

That was kind of adorable.

I didn't wait for her undivided attention, though. I took the distraction as a chance to attack.

I charged full speed at her and she looked at me keenly but didn't move. I opened my jaws to grab her by the throat, but when I snapped them shut, there was nothing but air.

She was gone.

No. Not gone.

She wrapped her very naked human body around my fucking neck like she was some sort of sloth along for a ride. I couldn't see her, but I felt her slight weight.

I noticed as each of her fingers slid into my fur. Then, she grabbed me by the scruff of my neck and slammed me to the ground harder than any male alpha ever had.

I wiggled, trying to dislodge her grip and get out from under her, but her strength was... insurmountable.

I couldn't believe this. She was what? Maybe 130 pounds. She held me down in wolf form like I was a rag doll.

She snatched me by my scruff again, gaining my full attention. Jerking my head over, she exposed my throat.

I kicked with all my strength, feeling my claws dig into her flesh. I could smell the blood. I knew she was injured, and it was all my doing. Trying to make her move away seemed to fuel her rage more than the blood did, though.

I felt her jaw open up and clamp around my neck, the slightest pressure of her very human teeth set with her wolf's canines. She pulled up and looked into my right eye.

"Submit," she demanded, but I wouldn't. Not yet.

I wiggled again to get free. She loosened her hold on me and let me up. I did *not* like that.

I snarled as I shifted back to my skin.

She launched at me the moment I got my human legs underneath me. I was on my back in the grass, and I had no idea how it happened so fast.

I was standing one second and then flat on my back the next. I never felt her impact, but I felt the slam knock the breath right from my lungs.

She landed on my chest, straddling me, with her left hand wound tightly in my hair. She jerked my head to the left, leaving the full length of my throat exposed a second time.

"Submit," she demanded impatiently. I still wasn't ready to admit defeat.

I flipped us over, throwing her back onto the unforgiving ground. My thighs caged her arms in and my dick rested wholly against her perky tits. I wanted to enjoy the view, but when I glanced down at her, she was wearing a smug grin.

I had a brief moment to furrow my brows and wonder what she was thinking before she slung her legs up. Her heel hit me in the throat while she used her legs to slam me backwards.

All the air whooshed from my lungs painfully fast. She followed me to the ground and sunk her teeth into the left side of my throat, piercing the vulnerable flesh.

I felt the warmth trail down my neck into the grass beneath us, and my dick woke from the violence.

She had her body stretched out between my legs. Her knees were jammed into the soft spots on either side of my groin, cutting some of the circulation off as she put more of her weight on me.

She had me beat. If I moved my head, she could rip my throat out. If I wiggled my body, I'd take a knee or two to the balls, and there was still the throat thing.

I had no doubts that she was holding back, too. That was a bigger turn on than the position we ended up in.

Her power was intoxicating.

"I submit," I blurted, my voice like gravel.

She pulled her teeth out of my skin and licked the wound her bite left. She ran her tongue all the way up my jaw, to the corner of my lips, where she hovered over me in the sexiest fucking way.

Her long bluish hair curtained around us, making it seem like we were the only people there as she stared straight through to my soul. She didn't kiss me, but her lips were so close that I felt her smile down at me.

Her lips brushed mine in the most delectable way as she uttered, "You taste delicious."

She peeled herself off of me and began to dust the grass and dirt from her naked body.

"That took longer than I thought it would," she acknowledged as I lay in the grass staring at her while I waited for the bite to heal.

When she looked down at me, she had the most sinful smile I'd ever seen on her face. Her lips were stained with my blood, and I had this primal feeling of satisfaction knowing that my mate thought I tasted good.

I might have lost the fight, but I'd never received a compliment quite like that before. I gave her a self-satisfied grin, and she cocked her hip at me before she added, "Well, come on. We have shit to do today."

She offered her hand, and when I took it, she pulled me upright.

She didn't let me go immediately. She kept my large hand held tightly in her small one while she looked up at me, studying my face and, oh.

Was she checking me for injuries or checking me out while I was naked?

The tattoos that covered my body left little skin unmarked, but the glint in her eyes showed me she was intrigued by what she could see.

She saw me watching her and snapped her fingers. Cold magic brushed against my skin, making all the bruises and pain fade away. When I looked down to examine my body, I noticed that we were both dressed.

Damn. I couldn't check her injuries now. Lame excuse, right?

"Thanks, Doll." I marveled after her as we took our time getting back to the patio. I didn't know if I was thanking her for dressing me, healing me, or kicking my ass.

Probably all three.

"I'll be taking that," Novak declared as he took Jack's money from the table. "A pleasure doing business with you, Jack."

"You should know better, Jack," Sloane chastised him while shaking her head. "You're not a gambler. That's why I always make the bets, babe."

She picked up a peach from the basket of fruit in the middle of the table and took a big bite as the oldest vampire I'd ever seen strolled onto the patio and addressed her.

"Madam, I've set up the rooms and given the mage a room with access to the library. I put weapons and a change of clothes in the back of the Audi for you. It's parked out front with keys in the ignition. I informed Simon that Jack will be accompanied by a friend to search the bar, but may I suggest you lose the robe, Sir."

He turned his attention to Grim for a moment before continuing, "The hounds are patrolling the grounds and Atlas will be inside tonight. I have news that Taylor Caplin is out of holding as well."

Another bite had the juice dribbling over her full bottom lip.

I had to wrestle myself under control before I lunged to catch the drop that was rolling down her chin.

Another bite.

I turned my back to her and popped the cork on a new bottle of bourbon sitting on the black cart she'd rolled out earlier.

Another bite.

I didn't see that one, but I heard it. I poured myself a glass before I turned around to face her again.

"Thank you, Franklin," she politely replied with a nod of her head while that peach juice rolled from her chin to her chest. "We'll let you know if we need anything else."

"Thank you, Madam." He bowed his head before walking off.

She grabbed a napkin and ran her fingers under the neck of her shirt, between her tits, to catch the juice that was on my favorite kind of trail.

We were all watching her.

The reaper shook his head at her as he started to remove his robe. Jack was rolling his eyes with an amused grin on his face. They were used to her antics, but we were not.

We were all feeling the bond pretty fucking hard right now.

I bet every single one of us was thinking about the sticky path that peach juice left. I knew all five of us would end up discreetly adjusting our pants, too.

"Okay," Sloane tossed the peach pit into the trees behind her and clapped her hands together, "We should get moving. We've got shit to do, yeah?"

And that... was that.

I met my mate. I got my ass kicked by said mate. I had blue balls because of that mate. And I was going to hunt some rogues with Stone and my mate.

My mate. It still felt weird to say.

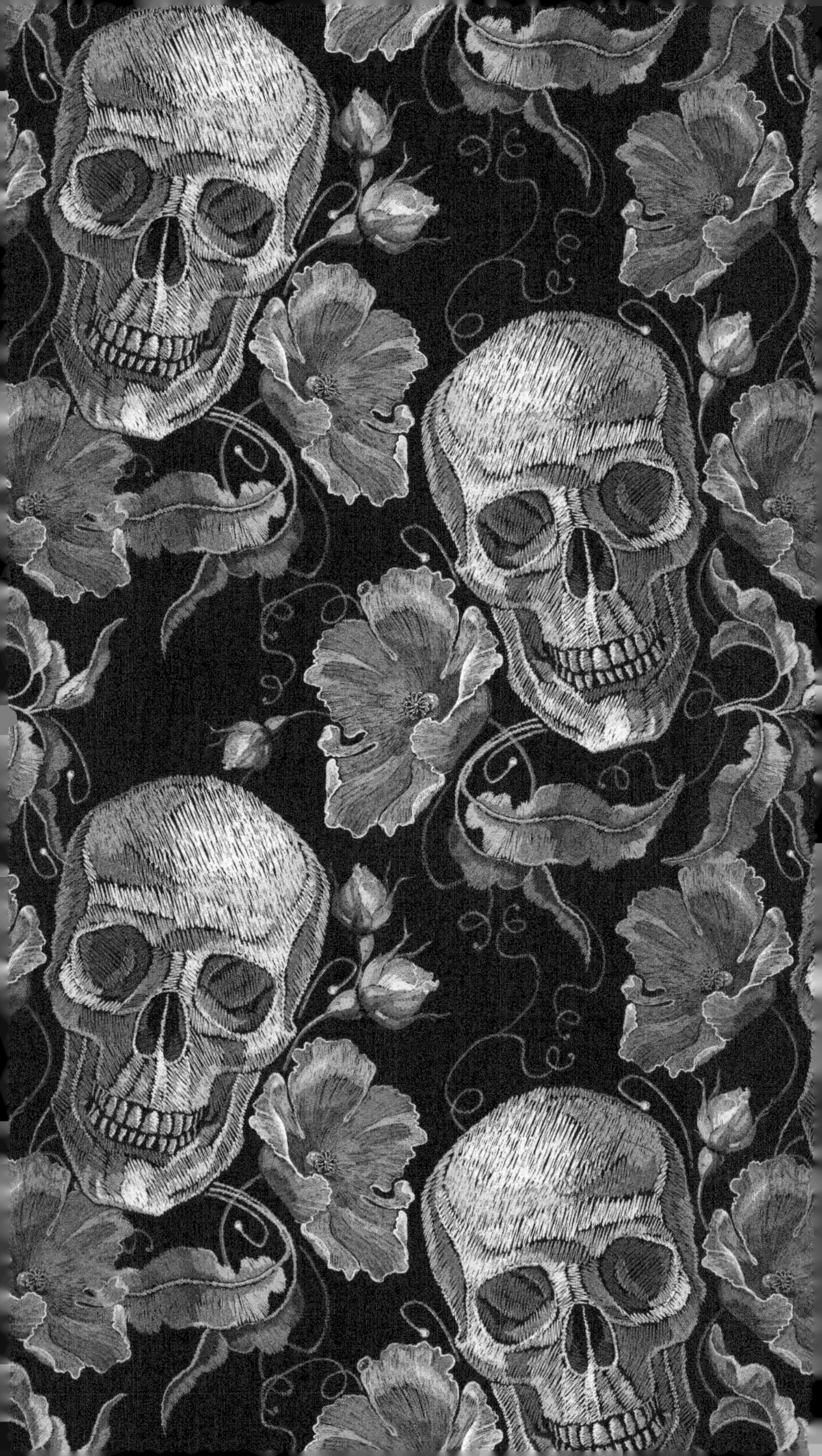

CHAPTER 11
Sloane

Saturday, May 16th
Midday

I have mates. I. Have. Mates.

Focus. We're going hunting.

The thoughts kept circling my mind as Stone drove my Audi SUV due south so we could cut off the rogue pack.

They had been given the injection that we were all actively trying to stop. They were a danger to themselves, each other, and everyone else.

There *was* no antidote and no way to save them. Our only option was to destroy them as quickly and as painlessly as possible. How much longer until they started hunting humans? How much longer until they exposed us to the rest of the world?

Holy fucking shit balls. I have mates.

I couldn't believe Father told me that in a letter. I couldn't believe Papi, Dad, and Jack all knew and didn't tell me.

I kept reading his letter over and over. I knew the ink would disappear soon, and I'd have nothing but a blank sheet of parchment. I read it again and again to see what I could decipher from it.

The conversation I had with my father when I went inside played on repeat in my head between the bouts of *"Oh gods, I have mates,"* and *"fuck, I need a drink."*

"Hello," Father answered his phone in an unusually clipped tone.

"Hi," I responded shyly, thinking maybe I caught him at a bad time.

"Did you not read the obituaries?"

"No, I haven't yet."

"Read them and then we can talk. I'll be sailing for a couple weeks."

He hung up on me after that. He was oddly short, but I recognized the code.

I searched for my purse, remembering that was the last place I put the letter.

I found it in the kitchen and opened it up to seize the envelope while making myself comfortable on the kitchen island. Kicking my feet like a small child, I nervously stared at my name scrawled on the front.

I loved Father's handwriting. It was a beautiful

calligraphy style cursive that I knew he picked up hundreds of years ago.

The S was large, and the ends looped around to make a twisting design that connected to the L. The O in my name was a bleeding heart. He only did that when he wrote letters to me. The ANE connected together perfectly, and the end of the E trailed off into a small series of loops that mimicked the beginning of my name.

I'd recognize his handwriting anywhere. It was uniquely Nathaniel in all his Renaissance flair.

I gently broke the wax seal with the elaborate K and tugged the thick cream-colored parchment out. Laying the envelope to the side, I unfolded the letter and started reading.

My Dearest Little Lo,
I have a few important things to tell you, but you mustn't call me unless it's of life or death importance. I know you'll understand.
My phone has been bugged and I am using it to feed whoever it is false information. We can't trace it yet, and we don't want to tip them off. Please send all correspondences through Samuel. He will get them to me. Ask Charles and him if they have any bugs before you speak freely, though.
You know the code.
First, you should know that I'm following a tip that mentioned your mother. I'm in Oxford, staying in a hotel near the Fae realm right now, but I haven't been successful in crossing over.

I think my dear Amelia is in the Summer Fae Kingdom. I suspect a mage and a summer fae are working together.

The research you sent me looks to be magically manipulated, but it would take more than a single mage to collect that much power. They would need a vessel of sorts to store it in as well. I haven't found proof of this yet. Call it instinct, if you will.

Second, keep up your appearances. You're being followed.

*I've asked Simon to help you run the darker side of the family businesses. He is at your disposal. You will receive all jobs through him that revolve around the **other** side of club matters as well.*

I have informed Jack of the issues. He will remain close by until your mates arrive. You should have met another today, and some of the others tomorrow, if not the rest of them.

Third, yes, My Dearest Little Lo, I said mates. Plural.

Charles, Samuel, and I have been training a few of them for quite some time now. They are interesting fellows, though I've only met the Winter Prince once in person.

Don't be mad at us for keeping it from you. It wasn't time to tell you. Your mother left us strict instructions. I'll show them to you when I arrive home in a couple weeks.

You met your Druid Prince before it was time.

When you find him, you'll have to work hard to move past your heartbreak.

He didn't leave because he wanted to. I fear he was taken. We haven't been able to find him. With your mates' help, though, I believe you'll find him soon.

Trust them, Little Lo. Trust your instincts. Keep those hellhounds near you when you're alone. They will be useful in the coming months.

Figure out how to change their appearances to other animals that you can keep with you. You'll need them, Lo.

You'll need your mates. You'll need Jack and Grim. You'll need Franklin and Simon, too. Always keep someone near you, but don't always make it obvious.

Stay aware. Stay observant. Use more than your eyes, ears, and nose.

A bloodbath is on the horizon and you will need all the alliances you can get. It's time to build an army. ***Only you can do that.***

I love you, My Dearest Little Lo, with all the blood in my body.

-Your devoted Father.

I read it over and over and over, trying to pick up any subtle clues.

I wondered briefly if he had known this whole time that the druid was missing, if Papi's phone was also bugged, and what my mother's instructions were. I would call Papi to find out.

It was the bloodbath, alliances, and army parts that really confused me, though. What kind of bloodbath? Alliances with whom? An army for a war? I had too many questions and zero logical answers. *Time to call Papi*.

I slid my cell phone from my pocket and hit the side button.

"Call Papi," I requested.

Stone and Briggs both looked at me but kept quiet. Stone knew Papi, but I didn't know if Briggs did.

The ringing came through on the car speakers while I pondered about who knew whom. I cut the settings off and opted for the speakerphone function instead.

I didn't want to have a conversation that could be heard outside of the car. That was what happened when you talked through your speakers. *Just FYI, people. We could hear it all.*

Stone and Briggs were my mates, and my instincts said I could trust them. I was just waiting for my brain to play catch up. *It was a little slow to match sometimes.*

"Hello?" Papi answered on the third ring.

I heard him shuffling papers and people speaking in the background. He must be busy, but I was on the fence about whether or not I could wait.

"Papi? Are you busy?" I reluctantly asked.

I did need to speak with him. It couldn't wait for tomorrow's dinner. My mind was made up. I didn't really want to say anything if he had an office full of demons.

Sloane

"For you, My Sweet Little Devil? I'm never too busy to talk to you, but I will unfortunately be missing dinner tomorrow," he disclosed with a sigh. He hated canceling dinner, but with everything going on, it was probably best.

"It's okay, Papi. I was just calling you because I got Father's letter last night."

"Oh, good! Good! You've met your mates, then?" he speculated, sounding happier than you would expect from the Devil.

He loved me, though. He only ever wanted me to be happy, so of course he'd be thrilled that I'd found my mates.

"Yes, sir. Did you know the druid is missing?" I kept my voice level, but for some gods-awful reason I had to swallow a lump in my throat before I spoke.

I was still so angry with him, even with the knowledge that he was missing. Knowing my mate could be in danger was profoundly upsetting. *And confusing*. It fueled my anger in a different direction.

I was going to kill whoever was holding *my druid* captive.

"No. How long?" He abruptly became very stern and serious. His mood swing made it clear that he didn't know. "I haven't spoken to York in quite some time."

"A little over two years, Papi."

I heard his intake of breath before he rushed out, "You must find him, My Little Devil, and there's no need to be sweet when you do. He wouldn't just disappear without saying a word. He would have warned you if he'd had time."

That chilled my blood. Papi was right.

My heart pounded erratically in my ears the harder I thought about York and everything he could've been going through for the last two years.

That was a long time to be missing and have no one looking for you.

My chest burned painfully at the thought. Briggs turned to me with a concerned look on his face, but Stone spoke up before either of us could.

"We'll find him, sir, and there will be nothing sweet when we do."

Shit, I had completely forgotten to ask about the bugs.

"Papi, Father said he found some pests around. Are you having any issues?"

The guys both looked at me again and I placed my index finger over my mouth. I needed to know if his phone was bugged. If it was, then we'd already said too much.

"No, I haven't seen any pests since his last visit, but I'll check again. There are other ways to cross the distance, My Sweet Little Devil. You don't always need to go sailing to do so." He hinted, reminding me gently that I only needed to call the flames of Hell to talk to him.

"Yes, Papi. See you after my trip. I'll bring back a souvenir for you."

"I love you, Little Devil. Stay safe during your travels." He ended our call after that.

Sloane

My mind was still spinning, but I knew one thing I needed to do, and I needed to get it done as quickly as possible.

I hit the side button on my phone once more.

"Call Franklin."

When it started ringing, I looked at Stone and Briggs. "I hope you guys aren't too attached to your phones, because we're gonna have to ditch them in a moment."

Stone tossed his phone right out the window like it was no big deal, straight into oncoming traffic.

I was surprised it didn't hit a car. That would've been funny for us, but not so funny for the driver of said car.

He apprenticed under Papi, so he understood the code. Briggs should too, but we needed to wait a few more miles before tossing another phone. They couldn't be found too close together.

We'd need to switch direction at some point so we didn't lead whoever could be tracking us to where we were going.

Could be.

I wasn't one hundred percent positive, but I'd rather be safe than sorry.

"Madam," Franklin answered on the third ring. "What can I do for you?"

"I've spoken to Nathaniel and Samuel, and they seem to be having a pest problem, Franklin. Please call the exterminator and have him come by tonight at 10. Cash in hand, the highest grade poison he's got, and tell him to spare no expenses. I need him to sweep the entire estate. You know how much I hate creepy crawly things."

"Yes, Madam, I'll have the appointment set as soon as you hang up. Anything else?" Franklin reminded me subtly. He's always on top of things. I think I'd be lost without him.

"Uhm, yes, also have him set a couple of high quality traps. Throw the old ones out."

"Understood, Madam. It will be done."

Someone remind me to give Franklin a raise.

"Thank you, Franklin. That's all I need." I hung up and motioned for Briggs to toss his phone out. He looked down at his hand, shrugged his shoulders, and slung his phone like a frisbee at the trees.

"What's—" Briggs started, but I covered his mouth with my hand.

Stone gave him a wide-eyed look and zipped his mouth shut. I released Briggs after that, and Stone took us off the interstate.

The exit had no gas stations or fast-food joints. It was a disaster of a two-lane road going in either direction. Trees grew just feet from the edge, their roots breaking up the concrete and their canopies reaching for each other. It felt like we were driving through a tunnel.

After fifteen minutes of silence, staring out the window and letting my thoughts run wild, I popped the case off my phone so I could take the SIM card out.

Chucking my phone out into the wooded wastelands around us, I exhaled a relieved breath.

That was the third phone this year, and it was only fucking May.

"Can I talk now?" Briggs pleaded quietly.

Sloane

"Yes," I approved as I folded the SIM card up and tore it apart, tossing it out as we maneuvered off the desolate road and into a small town.

It was a rural area with a clever little setup. Everything functioned around the downtown area. The restaurants were in brightly painted historical buildings. The vehicles were all beat up. The town square sat in front of a quaint courthouse.

There seemed to be a festival of some kind going on. We got stuck in the small town version of traffic, but the town's police were efficient in keeping it from getting out of hand.

"What was all the code about?" He fretted aloud, sounding anxious and curious.

"Nathaniel said his phone was bugged, but it's probably someone hacking into it, because he never sets the damned thing down for someone to tamper with it. That's why I asked Papi if he had a pest problem, and why I called Franklin.

"He's searching the estate for bugs and he'll check all the camera feeds. After he does that, he'll grab some cash and go get new phones under an alias and pick up laptops," I explained.

I was surprised Charles never went over this stuff with him.

"Who is the exterminator?"

"Franklin is. He's going to take my laptop and collect everyone's phones, then take them to a guy he knows to have them searched. If he finds anything, he'll trace it and call Franklin. We also need to check all the cars." I felt my shoulders sag. "I'm surprised Charles didn't explain any of the code to you. Did you understand any of it?"

"He explained it, but it's been years and I've never heard it used," he assured me.

"Well, get used to it, because if what Nathaniel says is true, then we'll be using it more often than any of us thought."

"What did he tell you?" Stone queried, cutting his eyes to me in the rear-view mirror before returning them back to the road.

"He said to keep up my appearance, which means to keep my usual routine going until I see something that tells me otherwise. No clue what that could be exactly, but he also said to trust you guys and trust my instincts."

I knew that wasn't all he said, but the rest of the letter was for me. We could talk about my mom and all the wild goose chases we'd been on to find her later. I wanted to wait until we were all together so I could ask Vaughn about the Summer Realm.

I made a copy of the letter and gave it to Palmer before we left. I'd need him to help me research more forms for my hellhounds. I also felt like he'd have some insight into a few other clues within the letter.

"Head east when you get to the next stop sign, there should be a campground about four miles up. We can park there and track the rogues." I'd almost forgotten to give Stone directions.

Since we'd all thrown out our phones, I found myself feeling thankful that I knew this area so well. We may have been lost in a couple more miles otherwise.

I'd hunted here many times before. It seemed to be a popular spot for rogues to hang out. I worried the campers would eventually become easy pickings.

A pack of rogues this size was going to be dangerous and would do the maximum amount of damage if we didn't get the job done efficiently.

That meant no stragglers.

"Uhm, east?" Stone contemplated as he pulled to a stop at a four-way intersection.

"Left." Briggs chuckled to himself.

I felt like there was some kind of joke I'd missed. Stone glowered at him from the driver's seat with flared nostrils. Maybe Stone was directionally challenged. I'd never met a demon who didn't know his directions. *Interesting.*

"You're not good with directions, Stone?" I inquired. I really wanted to know what was so funny to Briggs.

"No, I'm not," he quietly admitted. His ire about the subject made me giggle. I tried to keep it contained, I truly did.

"I've never met a directionally challenged demon before," I choked out. "It must be difficult to find your way around the Underworld," I added with mock concern.

Briggs chortled loudly before he could smother it. "And Earth," he agreed.

Stone glanced at us with a flustered look as we drove into the gravel parking lot of the campground. He parked the SUV and got out, grumbling. Briggs and I shared one last quiet giggle before we followed him out.

We walked around to the back and popped the hatch of my Audi open to view the weapons that Franklin packed for us.

Briggs surveyed the area before stripping down, preferring to use claws and teeth.

Stone tested the weight and balance of a well-made katana, which felt pretty cliché to me, seeing as how he looked Asian. I decided to keep my mouth shut.

I strapped a couple thigh holsters on and loaded them with throwing knives and two of my favorite daggers. *Obsidian blades with intricately carved, bleached bone hilts.*

Franklin was a weapons master and always knew what would suit me best for my current job. I guessed the guys would be no exception.

There were a couple guns left under the black cloth. I assumed those were for Briggs if he wanted to fight in his skin.

Time to focus.

We were heading into a big pack, which was rare for rogues. They normally ran with two or three others, but never this many.

I hoped this wasn't the beginning of a trend, but I wasn't too worried about it.

The demon at my back looked like the quiet, lithe, and lethal type. He didn't make a sound as we ambled through the dense trees. His eyes darted around us, searching for movement. He was ready for an ambush.

The shifter in front of me was a brute of a male and a

colossal wolf. His jet black fur made him appear as a shadow against the darkened forest floor.

The trees were so overpopulated here that the branches formed together to look like a green ceiling above us. They let little to no light shine through from the sun beaming overhead.

Snarls in the clearing ahead of us caused Briggs to stop. I fingered my knives and extended my nails into my demon's claws.

I'm excited. It was all I could think as we swiftly approached the worn down path.

What made a bitch feel mightier than an outnumbered fight with senselessly overpowered shifters?

I'll tell you. Walking into a hive flanked by sexy killers.

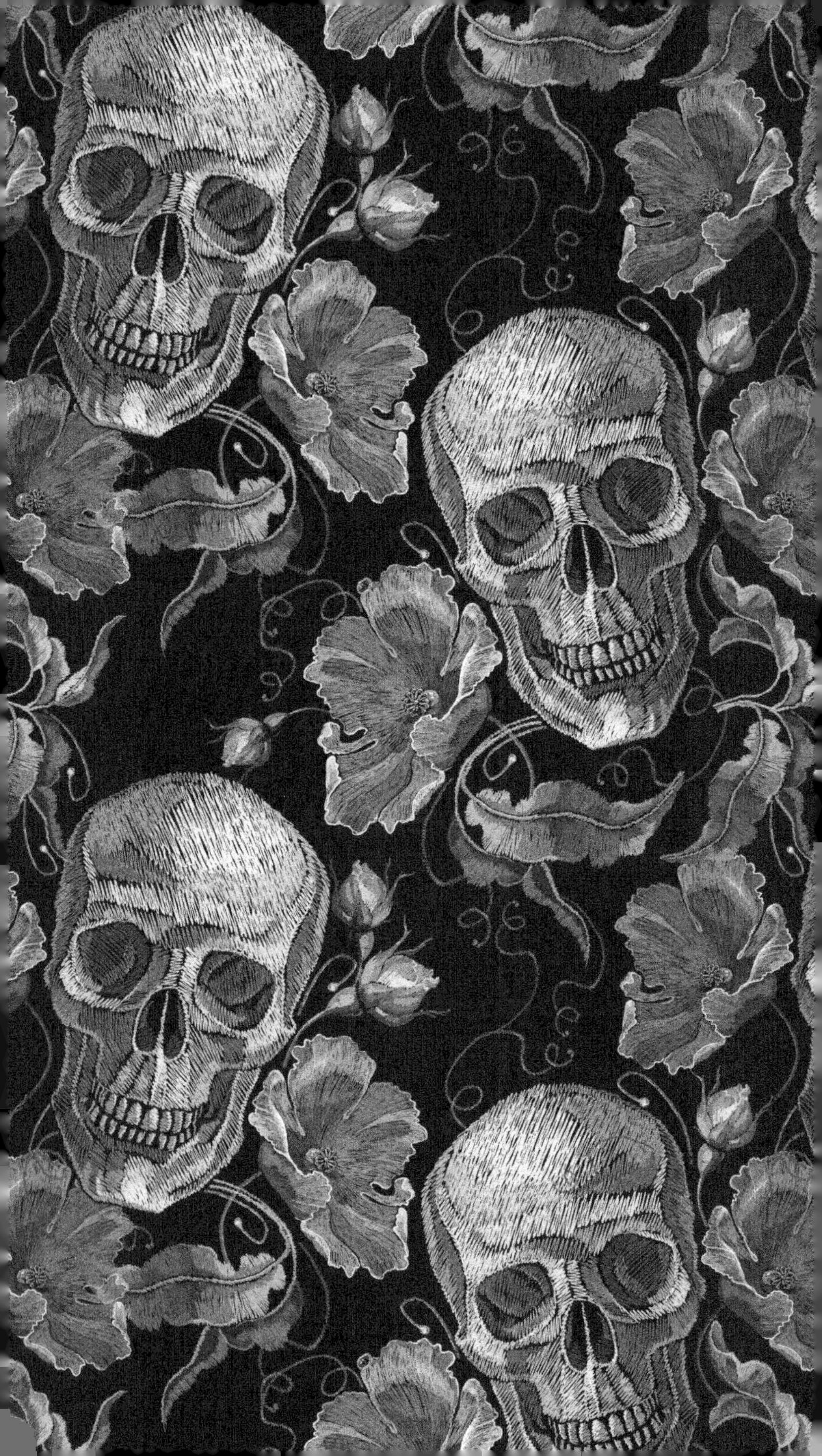

CHAPTER 12
Novak

Saturday, May 16th
Midday

I'd never been to Vaughn's office before, but let me just say, the whole fucking place was boring.

Everything was white or gray or godsdamn white. There was a larger-than-life picture hanging on the wall behind the front desk in the lobby. It was just three grown ass weirdos smiling at the twelve terribly placed chairs along the walls as you entered.

That was the only color to be found in the plain lobby.

We walked past the security guard sitting at the front desk. He was asleep. Vaughn hit the up button for the elevators, and the guy didn't even stir when the doors opened with a ping.

If I hadn't seen his chest moving, I would have sworn he was dead. I watched him as the doors jarred to a close. No movement, not even a flinch. They hired terrible guards to keep this place safe.

Once we were in the elevator, the fun began. Vaughn swiped Sloane's badge against the panel below the buttons. The metal death trap whizzed to life, halting when we reached the top floor.

There were no guards up here. There were a few plants in the hall that led to several offices, so the white on white decor was speckled with some color. *Some.*

The first two offices we passed were open and empty. There were two more after those with closed doors. I was itching to do a little snooping.

Sorry, breaking and entering.

Except, we were the Keepers of the Badge. The only badge in the entire company that opened every single door in the whole factory.

It really wasn't as fun as I thought it was gonna be.

I knew why I was here, though. So as soon as Vaughn got me in that Preston guy's office, I'd sit down and get to work.

I'd be able to hack into his computer and pull all his information.

Every email he sent or received, every website browser he opened, every individual thing he deleted — It would all be at my fingertips.

I just needed a few minutes to study the wear

patterns on his keyboard and a piece of paper to jot down some possible passwords.

Vaughn stopped at the second door on the right. He rubbed the badge over the shining, black glass piece attached above the fancy metal door knob.

A green light flashed, and we heard the latch pop open. Turning the handle, Vaughn took a deep breath and shoved at the door.

The door flew open, stopping abruptly at the halfway point, and slammed shut in our faces.

That was interesting.

We glanced at each other in states of amusement and confusion, but when I took a deep breath all my amusement died.

I smelled the tangy, metallic scent of blood. It came from something that was behind the door.

Vaughn slowly skimmed the badge across the black reader one more time. When the green light blinked again, he twisted the handle and eased the door open.

I poked my head in for a quick glance and immediately regretted it.

"If you start to get queasy, let me know, man. This place is fucking gory." I had to give him some kind of warning.

The last time we were anywhere half this bloody, he almost puked on me. *Not happening today, buddy.*

You could never fully comprehend how much blood the human body could hold until you saw it all on the outside. If I had to give a rough guesstimation, I'd say there were around ten pints pooling on the floor of that poor guy's office.

Vaughn gagged when he stepped inside the once white room. I did my best to avoid stepping in the blood while actively trying to move away from him.

The scene in front of us was nightmare inducing. The door was stopped by the torso of what used to be a man. One leg was on his office chair while the other leaned against a potted lime tree in the corner.

How did I know it was a lime tree? It had little green balls on it. Maybe it wasn't a lime tree, but it was some kind of fruit tree.

Also, not the point.

I tiptoed around the room to get a better view.

There was an arm hanging out of the bottom desk drawer, the one that should've been locked. The wrist joint was wedged between the desk and the drawer top.

I knew before I even looked inside that whatever was kept safe in that drawer was long gone. It must have been real fucking important to someone.

I looked up from my inspection to find Vaughn staring at the top of the desk in absolute horror. When my eyes followed his line of sight, a full body shudder flowed through me.

There was a dick on the desk. Just... a loose, dismembered dick flopped haphazardly across a cell phone.

"I'm telling you right now, Vaughn. I'm not touching it."

He fought a grin despite the macabre scene we were

in. "Let's call Sloane before we touch anything. I don't know how she wants to handle this, and I'm pretty sure she wasn't expecting us to walk into a murder scene."

Logical. We should call her. We also needed the information on that computer before the cops confiscated it as part of the evidence.

"Okay," I agreed, not focused on him at all as I walked around the room.

I avoided stepping on the bloody parts of the floor as I tried to take stock of what could've been moved or anything that might be missing.

I didn't see anything, though, so I started wondering if this guy was a loose end or a coincidence that had nothing to do with what we were looking for.

"Franklin," Vaughn acknowledged as he fumbled to hit the speaker button. "We just got into Preston's office at CBP and this place is a battle zone. He's dead, or someone else was murdered in his office. Sloane's phone is going straight to voicemail. What should we do?"

"Take the computer and anything else that looks like it could be of use."

Franklin exhaled loudly before he proceeded with our instructions.

"Go through all the drawers, shelves, books, and any cabinets or closets. Take all the files in his desk and check to see if you can find a cell phone or a wallet. Sloane has boxes in her office. They're full, but you can empty a couple of them to use. Just stack her stuff on the floor and I'll put it up on Monday."

A door closed in the background of the phone call shortly before a laptop beeped on.

"And don't leave any fucking fingerprints. Wipe down the door handles and the elevator buttons. Wipe down everything in that office that you touch too.

"Call me back as soon as you leave so I can clean up the security feed. Leave the office door ajar so the guard finds it on his next round," he paused, then added, "You have an hour to get it done and get out before he wakes up to do his next check." He hung up after that.

Awesome. Fantastic fucking Saturday.

"Okay." Vaughn dragged the two syllable word out for a full four seconds before he jumped into motion.

"You're lighter on your feet and can handle this," he motioned his hand around the room, "so I'm gonna go to Sloane's office and empty a couple boxes. Stack whatever we're bringing with us outside of the door and I'll load it up. Then let's get the fuck out of here."

He looked down at his feet and saw that he was standing in blood. I sniggered at his disgust. *Guess we're packing our shoes up too.*

Vaughn arched his head back and stared at the ceiling as he pulled one foot from his shoe, using the toe of the other, and took a large step backwards.

Once he had his clean foot on the carpet, the other still planted in a pool of blood on the office floor, he took his shirt off and wrapped his hand so he could brace against the door frame. Then, he lifted that blood-covered shoe my way.

I rolled my eyes at his squeamish behavior.

"Say please," I teased him with a saccharine smile on my face, "And I'll untie it for you."

All the muscles in his stout upper body flexed as he held himself up. He glared at me in agitation.

"Please, hurry the fuck up. We don't have time for games, Novak."

Yeah, yeah, I know.

I untied his shoe, and when it dropped to the floor, I used it to carefully prop the door open.

Fifty-five minutes left.

I traversed the office as Vaughn disappeared down the hall, barefoot and cursing under his breath. Who knew our mate would come with so much trouble?

I removed the computer from under the desk, delicately pulling all the wires and rolling them up together in a bundle that I wrapped in my shirt.

The wires had a little blood on them, and I didn't want to leave any on the floor when I set them down.

I left the monitor but removed the files from the bottom desk drawer first, the one that didn't have a hand hanging from it, so I could set everything on them.

Arranging them on the carpeted floor outside the door, I placed the computer on the paper file folders to absorb any missed blood and stacked the wires on top.

This wasn't my first time doing this.

The top drawers held nothing of importance, so I moved on to the last bottom drawer. The one with the hand dangling from it.

I used a pen to maneuver the drawer open, letting the hand fall naturally to the floor. I put the pen in my pocket so I didn't set it down anywhere and leave partial fingerprints.

I was already in the database, and I didn't want a murder charge pinned on me.

Inside the drawer was a broken, empty safe. Well, almost empty. I took my phone out and snapped a picture, then removed the envelope and placed it outside the door with the rest of the stuff.

Forty-five minutes left.

Moving over to the shelves, I visually scanned them for anything noteworthy. I picked out eight books with Latin titles, or what I thought was Latin.

They favored the books Palmer had in his room. I added those to my stack outside the door. I found three more books with old, worn leather bindings that looked like they could be something useful.

There were a few trinkets on the shelves that caught my eye as well, so all that went into the pile.

Thirty-seven minutes left.

Vaughn was making his way back to the office when I made my last trip, so I took his shirt to cover my fingers while I opened the rest of the books.

Nothing hidden in them. Boring titles of no concern. They all went back on the shelves where they came from.

I looked around the room one last time, spotting a jacket hanging on the back of the door. The pockets were empty, so that was a bust.

No cabinets and no closets. No hollowed out wall panels either, I checked.

Twenty-four minutes left.

The last thing I grabbed was the bloody fucking phone with some poor old man's prized possession lying on it.

Don't touch the dick. Don't touch the dick. Don't touch the—

The squeal that left my mouth was never to be talked about again. *I was not proud of it. Godsdamnit.*

I tried to pick the phone up from either side, but when I lifted it, that dead dick rolled right against the palm of my hand.

The dick touched me.
I was gonna be sick.

"What the fuck was that?" Vaughn whisper-shouted from the doorway as he packed everything into the three boxes he'd brought with him.

I hurled the phone into the box sitting on top of the two he had already filled and started untying my boots to slip out of the office.

"Dude, I touched the fucking dick."

I stopped what I was doing to rub my hands on my pants. *I could still feel it touching me.*

Vaughn let out a surprised hoot and shook his head at me.

"That's why you squealed? You've touched dicks before. I don't see what the issue is with brushing up against that one."

He looked me over like I was the biggest idiot he'd ever met.

He didn't get it.

"Yeah, but those dicks were warm and attached to

someone. That one is NOT attached to anyone," I whisper-shouted right back at him.

"It's cold and lifeless and severed at the end."

Another full body shiver worked its way through me as I described why I was freaked out.

That motherfucker was still laughing at me. He was folded over at his waist with his hands on his knees, sucking in breaths as he tried to contain himself.

It was not fucking funny!

I gave him my back and began wiping down the door handles on both sides of the door.

"Cold and lifeless, huh?" he jeered. "I thought you were describing your own dick for a minute there."

He handed me the open box full of computer equipment while he picked up the other two filled with paperwork, books, and random shit from the shelves.

"Get fucked, asshole. I'm scarred for life after that," I muttered to him as we made our way back to the elevator, barefoot and carrying boxes full of stolen shit.

I wish I could say this was the first time I'd done this, but I don't want to lie. It wasn't.

I glared daggers at Vaughn as he silently continued to laugh at me. His shoulders lifted up and down and his reddened face was canted to the side.

We stepped into the waiting elevator to make our way back down to that boring ass lobby. I set my box down and backtracked quickly to wipe the outside button down before the door closed.

I swiftly wiped the inside buttons and shoved

Vaughn's shirt in the box so I could pick it back up as we waited for the elevator to take us to the ground floor.

"You're being a really shitty friend. You know that, right?" I patronized him with a murderous look before turning away from him.

"Yep," he boasted, and I could hear his fucking smile with that single word.

I wanted to hit him, but my hands were full, so I'd have to wait.

The elevator dinged when it reached the main floor and we peeked around before stepping out. The guard was still asleep.

I didn't know why that shocked me, but it did. I briefly hoped he got fired for sleeping on the job, and then I remembered that he was about to find a gruesome murder scene in... *sixteen minutes.*

Damn, we made good timing.

Quietly setting my box down again, I grabbed Vaughn's stupid shirt and angrily wiped down the last button. I didn't put it back in the box because I knew I'd have to dig it out again to clean the handles on the doors leading outside.

What I really wanted to do was strangle him with it.

We made it back to the car and loaded up our stolen goods with no further issues or confrontation.

I mean, other than the dead body.

All fingerprints had been removed, and we were driving off company property. That meant it was time to call Franklin and let him know we were done so he could override the security footage of us being there. Then it was a done deal.

"Franklin, we're done and heading back," Vaughn confirmed as soon as Franklin picked up his end of the call.

He paused to listen and then sighed loudly. *He'd done that a good bit today.*

"Great, okay. We'll take the long way around. Tell Palmer we'll be there in an hour."

"What did he say?" I was too curious about what had his kacks in a twist.

I loved that word. Kacks. It was what Palmer called his panties.

His accent was light after living in the States for so long, but he still used some of his Irish slang. Most of it didn't make any sense to me.

Don't let him know I called him Irish. He'd give us the speech about how Northern Ireland and The Republic of Ireland are two different places. Again.

"He said to leave here and not head to Sloane's yet. We need to toss our phones out first. She told him Nathaniel and Samuel had bugs. Everyone else has already dumped their phones.

"So we'll head into town, grab some lunch, and toss our phones in the garbage before going back to look through all this shit we just stole." He sounded exasperated.

When we got back to Sloane's house, we'd have to lock him in a bedroom and force him to take a nap. *Nobody liked a grumpy fae.*

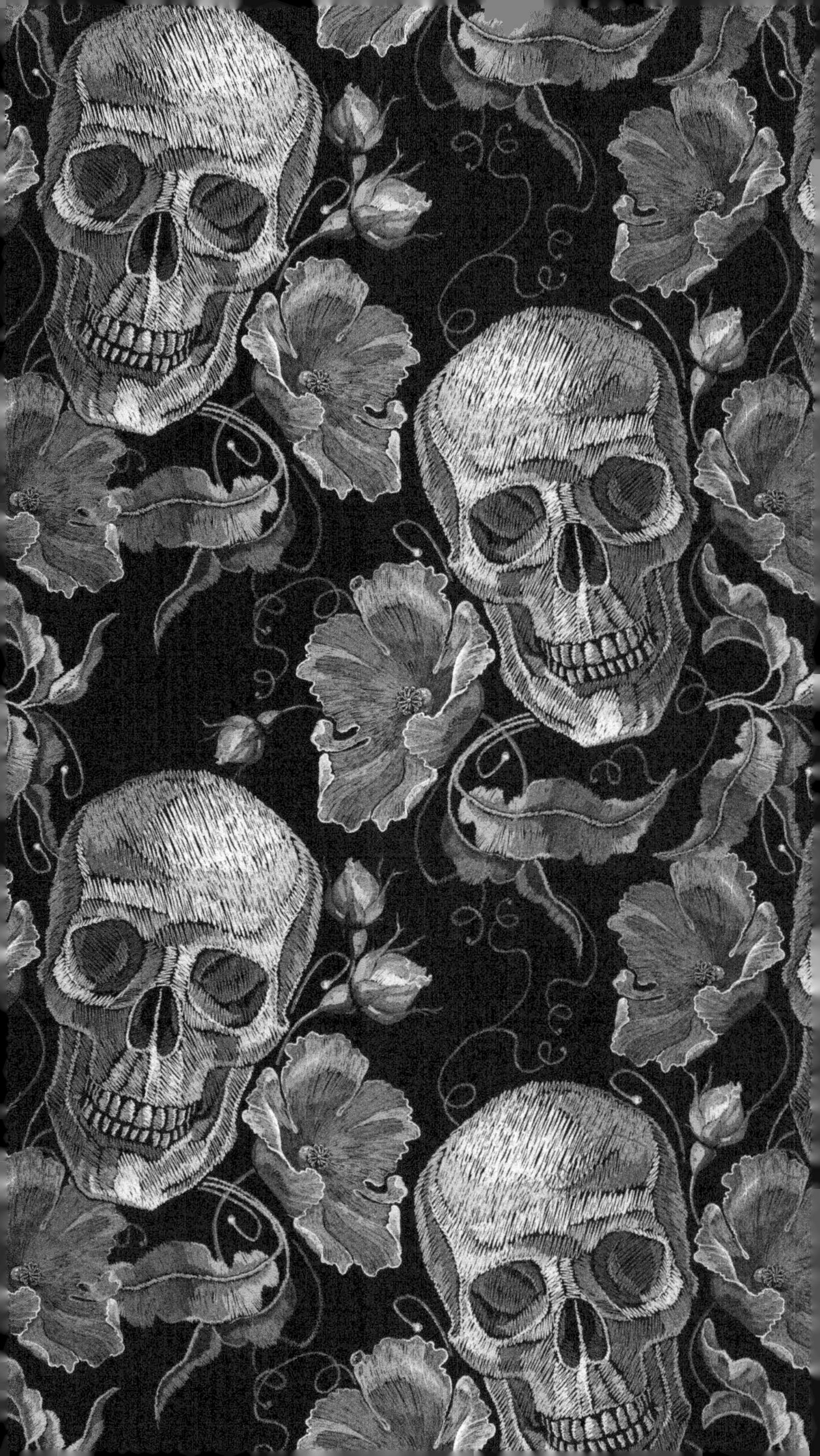

CHAPTER 13
York

Saturday, May 16th
Midday

E*ight hundred and fifty-seven days.*

That was how many days I'd spent in a cell being drained of my power. Slow and steady, so they could keep me longer than the rest of the prisoners they'd had over the years.

Every new moon and full moon they came down to get me, but I never got to see the sky, the stars, or nature.

They would knock me out with vaporous sleeping potions and drag me to the mock medical room where I'd first spoken to my mate.

Then, they'd strap me to the metal table with cursed

chains. No matter how hard I tried, I could never break free.

I didn't know what I'd do if I could.

I didn't have much fight left in me anymore. I was saving that for Sloane.

The new moon was in three day's time, and I feared it may be the last drain they got from me. Those fae crystals would suck out the rest of my power if they weren't removed while I had enough life force left to keep me alive... *yeah.*

After every drain, I grew weaker and weaker. I couldn't heal properly when I was down in the damp cell with no true earth to touch my skin.

I'd been here for so long that I no longer felt the wet chill on my skin or the bone deep cold that the winters brought.

I was used to the constant exhaustion that came from too little sleep on the stone floor with the threadbare blanket they threw me during my first winter as a captive.

Over time, it became increasingly easy to ignore my hunger. They fed me twice a week, if I was lucky, but it wasn't enough to give me energy or sustain me.

They liked to keep me weak so I couldn't fight back.

The only other constants I had in this place were the dripping dirty water that ran down the wall, leaving a trail of slimy mess in its wake, and thoughts of my mate.

I had to be careful when I thought of her. If Kelvin knew I was bonded with the powerhouse that got away, he wouldn't just drain me dry, he'd use me as bait to get to her.

Kelvin used to be my boss, when I lived as a free male in the campground and not a prisoner in this cell. I'd spent three years working up to be his right-hand man. I needed all the secrets.

I still needed the major secrets he never shared with me.

I wouldn't get them now. Though, maybe he'd pity me on my next drain and tell me before he killed me.

I stood up and stretched my stiff, atrophied muscles. My body ached, but it wouldn't stop me from moving to the opposite side of my cell and digging out the small stone fragment to make another mark on the wall.

Eight hundred and fifty-seven marks.

One for every day that I had been in this tiny piece of Hell on Earth.

I imagine Hell would be better than this cell. Especially when your mate was the Devil's daughter.

The door to the stairs creaked open as I eased the fragment back into its hiding place.

I wished I could say I was able to catch a whiff of the fresh outdoor air, but I never could. I didn't feel a breeze, nor did I see sunlight filter in. It was just stale, putrid air and the dim lighting from four bare light bulbs hanging outside the cell doors.

Levi walked up to my cell door and shifted uncomfortably on his feet. He was always too good of a guy to be in a place like this, but I was thankful he was.

He'd been my saving grace since he found me down here four months into my stay. He was the reason they gave me any blanket at all during that first winter.

He was the only one who brought me extra food when he was tasked with feeding the prisoners.

Just prisoner, now that I was the only one left again.

"Look, man. I don't know how much time I have before they start looking for me. I brought you some jerky. It should give you a bit of energy, and I was able to sneak in some flowers that I found. I remember you saying one time that you can pull life from nature to fuel your power. Is that right?"

He glanced at me as he spoke and then returned his attention back to the door. He didn't want to get caught. *I didn't blame him.* He was human. He shouldn't even be in the camp.

"Yeah," I croaked out.

My throat was dry. I hardly used my voice anymore. I didn't scream when they put those crystals across my chest to siphon my power. I hadn't fought the chains in so many months that I'd lost count of how long it had been.

"Here," he offered as he shoved a water bottle at me through the bars.

He released a clear bag of jerky into my hand and opened his jacket to expose the flowers he'd gathered. They had just recently been cut from their tether to the earth so they would give me a small boost.

I noticed he'd lost too much weight, too, and it made me wonder what was happening above me.

"Kelvin says he's going to kill you on the next drain. I know you said you have a mate somewhere, so maybe this is enough to reach out to her one last time. I don't know how that works, but I hope it's enough."

He roughly pushed the flowers to me the same way he did the water bottle. For the first time since I'd been here, I felt a spark of hope.

Sloane should have met her other mates by now. I should be able to slip into a dream and manipulate her Sight to latch onto a vision.

Should being the keyword there.

I hadn't been able to test my theory yet, but I *had* talked it out with Levi when he'd been on guard duty.

I guzzled the water down and took the jerky out, poking the bag into the bottle, and handed it back to him. He hung his head with a concerned look on his face, then he pivoted on his feet and quietly left like he was never here.

I sat with my back against the wall and gathered the flowers in my lap, enjoying the colors before I drained them until they were nothing but dirt. As I siphoned the life from them, the colors faded away.

I opened myself up to feel the things that I hadn't felt in far too long. I could feel the pain I caused the flowers, and I silently thanked them for helping me. I felt the light inside me flicker a little stronger.

I felt the snap in my chest as I released my hold over the mate bond.

Sloane and the intoxicating rush of her emotions filled my mind. Excitement, adrenaline, and mayhem followed by curiosity, then downright murder.

She felt me, too, and now she was angry.

I'd rather face her wrath every day for the rest of my life than die in this dungeon on that cold metal table.

I closed my eyes and began to meditate.

First, I evened out my breathing, slow and deep. Second, I focused completely on her, picturing the last time I saw her.

She was asleep when I left that morning, her silver hair flowing around her face on the pillow, her naked body half exposed under the jet black sheets on her bed.

Her face was peaceful as she took the little rest she needed after a long night of arguing and makeup sex.

I kept that image of her in my mind as I opened up the flow of power and forced my dream-like state on her.

It wasn't a dream like humans had, but it also wasn't a prophetic vision like Sloane usually saw. It was a real-time image of me, not the past version of me and not manipulated. She'd see me exactly as I am, and where I was at.

If I was lucky, I'd have a few minutes where I could speak to her. I had to tell her where I was and what was happening, even if she decided not to come for me.

"Sloane? Sweetheart?" I sought her out softly, hoping to gain her attention.

The feeling of disbelief flashed through me and smothered her mounting anger.

I'd found her. Thank the gods.

"I don't have much time, and I know you're angry with me. I'm so sorry. I'd never willingly leave you."

I didn't really know what else to say. I'd rather tell her face-to-face and explain everything that happened. I needed her to find me.

"Where are you? Why are you just now reaching out to me? What happened to you, York?"

Her emotions were a tangled mess, making it hard to sort through them. Determination, worry, heartbreak, and that ever present anger when it came to me were all present, but more lingered under the surface.

"It's a long story, Sweetheart, and I'll tell you all about it, but I don't have enough power to keep you long. I need you to find me before the new moon. I'm somewhere near the Red River Gorge in Kentucky. I can't explain exactly where, but I'm in a cell underground.

"I've been trying to help you remember what you've forgotten, but I'm just not strong enough anymore. Have the fae open your mind. He can do it, but you'll have to let him in. I'll see you soon, Sweetheart. I love you."

The connection I held was gone, but hearing the soft rasping quality of her voice made me miss her more than ever. I shut the bond down and saved what little power I had left to open the connection again.

I'd wait two days.

Two days, and I'd open the connection back up to see if she was near me. If she was, then I could lead her to my location.

If she wasn't... then, at least I got to hear her one last time.

Sloane

We had just finished up with the pack of infected rogue shifters when that ever present ache in my chest snapped so hard that it doubled me over.

I placed my hands on my knees and sank to the ground. Stone came rushing forward at a speed that would terrify any creature.

He was as fast as a vampire. That was unusual for a demon.

"Are you okay?" he asked me earnestly with concern etched all over his sharp features.

His cheekbones were high over his square jawline, brows creased low, covering his beautiful black and lapis colored eyes.

If the sun weren't so high in the sky, it would be easy to miss that deep blue starburst around his pupils.

York

"I just, uhm." I released a frustrated groan. "I think I just felt another bond snap into place, Stone. I haven't felt York's end of it in years. I thought he was—" I couldn't finish that sentence, and Stone seemed to understand all too well what I wasn't saying.

He nodded his head sympathetically and dropped to the ground in front of me before placing his hands on my shoulders. That extra touch exposed a vision, one that I desperately hated seeing.

York was sitting on the ground in a stone cell, his back against the damp wall with his legs crossed in front of him.

A stone cell that I was very familiar with.

It had plagued what little drunken sleep I'd received since he'd been gone.

"Sloane? Sweetheart?" I heard his voice, soothing but shaken.

It was him, but he didn't hold that velvety smooth quality to his voice like he'd had when I'd last heard him. He sounded broken and hopeless, and it had tears pooling in my eyes.

Stone slowly put me in his lap, careful not to jostle me out of the vision. I briefly wondered if he knew what was going on, but I snapped my attention back to York.

I was so fucking pissed at him.

"I don't have much time, and I know you're angry with me. I'm so sorry. I'd never willingly leave you." He rushed the words out, and his sincerity had my attitude dissipating.

Longing and self-loathing followed slowly on the

crest of his feelings. It ripped open my heartbreak all over again.

The jagged wounds left when he never returned had the unshed tears streaming down my face. I was still mad at him, but I wouldn't let anything stop me from finding what was mine.

York Briar is mine. Was? No, IS.

"Where are you? Why are you just now reaching out to me? What happened to you, York?"

Seeing the state that his body was in had me worried for his life. He looked like he'd been starved and beaten.

It fueled the fire that was my anger to new heights. The demon I kept under lock and key crawled to the surface of my skin, ready to rampage through the streets to return to me what was lost.

My wolf howled her outrage with her hackles raised and teeth exposed.

"It's a long story, Sweetheart, and I'll tell you all about it, but I don't have enough power to keep you long. I need you to find me before the new moon. I'm somewhere near the Red River Gorge in Kentucky. I can't explain exactly where, but I'm in a cell underground.

"I've been trying to help you remember what you've forgotten, but I'm just not strong enough anymore. Have the fae open your mind. He can do it, but you'll have to let him in. I'll see you soon, Sweetheart."

Either his connection or his power was fading with each word, and I caught the barest hint of "I love you" before I lost him completely.

The pain in my chest left with it. I was finally able to take a deep breath and push through all his emotions still lingering in my mind. His pain, torment, fear, and his own heartbreak over what we had and what happened between us were so heavy that I didn't realize I'd been holding my breath.

I used the sides of my hands to wipe my eyes and steadied my head on Stone's shoulder while I tried to calm down.

He had his lean muscled arms wrapped around my waist and above my breasts with my back held firmly to his chest. I let myself enjoy the feeling of being held intimately after avoiding it for so long.

His body radiated heat. He smelled of spicy cinnamon and charcoal.

If I didn't get out of his lap soon, I might make us both a bit uncomfortable. I couldn't stop the swell of thoughts from lashing out.

His flaming hands trailing up my spine. His teeth sunk in my shoulder. Him pounding into me from behind while I smothered my face with a pillow to quiet my screams. Nothing but a pair of red pumps on.

He dipped his head and buried his face against my neck. He inhaled deeply before I felt his lips morph into a smile on my heated skin.

"I was able to see what you were seeing." His dark confession sent tingling pleasure racing through me.

"We need to go to Kentucky," I asserted, but I made no move to leave his lap.

I canted my head and his hair tickled my cheek. It

was soft and silky, and I wanted to run my fingers through it until it was a tangled mess.

"Mmm." His hummed agreement teased the skin where his face still touched me and sent shivers down my back that I didn't bother trying to hide.

The demon grinned again as he leisurely ran his fingers up and down my arms, goosebumps trailing behind his touch. When he stopped, he twined his fingers together with mine and then stood, bringing me with him.

I released his hands and twisted my body into him, putting us chest to chest. My peaked nipples rubbed the inside of my bra with the pressure.

I wrapped my arms around his waist, holding him close and looking up at him with my chin resting on his chest.

He skimmed his hot hands across my back. They left behind a path of embers licking at the flesh under my thin shirt.

Those sensual shivers wracked through me again, and when he tilted his head down at me, he had the most sinful smile playing across his seductive lips.

A crunching noise sounded from behind me, popping our lust bubble. When I reversed my position in Stone's arms, I saw Briggs standing before us in all his four-legged glory.

His black fur was shining and matted with drying blood. Those forest green eyes sparkled in his large canine face. His exposed teeth translated into a wolf-like grin and would send any lesser beings running for the hills.

He was bulky, broad and beautiful, just like the human skin he wore, but his wolf wasn't as broody as his male counterpart.

He trotted over to us, nosing Stone's arms off my body, and sniffed at me for injuries. He pitched his head forward when he looked at my face.

I placed my hand between his ears and ran my fingers through his course black fur. He growled low in his throat and I simpered.

"Fine, I won't pet you." I started to retreat, only stopping for a moment to slap his flank.

Stone let out a surprised chuckle, and I smiled to myself. Briggs struck back by nipping my ass cheek with his front teeth before trotting away with his tail lashing side to side.

"That's going to bruise," I yelled at him, rubbing the sore spot on my ass. *Bruises didn't heal as quickly as cuts did.* I was going to be sitting on that bruise for an hour while it tried to heal.

"I'm a little jealous right now," Stone admitted to me as he jogged to catch up. He tugged my hand into his as we strolled down the path to get back to the gravel parking lot of the campgrounds.

"You could always rub it for me." I smirked as I teased him.

It backfired completely when that fire-laden hand of his began rubbing circles across the tender flesh of my buttcheek.

"You're going to be the death of me, aren't you?" His baritone voice whispered the words in my ear, and the throaty quality made my core throb with need.

"Not intentionally," I affirmed in a breathy rasp that did nothing to hide my growing need for him.

His voice was the sound of sex, and it made me want to jump him every time he spoke. I didn't care that I'd just met him today.

The tips of his fingers stroked higher and lower with each pass over the bruise until eventually his path started at the waist of my pants and ended at the junction of my thighs.

Over and over again.

The walk back to the car was torturous for me, *possibly both of us,* but I was quick to decide that if this was what fate had in store for me, then I'd be just fine.

This was MY demon with his hands on me. These were MY mates. We may have just met each other, but I couldn't deny how right it felt to be with them. I knew that would only intensify the longer we were together.

Now I needed to get MY druid back.

Step one: Plan a trip to Kentucky.

Step two: Save the fucking druid.

Step three: Kill him myself.

And somewhere in between those steps...

Get rid of this godsdamn ache.

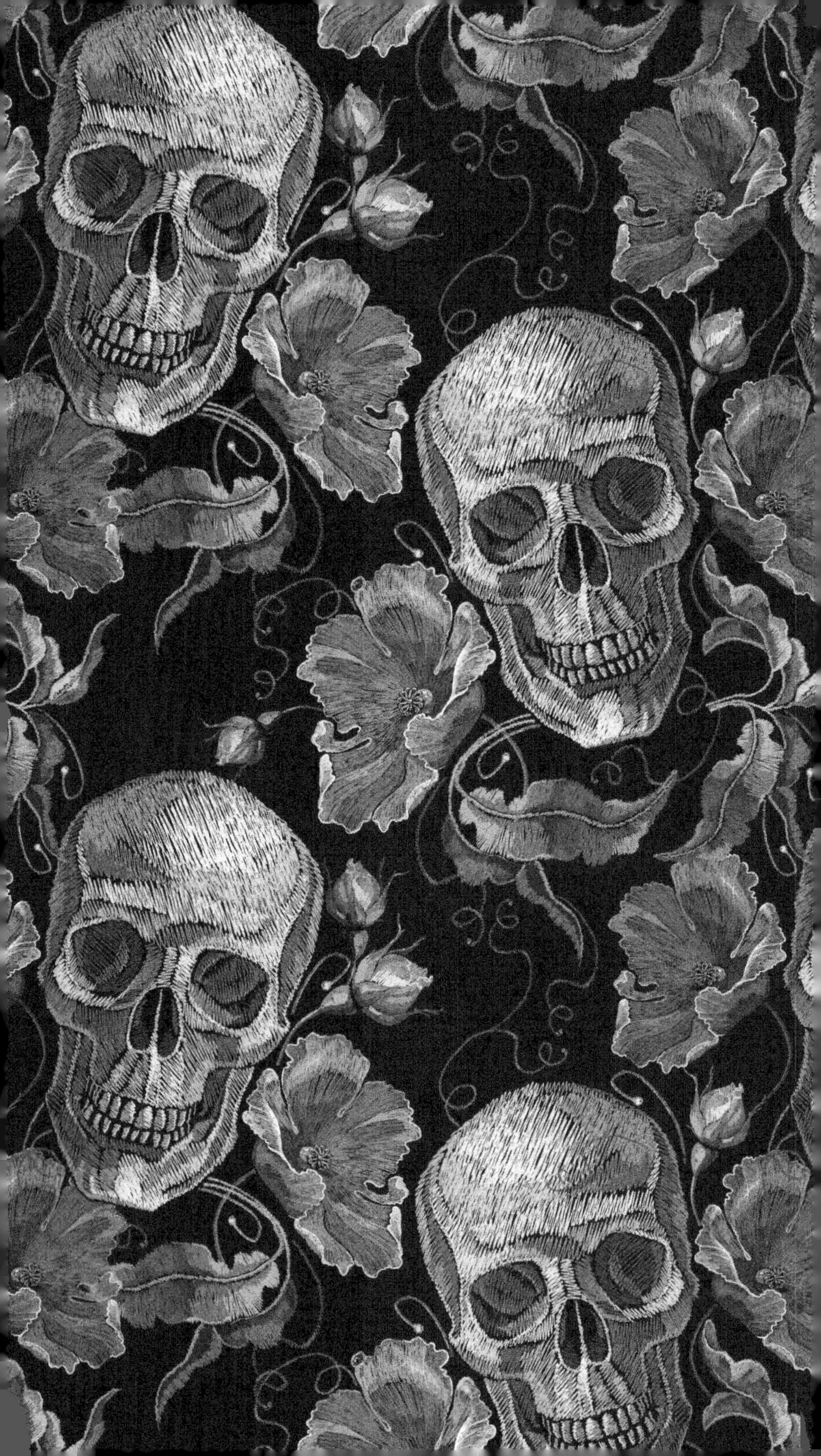

CHAPTER 14
Sloane

Saturday, May 16th
Afternoon

The car ride home was exactly the same way the walk to the car was... *agonizing torture.*

The demon's dexterous hands were on the steering wheel instead of my thighs. *I wasn't sure if that made the ride better or worse.* Even though it was only a little over an hour, I felt like I was ready to explode.

As I shifted uncomfortably in the back seat, Stone eyed me in the rear-view mirror. I wanted to throat punch that demon for the havoc he wreaked on my libido.

Between that and the pent up frustration from months of self-induced orgasms, need was going to kill my immortal soul.

I glared at him and he fucking smirked at me. I knew then and there that not only was he trouble, but every single one of them were.

I would either die horny or I was getting laid tonight. I knew I sounded dramatic. I didn't care, though.

Don't get me wrong, I wasn't one to rush into things, but these were my mates. What was that saying about test driving a car before you bought it?

Yeah. I'd like to test drive my mates before I sealed a bond with them that would last forever. *I didn't even know how long forever was. What if it was like five hundred years and I ended up hating their guts!?*

We were stuck together until one of us died...

Like that fucking druid. I cared about him once. Loved him, even.

Was he good in bed? *Yes.* Would I be welcoming him into my bed again? *Nope. Not for a long damn time, if ever.*

Would I save his ass from certain death?

I sighed as I thought about it. Part of me wanted to let him sweat it out a little longer. The other part of me knew he had been sweating it out for the last two years, and he'd only reached out because he was about to die.

That thought made me angry. Why not reach out to me before?

As if the day hadn't been hectic enough, the moment

we parked in front of my house I noticed Franklin was waiting outside the front door for us.

What's worse?

Well, he had two glasses of whiskey, one in each hand.

Whiskey was our 'it's been a rough day' drink.

As I dragged my ass out of the back seat, he took a sip from one. He handed me the other and took my elbow to lead me inside, never saying a word.

Stone and Briggs followed us from the front entrance, all the way through the kitchen and into the pantry where a spice shelf doubled as the hidden entrance to one side of the basement.

The basement had been spelled soundproof. No audio could penetrate the walls. No security feeds picked up down there. Not even the cell phones would have reception.

I knew whatever he was about to tell me wasn't good.

We pushed into a bubble of sorts at the top of the staircase. *It felt a little like walking through electrified water.*

It made the hairs on my arms and neck stand on end, but it didn't hurt. Once you moved past the popping sensation, everything would return to normal.

We wandered soundlessly down the stairs, listening to the flurry of conversation on the other side of the barrier. When we stepped off the last step, they all ceased talking at once when they spotted me.

Novak, Vaughn, and Palmer all scanned my body, up

and down and back again, as Franklin corralled me to the new table that had appeared in the open room since I was down here days ago.

Before my ass had time to even hit the seat, Vaughn jumped right in.

"David Preston is dead. Murdered. In his office, no more than twenty-four hours a—"

"Why didn't you call me?" My concern was evident in my hushed demand.

"Your phone went straight to voicemail," he supplied.

"Because she threw it out the window after talking to Samuel," Stone confirmed, like it was the most important detail of the day. "We all did."

"Right, we've all ditched our phones too, and Franklin gave us new ones before he took Palmer's laptop. He's not happy about that, by the way. Now he has to start his spank bank all from scratch."

Novak pouted his lower lip at Palmer. Palmer threw a pen at Novak, hitting him dead in between his eyes.

"Ouch!" Novak whined as he rubbed at the red mark the flying projectile left.

"Oh yeah, it's all about ma spank bank and nothin' at all ta do wit' the spells I've been workin' on an' have saved on me lapto—" Palmer defended himself before being cut off.

"Right," the other four muttered in unison, disbelief clear on their faces.

"Okay, let's get back on track. New phones? Great. Murder at CBP? Not so great. Tell me what you saw."

Vaughn swallowed hard as Novak rolled his eyes and began to describe the gory scene.

"Vaughn can be a bit squeamish, so I gathered everything that I could find that might be useful in the office. Then we loaded it up and left."

He finished by pointing to a few stacked boxes on the floor and a computer plugged into a television that had not previously been down here.

They'd been busy.

"Yeah, and tell them about how you touched the dick." Vaughn grinned triumphantly.

"What dick?" Briggs inquired. "You can't just go around touching dicks, dude."

"I think ya mean whose dick," Palmer replied.

"It's not important," Novak argued.

"It could be," Stone countered in a tone that said he was urging him to finish the short story Vaughn had started.

"It's not!" Novak shouted at them.

"So, you had to touch the dead guy's dick?" I clarified just to make sure we understood the situation at hand.

I gave him an innocent look and motioned with my head for him to keep talking.

"Yes, okay?" he conceded.

"I needed to get his cell phone and his unattached dick was lying on top of it. It brushed my hand and I've scrubbed them until they're fucking raw. Look!"

He showed us his pink palms. We all struggled not to laugh at his expense.

"Dead dicks are not my thing. That's a hard limit for me," he informed us all.

He was looking at me so seriously while he confessed that I *almost* thought about what came out of my mouth next.

Ah, fuck it.

"Good to know. I'll mark necrophilia as a no-go with you." I winked at him after my smart ass remark and his golden orbs flared, not finding the slightest bit of humor in it.

"Okay, have you guys found anything on his computer yet? I mean, I'm assuming that's it." I pointed, canting my head in the direction of the other new additions.

"Of course we brought it," Novak mused at the same time Vaughn divulged, "No, we haven't found anything on it."

"Great, what other news?"

"Well, what I can tell from all the research on the injections is that it appears that a mage is powerin' them, but it's too much power for one mage alone. So, either there are multiple mages willin ta commit suicide ta see this drug through, or the mage who started it is stealin' power from other sources. I haven't had enough time ta find anything else though."

Palmer never looked up from the papers spread out all over the table as he spoke. He was deep in thought and trying to stay on task.

"Right."

I thought it through slowly, the pieces starting to be

more visible to me. I was still missing too many to see the full picture, but if what was happening to York was any part of this—

"We need to plan a trip to Kentucky," I blurted as I looked at Stone, and he nodded his head.

Everyone gave us their undivided attention while waiting for the explanation to my sudden outburst.

"We found York, or well, York found me. He told me the rough location of where he's being held."

I streamed some images to their minds. Since I couldn't read them like other people and supes, I simply left it at the edge of their mental barriers like postage being delivered to their doorstep.

If they wanted it, then it was there, but if not, then—

The sharp intakes of breath and muttered curses let me know that they saw the images. They knew we needed to move fast.

"He said we have three days until they kill him with the next drain. It's at least a five-hour drive from here to the nearest campground, then miles and miles of park to hike through.

"Palmer and I can try some locator spells when we get closer, but he gave me the rough estimate of where he is, so maybe we can narrow it down from there. The permanent camp he's in is near water but out of sight.

"That's not the best information; however, it does cut the search area down. We need to leave in the morning, so you guys need to get some sleep."

"And what are you planning on doing?" Vaughn questioned me with suppressed authority.

He wasn't trying to step on my toes but *was* clearly used to calling the shots.

"I'm going to work, of course. I have to be at the club on Friday and Saturday nights." I arched my brow at him as I spoke.

We *just* talked about this last night.

"About that, Madam," Franklin cut in, dread lacing his normally chipper voice. "The usual Saturday night DJ called in while you were gone. It appears he has the human flu."

"Oh." I'm stunned.

That's really short notice to find a new DJ. *What the fuck was the human flu?*

"Yes, I've called around, but—" Franklin began, but Novak's beaming face drew my attention away from the matter at hand.

"Why are you smiling like that?" I reluctantly asked him. His mischievous look only grew wider.

"Well, you see, I wasn't supposed to be back in town until later tonight, and I had planned to take the weekend off," he started.

This was not the time to have this conversation. I had real issues to deal with.

"Yes, and?" I questioned him impatiently, not really seeing where he was going with this.

"Yes, *and*, Novak Malin at your service, mademoiselle." He bowed. As he straightened, he blew a kiss at me and said, "Je suis Gourmandise."

What the fuck did that mean? I knew it was French, but what—

Sloane

"Oh. Ohhhhhh... Wait! Noooo." My voice rose and fell through so many different levels that I sounded like a teenager while I tried to comprehend what he said. I was stupefied.

"Is she having a stroke?" Briggs leaned over to ask Palmer.

"Nah, I don't think so. She thinks he's havin' 'er on," Palmer stated emphatically.

"We thought the same thing. You two made him prove it before you believed him," Vaughn mentioned as he shrugged his shoulders dismissively.

"Yeah, I know how she feels," Stone informed them before he directed his attention to me. "Sloane? You okay, Kitten?"

I was still staring wide-eyed at Novak. I was pretty sure I hadn't even blinked.

There's no way he was the DJ that everyone's been after.

The guy never spoke English at any of his gigs. People were going crazy over him and promoters were paying—

No. *I had a shit ton of questions right now.*

"I want to believe you, but also I don't. I have questions." I shook my head, lost but finally able to translate what he said.

I'm Gluttony.

"Naturally," he interrupted.

"You're French? You speak French?"

"That's where you want to start?"

I threw my hands up. "Uhm, yes. No. I don't know!"

"Yes and yes."

"And you, Novak," I pointed at him, "are the French DJ, DJ Gluttony?"

I was filled with disbelief. When did a DJ *ever* just fall into my lap? *What else could these guys do?*

"Also yes."

"Are you going to explain any of this?" I propped my elbows on the tabletop and folded my hands under my chin.

"Are you going to ask me a question where the answer needs to be given in more than a one-word statement?" he smarted back at me as he matched my position.

Okay, he had me there.

I filtered through my questions and realized that most of them could wait.

"Right," I addressed myself.

Flipping to professional Sloane, I started up the negotiations. "Let's get down to business then. How much is this going to cost me and what stipulations do you have?"

"Hmm." He reclined his head towards the ceiling as he made a show of thinking about my questions. He subtly adjusted his body so he could face me better before dropping his eyes back to mine.

"I'll just require your company... *this time*." He smirked at me.

"Why don't you sit in my booth tonight instead of yours? I'll answer all your questions while I set up, and in between pushing my fancy buttons you can answer mine. Deal?"

He waggled his eyebrows and extended his hand across the corner of the table for me to shake. I debated my options for a moment, but honestly, spending time with Novak sounded like fun.

I hesitantly agreed to his terms. The playful look in his eyes was enough to give me pause over my decision.

Whatever. I'd take the consequences as they came.

There wasn't much time left to plan anything out. It was 5pm already, and we needed to be at the club by 8pm for him to have time to set up. We needed to go to their apartment and get his equipment. We had to get ready.

Well, I had to get ready, and he needed shoes.

"Right." Franklin intercepted what was sure to be an awkward moment where I was still trying to believe what I'd just discovered and agreed to.

"Here are the new cell phones," he spoke as he started handing us phones with sticky notes indicating our names on their cases.

"These are for Jack and Grim," he directed as he passed me two more.

"Your new laptop has already been set up and left on your desk. Palmer has another, and when you and Novak return in the morning, we can transfer his stuff to this one for him to use while we send them off to be checked.

"I'll have the search of the property done before you get back, and I'll text you if I find anything. Though, I don't expect to."

"Novak and I will head to the apartment and pack a few bags. Text me what you guys need," Stone spoke to the group.

Vaughn looked exhausted, and I didn't think he'd had any sleep.

Palmer was messing with the computer from CBP and didn't seem to hear a word Stone said.

Briggs was already dozing in his chair with his head resting on his arms where they sat crossed over the tabletop.

They needed sleep.

"I'm gonna go jump in the shower and wash all this filth off." I motioned my hands around my body. Stone and I had come in covered in dirt and dried blood.

"Franklin can show you guys around the house when you're ready. Make yourselves at home." I had too much shit running through my head to be any more polite than that.

"Franklin, when I'm done, you can drop me off with Novak. Then, go buy whatever supplies we may need for the trip to Kentucky that we don't have here or in storage. I'd like to have all the weapons and bags packed so we can leave in the morning.

"Also, get a rental van too. I don't want to take any personal vehicles that can be traced back to us. Am I forgetting anything?" I'd been slowly backing up to the door as I spoke.

The dried blood didn't really bother me, but the dirt? *Yeah, I didn't like it.*

Sloane

Tomorrow was going to suck so bad, but I'd get to kill some bad guys, so that would help.

Then it would suck some more as we made our way back to wherever we ditched the van. I wondered briefly if I could teleport people.

Probably best not to practice that on my mates.

"I'll have everything ready, Madam," he assured me before my mind really derailed.

"One last thing." Palmer regarded me before he continued. "I, ehh, think I may have found a spell ta turn yer hellhounds into somethin' other than dogs. I don't know what yer limits with magic are, but I could probably change them into somethin' like mice that would fit in yer bag."

"Thanks, Palmer." I smiled coquettishly at him.

I hadn't found a limit to my magic yet. I'd have to explain that, eventually. *But not right now.*

"Send me a picture of the spell when you get a minute, and I'll see what I can do." I winked at him as I exited the basement and made my way back to the ground floor of the house.

As I leaped up the stairs that led to my bedroom two at a time, I let my mind wander over the last two days. Too much had happened, and I hadn't had a moment to digest it.

I started shedding my clothes as soon as I shut my bedroom door. I made it to the bathroom and stepped into the shower before I even turned it on.

The blast of Baltic water brought me back to reality

for a brief few seconds before I nose-dived into the rabbit hole of spiraling emotions all over again.

Except this time I let it happen.

I didn't stop the tears that fell from the corners of my eyes. I needed this breakdown to happen now, not tomorrow when we walked into an unknown situation, and not later tonight when I wasn't alone.

Right now.

It was going to happen and then I was going to move the fuck on.

Let me list the shit I was dealing with:

1. I bought a company to put a stop to a horrible drug that had hit the black market, then realized the previous owner's son had started stalking me.
2. I found out I had mates. *Plural.* And one of those mates was the asshole who broke my heart two years ago.
3. I found out my parents may have been bugged, and I was being followed by someone other than the stalker I'd carelessly collected.
4. I needed to make alliances and build an army, even though I had no idea what that meant.
5. Then, I found out the fucking druid mentioned above was kidnapped and in deep shit, *and* we had to rescue him before he was killed.

The thought of bringing York back into my life was

what had me really and truly twisted. I wasn't ready to face him. Not by myself anyway, but also not with an audience.

Time to pull up my big girl panties and dry my eyes. I had shit to do. The rest of this breakdown would have to be penciled into my schedule for a later date.

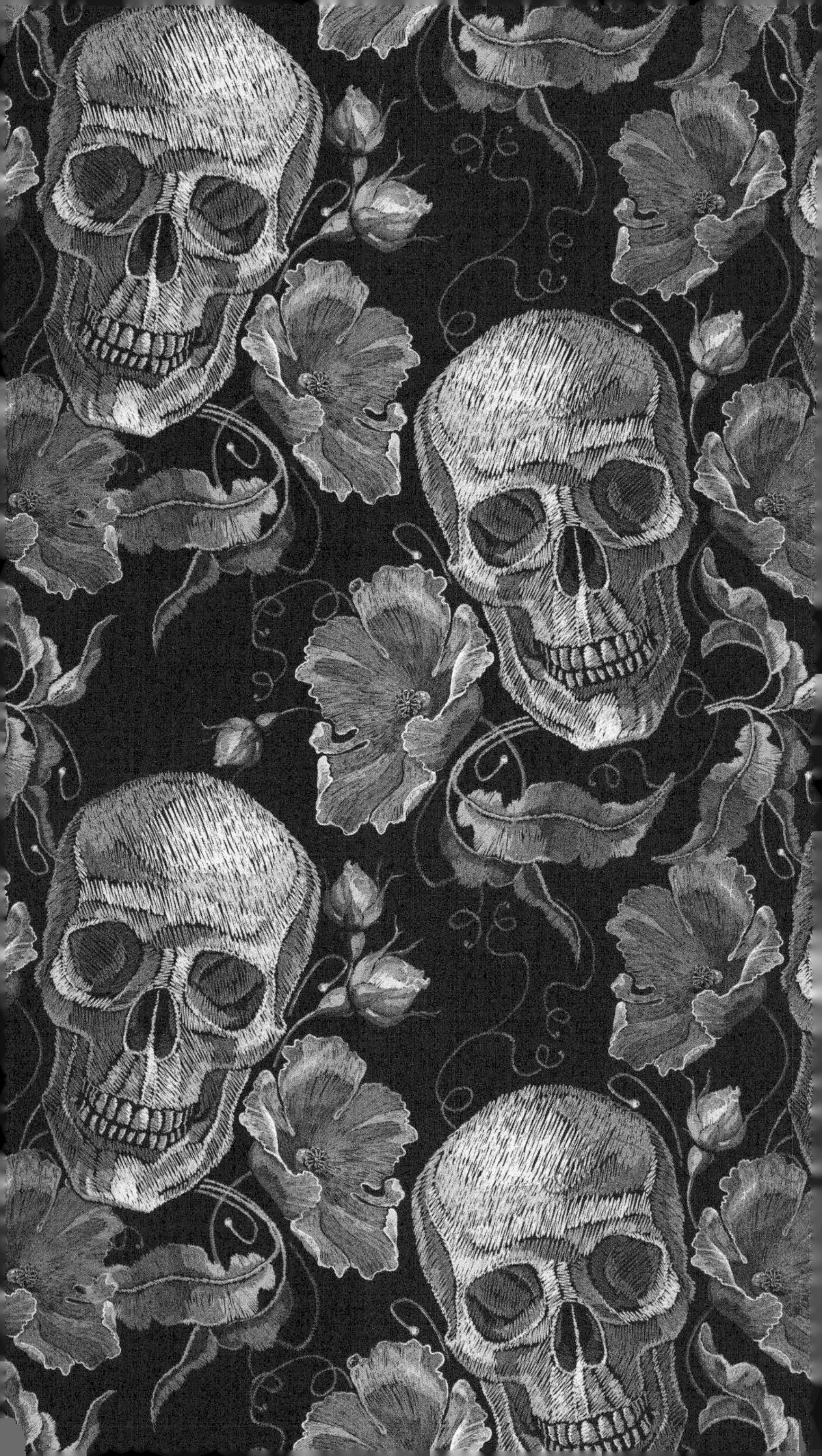

CHAPTER 15
Sloane

Saturday, May 16th
Late Afternoon

I threw on some light gray jeans and a black crop top when I got out of the shower.

This was one of my favorite tops.

It crisscrossed between my breasts and wrapped around my neck and waist. The back was open and exposed, and the fabric felt like a well-worn t-shirt.

I admired the way it hugged my chest as I waved my hand around my hair and magicked that shit dry. I then twirled my fingers to add some beachy waves to my straight silver locks.

Sometimes I found myself loving magic. Sometimes, I was bitter that I had to learn it on my own and not from my mother. That was the cycle of my life on any given day.

Snapping my fingers, I applied my makeup. There was no way I could do makeup so effortlessly by hand.

Magic was cheating, I know, and I don't care. You use what you've got.

Now I just needed shoes, and I'd be ready to leave.

Wait, scratch that. I stuffed a short black skater skirt in my purse first, and then I started searching for shoes.

Shoes, shoes... *Why could I only find one of almost every pair of shoes I owned? Mother fu—*

"Helios!" I snarled his name as I marched down the stairs and stomped through the house.

"You rotten fucking hound! Where are my shoes?" I yelled, completely forgetting there were actual, live people in my home who would hear me screaming at the hellhound.

"Here." Palmer tossed me one of my black Vans and a half-chewed tennis shoe. "I've no idea who's who, but I snatched these from the red one before he made it out the back door."

"That's Helios. He didn't burn you, did he?"

Palmer didn't realize how lucky he was to still have eyebrows, or pants. *Or fucking skin.*

He was a brave one to go toe-to-claw with Helios so soon.

"Nah, but you've got a burn mark on the outside of yer door now, because I slammed it right in his fire breathin' face." He huffed a laugh and rubbed his hands together, looking embarrassed.

"Thanks. That asshole stole half of my shoes. Atlas will bring them back, though. He's the fawn one. He'll be nice if you see him running around. Cronus is the brindle one, dark with stripes in his fur."

"Yeah. I, ehh, don't think I'll be gettin' too close ta them if the others are gonna be tryin' to light me on fire as well."

"Atlas will like you. Cronus is hit or miss, and Helios is almost always a miss. They'll stay outside while I'm gone, but Atlas might come inside. He likes company. Just, uhm, text me if the other two are being rude. I'll tell them to stop."

It was my turn to be embarrassed. I didn't typically admit to being mentally connected with my hounds the same way I was connected to Jack.

After some time, I'd be able to make that connection with my mates too.

"Oh yeah, what're ye gonna do? Text 'em?" His smartass smirk relayed to me that he thought this was funny.

Maybe it was.

I could count on my hands how many people knew about my mental connections, though, him being one of them.

"No, of course not. They don't have thumbs to text me back," I sassed and rolled my eyes as I started walking towards the kitchen.

"Mmm-hmm," he hummed in amusement and trailed behind me.

It was so fucking sexy to hear him hum with his lyrical voice.

I snatched a water bottle from the fridge and rested my back against the island so I could face him. *Check him out.*

His short, dark auburn hair was messy. His eyes were the color of gray storm clouds. He had a light dusting of facial hair across his jaw, and his fitted button down was nearly the same color as his eyes.

I bet he looked edible in a suit.

He was lean and sculpted, and I'd wager his abs were so ripped that tape wouldn't even fix those tears.

I was on the verge of fanning myself when he slyly asked, "Checkin' me out, are ya?"

"Mmm-hmm," I hummed back at him.

"And do ye like what ya see?" he inquired with a knowing look on his face.

Instead of answering him, I leaked some images into his mind to test out these two theories I had.

Purely for scientific reasons, of course.

Me on my knees with his finger under my chin, tilting my head back to look up at him from my kneeling position.

Him circling the bed I was strapped to with a black leather flogger in his hand, taking his time to work me over.

Me dangling by my wrists, blindfolded, and him edging me.

Him wrapping my legs around his waist and giving me that release he kept denying me, driving into me until I screamed so much my voice was hoarse.

Totally scientific.

"Does that seem about right?" I questioned him breathlessly.

Teasing him turned out to be bad for my sex drive. I was regretting the decision to skip panties real fucking hard too.

I could get in his mind, but not the others'.

Smirking, he crossed the three steps between us in two long strides. He took my hand gently before spinning me around and pinning me to the island.

He ran that stubbled jaw of his up the side of my neck and rumbled in my ear, "That's just the tip of the iceberg, Love."

Then he ran his face back down my neck. When he spoke next, his lips barely caressed my skin, but it was enough to send tingles storming through my body.

"An' don't ye forget that ya started this when it comes time for yer punishments for bein' a bad girl..."

I groaned hoarsely as he pushed himself against my back and reached around to run his fingers just below the waist of my jeans.

Why was I in jeans right now!? Why did I need to leave?

He twirled me back to face him and his left hand slipped through my hair before he tugged it harshly and kissed me softly. He didn't remove the fingers of his other hand on their trek along the top of my pubic bone.

After a few heartbeats passed between us, he broke the kiss and backed off, returning to his original spot, propped up and looking unfazed except for the large bulge in his khakis.

"I'm a patient man, Love. Don't start thinkin' I won't tease ya as hard as ye tease me." He winked at me. "Now, go keep the Vampire out of trouble and have a little fun tonight."

Then he just fucking sauntered off, adjusting his package and leaving me breathless and wet.

This wasn't teasing, it was godsdamn torture!

The trip to meet Novak at their apartment was an excruciating twenty-eight minutes.

Unfortunately, every car ride I'd had today had felt the same way.

I was so flustered and soaked that I shifted mercilessly in the back seat. Wearing jeans with no panties only made it worse. Every time I moved, the friction drove me further insane.

I was going to die a frustrated, miserable death at this rate.

I lifted my hand to knock on the door as I surveyed the hallway around me. I didn't even connect my knuckles to the wooden surface of the door before it swung open.

Sloane

Stone appraised me, his nostrils flaring as a knowing smirk settled on his chiseled face. Then he nodded his head in that "come on" way that guys do sometimes. When I entered, he grabbed a few bags off the floor and exited, closing the door quietly behind him.

Novak came around the corner talking to Stone. "Palmer is gonna want those books on the coff—Hey. When did you get here?"

"Just now," I informed him.

"Awesome, I need to grab my laptop and then we can go."

He was gone and back in the blink of an eye, patting his pockets down while mumbling "keys, keys, keys," like the chant would help him magically locate them.

I watched him fumble around for a few minutes, trying hard to keep the smile off my face. *He was so hot, even when he was talking to himself about where he'd left his car keys.*

His chestnut hair flopped in his eyes, and he pushed it out of the way with one heavily tattooed hand.

The colorful art mingled together, from his fingers to his forearms, where they got lost in the scrunched up fabric of his black, long-sleeved t-shirt.

As he kneeled to look under the coffee table, the back of his tight shirt rode up a little. I saw that those striking tattoos appeared to cover him from neck to waist as well.

I wondered if his whole body was covered in them like Briggs'.

I wanted to run my fingertips over the intricate

artwork and memorize all the images, but I'd have to make time for that another day.

His septum was pierced. It drew my attention to his plump Cupid's bow lips that he pulled to the side as his eyes roamed around the room.

Those gorgeous, golden irises bounced from surface to surface while he ran his hand through his hair in frustration.

"Would you like some help?" I called out to him as I battled with myself to keep a smile at bay.

"I mean, as much as I'm enjoying the view, I feel like I could use a locator spell to find your keys."

I could've already found them, but looking at him had been a pleasant distraction.

His fitted jeans made his ass look amazing and showcased the bottom half of his sinewy physique.

His muscles bunched and tensed as he walked closer to me, his predatory gait turning me on even further after my perusal of his body.

"Are you telling me you know how to find my keys *and* you've been checking me out while I search for them?" He stalked closer as he playfully questioned me.

His graceful movements could be compared to a feline. No motion was wasted. Every step he took was purposeful, powerful, and sexy as hell.

"Absolutely," I purred at him. "That's precisely what I'm saying."

I gave up completely on fighting my expression as he took one last step, crowding my personal space. His sandalwood and sage scent invaded me, momentarily making my brain short circuit.

"Describe your keys to me." My whispered request came out husky with desire.

My deceitful body had done nothing but betray me since I'd met these males.

"Well," he glanced down to where my taunt nipples brushed his chest with each inhale I took.

"My key is…" he continued to watch my chest move as I fought to control my breathing.

He left his sentence hanging, and I desperately searched for a distraction while I waited for him to start describing his keys again.

"Unyieldingly firm." His voice dropped to a deeper tone as he peered into my eyes and settled his hands on my hips.

"It's got a few silver rings attached to it and there's some writing around the base. It slides in the ignition with a bit of resistance, but with a twist of my wrist she turns right on."

I let out my second frustrated groan of the day. The victorious look on his face was enough to make me want to kiss him, or slap him.

I wasn't sure which one I was going to choose yet, but then he leaned in so close that I thought maybe he'd decided for me.

Instead, he hovered over my lips as he whispered, "Found them."

On the table in the small foyer, right next to where I'd set my purse, was a set of keys.

"Time to go, Trouble."

Fuck. Was he joking?

Why was it always suddenly 'time to go' when things were getting hot!?

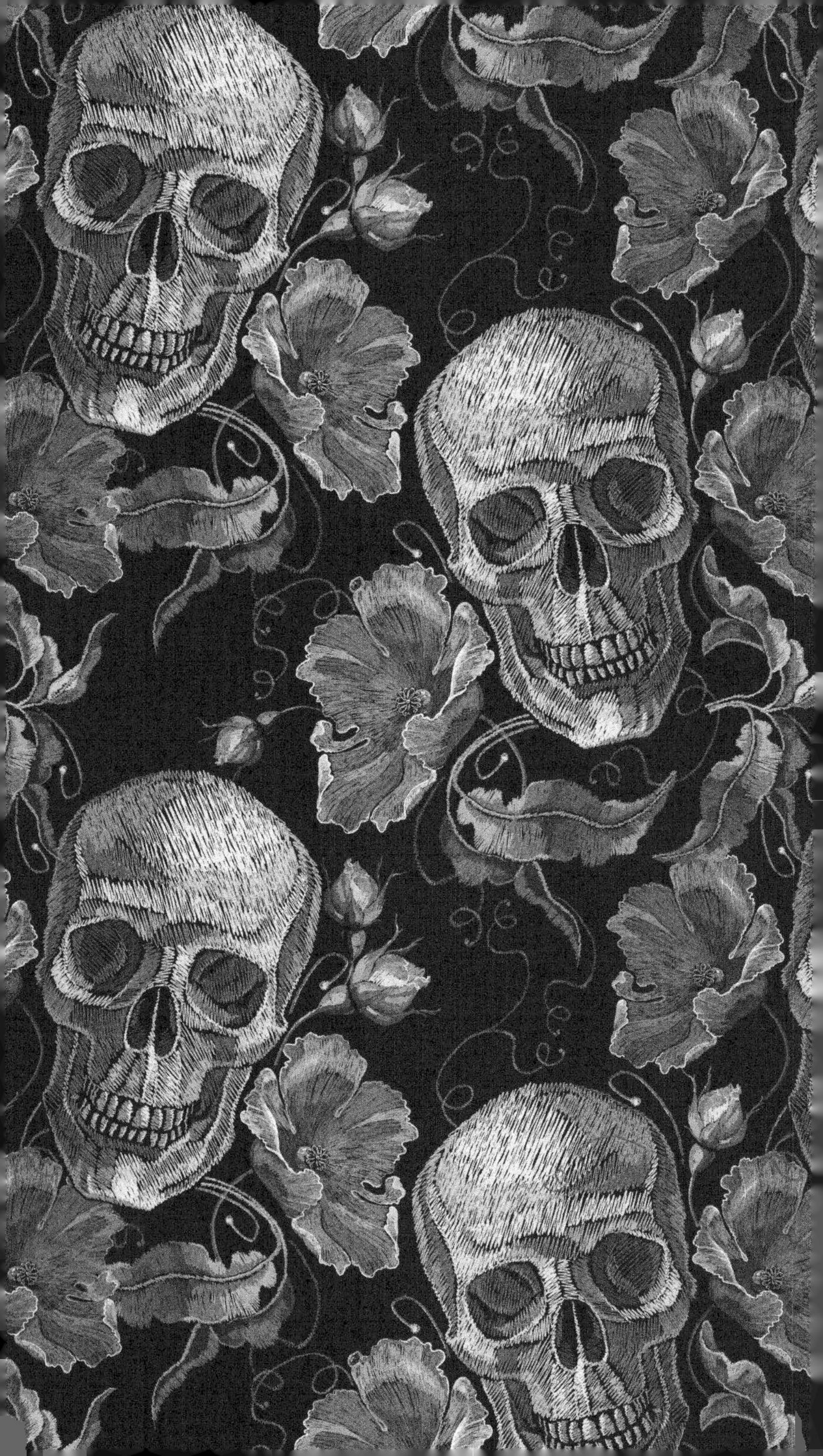

CHAPTER 16
Sloane

Saturday, May 16th
Evening

The club felt desolate outside of opening hours. With all the lights on in the building, it had an emptiness to it that made me uncomfortable. It was typically wild with life and music, but there were still two hours before we officially unlocked the doors to the public.

A quietness rang through the barren establishment that was both haunting and peaceful, yet it was so abnormally cold that I couldn't stand being on the main floor. I left Novak and Simon to their various setups after introducing them and headed upstairs.

The rooms up there weren't meant to have the same party atmosphere as the main space.

They were homely and warm. Not temperature wise, but that feeling of warmth you got when you walked into a well-used room that showed the owner's pride in their area.

I walked into the office and stretched out in the chair behind the sleek, modern desk. There was a folder full of paychecks that needed to be signed and an inventory checklist to be looked at and initialed so we could send off for our weekly orders.

I got all of that done and out of the way before writing out a few other notes. I waved my hand above each of them with the intention of sending them to the rooms my mates would be staying in.

When I knew they had all reached their destinations, I relaxed once more in my chair and picked up my phone to text Jack.

A phone chimed from my purse, reminding me that I had new phones for Jack and Grim in there, and no way to get in touch with them until they showed up.

Other than reaching out mentally.

I didn't want him to freak out over the turmoil rolling around in my mind, so I decided to wait out my boredom.

I exited out of the one-sided conversation with Jack and saw that Franklin had texted me. All preparations had been made for our trip in the morning, and that filled me with nervous, jittery energy.

I would rescue York, but I would not be ready to talk about how his disappearance made me feel.

Sloane

I knew he'd want to talk sooner than I would. He was always like that.

Often I needed time to put my feelings into words. Other times, I just needed that distance to keep from getting angry. He understood, but he'd still push me.

Together we were like a brushfire waiting to happen, dry grass and one misplaced burning match. He kept me grounded, and I kept him wild.

The adventures and excitement I experienced with him had felt endless, until they'd abruptly ended.

In hindsight, I should've known something was wrong. I did look for him, and I hired people to find him, but there was nothing.

His cell phone was wiped clean by the factory reset, then cleared of fingerprints and left to be found on a bus station bench. I didn't know what happened to his car or the stuff he had at his house.

Now that I was really thinking about it...

I remembered I still had a few boxes of his things in the attic. Franklin packed his stuff up and moved it all out of my room after a couple months of not hearing from him.

I didn't know what to do with it. So it had been sitting there the whole time he'd been gone.

I guess, if anything, he'd have clothes when we returned.

Out of the mega load of crazy shit that had been dumped on my plate recently, I think finding out that he was meant to be my mate had me the most tied up.

All that time together, and I never thought to ask

about what I was feeling. Had we already sealed our mate bond, and I just didn't know what to look for?

I didn't really know anything about it, and I wasn't sure where to start looking.

Although, I suppose I did have five other mates I could direct those questions to.

Almost twelve hours ago I opened my home up to them, and now I felt like I'd be living in a hotel full of sexy males with a variety pack of personalities and powers.

Taking on mates wasn't the scary part, though. Taking on the responsibilities that came with said mates was the kicker.

If I sealed the bond with Palmer first, then I'd have to step in and take over as High Priestess of the Guilds.

I wasn't ready to give up my freedom, or my jobs, to take on being queen bitch to a bunch of uppity supes, but I guess that was happening whether I was ready or not.

I mean, it wasn't like I could put them in a particular order and expect it to go the way I planned. I wouldn't know who to choose first either.

I'd rather that happened organically, but if what Father said was true, then I may not have as much time as I'd like. I could always get to know them later, but that sounded mortifying.

What if I mated with one of them and then I found out I didn't like him as a person, or that he didn't like who I was?

Looks were one thing, but actually knowing someone? That was totally different.

Sloane

We weren't talking about getting married on a whim and being able to get divorced.

No.

The bond lasted until death, and for us that was a lot longer than your average lifespan.

My thoughts were starting to twist into each other again, and I felt like I was on the verge of a panic attack.

I closed my eyes, and I fought to slow my breathing, focusing on happy thoughts when I picked up Jack's mental trail.

Thank the Devil. I needed him right now.

I needed him to calm me down, and then I needed to consider a vacation.

Or maybe not.

I didn't need to be by myself. That would've given me too much time to think about all th—

A knock at the office door jerked me out of my head, and I smiled thankfully as the door opened. Jack strolled in, followed by Grim and Novak.

The latter was looking at the de-robed Grim Reaper like he'd never seen a male before. I wondered what was going on in his head, but just like with the fae, I heard nothing.

When he looked at me, his gawking eyes said, *"I thought this guy was a skeleton,"* and I struggled with the urge to laugh.

I'd met many reapers, but Grim had always been my favorite.

That wasn't his real name, but it was what everyone called him because, well, he was pretty fucking grim.

He was the complete opposite of his bubbly demon boyfriend, and yet somehow they fit together better than Jack and Coke.

Novak shut the door behind him and sat in one of the chairs on the other side of my desk while Jack and Grim remained standing. They all looked annoyed, which had me sitting up straighter in my chair.

What had they found?

Grim snapped his fingers and a smoky gray bubble appeared around us.

Oh, great. Just what I needed.

"We found a mini camera and a few bugs downstairs, but nothing up here. Grim took them to Franklin to see if he could trace them. But we won't know for a few days." Jack cut straight to the bullshit.

"Okay. I can send the security footage off and see if we can spot any suspicious activity, but I don't think that's going to get us anywhere."

"Sloane," Grim addressed me formally, and I didn't like his unusual tone. "The camera was facing your booth."

"I figured that was the case. Nathaniel told me I was being followed, so it doesn't surprise me that this would be a step they'd take. Whoever *they* are."

It aggravated me to no end to know that I was being followed, but not closely enough to be able to determine exactly who it was.

"How are you so calm about this?" Novak inquired with some anger lacing his voice.

"It's not the first time," Jack countered.

"Not even the second. Though, this time it does feel more serious," I answered Novak, bouncing off what Jack said.

"Oh, before I forget, I need to give you guys your new phones. Franklin set them up."

I passed the phones to Jack and he handed one to Grim, who gave zero fucks about technology. We could've given him an old flip phone and he would've held the same level of excitement.

He nodded his head in thanks and let the smokey dome drop.

"I'm going to get changed for tonight and Grim's leaving. He has some reaping business to handle." Jack chuckled at Grim.

*We knew what he did, but we didn't fully know **what** he did when he left, you know?*

They exited the office together, and I heard Grim telling Jack, "I'll see you when you get home in the morning."

They'd moved into an apartment together a couple months ago, leaving me in that big house all by myself.

It was fucking adorable and annoying.

I had heard all about how Grim didn't get all his beard trimmings out of the bathroom sink, and how Jack left his dirty clothes in a trail through the house.

But they were happy, and that was what mattered to me.

"So, what was going on in that pretty mind of yours when we walked in? You looked a little panicked, Trouble."

I decided Novak was too attentive after that question, but I was also weirdly comfortable with that too. I found that I wanted to answer him, and I briefly wondered if he was compelling me, but wrote it off as soon as it crossed my mind.

No vampire had ever been able to compel me.

"I don't want to talk to York tomorrow. I mean, I want to save him, yes, but I'm not happy with the idea of addressing feelings I buried years ago. He's going to want to sleep, eat, and talk. Probably not in that order. I want to avoid it until I can have a calm, rational conversation. I feel petty for wanting to avoid talking to him and irrationally protective at the same time. I don't like it."

Uhg, I didn't like it even more when I said it aloud. I folded my shoulders in a little and let my head fall to my desk.

"Are you nervous about the rescue mission?"

"Absolutely not, but I also don't want you guys to freak out if I walk in and kill everyone. It's not really the kind of impression I want to give the males who are supposed to be my mates."

I shrugged my shoulders in deference, but it felt weird with my forehead flat on my desktop.

"I think it'll be hot, Trouble. Stone told me about you guys taking out the rogues, and I'm pretty fucking excited to watch you work," he admitted.

"Why do you call me that?"

"What? Trouble?"

"Yes, that." I pulled my head up and rolled my eyes at him. What else would I be referring to?

"Because you *are* trouble. The fantastic and terrifying kind. The kind that makes mere men want to move mountains with their bare hands. The kind that makes males like us want to kill anyone who gets too close to you. The kind that comes into your life and makes the axis of your world tilt, changing all your notions and beliefs in a single glance."

The smile on his face was sweet, but the heat in his eyes was something completely different.

"And right now, am I the good kind of trouble?"

"There's no need for good trouble with me, Sloane. I'm not like the other guys. I thrive off mischief and chaos. I love walking the line between good and bad, but I always lean a little. I lack in some of the moral standards departments."

He shrugged noncommittally.

"I don't want you to be the good kind, I want you to be the addictive kind. The trouble that has me itching for my next fix. The kind that does really bad things with me, but also forces me to be a better version of myself at the same time."

"That makes this sound sweet and dirty." I gave him a sidelong glance with a smirk on my face. "I'm not exactly one with a high moral standing either. I do worry about that causing issues with some of the others, though."

"Let me elaborate a little on your mates, Trouble."

He ambled over with that feline grace, slowing his steps for me as I stalked his movement around my desk. He scooped me out of my chair and set me on the desktop as he took my chair.

He moved so his elbows rested casually on my knees and he could look up at me with his glorious, golden eyes.

I couldn't take my eyes off his mouth when his fangs started to slide out and the tip of his tongue brushed across them.

"Palmer? He likes to dominate, and Vaughn likes to be dominated. They're both control freaks, but one likes to lose that burden and the other has to maintain it.

"Stone likes a rough ride. He's a bit of a sadist who will occasionally switch, but pain is his game. Briggs will play hard to get. He'll make you feel like you have to work for it when really he's been ready to give in from the jump.

"Me? I'm easy, I like it dirty, Sloane. I want to fuck you on the dance floor in front of everyone. I want to lock you in the bathroom at your parents' house and test how quiet you can be, or have you in my lap as we drive through town during rush hour. I like watching and sharing as much as I'll like having you to myself."

Yes, please. Sign me up! If he was trying to deter me with his public sex and sharing comments, then he had to work his angles better.

I locked eyes with Novak, the space growing smaller between our bodies.

"Are you trying to talk me out of wanting to fuck you?" I questioned him in a whisper as I ran my nails gently up his arm and weaved my fingers through his thick hair.

He growled low, letting his fangs fully extend. I let mine slip out and bit into my lower lip.

"Not at all," he assured me with a slight shake of his head. "I'm just telling you what I like, so you're prepared."

"I'm no angel, Novak. If you knew half the shit that ran through my mind, you would've ripped my clothes off and fucked me on the floor in your apartment while the door was still wide open," I informed him with a single raised brow.

"I take what I want, when I want it, and I'm not afraid to tell you exactly how I want it." I winked at him as I scooted forward and slipped into his lap.

"You see, unlike all the girls you're probably used to, you can't hurt me. You can try. I've enjoyed it in the past. You can bite me, but you can't compel me to forget it happened. You can't drain too much from me and you can't turn me."

He stared at me intently as he listened. I grazed a fingertip against one of his fangs and brushed my other hand over his cock.

"These don't scare me," I added as I pushed his fang into the pad of my index finger, "and this," I asserted as I leisurely stroked him through his jeans, "makes me wish I'd changed clothes sooner."

I glided my bloody finger across his lips. Popping it into my mouth before pulling myself up, I grabbed my skirt from the side of my desk so I could change.

The growl that followed in my wake was a thrilling, feral sound that sent heat coursing through my whole body. Goosebumps raised across my arms, and my nipples pebbled painfully.

I was so wet right now that I'd need to clean up before I went downstairs.

A room full of humans wouldn't notice, but mix in some supernatural beings, and I'd have too much unwanted attention.

"Oh, you're the wicked kind of trouble," he confessed to me as I sashayed to the other side of the room.

I *was* headed towards the bathroom to change and give us both a few seconds to chill out. *I think I'll just change right here.*

He thought I was *wicked*, but I knew exactly what I wanted right now and how to get it.

He didn't move a muscle when I unbuttoned my jeans. He tracked my hand, like a hawk watching a mouse, as I tugged my zipper down at a torturously slow pace.

I pushed my fingers into the waist of my jeans and started to ease them down. They got no further than mid-thigh before he broke.

He was across the room and had my bare ass sitting on the desktop in a flash of inhuman speed.

In one swift movement, my jeans were off my body and hitting the floor as he stretched his hands around the tops of my thighs.

Novak dug his fingertips in my flesh so hard that I'd be left with fading finger shaped bruises in a moment.

I drew a small circle with my left index finger and traced straight down, using my magic to open the button and zipper of his pants.

He dragged me closer to the edge of the desk before

sinking two fingers into my dripping core and rubbing his thumb across my clit.

I moaned at the contact, and he muffled my sounds with a frenzied kiss as his fingers curled and sped up.

I wasn't the least bit embarrassed by how fast I came.

His fingers moved as fast as a vibrator but felt a hundred times better.

I rode his hand through my orgasm. Every flick of his thumb felt like it dragged another shudder from my body.

When he was satisfied with what he'd done, he lifted me off the desk. I wound my legs around his hips as he shoved my back against the wall behind my desk.

He held me up with one hand while he jerked his jeans down with the other.

I mentally whispered a birth control spell. I hadn't had sex in months, so I hadn't kept up with the protection magic.

I guess I should work on a more long-term version now. Maybe I'd ask Palmer to help me.

"Fuck," I breathed out as he impaled me slowly, stretching my walls with each inch.

I moaned louder at the new sensations. *He was not lying when he said his, uhm, key had a few rings on it.*

He stilled when he was fully seated. I gave him a moment to enjoy the feel of my tight channel before nudging my hips to get him moving.

"You're so tight," he groaned, throwing his head back as he pulled out almost completely before slamming home harder.

Each thrust had him picking up speed, driving into me

with more and more strength. My office filled with the sound of slapping flesh, grunted curses, and cries of ecstasy.

I was a gasping mess. My inhales came in short bursts of breath, and my exhales hissed out every time my back hit the wall.

His punishing rhythm would have bruises forming across my shoulders, but I didn't care. They'd heal, along with the other ones, before the night was over.

Another orgasm began to build, growing in intensity until it came barreling to the surface. He slowed his movements as I tightened around him and screamed out his name with my release.

When I loosened my hold, he placed his forehead against mine to catch his breath, then started up again.

His body was merciless, and despite my fast healing, I was sure I'd still be sore tomorrow.

I felt him start to swell inside me, and it had my passion building up all over again. Novak dragged his fangs across my neck before piercing the skin.

He sucked deeply on my flesh and I moaned low against his ear. The venom in a vampire bite was an instant aphrodisiac. The moment it flooded my bloodstream, my entire body lit up like a Christmas tree.

The orgasm hit me so hard it nearly gave me whiplash. He came with a long groan, pushing in as deep as the position we were in would allow.

He pulled his fangs out of my neck, licking my skin to seal the wounds before they had a chance to heal on their own.

Sloane

He didn't set me down though. Instead, he backed us up, and we fell into the desk chair with me sitting astride him.

Placing one hand on my lower back and the other in my hair, he kissed me with a gentle desperation. I returned it with all the pent-up emotions that possessed me.

I loved the way he held me tightly. *I wasn't much of a cuddler after sex, but this...* It was caring yet possessive. I felt like we belonged to each other, and it was a heady fucking feeling.

I was naked from my waist down and his pants were halfway to his knees. The near-clothed state of our bodies didn't change the feeling of that romp being more than either of us intended.

As we sat in the chair, his face rested in the crook between my neck and shoulder. I leaned my cheek against the side of his head while I ran my right hand through his hair.

We stayed like that for minutes, and it felt like hours. I couldn't tell.

A knock at the downstairs door brought us back to the present. We scrambled to get dressed before the door swung open the rest of the way, and someone came into the office.

It was Simon.

He walked in on our intimate moment to tell us that they were about to open the doors for the night.

My heart was still frantic, but my breathing had

finally evened out from the panting I was doing a few minutes ago.

I glared at Simon while I checked myself for any dried blood in the mirror by the door. Snapping my fingers to fix my hair and makeup, we began to venture downstairs.

"Next time, Trouble, I want to do that in the DJ booth with a room full of people around. The light show flashing across your ecstasy-filled face, disguising the movement of our bodies, and your moans blending into the music. What do you say?" Novak spoke between the kisses he left across the back of my neck.

Gods, that sexy, sultry whisper was sending fireworks sailing through my body.

"Keep whispering in my ear while you kiss me like that, and it will get you anything you want," I groaned out.

It was the honest to gods' truth, too. *If he didn't stop, we wouldn't be going downstairs at all.*

But that was exactly what we did, and that was exactly what he got.

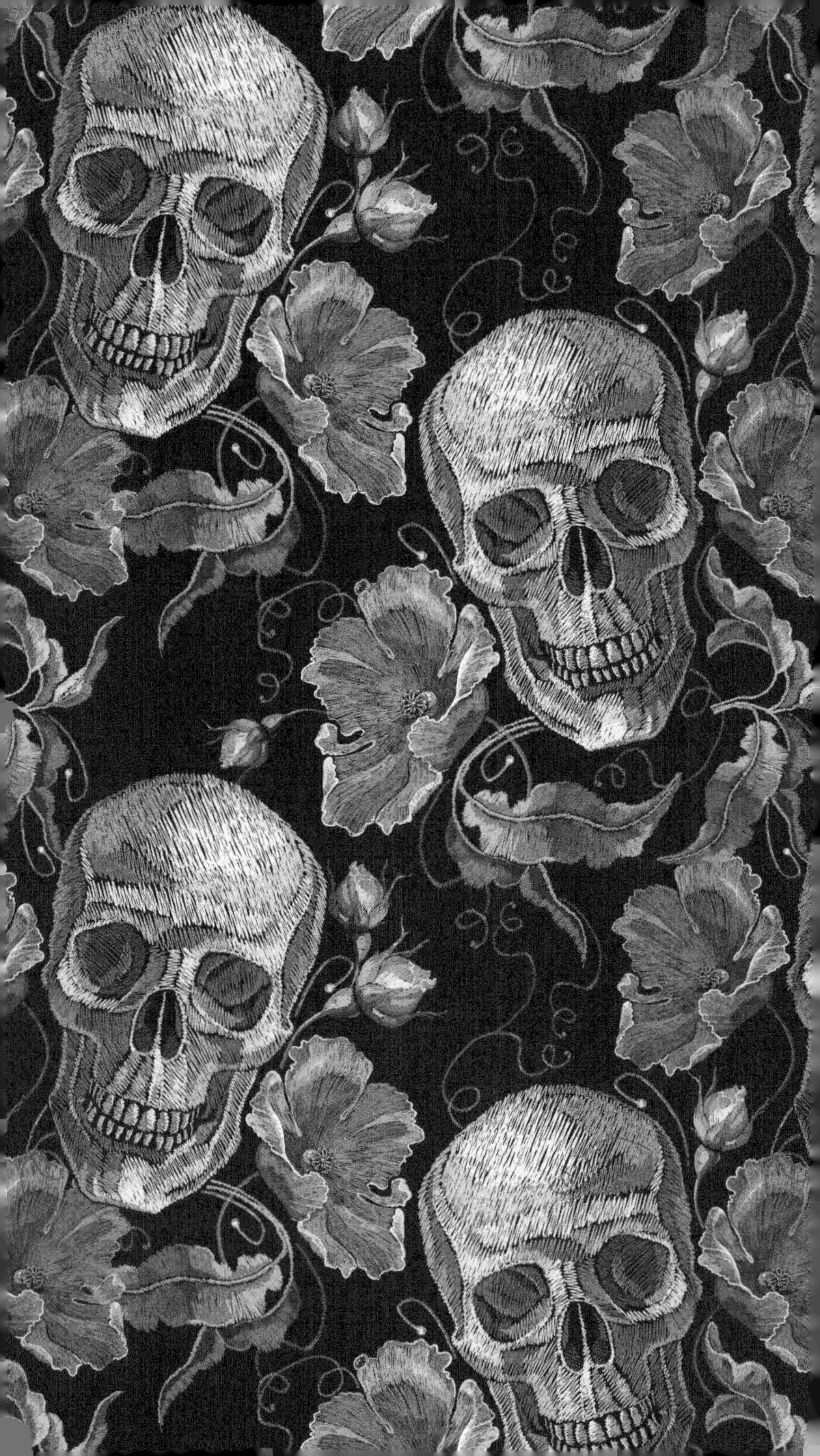

CHAPTER 17
Stone

Saturday, May 16th
Late Night

The day's events piled up in my mind as I sat at the edge of the steps on the back patio.

Oddly, this dark mansion felt more like home to me than our apartment did. It had nothing to do with the size of the place, though.

I looked out over the midnight blue sky lit with stars and tried to imagine how much my life was about to change. I'd come to terms long ago with the fact that I was the Devil's apprentice, and I was to be bonded to his daughter.

What had really been irking my nerves was that we could be taking his place soon.

Was I ready to give up my career to become the next ruler of the Underworld with Sloane?

Actually, I didn't mind the thought of not working my day job anymore. I'd still own the dental practice, but it wouldn't kill me to give up my patients and hire another dentist to fill my absence. I only went in twice a week anyway, unless I was covering for someone who went out of town.

I could still do that if I needed to. *I'd need to keep my license up to date, but that was it.*

I think I'd rather stand by the side of the next Devil Spawn and rule the Underworld with her.

The tapping of shoes brought me out of my headspace as someone approached from behind me.

Franklin came into my peripheral vision and handed a glass of brown liquid to me before speaking. "Glenfiddich twenty-six, sir."

He inclined his head to the glass in my hand.

"If you'll follow me, I'd like to give you a proper tour and then show you to your suite. You have full privileges to everything on the property, but please be wary of Helios when you're outside alone. He likes to set things on fire and unless you're with Sloane when he finds you, then you're free game in his mind. Until he decides if he likes you or not."

The obsequious nature of his smile had me scanning the yard in search of the hellhound in question. I wasn't

Stone

worried about him lighting me on fire, but he could still bite me.

Franklin turned and started making his way to the back door as I stood. A back door that wasn't burned this morning, but was now covered in black scorch marks, making us both pause to study it.

I wondered briefly what happened there, but Franklin muttered, "That fucking hound," under his breath, and I had my answer.

I obediently followed Franklin through the house, making note of certain rooms and dismissing others completely.

This place was a never ending maze. I'd need a map to get around for the first couple days.

The mansion was positioned on the side of a slope. The yard was tiered, so each floor had its own access point to the outside.

The basement had a pool that was both indoor and outdoor, along with a gym and a small theater room.

The first floor was the main area of the house with a large den and TV area in an open concept floor plan that connected to a restaurant style kitchen and dining area. It could have easily sat twenty people but only held ten chairs.

Off the side of the kitchen were two black doors. One led to an attached three-car garage while the other opened up to a smallish room with a sleeping hellhound inside. It had a dog door attached to the outside wall where we just glimpsed the fire-tipped tail of a large dark beast leaving the sleeping quarters.

The second and third floors of the house had three suites on each floor. Franklin told me that Vaughn, Palmer, and York had rooms on the second floor while Briggs, Novak, and I all had rooms on the third.

The second floor was home to a gloriously filled library, and the third floor housed an incredible game room.

The fourth, and final floor, of the monolith mansion was where Franklin pointed out yet another black door. That one led to Sloane's suite.

All the doors in this place were black. How was I supposed to tell them apart?

The last floor also had a greenhouse with a waterfall that cascaded down the side of the exterior wall and into the part of the pool that hung out of the basement.

The doorway at the opposite end of the fourth floor hallway led to a rooftop patio with a large black telescope set up in one corner and lounge chairs scattered across the opposite side.

Real grass grew on the surface, and I could only imagine what kind of sight would await us when that grass needed to be cut.

It's really unrealistic of me to imagine the old Vampire scaling the side of the house with a push mower strapped to his back... but that's exactly what I was seeing.

Franklin's last stop took me to what I assumed was my suite. He disappeared before I opened the door. I inhaled a deep breath, turning the knob slowly.

Upon entering the suite, the first thing I noticed was that it had my tastes and personality written all over it.

Stone

Nearly the entire space was black and charcoal gray, but there were some occasional splashes of red, orange, and white around the den.

There was a dry bar in the right corner that hid a mini fridge under the black marble countertop. A concrete shelf held smokey colored glasses in a variety of shapes and sizes.

The sitting area had a black leather couch with gray furry pillows and a white knit blanket tossed over the back. A coffee table sat in front of the couch with a large glass top and a thin metal frame that showcased the rich burgundy rug underneath.

Across from the doorway was a room-length window that had black curtains tied back on both sides. The left side of the room was home to a tall cactus in the corner by the window, a fireplace with a TV above it, and another closed black door that blended in with the wall.

I twisted the handle on the door, readying myself. It led to a massive bedroom with a sleek desk positioned against a wall of glass.

The window seemed to continue through the wall of the living space. A floor to ceiling bookcase was nestled to the right of the desk where the window finally ended. One shelf was stacked full of classic books. The rest of the shelves were bare and waiting to be stocked.

The bed was all black. Ebony headboard. Pitch black bedding with pillows to match. And one vermillion throw pillow in the center that had the words *"Wanna touch my horns?"* in tiny black glass beads.

It made me smirk to myself. *It was dirty demon humor that lightened the room.*

I could imagine Sloane had a good laugh when she picked it out.

I walked closer to the bed, and the deep gray rug on the floor melted around my feet. It was warm compared to the cool, concrete-coated flooring that flowed throughout the suite.

The bed looked inviting. As I sat on the edge of it and threw myself back, the mattress dipped with my body weight and gave me the sensation of laying on clouds.

When I turned my head to the left, I saw a brick fireplace ready to be lit with a black fire iron jammed into the wood neatly stacked inside. Tied to the handle by a white ribbon was a red piece of paper.

I got up to grab the note, but the sight above the mantle had my footsteps halting.

Above the fireplace, across from my bed, was a large picture of a burning field from the Underworld.

I knew that place intimately. It was where I grew up, before my parents were murdered. That exact field was the view from my bedroom window.

Written in the fire were the words, *"The valley is mine"* in black, dripping ink. I watched, mesmerized, as the ink dribbled down. The fire from the picture made it sizzle and disappear, over and over, but the words never ran or faded.

The magic in this picture was breathtaking.

I figured out how to make my feet move again after

several minutes of staring. I strolled over to snatch up the note and the delicate white ribbon.

As I pulled it free from the fire iron, the fireplace roared to life. The hellfire inside licked at my fingertips but didn't burn the paper. I unfolded it gently and viewed the blank page for a moment before handwritten words magically began to appear one at a time.

Stone,
This space is yours for as long as you want it.
The magic in the walls is tailored to you, and you alone.
If you desire a change, then all you need to do is speak it aloud and it will happen.
I hope you enjoy it.
-Sloane.

I was very much enjoying the suite. It was ridiculously spacious with minimal decor. Exactly what I liked.

It was a gift that I didn't deserve yet. I intended to show my soon-to-be mate otherwise.

I thought about all the things I'd like to show her as I proceeded with the rest of my exploration.

The only door I hadn't checked was on the far left of my new bedroom. It opened to a well-lit bathroom with a pocket door that led to an attached walk-in closet.

Black towels were rolled up and snugly secured on a shelf near the entrance to a glass-walled shower. A large mirror showed my wide-eyed reflection, and after looking at myself I decided I'd had too much excitement to sleep tonight.

I exited the suite in pursuit of a nightly activity. I didn't need as much sleep as everyone else, but I did need a little more sleep than Novak's none.

Did I want to go outside? No. No, I didn't. What to do, what to do?

I started by looking at the other rooms. I liked to know who was where in the setup of things like this.

Call me nosey, but I couldn't help it.

I wondered if the others had rooms designed for them as well. I was pretty sure they did, but I wanted to see them, anyway.

Then I would poke around the extra rooms. Maybe I'd see what the game room was all about, find out what books were in the library, or check out the movie selection in the theater.

I didn't know. I was a curious creature, so I'd just see where my feet took me.

There was a door on the right and the left of the hallway. *Black doors.* I started with the left.

That suite had Novak's name all over it. *Not literally, but it was his style.*

The suite was completely different from mine. It still had a black theme to it, though his was more vintage to my modern. All doors led to the left in his suite as well.

As I walked through, I noticed the four-poster bed had a blood red pillow on it. It looked like someone had smeared *"No pencils allowed"* in black paint, and the humor surprised me.

I didn't know if that was a euphemism or if it was about wooden stakes. I didn't even know if stakes actually worked on vampires, but it was funny either way.

Sloane had a dry and insulting sense of humor with some of the guys. I was finding that I loved that about her. I couldn't wait to see if that was a recurring theme in all the rooms.

I really hoped it was.

Briggs' suite sat on the right side of the third floor. His space had a woodsy feel to it. There were a few potted trees and plants, and the furniture was earthy and rustic.

His suite doors opened to the right, and I followed them to his bedroom. His low bed sat against a brick wall and his pillow made me laugh out loud.

The stuffed white bone read *"Dog hair is totally trendy"* in rough threading. I knew he'd both hate and love it.

Instead of a balcony like Novak and I had, his wall of windows led to the tier of yard that was laid out for this floor. *Perfect for a wolf.*

I left his room with a relieved smile on my face. He should warm up to Sloane in no time.

Making my way down the stairs, I noticed that they lit up with each footstep. *Clever for those without night vision.*

The room on the far right of the second floor was no doubt York's room. It was filled with plants and had an earthy green and orange vibe that was broken up with touches of other colors.

His room didn't have an empty closet like the rest of us. It was half-filled with clothes I hadn't seen in years. It reminded me that the druid had a girlfriend before he went missing.

Now I definitely knew who she was.

My guess would be that Sloane didn't move his stuff back in, though. Franklin did.

His bed sat diagonally across his room with a large flowing plant hanging over the head of it. The pillow on his bed, yeah, it made me laugh more than Briggs' did.

It was controversial and would certainly piss the druid off. His insulting pillow was such a dark green that it was almost black. It was hand-stitched with *"The earth is flat"* in bright orange threaded letters.

The center suite on the second floor had to be Vaughn's.

It was more minimal than mine and all light to my dark, with one faded navy blue wall in each area. Everything else in the suite was white, cream, or light blue with touches of dark navy and royal blue.

His pillow was the color of twilight and popped against his stark white bedding. It was also the most insulting one yet. I was so thankful I decided to be nosey because I hadn't laughed this much in months.

Here lies a fairy" was printed on his pillow in a powder blue, swooping, girly script. I took a picture of it with my phone and sent it to Novak before leaving Vaughn's space.

I only had a few minutes before the guys went to

sleep. It was after 11pm, and I heard Franklin walking them through the tour of the main floor.

Palmer's suite was to the far left, below Novak's room. When I opened his door, it immediately screamed bookworm. His living space walls were either shelves or windows.

The rooms had a navy, gold, and burgundy theme to them that suited him so well I would've assumed that he designed it. His pillow was so specific to him that I had to smother my laughter so they wouldn't hear me as they trailed up the stairs after Franklin.

"Know your safeword" was printed in a neat, blocky script on a burnt mustard pillow in the center of his tall canopy bed. It was perfect for him.

This was all perfect for all of us.

I let that thought sink in as I slowly hiked the stairs to the top floor and stopped at Sloane's door. I wanted to snoop around, but I didn't want to invade her space.

The guys were different; we had lived together for years. I didn't feel bad about checking out where they were staying for the next... however long.

Sloane's room was a gray area for me, but I reached for the knob, anyway. *I was too curious of a creature to not look, but I wouldn't touch anything.*

Her suite was the same size as ours, but where we had sitting areas, she had a cluttered office with a purple velvet couch against the wall. Her large desk was filled with files and half chewed pen tops.

Everything was a gloomy gray, but the pops of color

she had in there brought some much-needed life to the room.

The end tables on the sides of her bed were bright pink. The edges of her black doors were all electric green. The rugs on her floor were layered with the same vibrant colors plus yellows, greens, purples, and blues that jumped out.

The colors made the room look busy compared to her gray cushioned headboard and plush black bedding.

I didn't miss the pillow thrown haphazardly onto her barely made bed. It was my favorite out of all the ones I'd seen in the rooms. *"Cute and psycho"* was scrawled in fancy black cursive on a bright pink pillow.

Her space had as much character as she did. It's just all hidden behind a solid black door.

As I eased myself away from the snooping, I decided the rooftop patio seemed like a good place to chill out and think through my convoluted thoughts.

I walked down the long hallway, to the right of Sloane's room, and up a lit stairwell to the door that led to the patio.

The late night air hadn't grown humid from the invasion of summer temperatures yet. The end of a Tennessee spring was hot during the day and chilly at night.

I picked a lounge chair near the brick firepit, tossing a ball of hellfire in it as I crossed my arms behind my head, and began to stargaze once again.

The thoughts swirled through my mind, but I basked in the chaos and nearby heat. It was a wonderful night to let my thoughts roam free while I counted the constellations in the night sky.

The stars were bright, and the moon was almost gone. Crickets chirped on the ground below, mixing with the waterfall from the greenhouse and crackling embers while making the most enchanting background music.

My mate was astonishing, and also not my mate yet.

She hadn't tried to force me to talk, and when I did speak, she listened intently. She didn't get mad that I was able to see her vision of York.

York. I missed that fucking druid.

He had been my closest friend. I knew he didn't just leave. He told me he was being followed and asked me to move all his stuff into a storage unit on the outskirts of town.

I thought he was going crazy until he came up missing. I would've spoken up if he hadn't made me swear a druid-style blood oath of secrecy.

Did I know if druid blood oaths worked on demons? No. Was I willing to chance death to find out? Also no.

I knew Sloane was apprehensive about York's rescue. I was looking forward to seeing him again, though.

The guys would be mad at me if they ever found out that I knew what happened. I didn't know much, but it could've been enough to rescue him sooner.

Sloane would surely be pissed.

In my defense, I didn't know where he was, just that someone was coming to kidnap him and they succeeded. After Sloane's vision earlier, I thought it might be best to pick up some of his things.

I stopped by the indoor storage unit, when I left her and Novak, to grab some stuff for him.

The old leather-covered box of druid artifacts being the first thing I stuck in the bag, followed by clothes and the keys to my beloved motorcycle.

I had been driving York's Bronco around since mid fall, when it started getting too cold to walk the six blocks to work twice a week. I loaded my bike carefully in the back and drove to Sloane's house.

Both vehicles now sat in a once empty detached garage.

I vaguely remembered hearing Samuel help plan the build of this monolithic estate, with his fellow mates, a few years ago.

Now that I had seen it with my own eyes, it felt like they built it knowing that Sloane would have multiple mates.

Of course they did. Why else would they put their only child in a house this size?

From my view on the rooftop, I caught a glimpse of movement in the trees and felt the presence of creatures similar to demons.

The hellhounds patrolled the grounds with keen fire-lit eyes and monstrous appetites, just waiting for some poor fool to pass through the barrier that divided them.

In the distance, a dark figure darted across the driveway and let out a bone chilling version of a bark before I heard the gate to the property open.

Think deep and throaty mastiff bark mixed with a

lion's roar, then mixed with the snarled warning of a wolf. Yeah, bone chilling was accurate.

I checked my phone, and it read 3:38am. I was lost to my thoughts for longer than I realized.

Novak's boxy black Mercedes slowly crawled forward with a hellhound trailing on either side to usher them in. When they pulled into the detached garage, the hounds dispersed and went back to their nightly patrol.

I took a moment to admire how well-trained they were. I had never heard of anyone training a hellhound, let alone three. It boggled my mind that *my mate* had done it so well.

Sloane and Novak stepped out of the garage, and the door started to close as they strolled towards the house. I grinned like an idiot as I watched them giggling.

She was barefoot, and he was holding her hand in one of his with her shoes in the other.

It was not typical Novak behavior, but she seemed to be bringing out our best qualities at breakneck speed.

Vaughn didn't argue when she took charge. Briggs didn't throw a fit when she beat him in their alpha fight.

I wondered what a few more days would bring out, or what a few months would show us?

What about years?

I waited for them to get closer as I swiftly moved to the edge of the house. I dropped from the rooftop patio to land silently on my feet behind Novak.

Sloane leaned over his shoulder and gave me a lopsided smile. "You can't sneak up on me. Even if I am tipsy, I can still hear you."

She blew me a kiss before winking at me. I was stunned, watching her with heedful eyes.

Novak hadn't heard me, so how had she?

"Did you get any rest?" Her stubborn look said she wouldn't take no for an answer.

I didn't have the chance to tell her anything before she continued her questioning. "You know we're leaving in two hours, right?"

She sounded so much like Samuel, but I knew better than to point that out.

"Yes. I need more rest than you two do, but not as much as the others."

"Uh-huh..." she responded with a small smile on her red lips. "So, what you're saying is, you'll rest on the trip there."

"No," I responded while shaking my head, "That's not what I'm saying."

"Are you tired?"

"Not at all."

"Do you want to go swimming?" She narrowed her eyes and looked up at me through her lashes.

Her line of questioning threw me off balance.

It was four in the morning. Why would I want to go swimming?

The coquettish look she gave me had me surrendering with no more hesitation, though.

"Lead the way, Kitten." I held out my arm for her to walk in front of us.

Novak winked at me as he matched my stride. He

was acting weirder than normal. I wondered what he had been up to as we followed Sloane inside.

She traipsed through the darkened house without missing a beat. When we got closer to the basement door, she started stripping off what little clothes she was wearing.

Her shirt came first, and we were looking at nothing but her bare back and her legs covered only in a skirt. She tossed the tiny top over her head.

Before it hit Novak in the face, he yanked it out of the air and threw it behind us along with his own shirt.

Her skirt flew towards us next. I grabbed it as it made contact with my chest, dropping it to the ground and removing my shirt as I tried not to stumble at the view.

Her body was thin and lean. Her muscles bunched delicately as we continued our trek. She was incredibly built with long legs, a slim waist, and a tight, round ass.

I wanted to groan at the sight before me.

When we made it to the pool, Sloane danced around to the far end. She gave us a saucy look over her shoulder before leaping into the water in a graceful arch.

Her back and leg muscles coiled with the movement. Her feet flexed like a gymnast as she dove with her arms straight over her head. She swam under the water to a glass wall that separated the interior pool from the outside.

Novak and I watched in fascination, then side-eyed each other.

I didn't want to swim. I wanted to watch her refined

motions until the sun came up and we were forced to leave.

We both finished removing our clothes in record time and jumped in after her. Once I was on the other side of the glass, I tracked her movement under the water.

She was a predator on land and in the water. Her naked body pulled me to her like a magnet. I felt myself becoming the prey.

As I watched her body flow through the water like clouds in the sky, I knew I'd die a happy demon if she was what death had in store for me. I'd be her prey any day of the week.

She was my devil, my vice.

I had no doubts that I'd move Hell and Heaven for her if that's what she desired.

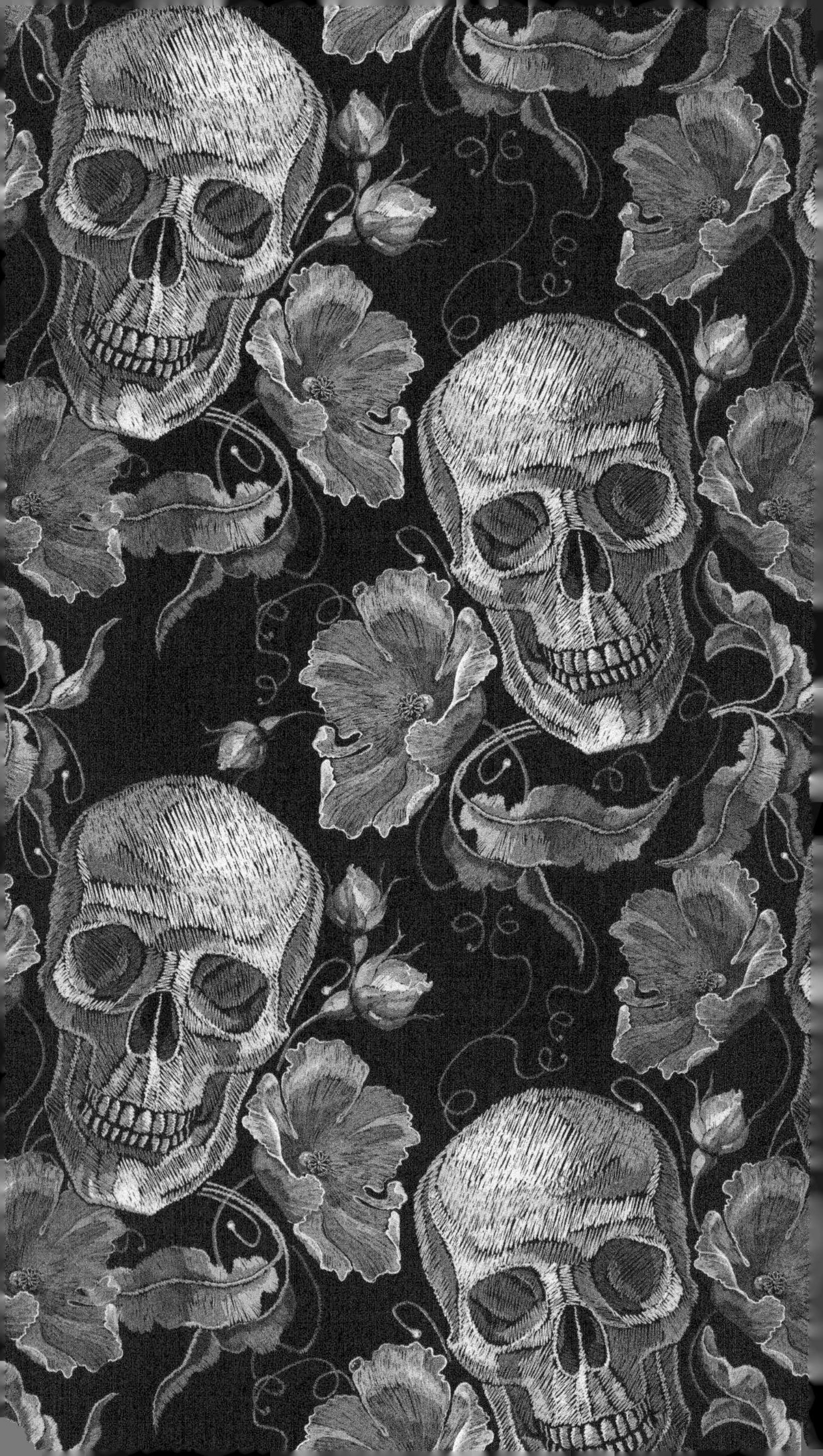

CHAPTER 18
Sloane

Sunday, May 17th
Early Morning

I spied the encroaching dawn and wished that we could spend the entire morning in the pool. Things were just getting interesting.

I was sandwiched between a naked demon and a naked vampire when Franklin walked in and cleared his throat.

Right. Time to go. Ugh.

As Franklin closed the door behind him, we begrudgingly dragged ourselves out of the warm water. I walked to the tall cabinets on the far wall to grab some towels.

We made our way upstairs as the others were walking down, and Briggs stopped to take in the state of our towel clad bodies.

"What were you guys doing?" he questioned us with a pointed look.

"Swimming." Stone's face was a mask of innocence, while Novak and I wore the complete opposite.

"Something like that," Novak coughed out.

"Yeah, whatever you say." Briggs stalked down the stairs and called over his shoulder, "We're leaving in fifteen, so get dressed."

I snagged Stone and Novak's hands and hustled up the stairs with them fumbling behind me. I dropped their hands when we reached the top of the third floor stairs and continued up the next flight two at a time while yelling down, "Show him his room, please."

I rushed into my bathroom for a five-minute shower and sped through getting dressed as I danced around in my closet.

Combat clothes were my absolute favorite.

I found my enchanted fishnets that repelled knives and bullets, snatching them up my smooth legs. Jack had given them to me for Christmas last year, and we'd had a blast testing them out.

This was the best gear a bitch could ask for.

I added a black pleated skirt over them, because I needed freedom to kick ass, and topped it with a tight black t-shirt that said *psycho*.

It didn't make much sense now, but it would later

today. I knew how I got, so it would serve as a warning. Maybe.

I stood on my tippy toes to reach for my combat boots on the top shelf in my closet, but I still couldn't brush the edge of the box. I snapped my fingers, and the shoebox dropped into my outstretched hands.

These boots were glorious.

They were made by a demon friend of mine in a small city called Stars in the Underworld. The leather was scaled, but I had no idea what kind of animal they were made from.

I also didn't want to know.

They had compacted two-inch rubber soles. Thick silver covered the heels and tips of the toes with inch-long spikes across the tops that were embedded into steel-toe plates inside them.

Let's be honest with each other. It wasn't rubber, silver, or steel. They're materials from the Underworld, but that was the closest resemblance to the earthy stuff.

I was officially ready and getting excited about the upcoming fight.

Slaughter? Nah, we'd call it a fight for now.

I really wanted to try the whole teleporting—disappearing and reappearing somewhere else—magic before we left. I'd never done it before, but I was damn well gonna figure it out.

I stared at myself in the mirror and tried to motivate the hungry bitch looking back at me.

"You can do this, Lo. You're hungry, you're full of energy, and you have no limits to what you can achieve."

I closed my eyes and kept right on talking.

"Just imagine yourself breaking down into particles and rushing through the Void, then coming out of the Void as those same particles and forming into a whole you again, except in the kitchen."

Breathe in. Breathe out.
Calm your mind.
Envision your destination.

I felt my body start to dissolve, and I focused hard on the kitchen. The stainless steel appliances. The black marble countertops. The coffee maker as it dripped scalding black life. My favorite mug beside it. The basket full of fruit on the counter by the sink.

I anticipated the familiar feeling that I knew so well, and as soon as I passed into the Void, I reveled in the bitter cold that washed over my body.

The warmth returned to my limbs quickly. I twitched my fingers and peeled my eyes open.

I'd made it! Fuck yes!

Six sets of shocked eyes stared back at me, and I gave them a confident grin.

"You guys saw that, right?" I nonchalantly gloated as I skipped around the kitchen island to the coffee maker. Taking my *"This is the blood of my enemies"* mug from the countertop, I filled it with coffee and sugar.

Franklin was the first to somewhat recover. He completely bypassed what just happened and set my hot pink duffel bag on the counter without a word.

The clatter of weapons was like music to my ears. I

knew from the sound that he'd included a few new instruments in the bag.

The noise of the weapons hitting the counter broke everyone else out of their ill-repressed stupor. Four voices spoke up at once.

"Well, that's some trick right there." Palmer.

"You just misted." Vaughn.

"That's a fae thing, right?" Briggs.

"Your bag is pink?" Novak.

Stone turned to Novak. "That's what you want to know? She just appeared as a silhouette of water in the middle of the kitchen and *you're* wondering about her pink bag?" His tone was incredulous.

I flashed an impish look at them before addressing the elephant in the room. "Yes, my weapons bag is pink. No one has ever stopped me about my suspicious looking pink gym bag before. Imagine an officer pulling me over and seeing my bag in the passenger seat."

I deepened my voice to imitate a man. "Uhm, ma'am, that pink bag definitely looks like it's holding enough weapons to take down a commercial aircraft. Can I take a look inside?"

Returning my voice back to my normal rasping tone, I continued. "Ha. Yeah, that's never happened before."

"I have so many questions about that statement." Novak's delighted laugh rang out through the silent kitchen. "They can wait for the car ride, though. I do have an important one that just can't wait." He held up his index finger, indicating his one question.

"And what's that?"

"Do you have a ouija board on your kitchen wall that says *"Drink Coffee & Hail Satan"* or am I imagining that?" He blinked a few times and turned his head in the direction of said decor.

"Oh, that was a housewarming gift from Papi. He thinks that stuff is funny and it aggravates his father. You see, Satan was Lucy's second-in-command before he tried to overthrow him a few millennia ago. It did not end well for Satan," I informed them with my brows raised, fighting with every ounce of self-control I possessed in order to keep a straight face at their confusion.

"Who is Lucy?" Vaughn's intrigued tone had me twisting my head to him and giving up my fight.

"Lucy is what I call my grandfather. I couldn't say Lucifer or Lilith when I was little so Papi told me to call them Lucy and Lil. You know we can talk about this in the van, right? We should really get on the road."

Franklin finally spoke as I started heading for the garage door. "Everything else you should need is already in the van. We'll take two vehicles to two different locations. I'll drop three of you off a block from the van and you'll pick the other three up."

"Perfect. Thanks, Franklin," I sang back to him when I made it to the door.

A thought nailed me right in the face as I placed my hand on the handle. "Palmer, can you show me that spell real fast?"

"Yeah." More confusion rolled across his handsome face as he reached for his phone. He opened the photos app and turned his phone to me.

Oh, that would be simple.

"Thank you," I exclaimed cheerfully, already mentally reaching out for my hellhounds. *They might be helpful today.*

I was already preparing the spell as they appeared in the garage doorway. *I'd turn them into puppies.*

They were still big when I got them, but only a fraction of their size now. I scooped them up and set them in the backseat between Palmer and me. Franklin took the driver's seat and Vaughn climbed in the passenger side. Then we were off.

Next destination, please.

The van was roomy and *super* white outside the tinted windows. Vaughn drove, and Briggs sat up front with him. Stone and I sat in the middle with Novak and Palmer behind us in the third row.

The first two hours progressed in comforting quietness while everyone rested up for our miles-long hike through the wooded terrain.

All was well, until the hellhound *puppies* woke up and began climbing around the van.

Atlas was barking and yipping at Novak, who snatched him into the back to play. Cronus ended up with Briggs in the front since I was ignoring him. Stone and I struggled to contain Helios. He'd do the most damage.

It was called priorities, okay? Did we want the inside of the van to catch fire? No. Then this was the one I chose.

"Sloane, would ya tell me why the hounds are taggin' along again?" Palmer irritatedly questioned as Atlas tried to lick the side of his face.

"We might need them," I admitted as the wiggling puppy wedged his way out from under me.

"Doubtful," Vaughn muttered.

Helios growled at him before lunging across the consol into his lap and huffing little gray smoke clouds at him.

"Fine, but make them smaller," he conceded.

"Okay," I snapped my fingers and three flies landed on his face. "There you go."

"Smaller, not annoyingly annoying," Vaughn argued.

"Fiiiiine," I dragged out in a sarcastic tone as kittens landed in his lap.

I almost changed them into Boston terriers. I was so close, but the kittens had claws.

Next time, definitely.

"Are you serious?" Vaughn raised his voice at me and everyone broke out in laughter at his expense.

The kittens clawed up his chest and hung from his arms, turning the large fae into a playground.

"You change them then, Oh Great and Mighty Mage. Oh wait, you're not a mage, so you can't." It was hard to be condescending whilst giggling.

"Fuck. Just keep them back there. I'm trying to drive," he growled out.

"They're cats. They do what they want." Novak cackled harder.

"Turn them into turtles so they'll just fucking sit there." Vaughn's voice was laced with exasperation at the situation currently crawling all over him.

"Have you ever been bitten by a turtle?" Briggs inquired, but I was already making the magic happen with snapping turtles in mind.

"FUCK! That hurts!" Vaughn shouted. We were all gasping for breath as we laughed hysterically.

I tried to compromise, but I was having too much fun with my new trick.

"Okay, okay. Just hand them to me."

When he started to grab one of them, I changed them to butterflies. Another bout of laughter settled over us as they landed in his hair.

"Now you look like a fae," Stone teased.

Vaughn spit out, "Yeah, a fucking summer fae."

"They look so pretty in yer hair, though." A mock girly voice came from Palmer.

"I'm going to pull over—" Vaughn started

"And what? Spank me for being a brat?" I waggled my brows at him.

"Give you over to Palmer and Stone," he threatened seriously.

"Is that supposed to scare me out of my bad behavior? We can do that right here without stopping the van."

I wiggled in my seat and twisted to wink at Palmer

and Stone. Palmer smirked back at me. Stone rolled his eyes at my antics but couldn't hide the small lift of his lips.

Vaughn pulled over at the next gas station, and I got a little anxious about whether or not I was actually going to get spanked in the parking lot.

It didn't happen. *I'll admit, I was pouting pretty hard about the missed opportunity.*

"Ye can put yer lip away, Love. I'll spank ya when we get back home." Palmer's low whispered promise had me groaning my displeasure about waiting.

He leaned over the back of my seat and skimmed his hand up the side of my neck. His lips brushed the edge of my ear as he added, "Patience, Love," so softly that I felt the words more than I heard them.

They did nothing to help my patience, though.

Don't tease me with a good time and then leave me hanging.

Briggs, Vaughn, and Stone all rotated their seats and Vaughn ended up beside me in the back.

The new seating arrangement reminded me of what York had told me. *I needed the fae to open my mind. But how?*

"Vaughn, can I ask you a question?" I faced him fully, waiting for his reply.

"Yes," he responded as he gave me his undivided attention.

I wavered for a moment. "Can you erase memories?"

"Yes, but it's not something I've done often or like doing," he admitted. "It can be painful, depending on what you're locking away and how badly the person's mind wants to hold on to it."

That was informative.

Okay, question two.

"What about making someone remember memories that have already been locked away?" This was what I really needed to know.

"Well, that's different." He paused and looked down at his hands to find the right words. "It depends on who locked them, how long ago, and how badly the person wants to remember. Why are you asking?"

His quizzical look showed me that he wasn't sure where I was going with the conversation. Stone's silent nod from the front seat gave me enough reassurance to plunge right in.

"York told me to ask you to unlock my memories. I don't know who locked them exactly, but it was roughly five years ago. I need to remember them. I think York's location is hidden in them."

"Okay," he agreed while watching me. "I can try. It won't feel pleasant. Novak will have to help me get into your mind. I need you to open up to us and drop your barriers."

"I don't have barriers." *Surprise. My mind was just a vault.* I wanted to add that, but didn't.

"Novak can't read your mind." Vaughn furrowed his brows at his own statement.

"And I can't read any of yours either, except Palmer's on occasion," I informed him.

It had been bothering me since I met him.

"That's because I'm an excellent teacher and Palmer is a shit student when it has to do with anything requiring focus," Novak chimed in.

"Fuck off," Palmer told Novak. "I've no issues focusin' on..." he stopped to think through his next words, "*stuff* I like ta focus on."

"Alright." Vaughn interrupted what would have been a thorough argument on what *"stuff"* specifically Palmer was talking about.

"This is what we're going to do. Novak is going to open your mind. It might hurt. Then, he's going to pull me in so I can find the locked memories. That IS going to hurt. Just, try not to scream in your head, because that will make it harder for us to get them unlocked. Okay?" He grimaced at his request.

I knew he didn't want to hurt me, but there was no way around it. *The pain would be temporary. I was no stranger to it.*

"Okay," I agreed with a steady voice. "Do it."

I relaxed my brain to the best of my ability, getting rid of all the random thoughts that plagued me. Novak leaned up and gently placed his index and middle fingers on my temples.

His presence brushed the edges of my consciousness. Letting him in was surprisingly easy. His mind stroked against mine, and it felt like a physical touch.

It ignited the smoldering fire that was burning in my core. Images from last night flooded my mind and filtered into Novak's.

"Trouble," he warned me.

Sloane

"I can't help it," I whined.

"Is that what you want Vaughn to see when I pull him in?"

"Pull him in and I'll try to keep it PG rated." My honeyed voice said otherwise.

I hope Vaughn enjoyed the show.

"He will." Novak's rough voice inside my head spoke volumes to me. He was loving the replay from my perspective too.

"Ready?" Vaughn sounded nervous, but seconds later I felt his cool, calm presence alongside Novak's bright energy.

Everything after that was a bundle of mental pain that attacked my consciousness. I had to battle with my own will power so that I didn't shut them out.

I'd trained against mental attacks before, and that was exactly what this felt like. I just had to endure it until I got what I needed.

The moment those memories were unlocked, everything went black.

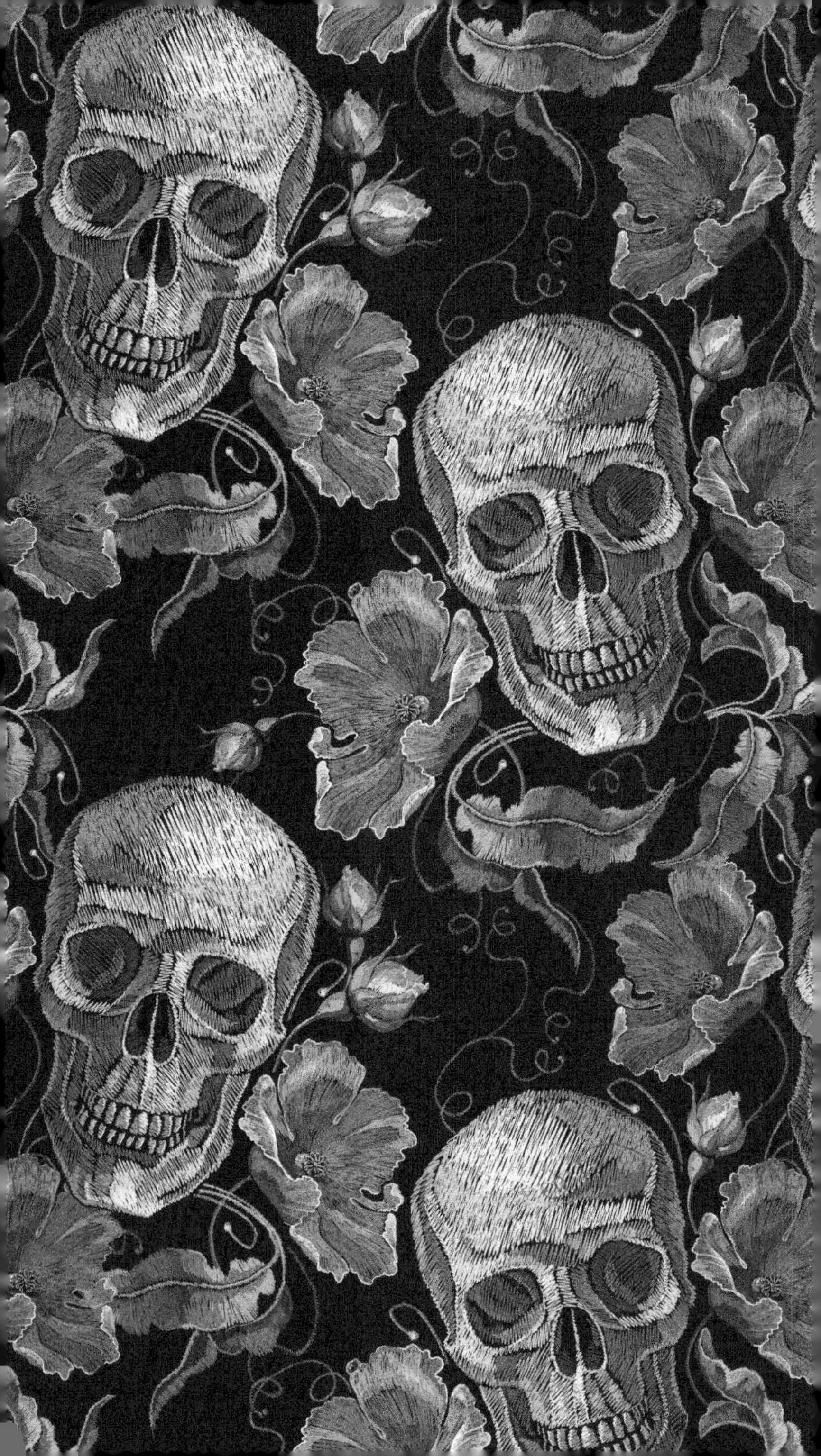

CHAPTER 19
Briggs

Sunday, May 17th
Midday

I had *never* been so worried in my life when I peeked in the rear-view mirror.

Sloane slumped forward as her eyes went totally white. Vaughn caught her without hesitation and placed her head on his thighs.

Novak squeezed his body over the back of their seat and slid her legs into his lap, casting a mortified glance at Vaughn. The fae remained calm.

"Did ye break her?" Palmer asked with an edge of nervousness to his voice.

"No, she's reliving the memories that we unlocked.

She'll be fine in a couple hours. Think of it as dreaming while napping," Vaughn replied.

"You could've warned us all that she'd pass the fuck out."

I wanted to throttle the emotions back into him. I'd called him Prince Emotionless one time, and he'd busted my nose.

I'd love to return the favor right now. Maybe he'd feel something afterwards.

Ten minutes passed in utter silence. The steady rhythm in her chest was the only thing that kept me from stopping the van.

Stone was turned around in the passenger seat with a look that screamed *"I'll kill you"* aimed towards the males holding the too-still hybrid between them.

If she didn't wake up soon, he'd go on a rampage. Sixty-two minutes in and he'd try to kill them both.

Thankfully, it didn't go that long. We were about thirty-five minutes in, and the only sound in the van was heavy breathing as we all tried to chill out.

A sharp intake of breath had me swerving into another lane. I twisted my head to look at Sloane.

She flew up into a sitting position and glanced around to get her bearings before leaning back into Vaughn's lap and staring at the interior ceiling.

"I'm going to kill that fucking druid," she seethed.

"How much time did ya get back?" Palmer questioned lightly.

"A little more than two days, I believe. How long was I out for?"

"Less than forty minutes. That shouldn't be possible, Sloane. It should've taken you hours to recover that much time." Vaughn was bewildered.

I didn't know why *that* surprised him. *She surpassed every magical and mystical boundary we'd come across.* Several times I'd caught myself wondering what else she could do.

"It's like speed reading." She shrugged nonchalantly. "Some of the time I was unconscious, so I skipped that and stuck to the important stuff, namely the parts where I was awake."

"What did you find out?" Stone was trying to remain cool and collected, settling his anger with the sound of her seductive, rasping voice.

"York had another prisoner erase my memory, but it wasn't clear as to why. He was fae. A king." She turned to Vaughn, "With your eyes," she added apologetically.

"I'm sorry, Vaughn. York made a deal with him: my memories for a phone call. He couldn't help him escape."

"I know this part of the story. He called me. It's okay, Sloane. Continue with the rest of it." Vaughn didn't ever talk much about his family.

His sisters called when they left the Fae realm, but that was it.

"There's not much more to it. When I regained consciousness, I checked on him and then ran. It's the beginning that we need to focus on. I know how to get to where we're going."

"How?" I interjected.

"Because I let them catch me and take me to their

camp. I was sent to kill them," she whispered. "All of them. And I didn't finish the job."

I focused on the road as she spoke. My anger surged with her story.

Damn York.

If he hadn't had her memories tampered with, then she would've killed those guys. They wouldn't have had a chance to kidnap him. We wouldn't be trying to rescue him.

My heart wouldn't have nearly fucking stopped when I watched her fall over while her eyes went all cloudy and shit. That was just the smaller scale stuff.

On the bigger side of the repercussions, there was one main issue. If those guys had been killed five years ago, then that rogue-inducing drug might not have been as successful. That could've saved hundreds, if not thousands, of lives.

I knew he was a selfish bastard, but he always had his reasons. Maybe he thought it wouldn't get that far, or maybe he was trying to protect her before he really knew her.

I'd fought against her *and* watched her fight, though. I knew she didn't *need* to be protected. If I had to pick anyone to protect *me*, I'd pick her before I picked any of the males in this van.

We reached our destination before any of us could think of something to say to her. She didn't seem like she was looking for comfort, but instead needed an outlet for her anger.

The address Franklin gave us was not what any of us

expected. I turned the van to the right by a large sign with the street numbers 5683 labeled on it.

We followed a long dirt road until we came to a minuscule gravel parking area. When I parked, we sat and viewed the scenery around us before we started opening any doors.

The heavily wooded lot was home to all manner of wildlife. My wolf inched to the surface of my skin, thrilled by the prospect of a bountiful hunt.

Nestled in the trees in front of us was an enormous treehouse.

The stairs began on the foliage-covered ground and led up to a platform which connected to a bridge suspended above a natural sandstone formation. The miniature bridge was only wide enough for one person to walk across it at a time.

I contemplated the safety of it versus climbing a tree to get to the wraparound deck that was attached to the house. The trees grew through cut out places in the deck flooring and appeared to also grow through the house itself.

This was the luxury side of camping, I guess.

We filed out of the van and started grabbing our bags. Butterflies flew around Sloane's head the moment her boots touched the ground.

She gazed at them for several seconds in blissful tranquility as they fluttered themselves down to chest height.

She snapped the fingers of her left hand and those massive hellhounds-in-disguise slammed their paws into the gravel patch she was standing on. They surrounded her in a protective formation, covering all angles as they surveyed the land for any threats.

With three clicks of her tongue, their gigantic bodies thundered through the woods in different directions to secure the perimeter around our temporary haven.

And run all the wildlife off.

We observed Sloane while she climbed the stairs, collectively holding our breath as she glided across the rickety bridge to the main deck around the house.

She looked strange with her bright pink backpack strapped to her back and the small matching duffle swaying in her delicate hand. I wasted no more time assessing her as I bounded up the steps and crossed the bridge in large strides.

The sooner I reached the other side, the quicker I could get off this death trap.

We were only here to drop off the van and our bags before we started the search for York.

Once inside, I didn't even admire the rustic decor as I found the kitchen table and set my bag of weapons on the top. I dropped my other bag to the floor and kicked it aside.

Within the bag that held my attention was brand new tactical gear. Franklin vehemently reassured me this morning that it would remain on my body between shifts.

I still didn't believe him.

I set the clothing and boots to the side and continued looking through the bag. He explained all of the weapons to me last night before we went to sleep and I'd been itching to try this stuff out.

Four magic-infused handguns were tucked neatly in pairs inside rough plastic cases. They didn't use bullets, and they never ran out of their ammo.

He'd included a handful of paper thin knives as well. They were so sharp I could probably slice through the tree that the kitchen table was built around.

The last thing in the bag was a five inch long black box that looked like it was made for jewelry. It wasn't anything Franklin and I had talked about last night. It was new.

Inside the box was a custom-made switchblade. The obsidian blade and bleached bone handle matched the daggers Sloane used yesterday.

Attached to the lid of the box was a short note in frilly handwriting.

Briggs,
This switchblade will never miss a target and
always returns to its owner. Use it with care.
Enjoy it often.
-Sloane

This was the most thoughtful fucking gift anyone had ever given me.

I tucked everything back in the bag and made my way into the first bedroom I found to change.

Behind the closed door, Sloane stood with one leg propped on the dresser. The other was firmly planted on the floor as she checked the knife hidden within the rubber sole of her left boot.

I started to leave but changed my mind. *She had already seen me naked, so what was the harm in sharing the space to change clothes?*

I set my stuff on the bed and pulled my shirt over my head while she watched me with a coy expression.

"How often do you pull a knife out of the *toe* of your boot?"

It seemed like an odd place for a weapon, but with her nothing was ever as it seemed. *See? I was learning.*

"I don't take it out. There's a sort of button inside my shoe that I press with my toe, and out pops the knife. It adds a fun effect to kicking."

She smiled at me. "Want to see?"

She didn't wait for my reply. She lifted her foot out towards me and the knife slid out slowly with her movement.

"If I move faster, the knife appears quicker. It's a nifty little trick designed by a friend of mine in Stars."

The female got excited about weapons. Now I knew to skip the flowers if she ever got mad at me.

"Good to know," I replied, but it was more to myself.

I took off my pants and started putting on the clothing from my bag. The tactical gear was breathable and tight, but fit me like a second skin.

The bedroom was too small to shift in, so I'd have to wait. I was eager to get outside and test the durability.

Franklin had mentioned that I wouldn't lose my

weapons as long as they were attached to the fabric, not in my hand.

The pants had thin pockets designed for the knives and wrapped up in the shirt were holsters for the guns. One set sat under each arm and the other set sat at each hip.

Sloane had matching holsters under her arms and her daggers tucked against her lower back.

Connected to her waist was a series of shiny chains hanging at different lengths down the front of her skirt. Each chain had an array of two-inch knives dangling from them.

Her shirt read *psycho*, and to be honest, the look of determined fury on her face said she'd be every bit of that description later.

Everyone was ready to go when we stepped into the living room.

We checked each other out, admiring the selection of weapons we carried, before maneuvering our way through the treehouse and across that unstable fucking bridge.

When Sloane reached the bottom of the stairs, she loosed a high pitch whistle, and I heard the hounds running towards us.

While we all waited, I shifted to my fur and back again, noticing that what Franklin had said was true.

All clothing and weapons were still in place. That's fucking awesome.

When I turned around to face everyone, the guys

were staring from me to Sloane and back again. They didn't know which was a weirder scene.

Me staying in my clothes after I shifted or Sloane holding three *huge* welded chains attached to hellhounds.

The links were easily the size of her fist and probably weighed more than fifty pounds each. They were not your typical hardware store chains.

She looked really fucking sexy and way more lethal than she did yesterday.

The hellhounds led the way with Sloane following soundlessly behind them, and the rest of us trailing behind her. *Staring at her ass.*

Hours passed, and the sun began to dip low in the sky. The terrain all looked the same. I started to wonder if we were walking in circles, but she seemed to know where she was going, so I didn't say a word to dispute our direction.

When the sun was gone and the night had descended, she stopped and passed a chain leash to Palmer and one to Vaughn.

She kept a tight grip on Helios, but he never jerked her as they hiked forward.

"Just the tips, boys," she called quietly to the hounds.

The tips of their tails lit with hellfire, helping guide the way since Vaughn and Palmer couldn't see in the dark.

"Just the tip, huh?" Novak questioned.

Sloane shot him a filthy, flirty look in answer and kept on walking.

It was after 11pm, and we'd been walking for a good

ten hours, when Helios switched directions to follow the bank of a small creek.

We were getting closer now. Attacking them at night would benefit us, I hope.

Out of the six of us, four had night sensitive vision. I was sure the mage had a spell for that too, so possibly five.

Another hour passed us by, and I could just start to make out faint talking in the far distance.

We were a mile out.

Sloane and Helios stopped, and she handed his chain to Stone as she strode closer to us. We circled around as she whispered our parts of the plan to us.

"When we get closer, I'm going to release the hellhounds so they can circle around to the other side of this camp. Briggs, shift and go with Atlas. I'll make them look like wolves and you can lead them into the back side for a surprise attack. You'll have full control over them, so use it wisely.

"Palmer and Stone, I need you guys to find and secure York. Keep him away from the fight. He may want to join, but he'll be too weak to stand his ground. Vaughn, can you mist with him to the treehouse?" She turned her head to Vaughn.

"Yes. That won't be a problem."

"Can you take Palmer as well?" she inquired.

"I'll need to make two separate trips, but I can do it."

"Okay, when the commotion dies down, take York and then come back for Palmer. The rest of us can move faster, so we'll come back on foot. Kill everyone except prisoners. And be careful. The male in charge is a vampire-mage hybrid. Not only can he read minds, he can control them as well, if you don't keep them sealed tight. I'd like to kill him myself, so if you find him, let me kno—"

Her word came up short and her attention shot to the right. All three hounds vibrated with tension.

My sensitive hearing picked up the snapping of twigs and crunching of the earth under heavy shoes.

Someone was out there, getting closer to us.

"Briggs, shift. Atlas, stay on his tail."

She waved her hand over him and smokey magic covered him. He transformed into a masculine charcoal colored wolf with a black dusting on the ends of his fur.

I shifted without question and waited for the command to leave.

She changed Helios into a burnt reddish brown wolf and Cronus into a wolf with a black face, tail, and feet that faded up to a dark brown body.

"Wait," she patiently relayed to the hellhounds, "Let him see us first."

What the fuck was she planning? I wanted to ask her, but I couldn't speak right now.

"Hey! You can't be out here," someone shouted from a short distance away.

"Go. Now," she whispered urgently.

We split up and sped away. The last thing I saw as I looked over my back was Sloane snatching something from her skirt and slinging a knife at the man.

It landed dead in between his eyes.

I heard her muted voice command, "Vaughn, glamor

yourself to look like him, then glamor our weapons, and lead us in."

I turned back and accelerated my speed with Atlas only a tail's length behind me.

We had to get into position and take out anyone in our path. The first strike had been made. The group was marching into camp as trespassers, with Vaughn pointing a loaded gun at their backs.

She was one tornado they wouldn't see coming.

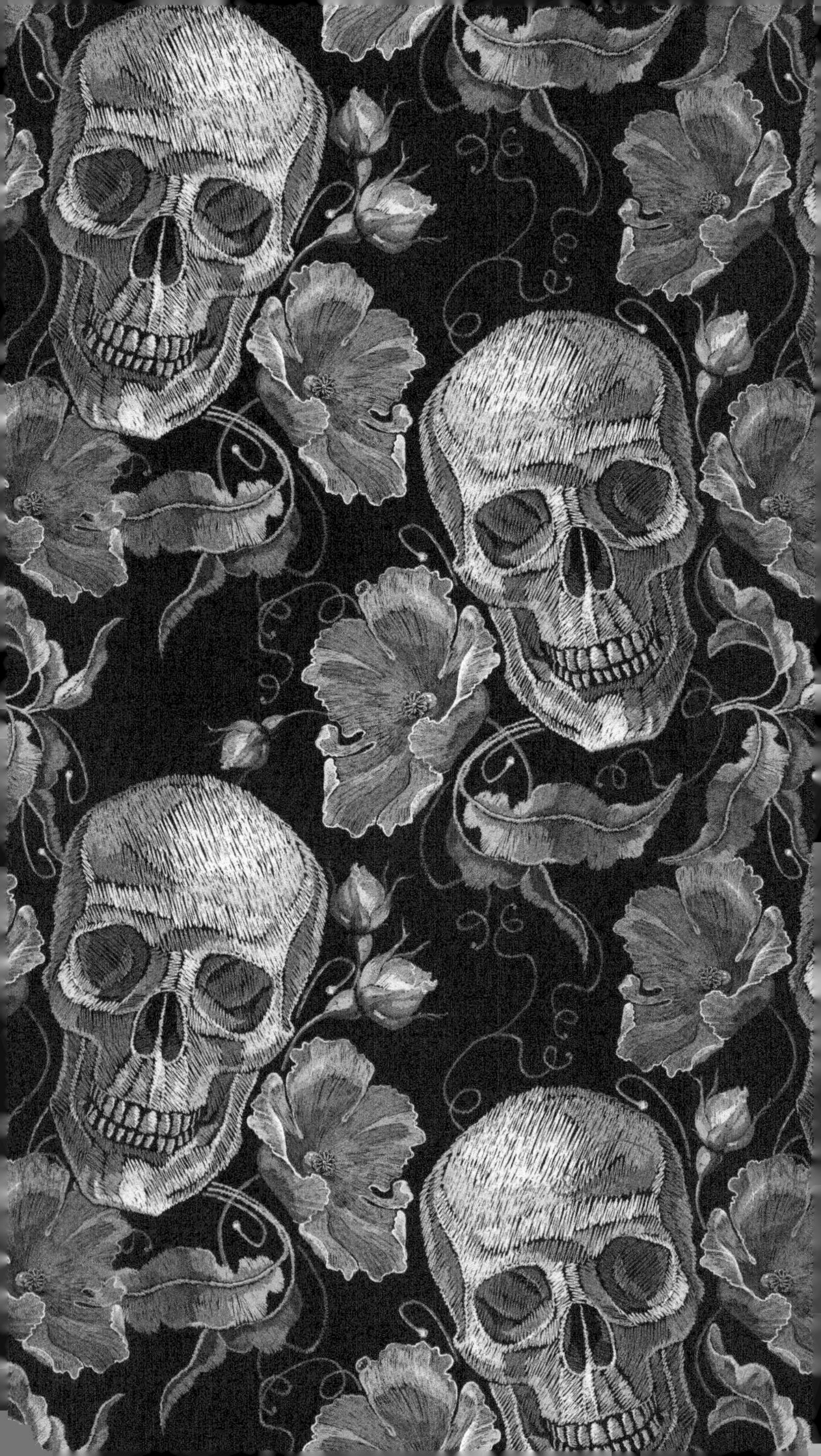

CHAPTER 20
York

Sunday, May 17th
Late Night

I listened to the dripping water as I stared at the newest mark on the wall across from me.

Eight hundred and fifty-eight days. I'd either be free or dead soon.

Alone in my cell, I let my mind linger on images of Sloane. I wanted to be free and wrap my arms around her again, but I knew she'd rather cut my hands off than let me touch her.

I had so much shit to make up for if I lived. My life was in her capable hands now.

Once she saw the state of my body, I knew it would

only be a matter of time before she went on a murder spree. I only hoped it was enough to bring her in my direction.

If I got out of this cell, I was going to kill Kelvin myself.

I needed to get Levi out of this mess too. He was scared to leave, I got it. *But this is no place for humans.*

The guard on duty tonight was sleeping soundly, sitting in a chair facing my cell. He was one of the more violent bear shifters here. He used that strength of his regardless of its need.

I'd kill him on my way to Kelvin. Over two years in captivity would have you planning murder on a daily basis.

He snored loudly, and I wished for the hundredth time that I had enough power to call up thick, thorny vines to strangle him in his sleep.

Having a time limit put on my life had turned me into a morbid version of myself.

Or what was left of me.

I feared that if I got to walk out of this place as a free male, I would never again be who I once was. I barely remembered what it was like to be free, to eat when I was hungry, or shower when I felt dirty.

I wanted the sun to shine on my skin and the grass to caress my back as I watched the clouds move through the sky. I wanted to climb the trees and speak to the birds.

I wanted to shave and get a godsdamn haircut.

My toffee skin was pale, wrapping around my bones from near starvation and no muscle usage. My once lean fingers now looked skeletal. My joints jutted out, showcasing how unhealthy I'd become.

It wouldn't take long for me to bounce back if I could get out of here. A couple of hours with my feet buried in the soil and the earth would feed me all the nutrients and power I needed to build myself back up.

The door to the cells banged open suddenly, and I flinched back into the shadowed corner of my cell. It scared the sleeping guard so much that he flipped his chair and landed on his ass on the uneven floor.

"Brad! Get the fuck up here. Roy just found some supes walking around the outside of our perimeter," was shouted from the doorway by an unknown camp dweller.

Brad, the shitty bear shifter, stood and dusted his ass off before slamming the door behind him, leaving me free of his snoring *finally*.

There were only a few minutes of tranquility before the door was opened again. Levi came into view with an armful of food and several bottles of water.

"Hey, man, did you hear what he said?" he quizzed me softly.

"Yay, more prisoners," I bit out sarcastically.

"The talk around camp is that it's a girl and a few guys. Roy said they had dogs with them, but when he yelled at them, the dogs ran off."

"Looks like these cells are gonna be more full than usual," I surmised.

"D-didn't you reach out to your, uhhh, girlfriend? Mate? Whatever you called her yesterday?" he stammered.

"Yeah," I acquiesced.

"Do you think it's her?" he whispered.

Did I think it was her?

I used what little power I had saved and opened my mate bond back up.

She was filled with a bloodthirsty rage, and so near that I felt like I could reach out and stroke her.

I sent a flare of earthy magic through our bond. She responded with a large dose of adrenaline-filled energy. It soared through my body, lighting me from the inside out. It was a painful pleasure.

She was here, and she'd brought the guys *and* hellhounds with her as backup.

This place was going to burn to the ground.

I sent her a rundown of the grounds and tapered my presence off so she could focus.

"It's her," I told Levi on a hushed breath. "She's here."

"Good, man. I'll go tell her where you are."

He stood, and I shouted, "No!"

He looked baffled before I explained. "No, if you go out there, she'll kill you too. She doesn't know who you are or how you've been helping me. If you want to stay alive, then you'll listen to what I say. Okay?"

"O-okay," he stuttered.

"Go to the top of the stairs and open the doors. *Do not* go out. Just swing the doors as wide as they'll go and then come back down here. Leave all the other doors open that lead to us. Grab the keys to the cells off the wall and pick one to sit in until they come to get me. I'll keep you safe, but you have to follow my lead."

He jerked his head in a nod and bolted for the stairwell. I didn't know if he was going to come back or not, but I hoped he would.

I hoped for a bunch of things at this moment, but I'd play it by ear.

Levi came through the last doorway a minute later with the keys hanging in his hand as he made his way to my cell. He opened the barred door and stepped inside, closing it behind him. He angled his head at me, terror clear on his stricken face.

"Take a seat. It should only be a few minutes," I enlightened him with a new vibrancy to my voice.

I didn't move from my corner, though. I closed my eyes and listened for the first sounds of rescue, the light padding of Sloane's boots, or the defeated screams of her enemies.

The first thing I heard was muted shouting, followed by a furious symphony of guttural growls.

"What was that?" Levi screeched loudly.

My ears rang as I forewarned him with a single word, "Hellhounds."

"W-w-what? What d-d-do you mean b-b-by hellhounds?" He was terrified.

With good reason.

Helios was frightening on his best days.

"My mate has hellhounds that guard her. They sort of look like regular dogs. Just, uhm, don't try to pet them, okay?" I teased him, remembering when he'd first arrived at the camp and attempted to pet a fox shifter.

"Y-y-yeah, no p-p-problem, man."

"Calm down, Levi. You're going to be fine." I tried to reassure him, but he looked like he was on the verge of passing out.

We listened to the yelling for a few minutes. Our position underground with all the doors open made it sound like the volume was turned way down.

From the stairwell, I heard a grunted moan, and a body rolled through the doorway. Two males walked in after it. I recognized them once they stepped under the light.

Palmer leaned over to brush blood from his khakis, letting out a frustrated groan when it smeared. Stone's pitch black demon body slowly morphed into his Asian appearance as he continued to walk toward us.

"Fucking druid," he drawled, looking displeased with me as I stood weakly.

It was more energy than I had before they got here, though.

"Fucking demon," I countered and was rewarded with a sharp-toothed smile.

"Pull your teeth back in before you scare the human to death, Stone," I chastised him.

"Who tha fuck is he?" Palmer eyed Levi.

"This is Levi. He's the reason why I'm still alive. We won't be killing him today."

"Aye, okay. I believe ye. I'll let ya take that up with Sloane. Keys?" Palmer's impatience was unusual.

York

He was either worried or wanted to fight. Probably both.

"Levi, hand me the keys, please," I requested gently.

He took his shaking fingers and reached in his pocket, setting the keys in my hand with widened cartoon-like eyes.

"It's okay. These are my friends, Palmer and Stone. They won't hurt you." I spoke to him like a parent would a small child while shaking my head.

He was panicking, but he nodded his head and let go of the keys.

I tossed them to Stone. He opened the door and sauntered over to me, pulling my arm across his shoulder to support some of my weight.

"Come on, Levi. Stay with us and whatever you do, *don't run.*"

"Sloane hasn't really gotten started yet. She caused enough of a scene for me to drag Palmer through the shadows so we could find you. We have strict orders to keep you out of the fight, though." Stone told me while helping me up the stairs and out into the fresh night air.

My first dose of fresh air in eight hundred and fifty-eight days.

Power seeped into my bare feet with each step I took across the dirt path. It crawled up my body at a snail's pace, awakening my dead limbs.

"When we get to Vaughn, he'll mist you to the treehouse. Stay there until we get back. There's a bag of clothes for you on the couch, and I stuck some soap and clippers in the bathroom so you could clean up. You need a hot shower and a haircut, Druid," Stone rambled as we walked towards the fight.

"Vaughn should be waitin' up ahead for ya. He can take yer man, too." Palmer waggled his eyebrows at me with his insinuation.

I wished I had the energy to waste so I could punch him in his smartass mouth.

"We'll figure somethin' out when this is all by." He waved his hand around and turned to Levi after addressing me.

"Do ye need to grab anythin' before we go?"

"N-n-no," Levi pushed out.

"Grand. Let's get ya outta here before we run inta any of those enemies Sloane was makin'." Palmer smiled excitedly as he led the way for us.

We wandered through the tents for about twenty more feet before Vaughn stepped out of one with Novak. They hustled to us, and Vaughn stopped before me.

"You look like shit," he complimented.

"You too, Fae." I almost thanked him, but I knew better. "Were you two sharing one last kiss before the fight starts?"

Novak made a kissy face at Vaughn and started leaning in.

"Fuck off," Vaughn chided as he shoved Novak's face with a palm to his forehead. "You ready to go, York?"

"Never been more ready in my life," I admitted with a laugh.

"And who's this guy?" Vaughn hitched his thumb in Levi's direction.

"York's friend. Human. Saved his life. He's coming back with us." Stone cut to the chase with easily understandable facts for the control freak.

"His mind is clean. Take him. Palmer can fight with us." Novak solved the questions Vaughn was going to ask before they spilled from his mouth.

"Alright, lets go." Vaughn wrapped his arm around my shoulder and Stone let go.

The cold passed over my body before I could even blink. We landed in an inviting living room full of wooden furniture.

Vaughn showed me where the closest bathroom was as he placed a hunter green backpack in my hands.

"I'll bring the other guy back. We should have enough clean clothes for him to wear. But, York, if Sloane freaks out..." he started.

"Yeah, yeah. I know. I'll handle her," I interrupted. "I couldn't leave him to die, Vaughn. He's the only reason I've lived this long."

"Handle her," he laughed.

"That's funny. We'll be back after the fight. Try to get some rest." His last words were spoken through water as he misted out of the hall and to the campgrounds.

It took him seconds to get there and back with an unconscious Levi in tow.

"I tossed him on the couch," he yelled to me through the bathroom door. "He passed out, and he'll probably be nauseous when he wakes up. I've never misted a human before."

Then he was gone again.

I inhaled a deep breath and looked at myself in the mirror while I waited for the water to run hot.

I did look like shit.

The heat of the shower washed away my anxiety as I stepped in. It swirled all the dirt and filth that covered my body down the drain. I hadn't been this clean since the day I was taken.

I lathered the soap and cleansed every inch of my body twice before rinsing and cutting the water off.

I looked a little better now, but I still needed a haircut.

I took the clippers and buzzed them over my head, leaving less than a half inch of hair behind.

Then, I trimmed my facial hair up and hopped back in the shower to scrub my scalp and wash the excess hair off my body. I rubbed my skin again and again, trying to get the feel of the underground cell off of me.

My skin was a raw, dusty pink color before I stepped out and dried off.

Now I looked like myself, minus the haunted look left in my eyes. I hoped that would go away with time.

It felt good to be clean. It felt even better when I sunk into the oversized recliner in the living room and popped the footrest up to get some sleep.

Until Levi woke up screaming.

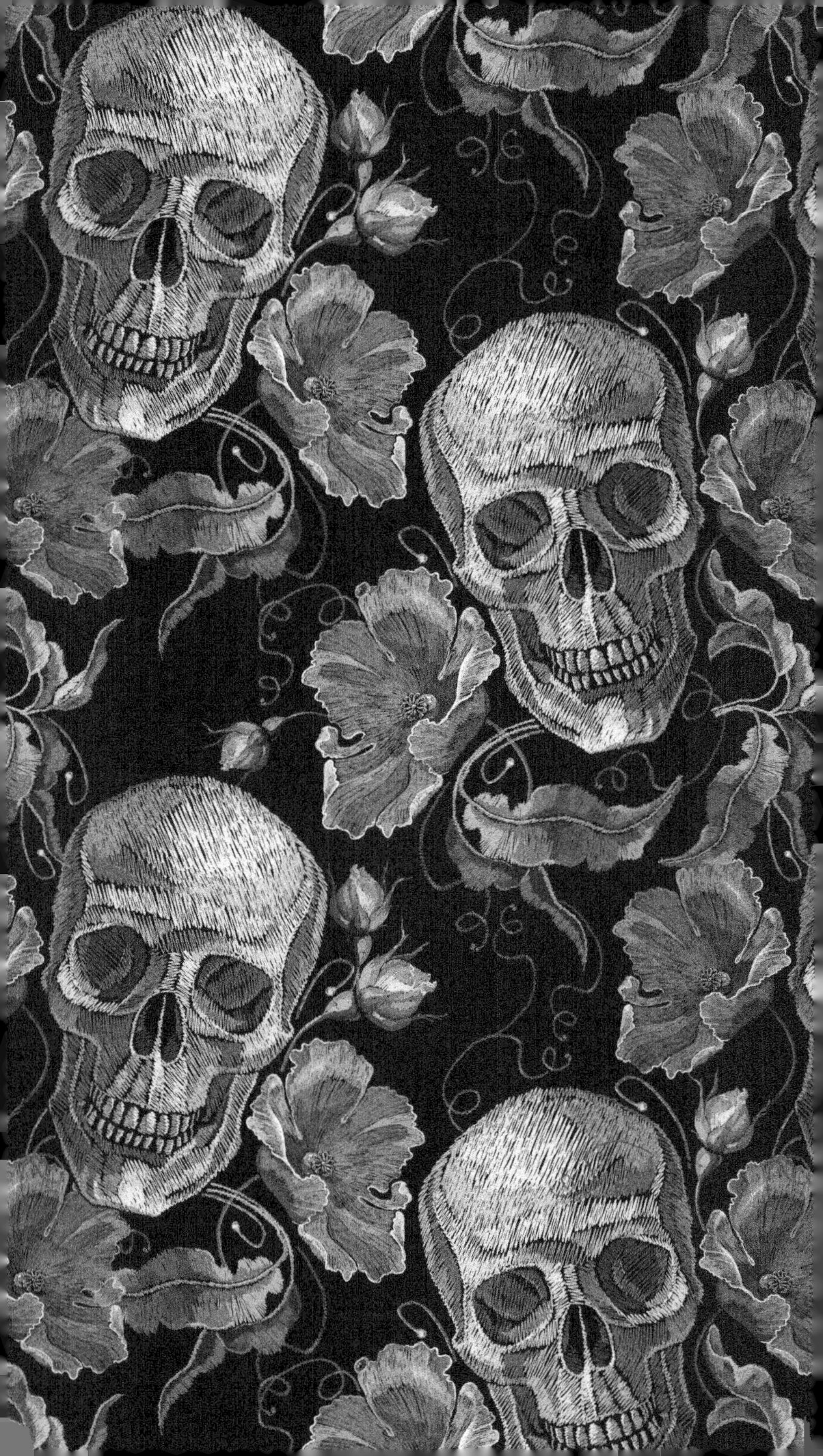

CHAPTER 21
Palmer

Monday, May 18th
Early Morning

After Vaughn disappeared with Levi, I turned my attention to Novak. "Where's Sloane?"

"She's playing hide-n-seek." He grinned at me like that was the answer I sought.

"What d'ya mean?" I didn't like the idea of her hiding or being by herself. I knew she was strong, but she should still have some backup.

"She killed a couple guys and then went for a joy run around the camp. They haven't been able to catch her yet. She's playing with them while she cuts them down," Novak explained a little better.

"Shouldn't we help her?" Stone asked us all.

"Yeah, Novak and I were checking tents for stragglers when you guys found us." Vaughn sounded like he was underwater as he spoke.

His body formed in front of us, and we all started walking while he kept talking. "She said to pair up and take them out. Briggs and the hounds are tightening up the perimeter, forcing everyone to the center."

A bolt of lightning struck right in front of my feet. We all jerked our heads to the left and saw a group of males standing together. It was a face off, but our odds were too good.

"Why don't ye keep goin'? Stone an' I will take care of these eejits."

"Yeah, we'll keep checking the tents," Novak proclaimed as they spun in the opposite direction.

Stone tempted me with an ecstatic, "Ready to kick some ass?"

When I nodded my head, he began to morph his lean 6'0 frame into the monster he kept hidden within.

Stone as a demon took some getting used to. If I had to put numbers on his growth, I'd say he was at least a foot taller and nearly two hundred pounds heavier.

His skin was so dark he looked like a moving shadow. His horns twisted out of the sides of his head, a few inches above his pointed black ears. They swooped out and up and curled towards each other behind his head.

His horns were pretty fucking cool.

Stone was enough to make any sane male run away in terror. He loved the thrill of a chase.

Apparently, just like our mate.

Three males turned and ran, leaving two gaping shamelessly. Stone unfurled his leathery wings and lifted to the sky, tail lashing back and forth as he slowly ascended.

The only way to see him in the sky was to follow the absence of stars as he glided through the night in search of his prey.

"Are ye for running too, or will ye stand and fight?" I called out to the last two males.

I didn't know what they were, but that didn't change anything for me. I wanted to fight and sling some magic of my own.

Maybe test out this medieval weapon the old Vampire showed me before I went to sleep last night.

I thought he had called it a dire flail. It was a three-foot pole with a foot of chain on either end. Attached to the chains were large metal spheres covered in spikes.

He said I could feed my magic through it. I liked the way that sounded and the ease at which I could sling the weapon around. It felt like an extension of my limbs when my power flowed through it.

No one moved, and I grew tired of just standing there, so I threw up my hands. "That's grand, yas don't have to fight me, but I don't fancy yer chances with the demon."

That got them moving. I waited until they got closer, then decided instead of drawing my weapon, I'd use my favorite move.

It was a classic.

I drew my fingers in so my hands looked like guns and aimed them both at the incoming males. With a childlike "pew, pew," I squeezed my bottom two fingers and shot bright orange magic rods straight into their chests.

The sound effects were for me.

They collapsed to the ground in heaps. I blew the invisible smoke from my finger guns for good measure.

Handy little trick, that was.

I swaggered over to them and pulled the magic from their weeping wounds before dissolving it back into my hands.

Laughter rang out behind me and I froze in my tracks. Sloane skipped over with a manic grin on her bloodied face.

She placed her hands on my chest as she leaned into my ear and whispered, "That was really dorky, but so fucking hot."

"Ye liked that, did ya?" I gave her a cocky smile, setting my hands on top of hers.

"Mmm, very much," she confided.

"An' if I did it again ta the gobshite that was followin' behind ya? What would ye do?"

"Do it and see." She waggled those silver brows at me, and her eyes twinkled with mischief.

My cock lifted to attention with a vengeance, straining to break free of its zippered cage. I groaned as my mind whirled in a terribly inconvenient direction for a split second.

I was a patient male, but I was ready to see her naked

and tied to my bed. I wanted to break out some toys and tease her until her moans turned to whimpers and they were all I could hear.

That would have to wait, though.

The guy behind her kept stalking closer. I let him move in as I memorized the details of her face. I leaned in and took her mouth in a fierce kiss, pulling her body against mine with my left hand while aiming my right.

After a flex of my fingers, we heard the thump of a body dropping. She broke the kiss to look over her shoulder and then back to me. I smirked at her with a smug attitude, waiting to see what she had in mind.

"Now what?"

Sloane snatched me so fast I almost stumbled over my own feet. She dragged me into the nearest tent and ran her fingers over my cock through my khakis before unsnapping the button.

As she sank to her knees, she took the zipper of my pants down with her, and my length sprang free from its confinement.

"This'll have ta be quick, Love. There's a wee battle going on outside."

She looked up at me through her lashes without concern as she traced her lush lips from the base of my shaft up to the head. Her silk tongue darted out to lick at the precum gathering against my tip.

She downed me fully in a single bob, showing me she had no qualms with her gag reflex. Then, she wrapped one hand tightly around my base while the other gently tugged on my balls, pushing and pulling as her mouth did the same.

Her teeth lightly grazed my shaft every few strokes, her tongue swirling around before every pump.

I plunged my left hand in her hair and grabbed her ponytail with my right. I started fucking her mouth in earnest as I grew closer to my climax.

She relaxed her throat and gave me control. My cock started to swell in her mouth and I slowed just enough to rasp out, "This is it, Love. If ya don't want me ta cum in yer mouth, pull it out now."

I picked my speed back up when she didn't move away. A few thrusts later, I felt the barest hint of her fang scrape across my head.

The intoxicating flood of vampire venom hit my bloodstream in a nanosecond. I came so hard my knees nearly buckled.

She pulled back and opened her mouth, showing me what I left. Then she swallowed, wiping the corners of her mouth with her fingers.

"I'll pay ya back for that when we get home," I panted while I fought to catch my breath and zip my pants back up.

"Yes, sir." She mock-saluted me as she walked out of the tent, fixing her hair.

That fucking mouth of hers. I didn't know if I wanted to kiss her or spank her for being such a smartass.

We crept through the quiet grounds until we got closer to the center. The fight was still going on, but the numbers had quickly dwindled.

Sloane raced forward, yanking a knife from her skirt. In her hand, it grew from a dinky two inches to nearly eight as she kicked a male, who was sneaking up on Vaughn, in the side of the knee.

He tumbled to his hands and his good knee, keeping weight off the new injury.

Sloane moved forward with predatory intensity, looking for her next target. When he tried to get up, she flicked her wrist backwards at her hip and sent the knife sailing through the air behind her.

It sunk into the side of the attacker's neck. The sound of slicing flesh was unmistakable.

She never stopped to look back, not even to aim or to make sure she hit him. I watched as he fell on his face in the dirt. With his last gargled breath, the knife shot from his neck into her outstretched hand.

She was fucking confident.

Stone and Novak stood in front of Vaughn, each one facing a different side. Vaughn was flinging icicles as fast as he could make them, while also covering Novak and Stone as they fought in close quarters.

Sloane and I weaved carefully between the guys, watching their backs as we scanned the darkness for incoming threats.

The last of the supernatural creatures came in a massive wave from one side. It looked like their bodies were being manipulated.

Their movement was too organized. They all stepped with the same foot and used identical stances. It was their downfall.

We wouldn't discriminate. We'd kill every last one of them.

They'd all fall tonight.

Sloane moved out of our formation and faded away. I couldn't describe what she did exactly, but it was like she turned into a ghost.

When she reappeared, she stood in the middle of the incoming attackers with no care in the world.

She was on a mission and this was taking too long.

The one person she was looking for hadn't been found yet. He was the one controlling the horde. I noticed the hounds and Briggs weren't here either. Maybe he had been found, and that was why she was in a hurry.

She flung her knives so quickly that it was impossible to track their trajectory. When one knife hit its target, another appeared in her hand.

She took out most of their numbers while standing among them. They never had a chance to notice before they dropped dead.

She was devastatingly gorgeous in her homicidal rage.

The last one left from the campground army came barreling towards me as I ogled Sloane. I swung my flail into the bear's head at the last moment, and Vaughn shot icicles through his chest.

We followed Sloane as she made her way through the tents and hanging tarps. We headed back down the path to where we'd found York.

The makeshift dungeon.

The cellar style doors had been ripped off the hinges. When we descended the stairwell, we heard Briggs talking and the guttural growls of the hellhounds.

"I can't call them off," he was telling someone calmly. "They don't listen to me. That one doesn't even like me."

Sloane smiled as she stopped to listen to Briggs.

"Please, please! I'll tell you what you want to know! I'll give you money! I'll-I'll..." A menacing growl quieted him.

"Don't beg *me*, man." Briggs chuckled as he verbalized why he was there. "I'm not in charge. I'm just babysitting you until the boss lady gets down here. She'll be on her way soon, and you can beg and squeal to her all you want."

Sloane exited the stairwell in a casual gait. The mask of composure she was wearing broke when she saw where York had been kept all this time.

She cut her hard glare to the male Briggs was talking to. All that homicidal rage I was talking about earlier reached its boiling point.

Her eyes were pure hellfire and glistening horns sprouted from her skull, coiling up from her hair like foot long S's.

It was a bad description, I know.

They came out near her forehead, curving up and back towards the backside of her head before sloping upwards with fine points.

A flame tipped tail popped out from the back of her skirt. It lashed agitatedly back and forth before it ignited with fire.

There was no flesh covering the bones, unlike Stone's tail.

We were shocked by her half transformation. I fought not to step back to give her tail space. It avoided us with agile precision.

I watched her shoulders rise and fall as she took a deep breath and addressed me without turning around. Her voice was a little raspier than normal and reminded me of how Stone's voice took on a deeper quality when he spoke in demon form.

"Palmer? Can you open the Void?"

"Yeah," I responded without hesitation.

"Good, take Vaughn, Briggs, and the hounds with you. We're going to dump all the bodies in the Void. Grim should be waiting on the other side. Atlas and Cronus will drag them over since they can cross without harm. All you have to do is hold it open."

"And what do we do?" Vaughn questioned.

She snapped her head to him, turning it a little too far for comfort. "Build a wall of ice around the grounds. We're going to burn it down before we leave, and I don't want the surrounding area to catch fire. Briggs, watch their backs in case we missed anyone."

"Yes, ma'am," Briggs replied with a small smile.

As he got closer to her, he leaned in and confessed in a whisper, "You look like the Demon version of Barbie right now. It's hot."

She grinned broadly at him, and all her teeth elongated to sharp points. The growth of her demon teeth caused her jaw to drop further than normal to fit their length.

They had to be close to an inch long and probably felt like razor blades piercing your flesh. I didn't want to be on the receiving end of that particular set of teeth. Ever.

They were what nightmares were made of. *I'd take regular teeth, thanks. Maybe vampire fangs, but those? Nope, no fucking way.*

Briggs rolled his eyes at her antics while Stone was in full boner territory.

The sadistic bastard.

He had a mouth full of those teeth, too. He just never wore them in his human skin. That was the part that freaked me out the most.

Cronus took the lead as we trudged back upstairs. I heard Sloane call Helios and then tell Novak and Stone to put good ol' Kelvin on the table in the next room.

We closed the door behind us, cutting off any reply or noise. I didn't know what she was going to do, but I knew holding the Void open had to be a better request than holding the Vampire-Mage down.

I also knew she didn't send Vaughn up here just to build an ice wall. *We all knew he was squeamish.*

Atlas and Cronus made quick work of dragging all the bodies into the Void. I caught sight of Grim and Jack several times, but they stayed pretty busy for a while.

I was bored outta my mind just standing here.

When the last body was passed over, Jack popped out

to ask how it went. He handed us some potion vials and said Simon sent them.

Who was Simon again?

We drank them like shots, but the nasty taste still lingered for too long afterwards. That stuff was like an energy drink on steroids. I pocketed the rest to give to the others.

"Where's Sloane now?" Jack inquired.

"She's down in the makeshift dungeon torturing the vampire-mage hybrid who ran this place," Briggs said nonchalantly.

Jack gave Grim a look that I couldn't read, and Grim nodded his head in return. I've only heard him say one word. He talked less than Stone did.

"Can you show us the way?" Jack's serious tone was unlike anything I'd heard from him so far.

"Aye, come on then," I answered uneasily, suspicion taking over my tone.

We took Jack and Grim back to the dungeon entrance. Grim waved his hand, and a robe appeared over his clothes.

Jack turned back to us and smiled meekly before speaking. "We're gonna go down and scare him into talking if she hasn't already. Vaughn, can you get these two back to wherever you're staying?"

"Yes. Are you sure we should go, though?" He sounded doubtful about leaving. I felt the same way.

"Go check on the druid. He needs to be warned that he'll have to give her some space after this. He can't start talking to her as soon as she walks through the door." Jack encouraged us with a pleading look.

"He has a friend with him. A human who kept him alive. How should we broach that subject with her?" Vaughn asked apprehensively.

"Ohhh, uhm, how was she when she sent you guys out?" he wondered.

"Royally pissed. Her eyes were completely red, horns popped out of her skull, and she grew a flaming bone tail," Briggs responded.

"Yep, then he," I pointed to Briggs with my thumb, "told 'er she looked like a demon Barbie before we walked out."

"Did she smile or growl at you after that?" Jack teasingly questioned Briggs.

"Smiled." Cockiness rolled off him in palpable currents, and before it could become contagious I muttered, "Oh yeah, before 'er teeth turned inta razor blades."

"Briggs or Stone," Grim said to Jack.

"Yep," he replied before facing us.

"Here's what you do; let Briggs and Stone talk to her. She doesn't often let her demon surface, so she's gotta be past her anger threshold." He shrugged.

"Briggs, when you get wherever you're going, talk to the guy. Get his story. Work that angle. If she gets pissed, back off and let Stone handle it from there. Demon to demon. She'll be back to her usual self in a couple hours. Sooner if she gets answers from this guy."

He shooed us off with a flamboyant flick of his hands. "Now, go. Get showered. Pack your shit back up. She'll be ready to go once she decides what to do with the human."

We all nodded our agreement, and Vaughn grabbed Briggs' elbow. They transformed from looking human to water silhouettes before disappearing completely.

I turned my attention back to Jack.

"You're sure she's gonna be okay?" I questioned him with concern.

"Yes, honey. She'll be fine. She'll never direct that anger towards anyone who doesn't deserve it. The druid, though; yeah, he'll catch some of her wrath when you guys get back home.

"When she knows he's not injured, she'll pretty much ignore him until she's ready to talk rationally. They were together long enough for him to know this, but he'll still try to push her. Don't be surprised by the tension. Give them a couple days to work it out."

Vaughn was back by the time Jack finished talking.

It was hard to drag myself away. I didn't want to leave my mate, but she was angry and I couldn't solve any of it for her. The best I could do was keep her and York separated until she approached him.

Or keep her tied up with distractions until she's too blissful to be angry. That's something I could do.

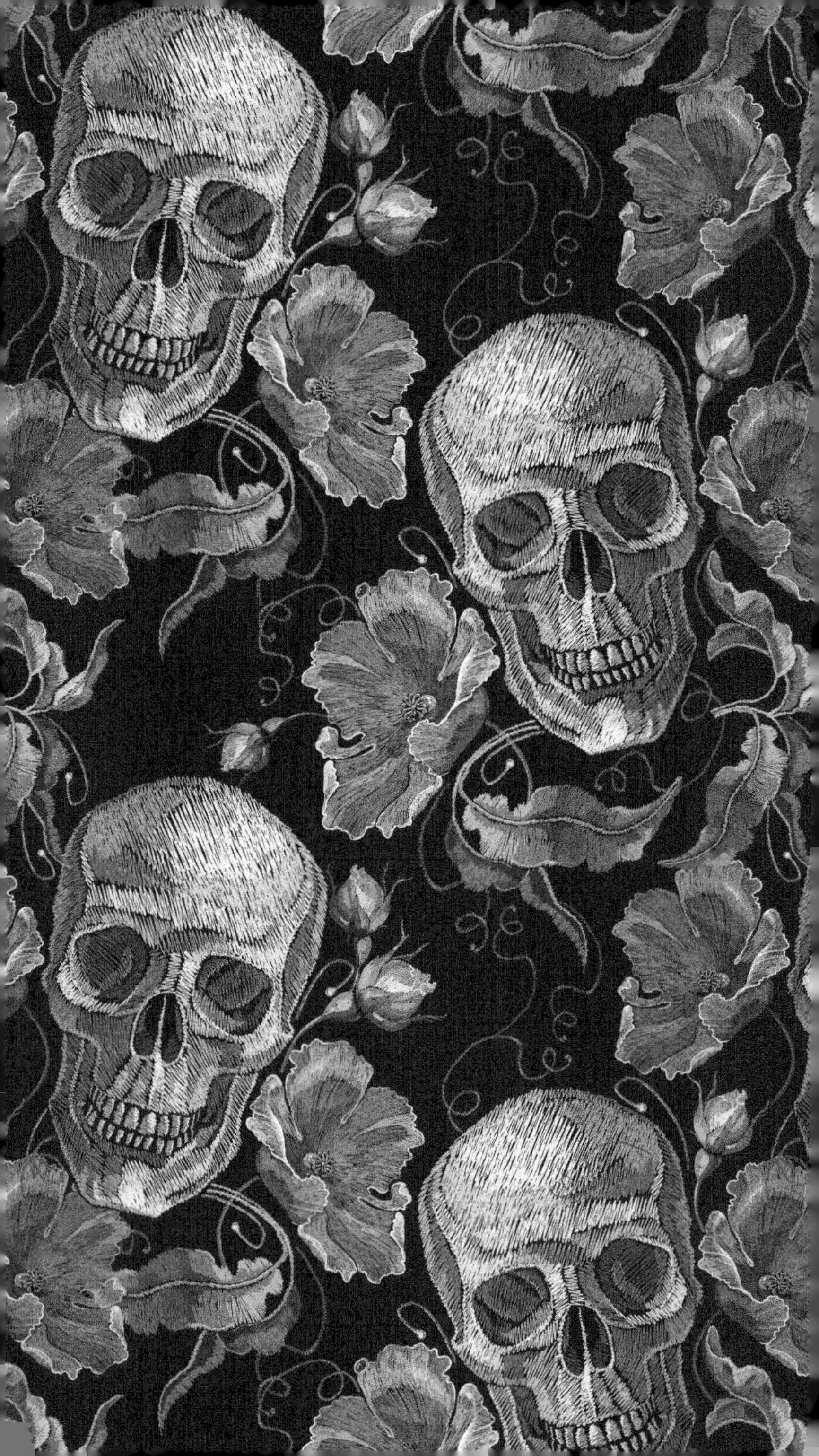

CHAPTER 22
Sloane

Monday, May 18th
Early Morning

I was beyond enraged when we reached the inside of the dungeon. It wasn't a real dungeon. No, it was dug out and bricked up inside.

I was here five years ago, and I was about to finish that fight, once I got a little information from Kelvin here.

Briggs' comment about me looking like the demon version of Barbie eased my anger enough for me to see straight. When he left, it all came rushing back tenfold.

There was a reason I didn't want him, Palmer, or Vaughn down here, though. I didn't think they'd be able to handle what I had in store for Kelvin.

Five years ago, I'd have given him a quick, merciful death. That was before he kidnapped and tortured one of my mates.

I called Helios off of Kelvin to give him a chance to stand up. He didn't take it. I ordered Novak and Stone to put him on the table in the other room. It was the medical table where they did all their power drains.

He tucked his knees under his chin and begged me, "No, please! I'll do anything. I'll tell you anything!!"

"Good. We're on the same page now." I smiled maliciously at him.

"Tell me who you give the power to," I demanded simply.

"I-I-I can't!" he cried out.

"Wrong answer," I stated, kneeling next to him. "The next wrong answer *will* cause bodily harm," I warned him, and he sobbed into his hands. "Who do you give the power to?"

"I can't tell you that," Kelvin said firmly.

"Are you sure? Because that sounded an awful lot like a wrong answer to me." I tilted my head as I raised my eyebrows.

If he wanted to play this game with me, then he needed to know that I'd win. I don't lose.

I snagged a knife from my skirt and rammed it through the top of his boot, into his foot. I heard the tip hit the ground beneath his shoe.

His wail made me cringe, my ears ringing loudly as he ended with a sniffle.

"Let's try this again, shall we? I'll even give you a

Sloane

minute to think about your answer," I gushed as I stood and surveyed my surroundings.

"Novak, would you please check that room over there—the one with the metal table—for any kind of crystals or artifacts?"

"Sure thing, Trouble." He giddily zoomed out of the cell while Stone stood stoic behind me.

"Now, about that question." I continued my conversation with Kelvin after counting in my head to sixty. *Quickly.*

"Don't tell me that you'll 'tell me anything' and then not answer the one thing I want to know. You gotta give me something Kel, or this is gonna get real painful real quick." I twisted the hilt of the knife in his foot.

"I can't tell you his name," he screamed out as he gulped. "You aren't understanding me. *I CAN'T!* Even to save my own life, I can't tell you."

Well, I *could* read in between the lines. I guess he was under some sort of blood oath to keep his mouth shut.

"What can you tell me?"

"Nothing, but I could be forced to tell you with compulsion, I believe," he squealed.

A look of regret passed over his pained features.

"You believe. Is that supposed to be reassuring?" I asked as I made focused eye contact with him.

Let's see if it worked.

"Answer my questions, Kelvin," I cooed to him. "What kind of monster is he?"

"He-he's a f-fae-mage hybrid." He fought the words as they spilled from his lips.

"Summer or Winter?" I let a seductive tone flow from my mouth as I started my interrogation.

"S-s-summer," he stuttered.

"And you know him how?" Maybe we could knock out the basics and narrow our suspect pool down.

"I c-c-can't tell you." He tried to break my hold by looking away, so I wrapped my hand around his jaw.

"Do you share mage blood?" I hardened my tone to keep his attention.

"Yes," he ground out.

"What's your father's name?"

"Alric."

"Alric who?"

"Alric Moore." He silently wept into his hands.

Now we were getting somewhere.

"When does your brother visit you next?"

"He-he doesn't."

That was interesting.

He didn't do his own pickups. So clearly he didn't travel from his base much. I twirled another knife in my hand as I proceeded with my line of questioning.

"Who does he send?"

"Kadence."

Who the fuck was that?

"Kadence Moore?" Novak spoke up from behind me, disbelief ringing clear in his words.

"Yes," Kelvin angrily bit out before a sobbing hiccup.

Sloane

"What does she have to do with this?" Novak dangled four glowing crystals in front of Kelvin's face.

Fae crystals.

He didn't answer, so I repeated it to him while maintaining the dizzying connection.

"She's doing the same thing—" hiccup—"just on a smaller scale." Hiccup. "I don't know what she does with —" hiccup—"them after she visits." Hiccup.

The man was a mess. *I'd barely touched him!*

I snatched the knife from the top of his foot. As he shrieked in pain, I let go of his jaw. I adjusted the angle of my body to face him head on.

"Do you have anything else you can tell us, Kelvin?"

"They're using the power for a magic mixed drug," he stammered out before another hiccup. "They've been testing it on the shifters—" hiccup—"for months, and they started trials—" hiccup—"on the vampires a couple weeks ago," he rushed out before he could hiccup yet again.

He tried to calm his breathing, and those fucking hiccups finally started to fade away.

"Is that all you know?"

"Yes! That's it!!" he screamed before lowering his voice, "That's more than they told me. I had to search their minds for some of that information."

"Thank you, Kelvin. I think you've extended your usefulness." I released the compulsion as I smiled awkwardly at him, showing more teeth than necessary.

They were retracting more with each word, but they wouldn't fully recede until I let go of my partial demon shift.

I sliced open the insides of my cheeks every time I spoke, and they knitted back together before my teeth tore through them again.

The minimal discomfort was nothing compared to what York went through down here.

"You're going to kill me!?" he bleated.

"Let me tell *you* something." I faked happiness that I didn't feel, kneeling before him again.

I reached out and stroked his head lovingly a few times while I continued to battle my rage.

"The druid you were draining—you know him, right?" He flinched. "He's one of my mates, and although I'm pretty angry with him right now, it doesn't make him any less my mate."

He looked up at me with wide, fearful eyes as I soothingly stroked through his hair.

"You see those marks on the wall over there? That's a mark for every day he was here. In this very cell. Eight hundred and fifty-eight marks."

I was losing the battle inside myself. It got harder and harder to fight with each calm word that rolled off my tongue. I petted his head rougher.

"My original plan was to mark you as many times as he did the wall and then paint this dingy cell red with your blood. That's why I sent my other mates out. But... you were so helpful, Kelvin," I praised him after my honesty.

"It's not nice to return your favor like that. Even though the Devil is one of my parents, I *was* raised with manners. The High Coven Master taught me those

Sloane

manners. The Supreme Alpha, however; he taught me how to get what I want," I admitted with a snotty attitude.

I stopped running my hand over his head as I summed up my mood swing.

"So, I changed my mind. I mean, I'm still going to kill you, but first I'm going to drain your power so I can make sure my druid is nice and healthy. Then I'm going to give you the quick death I had planned against. Sounds like a good deal, right?" I inquired sweetly.

He didn't say a word.

"Now, the last thing I need from you," I paused to make sure I still had his attention, "is for you to tell me how to release the power in these crystals. You think you can explain that to me?" I coaxed.

"No! You crazy fucking bitch! I'm not telling you a godsdamn thing," he raged at me.

"Got it," Novak whispered in my mind.

I tsked at Kelvin. "That's the wrong answer," I informed him politely before I stood back up. "I guess we'll just bury you down here. Would that be a better deal?" I pondered more to myself than him.

Thankfully Novak saw what I was doing. We had all the information we needed now.

He jumped to his feet before I stepped through the cell door, following the guys.

"You can't leave me down here!" he bellowed. "I'll just dig my way out. I'm not weak like that fucking druid," he spat.

"I'll never stay down here, and when I get out, I'll

come for you again," he threatened. "I'll kill you, bitch! And before I kill you, I'll make you watch while I kill all your mates."

Ohhh, that appeared to be a button of mine now. Here came the psycho. Just a little taste.

I spun to the right, pulling my knee up. As I pivoted on my left foot, I kicked it up and extended my left leg out straight.

Tornado kick, motherfucker.

It looked like I'd missed the mark with my kick, but the knife popped out of the toe of my boot, adding five inches to my reach. Just in time to slice through his neck.

His hands shot up to grab at his gaping throat in slow motion. When he dropped to his knees, I stepped forward and leaned in to whisper, "I told you what would happen if you gave me the wrong answer."

I sank my dagger through his heart. "And that, Kelvin, was the wrong. Fucking. Answer."

I twisted my weapon to punctuate the last three words. Then I jerked it out, slinging blood around the cell and sliced through the remaining tendons and skin attaching his neck to his torso.

His head rolled away just as Grim stepped through the doorway. He nodded to me, and his scythe formed in his hand while all his flesh began to disappear.

Fun fact about Grim Reapers: Their scythes are made from their flesh. That's why they look like skeletons when they reap souls.

Kelvin's soul was going to a special place in the Underworld. *My bedroom* in the Devil's palace. To sit in a glass display box like a signed fucking baseball on my shelf. His soul was forever mine.

I hope he enjoyed his eternal suffering formed by my own imagination.

Novak held my hand in his as we climbed the stairs to see the approaching dawn. Jack was waiting for me by the door, looking pleased.

"Go back to your clubhouse, babe. We'll take care of this and I'll get Helios home," he assured me as he kissed my cheek.

"Okay, just let me know if you need a hand."

My anger was fading with every step I took away from that horrid cell. The adrenaline of the night was quickly fleeing. I relaxed enough to force my shift back into my body.

Having a tail felt weird without my wings.

Parading around with gigantic horns on my human head gave me a headache. All I wanted was a hot shower, clean clothes, and coffee.

Gallons of coffee. And maybe a short nap.

"Come on, Kitten. I'll race you back to the treehouse." Stone nudged me with his shoulder as the three of us strolled side-by-side.

"You'll race *me*?" I pointed to my chest with my index finger. "Let's up the ante, shall we? If I'm going to race, then I want something out of it."

The idea of a small gamble had my mind distracted with all the things that could come out of this.

"What do you have in mind?" Stone wondered aloud.

"I don't know if I like the sly look on her face or not,

Stone," Novak confessed as he leaned behind me to mock-whisper to Stone.

"I'm feeling pretty confident," Stone retorted as he met Novak's concerned look. "So, if one of us wins, then you owe us both a lap dance. Three songs each. Winner's choice in music."

"That's all you're asking for?" Novak barked at him. "You're supposed to say if one of us wins, then we're having a threesome! Not getting three songs. Ask for something high and then work your way down to a lap dance."

I couldn't help the giggle that escaped me, and it had nothing to do with Novak's response. *Almost nothing.*

"Agreed," I chuckled as I made up my mind on what I'd ask of them *when* I won.

Because let's face it, I was about to win.

"And I want you both to wear frilly maid uniforms, feather dusters and all, when I win."

"Nope. I don't like this, Stone," Novak argued, but the demon ignored him.

"When? For how long? And in front of whom?" Stone always asked the right questions.

"Tonight... or tomorrow. Two hours. And, well, in front of whoever sees you." I took on his same business-like tone.

"Agreed." Stone extended his hand to make our deal official with a shake.

When I put my hand in his, he added, "And no misting or shadow jumping. We're just running."

"Agreed," I responded again.

Sloane

"Fuck it," the vampire declared. "I think I hate you both right now." He reached for my hand with a grimace as he agreed to our terms.

"Helios," I shouted, and he bounded down the path to greet me. "Start our race off with a bark and then go back to Jack and Grim," I commanded him.

He gave me his signature *"are you serious?"* look, and I rolled my eyes at him. "Yes, do it."

With a loud *woof* from the fiery hellhound, the guys flashed off. I stayed where I was and counted to thirty before chasing after them. We were miles from the treehouse rental.

I had time.

I spotted Novak ahead of me after a few moments and slowed my speed to run beside him. He stumbled when he saw me feet from him, and I tossed him a saucy wink as I blasted past. I could hear him cursing as he tried to catch up.

It took me longer to reach Stone. The demon was fast.

The fastest one I'd met.

He had a bit of a competitive streak, or maybe he just wanted that lap dance. I'd give him one either way, but the gamble made it more fun.

He was gonna look ridiculous in a skirt.

I pushed ahead of him as Novak caught up, and I cackled as they both yelled at me.

When I was sufficiently in the lead, I stopped and scaled up a tall tree. I used to do this to Jack all the time when we were kids. I moved as high as I could, keeping a clear path straight to the ground.

I heard them before I saw them, and as they rushed towards the tree I was in, I dropped down in front of them. Stone stopped dead in his tracks. Novak slid across the ground so quickly he couldn't catch himself before he went tumbling.

Stone and I keeled over with laughter as Novak stood and dusted himself off, muttering obscenities with each brush of his hands.

"Ha. Ha," He huffed at us. "That's got to be cheating."

"Definitely wasn't in the rules," Stone approved.

"Bye," I taunted with a wave as I took off again.

"FUCK!" Novak snarled. "Catch her! I'm not wearing a fucking skirt," he shouted at Stone, but his voice grew quieter the further away I got from them.

Stone was hot on my heels when I finally decided to stop playing around. The idea of them in skirts was fueling my motivation to win.

The losing side of the bet was nothing. I agreed with Novak, Stone could've asked for something *more*. I'd give them lap dances, that wasn't a problem at all.

I wanted to make a *memory*. Something that I would remember two hundred years from now.

I planned on taking some pictures too. Possibly show our kids when we're older.

Fuck. *Did I say kids? Slow down, Sloane.*

I slammed my metaphorical brakes on and stared dumbly ahead of me.

Sloane

I didn't want kids. Never had. So why had I just thought that?

Something solid collided with my back.

Not something. Someone.

We both went ass over tits for a few feet before we came to a halt. I was flat on my back, breathlessly gazing at the overly exuberant demon pinning me down.

"Got her!" he called out to Novak, who went racing by.

Oh, hell no, you don't.

I pushed my butt out to the left, twisting my body as I moved and threw Stone off balance.

It was called a shrimp in training.

I flipped him off of me and jumped up, not even bothering to get the twigs and leaves off of me as I started chasing after Novak.

The chase was my favorite part of hunting.

No more playing with them. *Nope.* Time to win.

I moved at the speed of light.

I thought I did, anyway.

It took me seconds to catch Novak again. He growled his frustrations in that feral way that had me so turned on it could melt the panties right off my body.

I accelerated to my top speed so I didn't stop to show him what that sound did to me. It took me a full four minutes of high speed running to make it back to the treehouse.

I may have gotten a little lost in my excitement.

I was breathing hard as I jogged up the stairs, pulling the debris from my hair.

I'd won, but I wasn't ready to be back so soon.

I didn't wait for them to catch up. I walked inside with a victorious grin on my face. Heading straight to the room where my bag was, I stripped down so I could shower and dress in clean clothes.

"Don't immediately tell them that I beat them, okay?" I sang out as I moved past everyone.

"Sure thing, Love," Palmer agreed readily while towel-drying his hair.

As I eased into the bedroom with the attached bathroom, I heard the front door open and close.

"We fucking beat her?" Novak questioned, disbelief pouring from his tone.

"Beat who?" Vaughn's confusion sounded honest.

"Sloane. We were racing," Stone informed them.

"Oh." Briggs was amused and let them bask in the glory of their victory. He drew the rest of his reply out after a minute break. "No, she's in the shower."

"Fuck!" Novak shouted again, and I couldn't wipe the smile off my face. "I told you that was a bad bet to take. But nooooo, you were feeling too cocky for your own good and you dragged me right into it," he complained loudly to Stone.

"What did she win?" York sounded healthier already.

My expression fell as my heart gave an abrupt twinge of pain.

"I don't want to tell you guys," Novak whined.

"You'll see tonight, or maybe tomorrow," was all Stone added before I heard the door to the bedroom open, and a very dirty demon interrupted my shower.

Sloane

A very welcome, dirty demon.

After our time in the pool this morning, I had been dying to get my hands on his lean physique again. I licked my lips as he set his weapons in a bag on the bathroom counter and started untying his boots.

I watched, transfixed, as he pulled his shirt over his head, revealing that delectable V cut and his hard lined abs.

The next few days were going to be shit while I worked through my issues with York. This moment with Stone was enough to make me forget about my worries, though.

The new demon in my life was one I didn't have to fight. I guess that was the difference between my life and a regular one.

While some people battled their demons daily... I got to live peacefully with mine. I got to touch him. Tease him. Fuck him. Love him. Yeah, my demon was different.

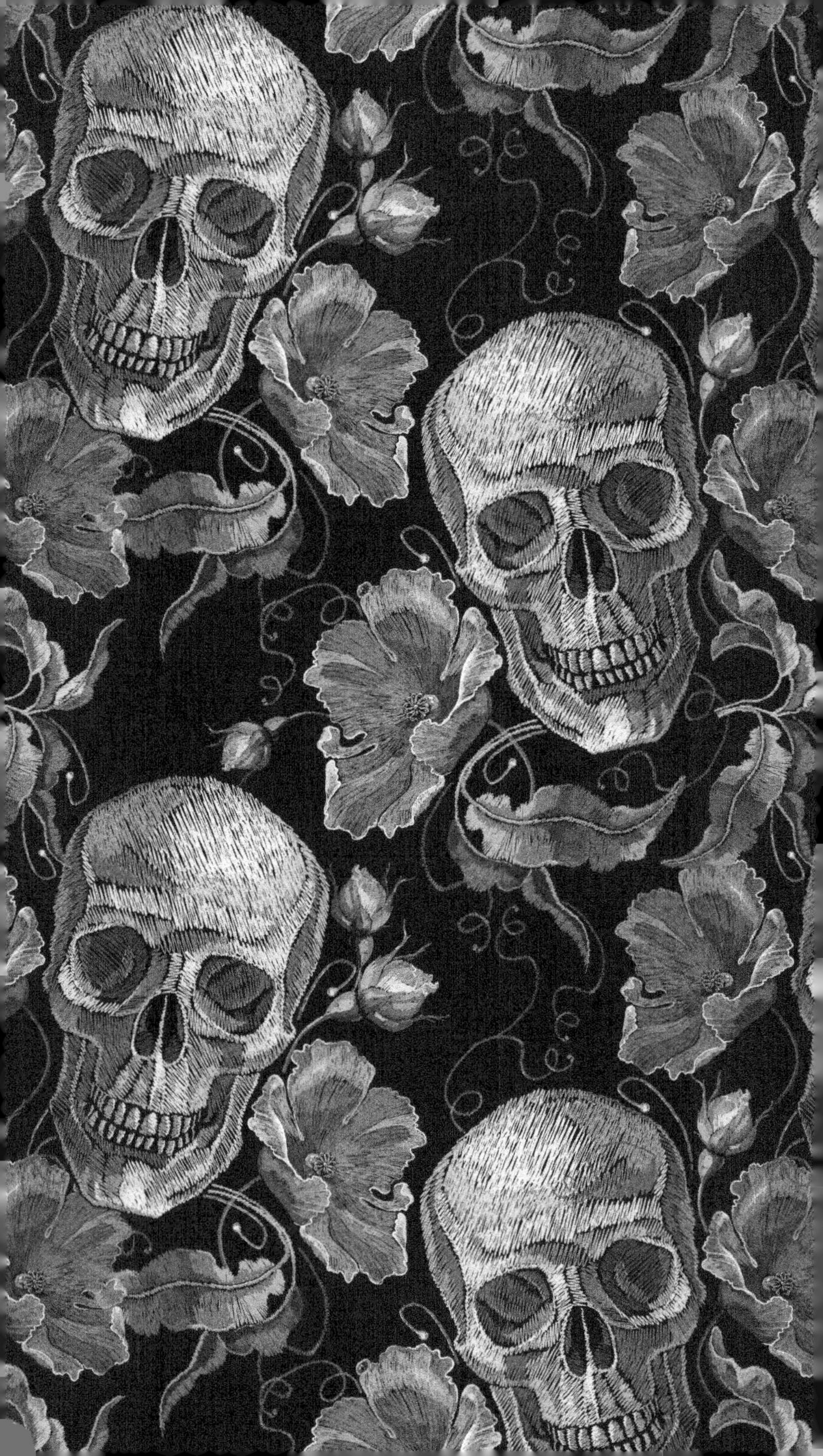

CHAPTER 23
Stone

Monday, May 18th
Morning

"Scoot over," I demanded of Sloane while she shamelessly drooled over my body.

"Mmm, come to wash my hair?" she teased me as I stripped out of my mud covered pants. "You'd make a lovely chambermaid," she continued, batting her lashes.

I rolled my hazy red eyes at her. My demon was still fighting for control after watching our mate wreak havoc.

"Only if you wash mine," I countered dryly, letting my long black hair fall down my back.

She moved out of the spray of water, suds running down her chest from her soaped up curls.

The tension of the night vanished between the scalding water and her hands on my back. They left lines of fire across my skin. I had to immerse myself in washing my own hair to keep from taking her there in the small shower stall.

Her hands took over from mine, and she ran her nails across my scalp as she massaged the shampoo into my tangled tresses. I eased my head back so she could reach better.

I'd never let anyone touch me like this. It felt more intimate than anything I'd ever been a part of.

Sloane made me realize that caring for someone ran deeper than a physical need.

We switched places several times, bathing each other until I noticed her tension rise.

"What's eating at you?" I finally broke the silence, hopeful that she'd give me an honest answer.

She exhaled loudly and turned to face me after cutting the water off.

"York. I want to forgive him, to not be mad at him, but it's harder than I thought it would be. All this time I thought he'd just left me. It was easier to be angry than heartbroken. Now, I'm about to walk out there and be face to face with him. I'm just not ready for the confrontation that I know he wants."

"I know he's going to want to talk things out sooner than you will too," I acknowledged, "But he's had plenty of time to think about what he wants to say. It's not a bad

Stone

thing that you want some time to think through your thoughts as well."

She stepped into me, resting her head on my shoulder. I wrapped my arms around her waist and held her flush against me.

Comforting wasn't really in my bag of tricks.

Seeing her vulnerability, even for a few seconds, was an odd sight when she'd been so confident. It was hard to keep my hands from roaming her naked body, but I wouldn't take advantage of the situation.

A little more stress and then we could go home.

I sighed gently as I rubbed my knuckles up and down her back. "Kitten, we have some more business to attend to before we leave."

She grinned against my skin, questioning me with a longing sigh. "It's not what I'm hoping for, is it?"

"Sadly, no," I replied wistfully. "We can pick this back up when we get home, though," I promised.

"What is it then? I can't think of anything we missed," she stated as she stared at the ceiling.

She looked as though she was calculating a difficult equation in her head, her eyes bouncing back and forth.

"Well," I started before I was cut off by shouting from down the hall. The voices were muted through the walls, but we were able to make out some of the words.

"You've got to calm down, mate. Everything is going to be fine." York must have been consoling Levi.

"None of us will hurt you," Briggs offered in his gravelly voice, not sounding the least bit sincere.

Sloane swung the bathroom door open and ran across

the bedroom. Just as she reached the door, I coughed obnoxiously, and she turned to glare at me.

"You're naked." I pointed at her and let my eyes linger on her body.

"Right." She snapped her fingers and ended my viewing pleasure. "Who's yelling?"

She ruffled her wet hair. It looked more gray in its dampened state than the usual silver and light blue mixture.

"Levi," I distractingly answered while looking down at her clothes. "Are you wearing purple?" I'd only ever seen her in black.

Confusion flooded her face as she nodded slowly.

"Yes," she drew out. "What's wrong with purple? Are my boobs hanging out the bottom of this crop top or something? Why are you looking at me like that?"

"Like what?" I tried to recover, blanking my facial features. "Your tits look fine. Purple looks good on you."

She eyed me suspiciously before opening the door and stepping into the hall. The shouting had calmed to frantic whispers.

Upon crossing the threshold in the living room, we were met with five backs leaned over the sofa.

"Uhm," Sloane began and five heads whipped around. "What the fuck is going on?"

"Palmer knocked Levi out," Vaughn supplied, nonchalantly tucking his hands in his pockets.

Sloane looked at me, and I gave her a guilty half smile.

"Uh-huh, and who is Levi?" she inquired, glaring at the others for an answer.

"Come on, Barbie. Let's go to the kitchen and I'll tell you all about it." Briggs ushered her out of the room while Palmer explained to us that it was just a sleeping spell.

"He'll come round in ten minutes or so." He rolled his stormy eyes skyward, then looked back at us in amusement. "Mmm, maybe twenty. I forgot he was human. I hit 'im pretty hard with that spell."

"What did you guys find out about him?" It's the only thing I care to know about right now.

York answered me with the man's entire life story. He had no family and nothing to go back to. No one had ever reported him missing. He was homeless when Kelvin brought him in as a human lackey.

Novak had already done a background check on him, which was pretty impressive to me. The guy was clean, no arrests and very little to be found. He was in a tight spot and got offered the world.

Not a bad guy. A good guy in the wrong place at the wrong time.

Levi jolted awake and scanned the room while he rubbed his temples. He took quick notice of everyone in the room before he landed on me. He wouldn't take his eyes from me.

It was unnerving to be studied like I was a rare specimen on display. He didn't blink. It felt as if he was waiting for me to change forms and thought he'd miss it if he closed his eyes for a split second.

"What are you?" He squinted and cocked his head to the side like it might change my appearance.

I wasn't holographic.

"I'm just a dentist," I shrugged. "How are your teeth? Any pain?"

I knew that wasn't what he was asking me, but I tried to be clinical.

I'd rather him be scared of me for being a dentist instead of a demon. Some fears were irrational, others weren't.

"Like fucking teeth, dude. How are your teeth?" His sarcasm could've been cut with a knife.

He didn't believe me. I flashed him a big smile, and he leaned closer to examine my human teeth.

"Where'd your fangs go?" His country accent grew heavy in his disbelief.

"I don't have fangs. I'm not a vampire." I rolled my offended navy eyes at him.

He laughed under his breath. "You had a mouth full of shark teeth," he informed me.

York and Palmer both turned their heads to silently laugh, their bodies shaking as they kept the sounds contained. Vaughn's crystal blue eyes danced with amusement. Novak was hysterical.

"I've never heard them compared to shark teeth," he blurted as he sat down to talk to Levi. "I take it you haven't seen too many demons in your time at that camp?"

"Uhhh, no." Levi scratched his neck. "Bunch of shifters. A few vamps and mages. That's about it."

Stone

"Well, Levi, Stone is a demon," Novak threw out with too much joy. "A very big, very scary demon."

"Yeah, okay. You don't look like a demon."

Right. Of course I didn't. That was the point.

He wasn't scared, though, so that was good.

"I told you, man, I'm a dentist." I tossed my hands up and went to walk out, but Sloane appeared from around the corner.

With a determined and serious set to her oval face, she tentatively approached Levi.

"I have an ultimatum for you. This is completely up to you, but think them both through before you answer." She smiled reassuringly as she sat beside him and grasped his hand.

He let out the breath he must have been holding, and his shoulders sagged with what looked like defeat.

"You know more about our world than most humans do, and that's both a good and bad thing. We can erase your memories of the last few years and feed you better ones. Memories where you've been living off the grid and enjoying life before you decided to go back home."

She held her index finger up to indicate that was the first option she was giving him.

"Or, you can keep your memories, and I'll give you a job so I can keep an eye on you. For your safety, of course."

She held up two fingers and then continued.

"Either one you choose is fine with me. I'll put you up for a couple months so you can get back on your feet. We'll make sure you don't have any issues getting an apartment or a car. Whatever you need, it's yours. I'll give you an hour to think about it."

Levi's mouth gaped open as he struggled for words. Shaking his head vigorously, he stopped her from standing.

"I don't need to think about it," he choked out before clearing his throat. "I want to keep my memories. I need to live with the things I've done. I need those lessons to learn from my mistakes. To remember that a bad guy conned me into thinking he was good and then turned me from a naïve teenager in a bad situation to one of the bad guys in a worse situation. If I forget that, then I'll go back to being the same person I was before all this began. I don't want to be that naïve person anymore."

Sloane grinned her approval at him. "That's a mature way to look at what you've been through, Levi," she observed. "Would you like to know what your new job is now?"

He hesitated for a moment before giving a squeaky "sure" in reply. Sloane told him all about the position of head of security at CBP.

She gushed about the changes she wanted to make and complained about the lazy guards that were currently employed.

I soon realized I stood alone listening to Sloane talk. I drifted out of the living room after a few minutes and found myself outside on the deck.

York was sitting with his back against one of the trees growing through the porch. His teal and green eyes were turned up to the canopy above us as he soaked in the rays of early morning sunlight.

He looked better than he did when we'd found him last night, but it would be awhile before he was back to himself.

I sank to the wooden floor beside him, content to observe nature unfold around us.

The Underworld had forests and oceans similar to Earth, yet none of it felt as peaceful as this.

We soaked in the quiet tranquility, and minutes passed before York heaved a resigned sigh and forced his attention to me.

"She's really mad at me, isn't she?" he questioned me softly.

I could hear regret twined into his words and his eyes closed as he waited for my reply.

"I think she's more hurt than anything, York," I admitted to him. "You didn't trust her. You didn't tell her what was going on. To her, you just disappeared. No explanations. No goodbye. Nothing." I grimaced as I told him the truth he needed to hear.

He opened his eyes, and they welled with unshed tears. He clenched his jaw to hold them at bay. When the first tear trailed down his cheek, he looked away from me and back to the sky.

"She's my mate. What was I supposed to do? Tell her? Do you know what she would've done, Stone?" he asked me with a hint of fear in his voice.

"Exactly what she did last night, except she'd have done it by herself. I couldn't risk her getting caught."

His tone was rough with emotion as he pushed the words out. His hands were fisted so tightly that his knuckles were changing color.

"We're all her mates. It's not like I don't understand your side, because I do. I also understand hers, though."

I wanted to remain a neutral party in their issues, but I knew he needed someone to talk to. York had been my friend for years. I would always be honest with him.

"No," he whispered. "She's not just a potential mate, Stone. We *sealed* the mate bond."

He paused to let his statement sink in and I turned wide eyes to him.

"I never said anything to her about it. I thought that she knew, but after some time I figured out that she wasn't aware of it. She's so powerful that she didn't notice any new abilities, but I did. My own power increased considerably. Magic I'd not been able to wield before was as easy as breathing, like second nature."

He blew out a strained breath, and I waited for him to continue.

He was frustrated with himself, but also with her. I got it. I probably would be too.

"I filled her greenhouse with plants from my kingdom. I shouldn't have been able to do that without seeds. I did, though, with nothing but the thought of missing my homeland. I grew them with no seeds or soil. Not even water. Look." His request was urgent.

York opened his hand, palm facing up, and as if out of thin air a flower bloomed.

Not an earthly flower.

Stone

It resembled a daisy, but the petals were twisted and warped. It was a deep plum color with a feather-like texture, and the stem it grew from curled around his wrist like a delicate bracelet.

Over the years of our friendship, I'd seen him create many things, but never from nothing.

"So," I started as my fraying thoughts began to form, "that time you and Vaughn were sword fighting in the backyard at our old house and you lost a couple fingers?"

It made me smile thinking about it. *Back then? Not so much.*

He chuckled as he nodded his head.

"I stitched my fingers back on with grass from the yard. That shouldn't even be possible. It wasn't sterile, that's for sure. Still, somehow the earth magic healed me. I've got no scars or suppressed motion. It's like it never happened. I healed as fast as Novak would have, but it worked more like how Vaughn heals his injuries with his ice."

He flexed his fingers and smiled down at them.

"And that was after you sealed the bond?" I needed clarification.

What could Sloane do if she had been practicing with his earth magic? Her possibilities really would be limitless when she was bound to us all.

"Yeah, man!" he exclaimed, breaking me out of my thoughts. "That's what I'm saying. Think about what could have happened if those idiots who kidnapped me had found out that we were mated. She was already powerful, and she'd barely dipped past the top of her well. Every time she takes another mate we all grow, not just her."

He stopped to let me think about what he was saying before he explained more.

"Draining her power compared to other supes... is like solar panels compared to AA batteries. We all run out of power eventually, but she keeps soaking it in.

"The same things that energize us will energize her, but there are six of us. We all feed off of different things. I'm not talking about food, Stone. I'm talking about walking across the dirt barefoot and replenishing my power.

"How fire makes you feel alive and ready to run a marathon. The same way shifting between forms never wears Briggs down. Think about that. Think about how strong she's gonna be, how strong we're all gonna be, when she's taken all of her mates.

"Think about being encased in ice and having your flames burn hotter than ever, not dying out. Look. See if your heat wilts this flower."

I summoned a small ball of orange and yellow flames into my palm and moved my hand closer to York. He didn't pull away as the fire danced across the space between us.

The flower didn't wilt. It was almost as if it were impervious to the flames licking down the petals and around the stem. York's skin didn't burn either.

I increased the heat, turning the fire light blue. *This should have melted the skin off him.* He never even flinched from it. The flower remained untouched.

Stone

I stared in wonder and disbelief as I sucked the flames back into my hand and touched the petals to see if they'd fall apart. They were hot, but that was it.

It felt like it had been sitting in front of a space heater, not surrounded by hellfire.

"Do you see what I'm saying now?" he quizzed me.

"Yeah," I acquiesced. "I see everything you're saying and everything you're not. This is a big deal, York. A huge fucking problem too, if the wrong people find out about this. You have to tell her."

I looked up at the streaks of sunlight as I thought about the ramifications of what he'd just told me.

Could we keep her safe? Would we be enough to keep her safe?

The threat was far from over. Sure, we took out a significant player in the power draining game. Other farms would arise, though.

More people would start hunting her when word spread about her being basically limitless.

Was she limitless?

We needed to test her. Push her to the point of exertion and see how far she could go.

We needed to ask Jack.

Palmer was right about training with each other. We could all take lessons from her on movement. She'd fought as effortlessly as water flowing downhill last night. Not one obstacle stood in her way.

We had to get stronger. For us and for her. We couldn't be the weaknesses that brought her down.

"I know what you're thinking, mate," York pointed out as my emotions teetered on a knife's edge.

My demon surged to the surface with barely contained anxiety over the mate we'd yet to claim.

"We won't be her downfall."

"You sound confident," I brooded.

"I am," he acknowledged simply. "You'll see. The Fates have spoken. The weapon is on our side. All we have to do is keep her out of the wrong hands and make sure she stays happy."

"Oh yeah," I laughed, "and just how do *you* plan to do that?"

"Well, I know this smooth talking Mage," he countered. "He's pretty good at working his magic. All I need to do is set the scene."

I could tell you now, I didn't want any part of his plan.

He was going to do to her what he used to do to Briggs.

Piss her off and let Palmer smooth things over so he could swoop in and apologize.

I didn't think it was gonna work on her, but watching him get his ass kicked should be fun.

Tomorrow.

"Tomorrow," I repeated aloud. "Do it tomorrow evening. She'll be in a great mood after Novak and I pay up on our debt."

I dreaded tomorrow for more than one reason. Watching them argue would suck. Knowing he'd planned it would be even worse. Wearing a skirt for two hours while I cleaned nothing? That was humiliating.

It'd be funny if it weren't me, though.

For once I was almost thankful that the druid didn't ask me what we owed, but that quickly turned to suspicion when I noticed his lopsided grin.

I made a decision right then and there. *No more bets with Sloane. I'd let the rest of them suffer.*

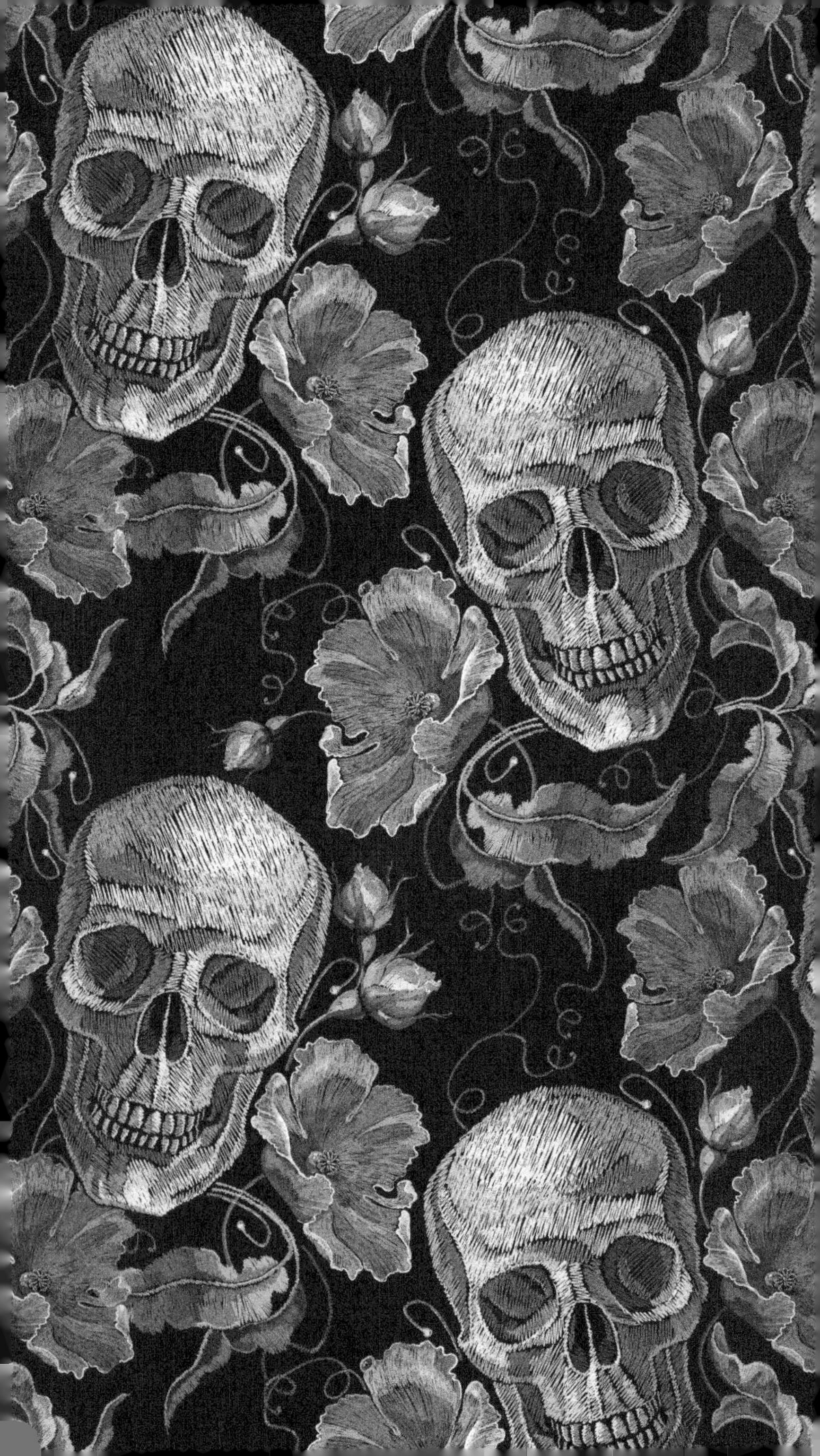

CHAPTER 24
Sloane

Monday, May 18th
Late Morning

I spent an hour or more talking to Levi about his new position and the changes I planned to make at CBP. He would be starting next week, and we were both excited about it.

Vaughn was freaking out because he didn't call into work and let them know he'd be out today, or late.

It was only 9 o'clock. He wasn't that late. It wasn't like I didn't know the boss or anything.

"Yeah, you should be worried. I heard your new boss is a dick," Briggs joked with Vaughn and me.

Novak whispered, "Magnet," gaining everyone's attention at once.

"What!?" he questioned us in a guiltless voice. "You were all thinking about it. I just said it aloud."

He turned to Vaughn with his brow raised skeptically. "You didn't notice when you were at the bar with her? Because I damn sure did."

Vaughn used his right hand to rub his left shoulder as he stared dumbfounded at the vampire. "Uhm, yeah, but calling her a dick seems a little rude, Novak."

"I didn't call her a dick," he gasped and slapped his hand to his beatless heart in mock horror before pointing to the shifter. "Briggs did. I just insisted she was dick magnet. And hello, look around us."

He spread his arms wide at the evidence of his words.

"I am right here," I admonished the group. "Are we going to work or not?"

Vaughn nodded his head vehemently as he walked around the table in my direction.

"Yes, I haven't missed a day since I started. This is the first day I've been late," he nervously admitted.

"I think your boss will understand," I stated dryly, "And since I fired everyone between your position and mine... I'm your boss. I won't write you up for being late today."

I winked at him, but he was *not* joking about his work ethic. *Noted.*

"I'll mist us home," he announced as he reached for me, placing his large, shimmering hand on my slim shoulder.

Sloane

"Right, you boys have fun on the ride home," I managed to squeeze out before we transformed into water.

We fled through the ice cold Void, landing in the foyer of *our* home.

That still felt weird to say.

Misting was a wild feeling. I could feel my body disintegrate into tiny particles, but I could also feel Vaughn's hand on my shoulder throughout the process.

There was a numbing chill that hit your bones before everything returned to the way it was before you misted.

When we landed, Vaughn looked down to his clothes. He moved to the doorway leading to the staircase as he spoke.

"I'll only be a minute. I need to change clothes."

Honestly, he looked fine. His dark jeans were work appropriate and his white t-shirt would be covered by his lab coat. He didn't need to dress formally to go to work.

I was starting to wonder if he just didn't want to be alone with me.

"You know, if you just told me what you wanted to wear, I could snap my fingers and pull clothes from your closet, right?" I informed him. I suppose he didn't know.

"If you could open your mind to me, then I could visualize it and that would be it. You'd be dressed and we could ride to work together. I'll even let you drive," I teased.

"You're sure that's a good idea? What if it causes problems? Are you ready to handle those kinds of accusations as soon as you take over? What happens when the factory floor falls apart because I'm not there to corral everyone?" His inquisition made me pause.

He definitely didn't want to be by himself with me.

I eased into his personal bubble and wrapped my arms around his neck.

"You need to relax," I murmured with my face inches from his. "There's no need to be worried about what anyone else says."

I pushed my body against his, and he moved his hands from his sides to my waist.

"I've handled worse allegations in a workplace, and none of those were true. The floor won't crumble without you there for an hour or two. Take a deep breath and calm down," I instructed him.

"That's really hard to do with you pressed against me like you are." His whisper soft breath caressed my cheek, making me arch into him more.

"Do you want me to move?" I inquired huskily.

My need amped up a notch with every second we touched. My skin felt like molten lava and his an arctic ocean.

As I waited for the steam to rise from our joined bodies, he mumbled, "We should go."

Those three words doused my core with icy resolve.

"Yeah, we should," I replied breathlessly. "But we're gonna finish this when we get to work," I told him.

I gazed at him with half-lidded eyes, hoping the look on my face would make my intentions clear. His eyes rolled back, and he groaned to himself before he dragged me in the general direction of the garage.

Sloane

Once inside, I strolled to the frame mounted on the wall that held the keys to a few different cars.

I had a problem. I was working on it.

I selected the set that belonged to my Audi R8 Coupe and tossed them to Vaughn.

He'd be the first person to drive this car other than me, but that's okay.

I wasn't in much of a driving mood. We both slid down in the smooth leather seats and the V10 roared to life.

Vaughn sped the entire way to work, and I couldn't decide if it was because he was enjoying my car or if he was just really that worried.

I tried to send a few emails, but typing correctly spelled words seemed impossible with him swerving between lanes.

When we pulled up to the gate, the security guard manning the entrance didn't even check our IDs.

Fucking ridiculous!

Security was getting revamped next week, so I'd post some hiring ads today. That was the least that I could do to help Levi with his new position.

So much for no firing sprees.

We parted ways at the elevators. Vaughn was going down, and I was going all the way up. This was the first time I'd be seeing my office as mine and not someone else's.

I knew I would be spending half the day unpacking things and setting it up. *That was the fun part, right?*

The corridor on the top floor was just as plain as the

rest of the structure. This place needed a cosmetic overhaul, but it could wait.

Not the top priority, Sloane.

As I strolled leisurely down the hall, I noticed a horrendous smell and an open door.

You've got to be kidding me!

Upon closer inspection, I realized the odor was coming from David Preston's office. That meant the weekend security never did their rounds on the top floor.

Fuck my life. I hated Mondays. Why did I even come in?

Knowing I wasn't being recorded by the shitty, outdated system that was in here last week, I decided to play it up a little bit. The new system that I had installed would catch every movement and breath.

I stopped walking and sniffed at the air, moving from door to door, before I got to the source. Rotting flesh had a way of making your stomach turn, and I found myself thankful that I hadn't eaten anything.

I paused at the door and knocked, making a play of leaning in to look through the crack Vaughn and Novak had left.

Raising a shaking hand to the handle, I pushed it open and screamed at the top of my lungs.

No one heard me. I was the only one up here.

I backed up until my ass hit the wall and fumbled for my cell phone as I slid down to the carpeted floor. I called 911 to report the murder, then called the security desk.

I had to call three times before anyone picked up. *They were all getting fired. Every last one of them.*

Sloane

The elevators pinged as they opened, and four guards stepped out. I stood and straightened my shirt.

My fucking crop top. I should have changed clothes, damn it.

"Don't go in there!" I had to shout at them as they bee-lined for the open office door. "What are you thinking?"

They all stopped as they noticed me. The guy who thought he was in charge stepped up. "We need to check the area out."

I did *not* like his tone. He clearly didn't know who I was.

"No, you don't," I snapped. "I've already called the police. What you need to do is have someone stand guard so no one can enter until they get here.

"I want one person by the door and one at the elevator. Do not touch that door *or* anything near it. The rest of you can come downstairs with me and wait for the cops to get here.

"They'll want statements from the guards who checked off on the patrol log showing they made their rounds this morning. We'll need to call in the guys that worked this weekend as well."

The man standing in front of me swallowed hard as his face paled.

"Of course," he affirmed, sounding both polite and disrespectful in those two words.

Or maybe I was just accustomed to being addressed properly.

I pointed to the three guys behind him. "You two take

up posts. You call the guards in from the weekend shift." I turned my glare to the main guy.

"You're coming with me," I bit out, clenching my fists at my sides as I sped to the elevator.

The cops showed up in heaps, parking all over the sidewalk in front of the lobby doors and filling the visitor parking spaces. They swarmed the top floor, using the empty offices to interview the guards and myself.

I signed my statement and gave them access to the security room so they could review the new camera feeds and old footage from Friday before the upgrades occurred.

Then, I told them that I had a meeting with an employee. I excused myself to my office after giving the officers a description of Vaughn, so they wouldn't stop him.

I spent twenty minutes picking up books off the floor and stacking them neatly on the built-in shelves before there was a knock at the door.

Vaughn came in before I could say anything. I set a handful of books down and leaned against my desk as I told him everything that had happened in the last two hours.

He sat in the chair across from me, listening intently while pressing the fingers of his right hand to his forehead.

"Why did you call me up here?" he inquired, confused. "There's nothing I can do."

I smirked at him and crossed the distance in two steps, plopping down sideways in his lap. "I seem to

Sloane

remember telling you this morning that I was going to finish what I started. Have you already forgotten?"

He repositioned me across his lap and tugged at the ends of my loose hair.

"Now?" He looked doubtful. "Are you serious?" His voice rose a little when I ran my hand down his chest.

"Shhhh, there are cops crawling all over the place." I grinned at him and started kissing down his neck.

"Sloane," he pleaded, the sexy kind of whine tinging his low voice.

"Ms. King," I corrected with my lips against his skin. "We *are* still at work."

He groaned deep in his chest before replying, "Ms. King. This is highly inappropriate behavior for the workplace." His face betrayed every one of his words.

"Are you telling me no?" I purred in his ear and his cock swelled beneath me. "Or are you telling me you can't be quiet?"

"That's not what I'm saying." His rebuttal was husky and laden with need.

"Mmm," I hummed my approval. "So you'll have no problem being obedient then." I spoke more to myself than him, but he nodded his head, anyway.

"Good." I got off his lap and stood by my desk. "Stand up and remove your clothes, Fae," I demanded.

He closed his eyes and leaned his head back, but did as I asked. When he was fully naked in the middle of my office, I circled around him in appraisal.

His naked body was glorious. His pale skin had a

shimmer to it that looked like fine glitter had melted into his flesh.

The royal blue tattoo across his back stretched from his broad shoulders to the top of his butt and hugged his obliques.

I could get lost in the intricate design. It was similar to a mandala but held symbols I'd never seen before.

I ran the nail of my index finger up between his shoulder blades and over his clavicle, causing him to shiver.

"Lie on my desk," I ordered him in a hushed tone.

When he was comfortable, I took my crop top off and covered his eyes, tucking the edges under his head so it wouldn't fall off.

"Don't move. Do you understand?"

I sucked his ear lobe between my teeth and he moaned out a soft "yes."

I slapped the inside of his left thigh as a reprimand.

"Yes, Mistress," I corrected him again as I rubbed the handprint it'd left.

His cock stood proud and his hands gripped the sides of my desk as his husky reply flitted through the air.

I moved over his body, alternating between my fingertips, nails, teeth, and lips.

When the first glistening bead of precum was visible, I sucked him into my mouth with a slow bob of my head. There was an audible pop when I pulled back to continue my sweet torment.

"*Fuck*," he whispered under his breath, so I slapped his right thigh, leaving a matching handprint.

"Shhhhh, or I'll have to find some other way to keep you quiet," I threatened, and he groaned loudly.

"Oh, you like that idea, do you? Let's see how loud you get when your mouth is busy."

I took my tights off and straddled his hips, sliding my soaked pussy up his chiseled torso. When I reached the base of his neck, I lifted up and placed my knees on either side of his head, and I sat on his face.

"Make me cum, Fae," I commanded him.

His hands darted up to anchor me down. His tongue was as soft as crushed velvet. It swept from my entrance to my clit, and his moan vibrated through my core.

He put his bare feet on my desktop, and I leaned my back against his knees to give him better access.

He did not disappoint.

His hands gripped my hips harder and his touch grew cold. His tongue felt like fire against my sensitive nerves while his breath was as icy as his fingers.

His hand snaked under my thigh, and he sunk a thick, frozen finger inside me before sucking hard on my clit. That icicle of a digit was my undoing.

I shook above him, covering my mouth with my hand as he sped up and prolonged my orgasm. When I couldn't take anymore, I shoved his head back and slid down his body, sinking slowly onto his wide girth.

He was so large that it took me a few moments to adjust to his size. Slow strokes stretched my walls, and I eventually turned my body around to ride him in reverse.

He sat up and twisted so his feet touched the ground.

My back pressed fully to his chest as his arms caged the front of my body in.

He pinched my nipples while he fondled my breasts, causing me to moan before I bit my lips closed. He thrust up to meet my downward motions in rough succession.

I mentally whispered that fucking birth control spell before I lost my godsdamn mind.

He nipped my shoulder, and I pulled his hand up to cover my mouth. The orgasm building within me would have me screaming his name.

I didn't want anyone barging through the door right now.

I fell into an ocean of pleasure. My walls contracted tightly around him, bringing my movement to a halt and making me shout around his hand.

He thrust faster in pursuit of his own release, and when he found it, he pressed his mouth against my neck. His seductive groan nearly tipped me over the edge again.

"Fuck," he repeated as he leaned his forehead on my back.

I straightened my legs out and slipped off him. Planting my bare ass on the desktop beside him, I put my weight on my elbows as I stared blurry-eyed at the ceiling.

"Fuck," I agreed breathlessly.

When my panting evened out to regular breaths, I hopped off my desk in search of our clothes. *And something to clean up with.*

Sloane

My cell phone chimed and Vaughn picked it up off the floor. *It was a text from Papi, but it could wait.*

We both got dressed, and when he was finished, he sat back down in the chair, his chest showing that he was still trying to catch his breath.

I eased back in his lap, running my fingers through his dark hair and kissing him gently, intent on keeping it simple. Vaughn pulled me closer, deepening the kiss.

After a few minutes of making out like teenagers in the janitor's closet at school, he broke the kiss. He grinned at me and stood, hooking his arms under me.

"Let's go get some lunch," he urged.

"Only if it involves going home afterwards." I winked at him, feeling insatiable.

"I'm sure my boss won't mind." His nearly English accent crept back in, and he chuckled to himself.

VAUGHN

I led Sloane out of the building and to her car, opening the passenger door for her to get in. She hadn't eaten anything since Saturday, so I was taking her to get some food.

Then home. Fuck everything at work. *It could wait.*

The ride into town had given me time to think about the last few days. *It had gone by so fast.* But in a good way.

Four days had felt like a couple hours. *It reminded me of that time I took the Fae hallucinogens that they love so much in the Summer Realm. Six days went by like six hours.*

That was a bad experience, though. This had been...

What was the word I was looking for? Crazy. Mesmerizing. Fantastic. Scary. *I wasn't sure.* It'd been the proper kind of mindfuck.

With every minute of time I spent with Sloane, I felt myself being pulled to her. The force felt like gravity. *It was natural.*

I could picture a future with her, and that part did scare me. I didn't know if she was ready to visit the Winter Kingdom.

I was not ready to go back and deal with Mummy Dearest.

When we sealed our bond, we'd have to visit. The Fae had traditions to uphold when royalty took a partner. It must be recognized by an elder of the temple, and we would have to be marked.

She'd bear a piece of my symbol, and if she were Fae, I could choose to bear hers. I would in a heartbeat,

Sloane

but since she wasn't, I didn't know how that would work.

It wouldn't stop me from sealing this bond, though.

Seeing her in action when we went to rescue York showed me her devotion and strength. I had no doubts that if my mother sent for me, then Sloane would find a way to cross the realms, or tear them down.

It was what I'd always wanted, and it was why I'd never been in a lasting relationship with anyone.

The moment my family thought that I was seeing someone, they'd start sending threats. My life. Her life. The rest of her mates, my friends. My mother would threaten us all.

I don't think Sloane would take kindly to that.

Sloane may be exactly what the Winter Kingdom needed. We could overthrow my mother. I could relinquish my claim to the throne to one of my sisters. Stay on Earth with her and the guys.

It sounded like a fairytale, but I knew with time it could be true.

I wouldn't let her go. I refused to bow down to my mother again.

At the first sign of another fae snooping around, I'd tell her everything. I couldn't keep my past hidden from her.

She needed to know why I ran, how my father was captured, the danger that came with being my mate. I couldn't keep her in the dark.

Just a little bit longer. I wanted to enjoy our time before I brought another fight to her doorstep.

It would help if the others could get stronger too.

I wondered what the guys thought about Sloane. *Did they feel the same way I did?*

I really needed to talk to Novak, but I knew how he felt. I could see it in his face this morning. Whatever happened last night, after we'd left, didn't bother him at all.

Quite the opposite, actually. That maniac was falling faster than all of us.

But I wasn't that far behind him.

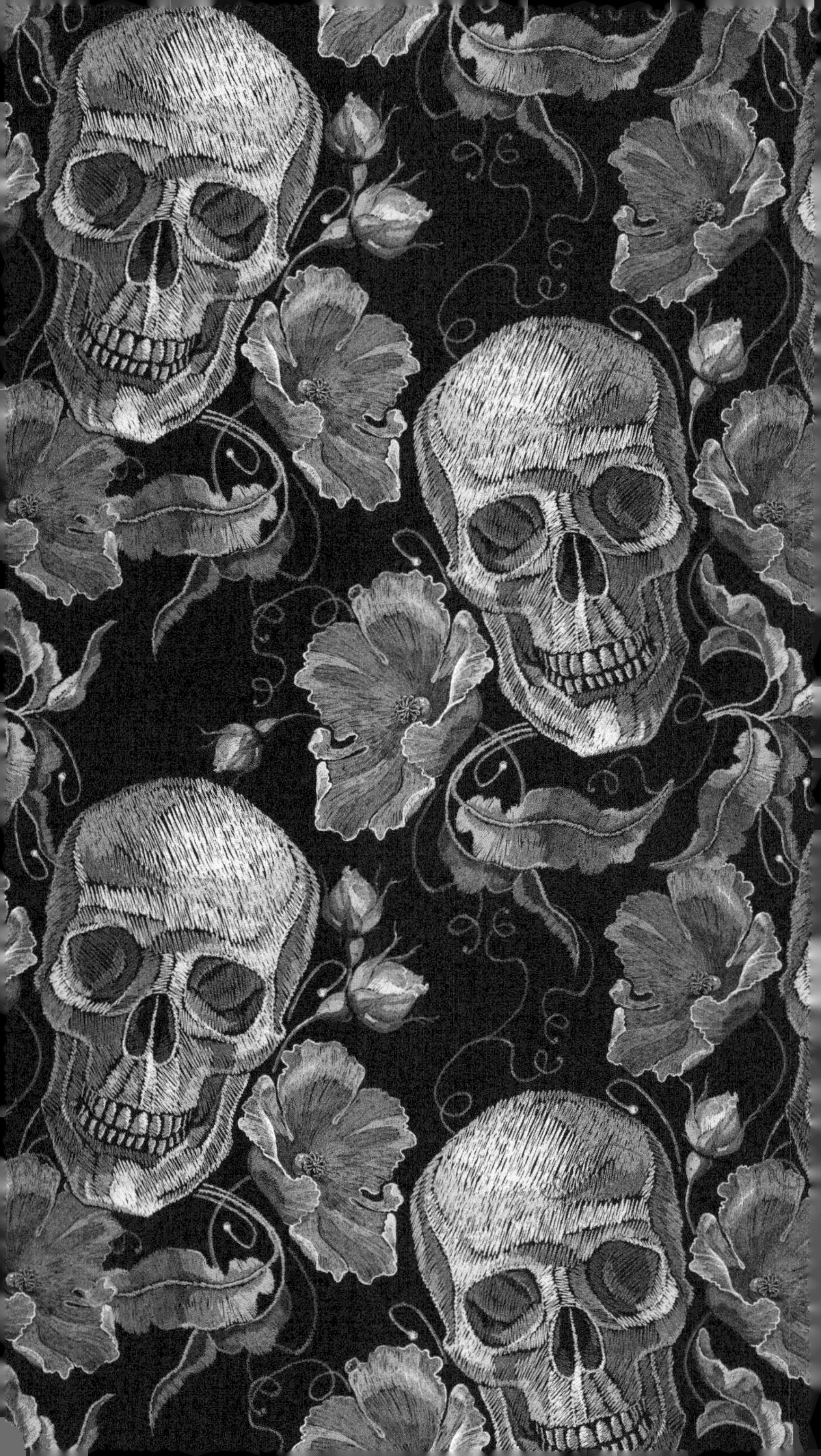

CHAPTER 25
York

Monday, May 18th
Late Morning

After Sloane and Vaughn misted out, Palmer worked hard to shrink the two hellhounds' sizes so we could all fit comfortably in the rental van the guys drove here in.

They loaded the bags as Levi and I climbed in the third row and Cronus' soot-colored body snuggled up to my side with his head in my lap.

Atlas clumsily clawed his way into the middle seat, with a boost from Palmer, and circled around the center of the bench to find the right position to sleep in.

Briggs and Palmer sat on either side of the drowsy,

fawn English Mastiff puppy. It was the first time I had seen them as anything other than gigantic, power-wielding versions of dogs.

They really could pass as ordinary dogs right now.

Novak shut the driver side door and turned the vehicle westbound down the rocky drive.

Six hours and I'd be home.

Sloane may be ignoring me, but that modern, monolithic mansion was still home to me. I wondered how much it had changed in the two years I'd been gone.

She'd just moved in a few months before we'd started dating. The place was barren, and any noise seemed to echo through the structure.

I spent the last year with her living there part time, bouncing back to the house I shared with the guys once or twice a week.

I was sure she had thrown all my stuff out, not that it mattered. It was all replaceable. I left Stone with the task of storing my important possessions.

He'd never let me down.

I could buy new clothing. My truck, on the other hand, couldn't be replaced. That '76 Ford Bronco was the first thing I'd purchased when I'd finally escaped the camp that very first time.

I'd put blood, sweat, and even a few tears into making her run. The matte paint job cost me more than the actual truck. That hunk of metal kept me busy and gave me something to focus my energy on instead of dwelling on the past.

She was sentimental.

I had few other things to my name that were irreplaceable. I could name them on one hand.

My truck. The handmade leather box filled with my Druid history. Sloane.

That was it. That list meant everything to me. *From least important to most.*

Living without Sloane in my life was worse than anything else that I went through.

I didn't know how to fix this yet, but the idea of picking a fight to make her confront me had been rolling around my brain for hours. I knew it wasn't right. I knew I should give her some time.

I was selfish, though. I needed her.

I didn't want to wait days, or weeks, for her to come around and talk about her feelings.

I would rather her scream at me and get this over with so we could work on fixing what I broke by not telling her the truth.

I wouldn't lose her. I knew that. It was irrational of me to think that she'd walk away. Before I was taken, I feared how deeply she loved, how protective she was, how consumed I was with her.

Now?

I feared losing her and not being by her side. My life without Sloane King in it was no life at all, regardless of my circumstances.

Without her, my heart wouldn't beat. The throne that awaited me would be nothing but a burden, a heavy weight on my shoulders that I was too weak to carry alone.

I looked at Atlas and thought of his namesake.

Sloane was my strength.

With her, I could endure the weight of the world in my hands. Just seeing her face woke the long destroyed resolve that I'd always held so near.

I knew I had to put the work in. She was mine once, and though I'd have to share her this time around, I refused to lose her.

I would do whatever it took to always be with her.

I could start with opening our mate bond back up. Maybe then she would be able to feel my determination to mend the fragile heart I knew I'd broken.

With my path chosen, my purpose was clear. I'd have to talk to Palmer about what I had in mind.

I thought it would work, but the other guys wouldn't like it.

They wouldn't help me with my idiotic idea, but they wouldn't stand in my way either. I scanned my eyes from face to face, happy to be with my friends again.

I spotted Stone in the passenger seat staring out the window, showing that he was deep in thought.

I'd bet that everything that was running through his mind right now revolved around Sloane too.

Stone

My demon was taking a life of his own around Sloane, urging me to take her as my mate and stop waiting.

This bonding business was tricky.

I didn't want to jump into it just days after I'd met her. I wanted to know her, her likes and dislikes, all the faces she made, the goals she hadn't reached yet.

I also knew that holding my demon at bay was getting really fucking hard. Especially after last night.

One would think such murderous tendencies in a mate would be frowned upon, but not to a demon.

Everything about her drew me in, like a moth to a flame.

I'd never been the moth before.

I wanted to enjoy my wings before I flew too close. The heat of that flame was enticing, though.

I didn't notice how cold I'd been until I thought about stepping away. The idea of moving farther, not closer, made me feel a physical chill.

She was more than any of us deserved, yet here she was. She held a strength that each of us lacked.

We all had something to offer in return. I couldn't be the things that the other guys would be for her, and I saw now that that was okay.

I could be her quiet place. The person who understood her without a single word. I could stand by her side and be the other half of the Devil Spawn that the Underworld needed.

I wasn't the kind of demon who would want to own and possess her.

I take that back. The possession part sounded like fun.

It was only a matter of time before my demon got a voice of his own. Then I wouldn't be arguing with just myself.

He wanted her. The moment her demon form began to pierce her human flesh, I knew that was it for me.

I spent the entire time I was in that cell with her struggling to remain in control.

Her ivory horns were magnificent. The way her tail looked made my imagination ramp up with thoughts of what her full form would be.

She was no ordinary succubus, I knew that.

I'd never seen another demon with a tail made of hellfire and bone, nor had I seen one command hellhounds. No other demon had ever made me lose my grip like she did.

It may be the bond hurtling my emotions through fast forward, but the more I learned about her, the deeper I fell.

I couldn't be the only one.

I didn't have the slightest clue how they were faring. I

wondered if the others were fighting against her as hard as Briggs was.

I didn't blame him. He fell in love quicker than any of us.

Soon he'd be so smitten that he'd follow her around like a pup with hearts in his eyes.

I peeked behind Novak to see if Briggs was asleep. He had his head leaned against the window and hellhound feet in his lap. He liked the monsters, even if he tried not to, just like Sloane.

His tension free face spoke volumes about his state of mind.

If I had to guess, I'd say that he'd been thinking of our mate too.

Briggs

I was gonna fall in love with her, godsdamnit. No matter how hard I tried to fight this mating shit, it was going to happen.

My wolf had chosen her the first time he'd scented her aroma floating across her yard. She hadn't even spoken yet, and I already knew.

I was fucked, plain and simple.

It would've been easier to hold off the itch to mate with her if she hadn't beaten me in an alpha challenge.

Now he was ready, but I couldn't wrap my head around it so fast.

I hated that I missed her fighting last night. I was also thrilled that I did. I wouldn't have been able to hold back the wolf's demand while not in my skin. He would've taken her right then and there.

Dead bodies littering the ground or not. Neither of us gave two fucks about an audience, living or dead.

If I could just tighten my leash on him until the full moon. *Two weeks, that was all I needed.*

Then we could make the smartest move, and that would bring both of our wolves to full power. I didn't even know what it would do to our power in our human skins.

That's something I'd have to research on my own. *If I ever got time to do it.*

I wasn't sure I was ready to jump into a new relationship after the way my last relationship ended. It'd been a couple months, but the wounds she'd inflicted were deep.

I didn't want to jump into this as a broken male. I didn't know how long it would take to heal from the things that bitch had put me through.

The cheating and verbal abuse barely skimmed the surface of her controlling behavior. If it hadn't been for the guys... I might still be with her.

Thinking about her now made a shudder ripple through my chest. How would Sloane handle the retelling of my past?

Probably not well.

I hoped real fucking hard that she never met any of my exes, the last especially.

I needed to get back in my rhythm. *Find my happy place again.*

The longer I spent with Sloane, the more I realized that she could easily become part of that place for me. It terrified and ignited me all at once.

How much of this was the mate bond and how much of it was my own feelings, though?

I fell in love so fast it was like jumping out of a plane. There was no parachute for me, though. When I reached the end of my free-fall, it always got nasty.

I didn't want that this time.

Fuck. I needed to get out of my head.

I'd wound myself so tight that I didn't know how to untwist the thoughts anymore. I needed to be in a kitchen somewhere. *Anywhere.*

Creating something delicious would occupy my mind and keep me busy. Taking care of everyone had always brought me solace.

Being a guardian. Providing safety.

Those were the things my wolf and I both needed. Palmer and I were similar on that front. He was a shoulder to lean on and filled with wise advice that he gave freely.

What kind of words of wisdom would Palmer offer us all about our mate right now?

Palmer

This had been the most intense three days of my life. It felt like weeks had passed us by, not mere days.

I'd spent two weeks in Belfast with my family and that had strung on forever. Every day I'd been ready to come home. The hours had ticked by agonizingly slow. All that time bled together, making me miserable.

This weekend had been different.

I still couldn't believe all the things that had

happened so quickly. Wednesday night I'd had an odd niggling that had made me want to speed home.

I'd booked the first available flight, kissed my ma on the cheek, and went to the airport three hours early so I wouldn't be late.

Here we were on Monday morning, and everything had changed.

I still couldn't figure out why we'd all felt that same need to be home. I hadn't heard from Briggs in a month, but he'd been in the apartment when I'd walked in.

Novak had flown back from spending time with his sister in France, arriving a couple hours after I did.

Stone had left a work convention in California. We'd met in the lobby of our building and came in together.

We all got home within hours of each other on Friday night. Then Vaughn had come in on Saturday morning to tell us he'd met his mate.

Our mate.

I didn't know what drew us in. We'd all had the same urge, but had felt it at different times. I wondered when we would've had the feeling if we'd been home.

Were the Fates at work, or was it a coincidence?

For the first time in a long while, I hadn't pieced the puzzle together as efficiently as Novak had. Seeing Sloane on Saturday morning was like a gust of wind knocking me off kilter.

I'd never wanted something so badly in my life.

It was an animalistic response that I wasn't used to. She made power crackle at my fingertips. Electricity flowed through my veins when she was near.

This trip home was giving me enough space to think, but I already missed her. It was an insane thought.

I'd just met her.

There was no doubt, though. This was it for me. *She was it.* I knew Saturday. *I definitely knew today.*

My feelings hadn't changed despite the things I'd seen and done. She wasn't who I pictured myself with. *She was better.*

My imagination had really let me down. The real thing happened to be so much more. *In every way.* It was hard to wrap my head around how perfectly we all fit with her.

She offered us all the things we needed. Each of us had qualities the others didn't. As a unit we covered all the bases, and then some.

It was more than that, though. *It was more than power.*

The aspects of a relationship that I sought weren't the same as what the other guys wanted, yet somehow she excelled in all of it.

I'd always looked for intelligence first and foremost, but also someone I could contemplate the universe with. I needed a mental equal, and I got one.

I enjoyed bedroom activities that some would frown on. She seemed enraptured by the prospects. *I was enthralled by her mind games.*

The thought of having her presence in my head, or mine in hers, made me ecstatic. I wanted our bond to be sealed at an organic pace, but I sincerely hoped that a mental connection flowed through us sooner.

My thoughts were in a twisted web now, but I knew as soon as I saw her this evening they'd untangle, and my body would become a traitorous bastard once again.

One smile or wink and my heart would beat wildly out of control for her. Laughter and a sassy remark would have my intelligence bested and my tongue malfunctioning.

My coherent thoughts would eventually turn back into a garbled mess that made it hard to communicate how this whole situation made me feel. It was hard to be consistent when she was so predictably unpredictable.

We were all thinking about it. I knew we were. Novak would be the only one with the balls to say it aloud, though.

I'd been driving this van for hours now, listening to all the guys' thoughts. They didn't realize that they had all circled around to the same conclusion.

Honestly, when would they learn the art of communication?

They were giving me a headache. We all knew we weren't going anywhere. It took me seconds to figure that out.

Mate with someone whose mind I couldn't read? Yes, please.

She was literally a gift from the Devil himself.

Maybe I was rushing into this, but I didn't want to wait around either. I would seal our mate bond today as long as she was ready.

I told Vaughn on Saturday—before we'd even started talking about her—that I was ready to meet my mate.

I'd meant it too.

I was done with the bullshit. I wanted no part in one-night stands or meaningless flings anymore.

Sloane was the best of both worlds for me. I could spend days with her and not tire of her company. When I wanted to be alone, she had other mates to keep her attention.

The guys were used to my occasional isolation, but I'd never want it to make her feel unwanted by me. I felt like that wouldn't be an issue now.

I'd never really dated because that was always a problem.

You went two days without being with your girlfriend

every waking second, and suddenly she thought you were cheating.

That wasn't the kind of drama I wanted in my life.

Sloane didn't strike me as the insecure type of woman. Her confidence was radiant and contagious. She made me want to be better, stronger, not just for her but for myself.

Her afflictions for blood and gore were a huge turn on for me.

I was a vampire. Of course it was. No surprise there.

The surprise came with how much chaos and devastation she'd caused in such a short amount of time. If my heart could beat, it would've sprung from my chest. My enthusiasm was palpable.

Watching her fight was one of the most tantalizing things I'd ever witnessed.

I'd wanted to fuck her in the middle of it all. Knowing she blew Palmer after he killed a couple males had had me hard as a rock for half the battle.

Seeing her wink at me while she'd fixed her hair afterwards? That had made my mind go feral with need. I'd wanted to watch, or join. Either would've worked, but we'd had shit to do.

Now that all that was over, the only thing left to do was pay up on the debt Stone and I owed her after she'd beaten us.

I still couldn't believe I agreed to that.

I knew it could've been worse than wearing a dress, but it could've been way more fun too.

It wouldn't matter.

Hearing York's thoughts told me exactly what was going to happen tonight. I'd be waiting for her when she was ready to blow off some steam.

Maybe Stone would join us so we could pick up where we left off yesterday morning.

My thoughts seemed to be more settled than the rest of my friends'. They all wanted her too, but none seemed ready to take the plunge.

I was already working my way in. I wouldn't be changing my mind. *I was ready.*

There was nothing I could learn about her that would make me not want to spend eternity with her. *I was hers already.* Now I just needed to make her mine.

Before my thoughts did that 360 thing like the rest of the guys', I decided it was time to speak up and call them all on their bullshit.

Too bad Vaughn wasn't here. I bet his thoughts were fucked up too.

"You guys know you're all thinking the same thing, right?"

"You're all thinking about pizza, too?" Levi's pained inquiry made me chuckle. "Or tacos? I can't decide which one I've missed more."

"Tacos," York supplied. "I've missed tacos more than pizza."

"Get your mind out of the gutter, York. That's not what he was talking about, and you know it. You weren't thinking about food. None of you were, not even Levi, until about ten minutes ago."

I knew none of them wanted to bring it up, but all of them needed to talk about it to work it out.

"I cut the radio off almost an hour ago and no one noticed. You guys are all so mindfucked right now that you keep repeating the same thoughts over and over. It's giving me a headache," I admonished them.

"Why are you thinking about Sloane?" Briggs turned in his seat to get a better look at Levi, who was sitting behind Palmer.

"Why wouldn't I be thinking about her?" he cautiously asked. "She just offered me a job and led you guys into a hive of aggressive supes to rescue York, who in turn rescued me. Should I not be thankful?"

"Leave him alone, Briggs," I chastised him. "At the rate you're going, she'll mate with Levi before she seals the bond with you."

"That's not funny," he growled out.

Stone turned to smirk at him. "It kind of is."

"I don't even know what mating is." Levi threw his hands in the air. "Is that like dating or something? Please tell me I didn't agree to elope with her. She's hot, but I don't know her well enough to get married."

The edge to his voice betrayed his frantic need for an explanation. He was genuinely freaking out.

I was loving it. Briggs was not.

"Calm down," York scolded him. "No one is getting married. You didn't agree to anything of the sort."

He rolled his eyes and propped his head up on his hand, making it appear like he was trying to go to sleep.

He shut his lids, and before anyone could speak again I called, "I hope your plan doesn't backfire."

"It won't," he responded quietly without opening his eyes.

"What plan is this?" Palmer gave him a sidelong glance before turning his attention to the dreaming puppy between him and Briggs.

York sighed and popped his right eye open to peer at Palmer. "You'll see later," was all he said as he closed his eye again and tried to ignore us.

"Yer draggin' me inta the middle of it, aren't ya?" Palmer pointed out with clear exasperation.

York didn't reply immediately, and I thought maybe he had finally fallen asleep. After a minute or two he admitted, "Yeah. Sort of. If you're not interested, then I'm sure Novak would be delighted to step in."

"Fuck yes, but I don't think I'll be as good a fit as Palmer would be." I cut my eyes to Palmer in the rear-view mirror. "At least you've got a solid backup plan. Though, if Palmer is going to do what Palmer does best, then I definitely want to watch."

"I honestly forgot how weird you can be." A faint smile touched York's lips at his admission.

"Oh, how you wound me," I dramatically declared, wiping fake tears from my eyes. "You've got a millennia to figure out how to share, Druid. I won't push you too hard too soon."

I stayed quiet after that. We only had two more hours of driving before reaching Nashville.

I'd drop York, Levi, and Palmer off at the first stop.

Then, Briggs, Stone, and I would park the van and stroll around downtown for a couple blocks before Franklin picked us up.

I liked the idea of going back to Sloane's house. *I guess eventually we'd all live there semi-permanently.*

Some down time sounded refreshing too. I wanted to spend the night with her gazing at the stars, swimming, or both. Watching a movie would be okay as well.

Sex sounded like an even better option. We could probably fit it all in since neither of us slept.

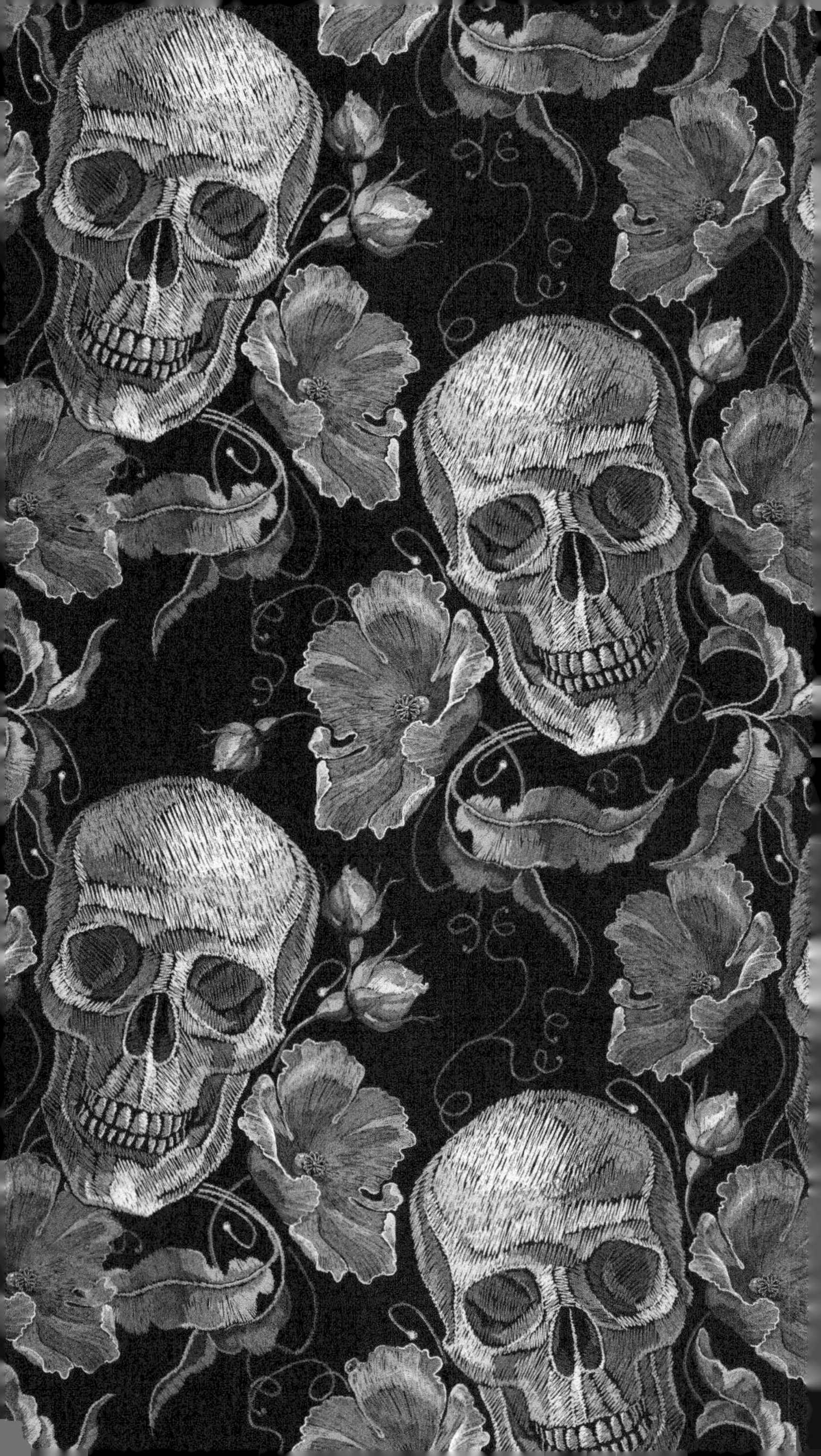

CHAPTER 26

Sloane

Monday, May 18th
Late Evening

I t was late in the evening when several cars started to enter through the wrought-iron gates of my estate.

Garage doors opened one at a time, and vehicles I had never seen before filled the once empty building. Males of all shapes and sizes exited through the side door, looking like my own personal lineup of GQ models waiting to be interviewed.

Shirts on. Too bad.

Briggs ran a hand through his untamable hair while he shoved Novak with the other.

Palmer strutted with his hands in his pockets like he was on a runway, his rusty auburn hair shining in the sun with a metallic sheen.

Levi appeared a little ragged as he stood in the middle of the group, gawking at my home.

Stone walked beside York with his usual blank expression. The latter was looking around with wide eyes as he surveyed the changes the landscape had gone through since he'd last seen it.

Vaughn waited patiently by the front door, welcoming them home by questioning their tardiness.

The guys were being Chatty Cathys as they all loaded up in the kitchen, opening beers and rummaging in the pantry for snacks.

Typical guy shit.

Palmer and Vaughn laughed obnoxiously at something York was joking about as they turned to an embarrassed Levi with large shit-eating grins.

I almost wished I knew what they were saying, but not enough to leave my laptop. I peeled my eyes from the bay windows before they caught me staring.

I'd been trying to power through the monotonous tasks that I did every day, but it was getting more difficult to focus.

The barest hint of their words echoed through the kitchen and out into the yard where I *was* trying to spend a lovely, sunny afternoon laying in the grass doing dumb shit by myself.

Shit like answering repetitive questions in emails that I had already answered a hundred times, or talking to childish employees who said they needed to come in two hours late because they were getting their nails done.

I should've passed this task off to Simon.

I shut my laptop and rolled on my back to watch for images in the fluffy, white clouds.

Novak plopped down beside me and broke the content quietness that had formed around me when everyone left the kitchen. The top of his head touched my shoulder, and he looked at the clouds with the opposite angle to my view.

"Did you know your back door is missing?" he asked with a carefree ease that only he could manage.

"No. I hadn't noticed." The dry sarcasm in my voice was strong. "Do you think we can find it or is it lost forever?" I gasped and covered my mouth, pretending to be upset.

He rolled his head over to smirk at me. "I'm sure it's hanging around here somewhere."

"That was really corny." I smiled at him anyway. That was the kind of horrible dad joke Charles would make.

"Are you going to tell the guys what you found out last night?" His inquisitive tone had me looking away.

I needed to tell them, but it was all mixed up with everything that happened at work today.

Going to lunch with Vaughn relaxed my mind enough to feel stress-free for a few hours. We did a little costume shopping while we were out.

Now two little black dresses hung in Novak and Stone's closets. Feather dusters included.

The stress I had escaped from came rushing back in. It felt like a current pulling me under. Every time I surfaced and took a deep breath, the chilling reality had me sinking further into the abyss.

"I suppose I should, but I don't want to. The information we got only leads to more questions," I told him honestly.

"With all the dicks congregating in one room, we should be able to figure it out in no time." He sounded confident, but that wasn't what caught my attention.

"Does it come with a side of orgasms?" I fucking hoped it did. "Because if it's all pillow talk and no orgasms, then I'd like to kindly decline." I scrunched my face up in distaste.

"Orgasms can be negotiated," he teased. "Just depends on how well you can work the crowd."

"I'd give everyone in the room blowjobs to avoid this conversation," I bartered.

It was true, too.

Of course, none of this shit would simply stop by taking Kelvin out. Soon we'd be on the hunt for this Kadence bitch too.

Uhhhg. Life was complicated before I'd found out about this fucking drug. Now it was a godsdamn disaster.

"Tempting," he confirmed, "But no. We need to work this out, Trouble. We can have fun later," he promised. "I noticed I have this new bed to break in, and since we won't be getting any sleep..." he trailed off, leaving that sentence open for my imagination.

Sloane

Mother. Fucker. Why couldn't we get dirty now and pillow talk as a group later?

"Fine," I bit out. "Round all the dicks up and make me stare at them while I'm frustrated. Wonderful idea," I pouted.

Novak climbed to his feet, stretching like a cat who'd been lying in a sunny window all day, and held out his hand for me. When I placed my hand in his, he hoisted me up, tugging me in for a tender kiss that left me wanting more.

"Tell them what you know, and then we can hide away for the rest of the night."

"Okay," I groaned. "But I'll only go willingly under one condition," I flirted, my voice misleading him about what I wanted.

"Mmm," he mumbled in my ear, "And what's that?"

"You owe me a debt. It's time to pay up." I raised my eyebrows and cocked my hip to the left, sass on full blast.

"Are you fucking serious? Right now?" His shock was *ahhhmazing*.

The next two hours were going to be the best. *They had no idea how much thought I'd put into those costumes.*

"Yep." I nodded my head enthusiastically with a broad grin on my face. "There's an outfit hanging in your closet, and one in Stone's. I'll get the others and see you in the basement in fifteen."

I kissed his stunned face and sauntered off.

Twelve minutes later... We were all sitting in the

basement, arranged around the table so we could see the entrance.

I was so fucking thrilled about what was about to happen that I could *not* physically sit still.

My feet were bouncing. My fingers tapped the table in rapid succession. I'd pretty much gnawed a hole in my lip while trying not to smile to the point that my cheeks ached.

All the guys watched me as they waited for an answer to a question that hadn't been asked yet.

"You'll see in a minute," I assured them with more exuberance than they'd ever seen from me.

"I'm starting to worry." Briggs' hushed voice vibrated around the room, and Palmer nodded his head slowly in agreement.

"What's taking Stone and Novak so long?" Vaughn propped his chin in his right hand as he narrowed his eyes at me.

"That's not the right question, mate." York grinned at Vaughn. "You should be asking her what the stakes of that bet were that they lost. It's probably something ridiculously hilarious and utterly embarrassing."

"You are correct," I informed them in my best game show host voice.

The smile I'd been fighting broke free once again, cracking open the healing cut from chewing on my lower lip.

The sound of footsteps on the stairs drew everyone's attention away from me. We could hear Novak cussing obscenities on the other side of the door.

Sloane

I was so fucking happy right now.

"I fucking hate you so godsdamn bad right now for peer pressuring me into that bet." He sounded mortified, and I paused to wonder if this was a bad idea.

Nope. Great call, bitch. Pat yourself on the back.

"I didn't pressure you into anything. You didn't have to agree, but you did. Now, suck it up and pull your skirt down. I can see your dick." Stone's voice was playful as he reprimanded Novak. "I can't believe you didn't wear anything under that."

Novak gasped. "What's under your skirt?"

"Stop that!" Stone barked out, and the guys turned quizzical faces to me.

"Worth it," I whispered in a singsong voice. I bit my lips together to stop my smile from spreading as the doorknob twisted.

The door swung open dramatically, slamming into the concrete wall behind it. Stone and Novak were standing just outside the threshold, looking pissed.

So fucking worth it.

After a solid minute of silence, a symphony of laughter reverberated around the room. Novak leaned down to look at the bottom of his skirt and grimaced as he tugged on it.

"Could you have bought a shorter dress?" he asked, annoyed with the peep show he was giving us.

"She tried," Vaughn wheezed out. "You should be happy I was with her when she bought them."

Those cosplay maid outfits were the jam.

The black dress was poofy at the bottom due to the

attached petticoat. The white apron had ruffled edges and crisscrossed in the back before tying off in an oversized bow.

Stone stood in his dress and combat boots looking completely unaffected, twirling his duster between his fingers like a baton. The frilly little headband in his hair was what really set my giggling fit off.

Novak's was tied around his neck like some sort of choker. He pulled at it while tapping the toe of his boot on the floor in agitation.

"I really hope the information you got was good, otherwise I'm going to be livid." The vampire looked pointedly at me, and I shrugged as I struggled for a witty comeback.

"It's not," was all I could manage as the laughter in the room started up again.

He was there for half of my interrogation. He should know it was shit information.

After a few more minutes, we all tapered off. I wiped the tears from my eyes and battled the urge to chortle when the demon took his duster and swiped it across Novak's face.

That pissed him off, and he swung the handle end of the cleaning device at Stone. He skirted to the side away from the blow, chuckling lightly at the angry vampire.

"Okay, okay," Stone surrendered. "I'll stop fucking with you. Sloane, please start talking so everyone will stop looking at us like that." He pointed to Levi's open mouth.

"Right, so, I was able to compel Kelvin into giving me

a few answers. Mostly they just lead to more questions, but this is the gist."

I took a deep breath before plunging in head-first.

"The person who is behind this drug is male. He's a fae-mage hybrid. His mother is a summer fae, and he and Kelvin were half-brothers on his father's side.

"He didn't come to pick up the crystals, instead sending his half-sister, Kadence Moore, to retrieve them. He said they started testing the drug on vampires a couple weeks ago, but there hasn't been any confirmation on that yet. Simon is looking into it now. Their father's name is Alric Moore."

"How do you know this guy's mother was a summer fae?" Vaughn was befuddled as he glanced around the room.

"I can explain hybrids to you," Stone started as he ran feathers over the desk in the corner of the room.

Clearly he was taking his job seriously.

"When Sloane told us Kelvin was a vampire-mage hybrid, she stated it in that particular order for a reason. In the supernatural world, outside of the other realms, hybrids come in a variety of mixtures. The mother's species is always listed first and the father's second.

"So, when you have a vampire-mage, you know the mother was a vampire and the father was a mage. If the species were reversed, mage-vampire, then the mother would be a mage and the father would be a vampire." Stone finished with a shrug of his shoulder and continued dusting the surfaces around the room in his short dress.

"What does any of the other information mean to us?" Vaughn inquired.

"By having his Da's name we can look him up in the guild headquarter's archives, but we'll have ta travel *to* the guild headquarters ta do that." Palmer didn't look happy about the possibility of going to Belfast.

"Right, but we also have his sister's name," I reminded him. "And we know she's a part of this too. Before we look for Alric Moore, we need to find Kadence and put a stop to the shitstorm she's going to cause with the vampires."

It was a logical move. Baton Rouge was closer and easier to travel to. I needed to check up on the coven council as well, since my father wasn't back yet.

I needed to call Papi, too, and tell him everything that's gone on.

"That's a solid start. I already know a little about Kadence Moore, but you aren't going to like it." Novak stopped pretending to dust the computer monitors to face me fully.

It was hard to take them seriously in those outfits.

I smiled at him.

"Don't start." He pointed his duster at me, feathers first.

I covered my face with my hands to smother fresh giggles.

"Anyway, I think Kelvin was her twin brother, or that's what I heard. She's on the coven council. Has been for decades. She's anti-Sloane when it comes to

Nathaniel stepping down, so she'll definitely be an issue if that's where we're headed. She is a *crazy cunt*."

He emphasized the last sentence in a deeper voice than his usual smooth tone. I didn't like the thought of going in unprepared. That wasn't enough information about her.

"We'll have Samuel and Charles meet us in Baton Rouge. Jack and Grim, too. She won't be able to contest my position. I outrank her as coven heiress. If she wants the position, then she'll have to challenge me just like an alpha fight."

I felt comfortably secure in my ebony tower, I could admit that. She wouldn't win, though. *I refused to lose*.

"The rules are different, but the outcome will be the same. If she challenges me, then she'll die. If she's behind this fucking drug being leaked to vampires, then she'll stand trial, with me as her judge. If she's found guilty, then she'll die by my hands with the same audience."

I was indifferent about the outcome. If she was *anti-Sloane,* then she'd eventually be on the receiving end of my special brand of punishment, regardless of her affiliation with the epidemic.

"You sound pretty sure of yourself," Levi commented.

I shot him a fang-filled, lethal grin. "I might not be the villain, but I'm the antihero of this story, Levi. My kill list is a mile long. I've been trained to use more weapons than I can count. I *am* the biggest, baddest predator on the planet. I'm not even bragging about that - it's just a fact."

I retracted my fangs and stood. As I walked to the corner of the room to grab a laptop, I spoke softly. "If I seem sure of myself, it's because I am."

I looked pointedly at him. "I'm faster, stronger, and smarter than she is. I'm an impossible combination of supernatural strengths. I've been molded for these kinds of fights my entire life. The supernatural world works very differently than the human world around us. Right now, you're in a room full of future leaders."

I let that sink in as I opened the laptop. I wanted to keep track of all the information we'd gathered so I didn't lose any with the coming mess.

Palmer took it from me and began typing everything out. The shifter was deep in thought and hadn't said a word since before Stone and Novak had walked in.

"What are you thinking about, Briggs?"

"I'm thinking about this: Why did a summer fae breed with a species other than their own? How many offspring does this Alric guy have out there? Where should we start looking to find this mysterious hybrid male?

"Who could be behind the shifters that were introduced to the drug? A drug that needs a name, by the way." Briggs ticked his questions off his fingers until he was sitting with only his middle finger in the air. "And, what can we do from here?"

He had many good points, and he was right. Those were questions that needed answers.

I didn't have them, though.

"We'll begin by looking for Kadence Moore. It's the

easiest starting point. Finding out who gave the drugs to the shifters will be difficult, but we could follow that path next.

"There's no way to know for certain how many children Alric has sired. Some of them may not be registered. I've never heard of a summer fae mingling outside their race, much less with a different species.

"I have no idea how to find someone that I know next to nothing about. We can't do shit from here tonight." That summed up all that I knew about his questions.

I wasn't happy about the unknown, but I was glad that I didn't have to walk through it alone. It had taken me no time at all to grow attached to having these guys around, and that scared me.

Except York. I still wanted to throttle him into next week.

I knew that feeling would change soon, and we'd eventually fall back into the easy contentment that we had before.

I just wanted to be mad at him for a little longer.

It was going to take more than a few hours for me to look at him and not feel my chest being ripped open.

I understood why he didn't tell me what was going on. What I cannot comprehend is how he thought *that* was the best decision he could make.

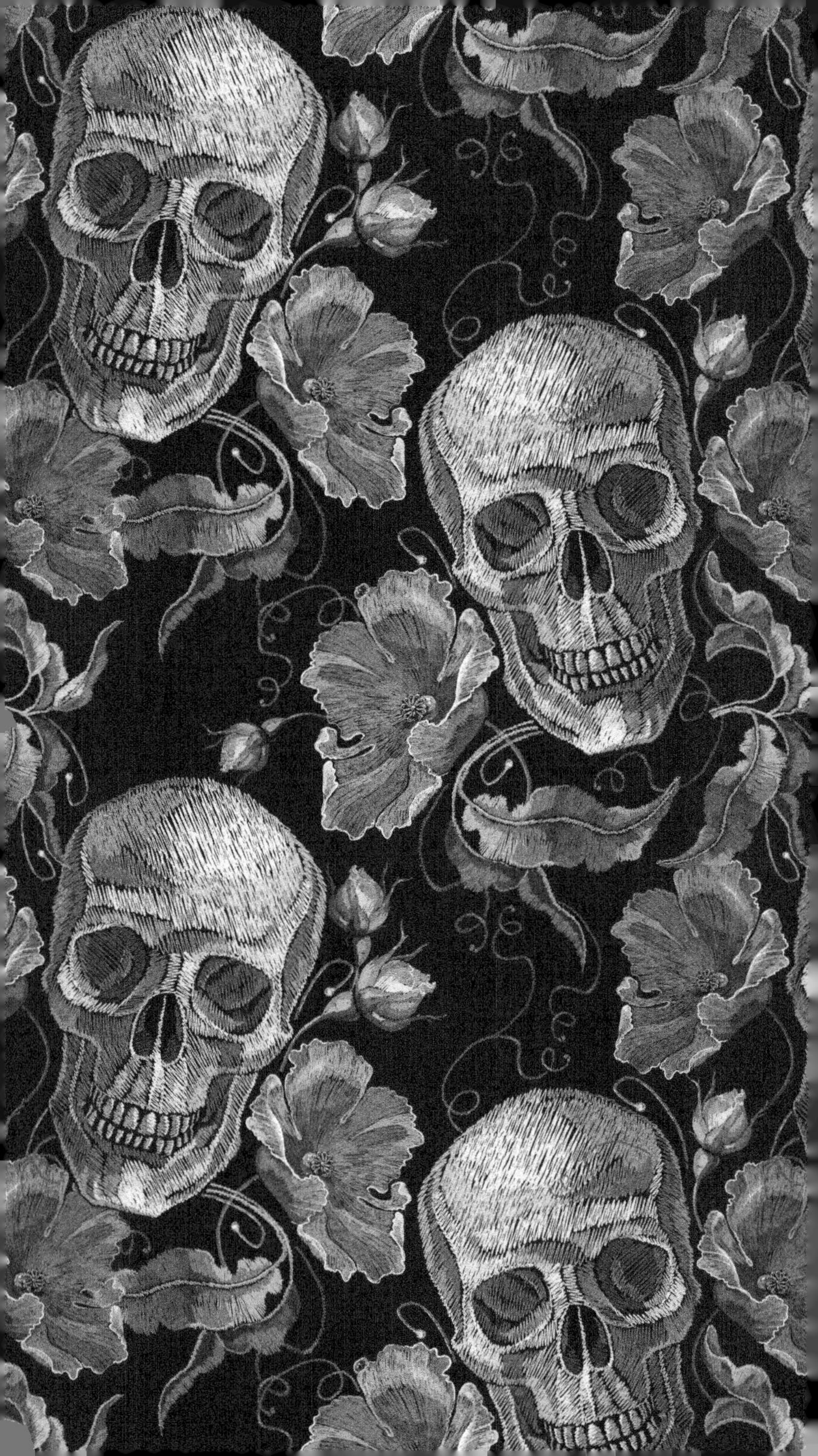

CHAPTER 27
Sloane

Monday, May 18th
Night

After I left the basement, I climbed the million stairs to get to the rooftop patio. The night sky was bright and there were more stars shining down on me than I could fathom.

I flattened myself out in a lounge chair and searched for constellations, doing the absolute most to keep my mind blank.

I didn't want to think about anything.

"I thought I'd find you up here, in the dark," York admitted from the doorway as he turned the outdoor lights on.

"I'm not ready to talk," I protested diligently, covering my face with my forearm. "Not even a little bit." It came out muffled, but I knew he heard me.

York huffed irritably and circled around my chair. "We need to talk," he persisted.

"No. We don't," I complained. "Not right now, please."

"Sloane," he pleaded with me.

"Don't *Sloane* me," I snapped. "Just. Don't."

"Sweetheart," the druid tried once more, his Australian accent thick in that one word.

"I swear, York Briar, if you don't stop now, I will push you over the roof's edge and not think twice about it," I warned him and stood to put more distance between us.

"You would, though," he mused. "You'd feel it, too, and then be mad at yourself for hurting me."

He approached me with long strides, stopping three steps away.

"Don't," I repeated, holding my hands up and begging him with my eyes to walk away.

"Sloane, we *need* to talk about this. You can't keep ignoring me," he chided.

"It's only been a few hours, York. Try again in a couple days," I informed him with narrowed eyes. Rage seeped into my pores as he continued to push me.

"Look, I'm sorry, okay?" He tossed the insincere apology out like it should mean something. "I get that I hurt you. I know you're angry with me." His nostrils flared with his admission.

Sloane

"Angry with you?" I spat out. "No, I'm fucking incensed."

My voice rose an octave, and I took a deep breath to calm myself.

"If you would've been honest with me from the beginning, then things would have been so very fucking different," I surmised.

"But, no. You lied to me, York. Not just once or twice. The whole godsdamn time. When were you going to tell me?"

I dared him to answer with a raised brow.

"Or, were you just hoping I'd notice? I overheard the shit you said to Stone. You've forgotten how much I can hear when I want to, or maybe you didn't."

He closed his eyes, and I kept going.

"When did we seal the bond? Why didn't you mention it when you noticed?"

"I thought you would feel it too. I didn't realize how much power you had until I felt it through the bond," he grumbled.

"So, you what? Thought you'd be mad at me for not knowing that I had earth magic coursing through me? With all the magic I have already? You only feel a tiny portion of it, York," I informed him.

"I have every right to be "angry" with you right now." I air quoted.

I took a ragged inhale as I prepared to let all my frustration out.

"If you hadn't had my memories locked away the first

day we met, then I would've finished my job. We both could have walked out of there. Together.

"Those hidden memories didn't just keep me from stopping all this shit sooner, they kept me from remembering what that bond felt like. Every time I thought about it too hard, my mind would clamp down."

I squeezed my hand shut in a tight fist to make my point a little more clear for him. I whispered the following words with more emotion than I wanted to show.

"The Fae King didn't just lock those memories down, York. He kept me from thinking about anything that related to them, even in his death."

I swallowed hard and tilted my head to the left. I hoped he understood how deep that mindfuck went.

"Until I met Vaughn on Friday. Then, those words and phrases that triggered the memory magic didn't freeze my mind in agony anymore. When Vaughn and Novak unlocked them, everything came hurtling to the forefront. I wanted to kill you for keeping that from me.

"For years you hid the truth from me, York. You weren't thinking about what was best for both of us. You were being selfish. Thinking only of *you*. No matter how you try to spin it."

I pointed my index finger at him, wanting so badly to poke him in the chest.

"So, forgive me if I'm not quite ready to hear about how you felt, or how you feel about any of this shit," I ranted in a stern voice.

Sloane

I heard footsteps approaching from behind me and knew we now had an audience.

Great. Let's give a big round of applause for Sloane's temper and York's inability to keep his mouth shut.

"I had to, Sloane." He shook his head at me like I wasn't understanding.

"I couldn't tell you. Charles told me it wasn't time for you to know. I didn't understand, but I promised to keep my word."

He looked up to the brilliance of the night sky above us and sighed.

"If you had known, then you would've done something stupid, like try to rescue me by yourself when they took me. I couldn't let that happen," he argued.

"*They want you!*" York bellowed before calming himself.

"If they had you, then they would've drained you and never reached an end. There is no death for you that way, because there is no end to your fucking power. Don't you see that?" he asked, astounded by what he thought was ignorance.

"I wasn't being selfish. I was being selfless. Sacrificing myself to make sure they didn't get to you," he shouted.

"Selfishly selfless, how noble of you," I sarcastically quipped.

"Did you ever stop to think that I could've handled myself better in that kind of situation because they couldn't weaken me to the brink of death?" I proposed mockingly.

Too many emotions were bouncing around inside of

me, so I resorted to being a smartass. My hands were shaking with unrepressed rage as I filtered through my feelings, noticing some of them weren't my own.

If he yelled at me one more time, this would turn into a knock-down drag-out and I would throw him right over the edge of the roof. Into the pool.

"No!" he shouted, and I fucking lost it. "They caught you once and—"

"Because I fucking let them!" I interrupted, seething and seeing red as I stepped closer to him.

"I had a plan, and it all flew out the fucking window when you had my memory tampered with!" I screamed and swung my left hand hard, connecting with York's nose.

The soft crunch it gave was a satisfying sound, but it made my hand hurt.

"I deserved that," York told our audience as he wiped at the blood running down his lips. He was harder than I remembered.

Fucking mate bond. He'd opened it up. That was where all these extra feelings were coming from.

"If you hadn't overstepped in the very fucking beginning, none of that bullshit would have happened to you!" I continued raging, unable to stop myself at this point.

"Those assholes would have been gone. Dead, York, they would've been dead! But, noooo. You had to take matters into your own hands. Matters that had nothing to fucking do with you! They were *my* godsdamn matters to deal with, and you took that choice away from me."

Sloane

I shoved him, but he didn't move very much.

What a great time for him to show me that he'd gained my strength.

"I deserve that too," he said to the males behind me as I finished screaming at him.

It just made me swing on him again.

He was being too calm now. I didn't like it. *This wasn't how York acted when we argued.*

"Fuck. Off." I spat the words at him.

"Well, I don't deserve that," he assured us all.

I heaved oxygen into my lungs until I couldn't hold anymore, and then I swung harder than before. The fae caught my hand before it connected with York's nose again, and I cursed under my breath.

"You guys need to calm down." He spoke to us like children, and I almost decided to act like one.

Instead, I snatched my hand away and stomped across the roof, ignoring everyone. *I'd throw my tantrum when I got to my room.*

I made it to the top of the stairs before Palmer grabbed my hand gently and tugged me down the first flight, leading me to my bedroom.

With a flick of his magic fingers, the doors opened and the lights turned on for us. He scooped me up and carried me to my bedroom, tossing me on the bed as he shut the door with his foot.

"Vaughn's right. Ya need ta settle yerself, an I know just how ta help with that."

I watched him wearily. Not because I was worried about what he had in mind, but because I wasn't sure if he was going to calm me down or get me more worked up.

Gods. If this didn't end with orgasms, I would blow a fucking gasket.

Palmer didn't ask me to strip, or even bother with my clothes. He moved his right index finger in a swirling motion in the air and cuffs tightened around my wrists and ankles.

I went from sitting up in the center of my bed to stretched out like I was on a horizontal St. Andrews Cross, naked and stunned.

I tested what I thought were straps, hearing them rattle. *Not straps, chains.*

He smirked at me while he unbuttoned his shirt. I raked my eyes greedily over his exposed chest and licked my lips. My brain did a happy little hip shake, tossing all my thoughts astray like a deck of cards catching in the wind.

He pulled a crop out of... where? *Where had that crop come from!?*

"Now that I have yer attention," he murmured, inching the head of the crop across my calf.

The cold leather was a stark reminder that I'd just been bested by the mage.

couldn't budge these fucking chains. The more I pulled on them, the tighter they got; until I reached a point where I could no longer move anything but my head.

His smirk held firmly in place as his attention centered on my bared position.

"Ya have to let go of that rage, Love."

A swift blow to the top of my right thigh had my breath hissing with my inhale.

"Ya can't stay angry with the druid forever."

The smooth fingers of his left hand rubbed circles on the small tender spot he'd left.

"I can try," I mumbled, knowing that I sounded like a petulant child.

"Did I say ye could speak?"

The Mage ran his glowing, orange-tipped index finger over my lips. When I tried to reply, nothing came out. My lips moved, but there was no sound.

This motherfucker just muted me!

"There. That's better," he whispered in my ear before leisurely gliding around my bed.

My eyes stalked his back-and-forth movement, waiting for the next strike to land.

"What he did may have been selfish in yer eyes, but it was also valiant. Ya can't always put yerself in the line of fire, Love, even if ya would've fared better."

The next swing struck my lower abdominal muscles, swift and gentle. It didn't sting, but the noise kept my predatory attention fixated on his movements.

Still, I could say nothing, only listen and feel. From the left to the right, he ambled around my bed, searching my body.

The aged, brown head of the riding crop stroking up one leg and down the other, across my peaked nipples, then dragging against my sides.

He was driving me wild.

I quivered with need as he continued to tease and castigate me simultaneously.

"Try naw ta be so hard on 'im."

The smack to the inside of my left thigh struck my pussy as well. The sting of the crop landing had me panting and frustrated.

"We all would've done the same thing ta keep ya safe. Especially if we'd all had the time between us that you and York had. Don't ya think for a moment that a single one of us would sit back and let anyone torture *you* when we could take yer place. We all feel that way."

His soft Irish accent grew thicker with the honesty and emotion in his voice.

The final blow was two quick strikes against my nipples that had me wishing I could do something more than lose my eyes in the back of my head.

He dropped the crop on the floor when he reached the foot of my bed. Crawling up slowly between my legs, he rubbed his clothed body on my naked skin until he was leaning over me.

The kiss he gave me had the intensity of a tornado, wrecking my mouth and destroying my mind.

"When ya make up with York, I'll give ya what ya really want," he promised after he pulled away.

I couldn't remember what I really wanted. *I was pretty fucking close to forgetting my name.*

Palmer slid back down my body, giving me a hellish grin. His tongue felt like satin as he lapped at my clit, and I could do nothing to show my appreciation.

I tried to moan, but I still had no voice. I tried to

squirm, but I had no freedom to move. I could only endure his form of punishment.

If this was what happened when I got mad, I was going to stay mad.

The fingers on his right hand eased around the entrance of my core, sending me into a spiraling feeling of bliss. He pushed two of those gloriously long fingers inside me and curled them like he was trying to touch his tongue.

I was a few "come here's" away from cumming right there.

His fingers were fucking magical.

When he felt my walls tighten around him, Palmer nipped lightly at my clit before sucking the bundle of nerves between his lips. That was all it took for the air to rush from my lungs.

His hold on the silencing spell dropped, and my newfound voice cracked as I screamed his name.

When my orgasm finally subsided, his eyes roved over my body one last time. He held a mischievous glint in those stormy gray orbs that I didn't quite like.

He got off my bed at an exaggerated pace before leaning over me to lay a brief, tender kiss on my lips.

Then he winked at me and moved for the door, only stopping to toss over his shoulder, "Now, be a good girl," he urged.

"I don't like goin' back on my word, and it's getting harder to maintain my promises." He adjusted the wondrous bulge in his khakis as he turned the knob to my bedroom door.

He was gone before I could say anything. I was *still* naked, chained to my fucking bed. *In magical chains!*

I'd never seen anything like these infernal things. I couldn't break or bend them. *I couldn't even move!*

I could hear him laughing as he walked out of my suite, leaving all the doors open behind him.

I shouted with a snarl, "You rotten fucking Irish bastard!"

His laughter increased, and I growled in a very unladylike way to release the frustration I was feeling.

A set of footsteps halted my tangent of creative curses. They were too heavy to be Novak or Stone, too light to be Briggs or Vaughn.

York. Fuck my life right now.

He knocked casually on my door.

"Come in," I conceded begrudgingly.

His head popped around the corner, the smile dropping from his face as he took in my predicament.

"I was going to see if you wanted to join me in the greenhouse, but I can see you're a little tied up. I'll just, uhm, come back later." He bit his lips together, and I wasn't sure if it was to fight a smile or to stop talking.

"I'm going to kill that fucking mage," I whispered to myself. "If you can get me out of these chains, I'd be happy to accompany you to the greenhouse."

That was a half truth. Would I go? *Yes.* Would I be happy about it? *Mmm, that was debatable.*

"Sure thing, Sweetheart." He walked over and uncinched the cuffs like they were just plain old leather constraints from the adult toy store.

Sloane

When I was free of my confinement, I looked them over, searching for sigils or magic symbols. *There was nothing on them.*

Fuck it.

I grabbed a pair of denim shorts and a t-shirt, dressing as I followed York to his favorite room in the house.

I dreaded the conversation that would come with this, but my anger was focused elsewhere at the moment.

He opened the door and closed it soundlessly behind me. The dim nighttime lights flickered on as we proceeded deeper into the druid's personal wonderland.

He stopped in the center of the room and turned to face me, his apology clear on his face before the words rolled off his tongue.

"I'm sorry. I shouldn't have pushed you. I don't want to talk about it anymore until you're ready." He held his hand out to me and gave a half smile. "Would you like to dance? It's been ages since we—"

"Yes," I cut in, taking his hand. "What are we dancing to?"

"Frank?" he questioned.

I didn't know if he was addressing Franklin or answering my question with another, but soon the music started up. Frank Sinatra's *Something Stupid* played just loud enough to hear the words.

The near perfect words.

He stepped to the beat, and I followed his graceful lead. His right hand gripped my left tightly. His left hand rested on the dip in my waist, and my right hand wrapped around the back of his neck.

He closed his eyes as we swayed around the small, empty space in the center of the greenhouse.

We used to dance for hours between the path and open space of the greenhouse.

This song and this moment brought back a rush of memories.

My chest tightened painfully as a tear rolled down my cheek. Despite everything that had gone on, and gone wrong, it was things like this that showed me how simple everything could be.

This. This was my York. Sweet, romantic, understanding.

We spent hours dancing, just the two of us, reliving our past together. The songs changed tempo and we switched our steps, moving in sync like we always did.

The bond between us was unmistakable now that I knew what to look for. I could feel his emotions as strongly as my own. His regret, pain, happiness, contentment, and exhaustion all took root in my soul.

When the playlist ended, he gazed down at me. The corners of his lips tilted slightly as his thumbs wiped at the tears trailing down my cheeks.

This was what we needed. It was where we should've started.

It was where we always started when we argued.

He leaned down and planted a kiss on my forehead.

"Goodnight, Sweetheart." His hushed breath was tired and filled with sadness.

"I'm sorry too," I confessed quietly to his retreating back.

"I know," I heard him admit.

His contentment sprouted, growing stronger and overshadowing his sadness and pain. I heard him descend the stairs, and when I was finally alone, I peeked around the humid room.

The plants looked healthier than they had when we entered. I swayed to the music still repeating in my head, circling the brick path and singing quietly to myself…

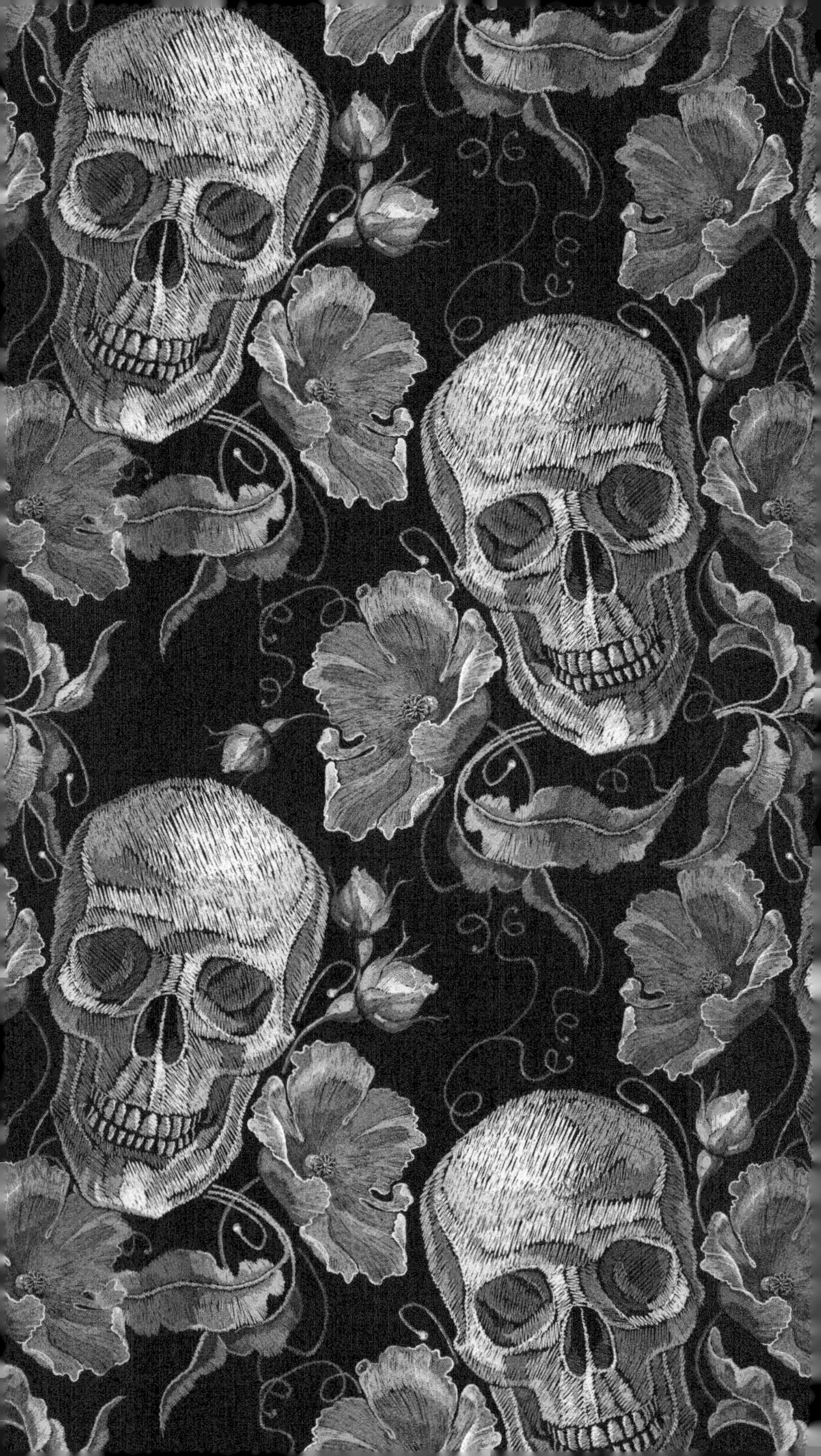

CHAPTER 28
Sloane

Tuesday, May 19th
Early Morning

Singing to myself grew lonesome in the still greenhouse, so I decided to enjoy the leftover night outside.

I putzed down the stairs one by one, watching the motion lights flicker on every eighth step, all the way to the basement floor.

I stripped out of my clothes and soundlessly dove into the deep end of the pool. I didn't come up for breath until I was beyond the glass wall separating the indoor section from the outside.

When I spotted Novak sitting on the edge with his

feet dangling in the water, I felt the instant relief of having company after everything the night had thrown at me.

The water was warm and welcoming as I floated on my back, gaining me the perfect view of the night sky above. Helios was stretched out beside Novak, to my surprise.

He'd always been a sucker for an ear scratch, though.

The vampire ran the fingers of his left hand through the dense reddish fur of Helios' English Mastiff form in slow, even strokes as he looked out into the woods.

"You make up with York yet, Trouble?" His whispered question had me flipping over to stand and look at him.

"Sort of," I admitted.

Was I still mad? *A little.* Was I getting over it? *Yeah.*

I started wading through the water, feeling a strong urge to be closer to him. Helios huffed smoke at me, becoming irate when I interrupted Novak's attention.

"I can hear some of your thoughts now, since he opened your bond back up." Novak continued with his gently spoken words, never stopping his rhythmic motions as he petted the hellhound's head.

"Your chest is glowing," he added, looking down at me where I stood in front of him and pointing with his right index finger.

He was right.

In between my breasts was a symbol I'd never noticed before. It was similar to a V, the usual straight lines bowed with the tops pointed out. A small, solid dot sat at the bottom and top left, almost touching the main symbol.

It was my mate mark. The mark of a druid.

As I stared down in awe at it, the glowing white light faded until it left a shimmering residue behind.

The longer I looked on, the more that glittering effect paled. The color stayed with it after the glow left, making it look like an inch-long, white tattoo.

"I wonder where the rest of our marks will go when you get them," Novak mused aloud.

"I wonder how we'll even find a mark on you, or Briggs, with all those tattoos covering your skin." I countered his musings with my own, and he grinned at me.

"I guess you'll have to search my body like an "I Spy" book," he chuckled.

"I certainly wouldn't mind that," I confessed while eyeing his shirtless torso.

"I haven't really been able to get a good look at what's going to be on your body for centuries." I grimaced, faking disgust when I spoke.

We both cackled, causing Helios to growl as he stood and walked away. He left scorch marks on the concrete around the pool with each step, and I shouted at him, "Don't you dare burn my grass!"

As soon as his paws touched the earth, little circles of fire appeared under them. *All the way around the side of the house. That asshole!*

I pushed myself up to sit on the edge of the pool beside Novak, and he laid his shirt down with such speed

I nearly missed the movement. Instead of my bare ass hitting the rough surface, I ended up sitting on his worn, cotton t-shirt.

It was thoughtful shit like this that kept a bitch on her toes, you know?

I rested my head on his shoulder while he leaned his cheek against my wet hair. We sat, unmoving, and watched the sunrise begin to streak across the night sky.

The navy backdrop, speckled with glistening stars, gave way to my favorite sight in the world. Twilight merged into purple, followed by fiery oranges, neon pinks, and brilliant reds.

The sun peeked over the mountain landscape, slowly bringing light to the darkened woods around us.

"You never opened this." Novak's hypnotizing voice rang out loudly after all the chirping of the crickets had quieted.

He casually handed me a crisp, white envelope with "Ms. King" handwritten on the front.

"What is it?" I examined the parcel as I inquired about its contents.

"It's the letter that was left in the busted safe in David Preston's office." He glanced at me before returning his attention to the morphing sky.

"I don't really want to open it," I admitted reluctantly, "but I guess now's as good a time as any."

I slid my nail along the seal, tearing the paper to expose the inside. With careful hands, I pulled the letter from the envelope and gasped as a piece of gold fell onto my lap.

Sloane

Novak caught it before it tumbled into the pool. I could only stare wide-eyed at it. Memories swirled around my mind with the single look I got.

I knew what it was, but I wouldn't get my hopes up.

"This belonged to your mother," the vampire at my side stated.

"How do you know?" I fought to suppress the panic I felt from rising.

There was no reason to freak out. Calm down, Sloane. You have to pencil freak outs into your schedule. You don't have time for this kind of shit.

"I told you earlier," he reiterated. "I can hear more of your thoughts. Before, I could only hear a word or two from time to time. But just then, I was able to get a glimpse of your memory," he confirmed.

"I saw you, as a little girl, staring at a picture of a woman who looks so much like you. She was wearing a necklace. The gold chain held this charm," he unclamped his fingers and dropped the charm into my hand, "and three others."

"She never took that necklace off." I sucked in a breath and thought of Father's current search.

"It doesn't change anything, though. She could still be alive, or she could have been dead for many years. Whoever sent this could've been waiting for the right time to bait me. I can't jump into anything blindly."

I rubbed my forehead with my free hand. "There's so much going on and even more to do. I need to call Papi."

"Read the letter first. Then we'll call him."

He took the empty envelope and the charm from me,

freeing up my hands. I unfolded the letter with a surgeon's precision, unsure if it held anything else.

> *Ms. King,*
> *It seems that the Fates have decided our paths shall finally cross. I do look forward to meeting you, but I thought a friendly warning might serve you well.*
> *You see, I have something that you're going to want. In return, I would've asked that you stop your investigation into my business endeavors. We both have the Sight to see that won't happen, so I'm giving you a deadline. If you want what I have, then you'll have to find me before the next new moon.*
> *While you search tirelessly for me, I'll enjoy watching you fail. Every move you make, I will have someone there to stop your best efforts. You will not win.*
> *We've already had unprecedented success with eradicating shifters. I'm moving on to the next species.*
> *Catch me if you can, Little King.*
> *Sincerely,*
> *-Mr. Moore*

"What the fuck?" I angrily whispered to myself.

Novak snatched the letter from my hand and read through the handwritten threat. The chicken-scratch writing was difficult—but not impossible—to read.

Sloane

Who the fuck did he think he was talking to!? I'm Sloane motherfucking King. I do NOT lose.

"Calm yourself," Novak chided, clearly hearing my current thought process. "There's plenty to be learned from this letter, and there's a possibility that Palmer can trace it."

"Like what? That he's proper because he signed it sincerely," I fumed.

I wasn't mad enough to skip mocking the fae accent when I said proper, though.

"No, Trouble. You're pissed and you're not thinking straight." He confronted me without a hint of regret.

I fucking loved that he wasn't tiptoeing around this.

He was right, though. I needed to calm down and think this through.

Think, bitch.

"He knows you won't give up, so he's had to switch his tactics," Novak started.

"And, he has to be in contact with a high-ranking demon to have access to the Fates," I theorized. "He's also using someone *with* Sight. That's a vampire trait, not fae or mage."

"Right. We found out about the potential next target with no hints from him." Novak smirked at me.

"And," he dragged out, "it sounds like he thinks you're doing this by yourself. He doesn't know that you have mates. He's not counting the people who will stand by your side."

His eyes spoke volumes as he picked apart the short letter.

"You're right." I tilted my head to the left, thinking through all the information.

He was very right.

"I read the copy of your letter from Nathaniel, the one that Palmer has. I think he was on to something. It's time to start building alliances, and we're going to start with the vampires when we go to Baton Rouge."

He was so certain and confident, but I needed to know if he knew what he was saying. I knew how I felt, and I knew the difference, now, between my feelings and the bond's urges.

The feeling of giddiness when he nudged me with his shoulder was ridiculous, but all mine. The need to be closer to him earlier was the bond trying to pull us together.

"Are you sure, Novak? I don't want us to rush into anything that you may regret later."

The look he gave me could've had half of Hell frozen in its tracks.

"I'm positive," he affirmed. "I was before reading that letter, I will be tomorrow, and I won't change my mind in a hundred years."

He leaned down and gave me a chaste kiss.

"If you're getting cold feet, you should take them out of the water," he advised.

"You know that's a saying about marriage and..." I paused as a provoking grin split his handsome face. "Oh. Ha. Ha. Very funny," I humorlessly supplied.

"Call your Pops. Let's make it almost official," he insisted, the smile never leaving his full lips.

Sloane

"Pah-Pee," I corrected him, slowly sounding the name out.

"Papi," he repeated, sounding amused with himself. "Don't try to stall now," he joked.

I smiled big at him, flashing a little fang, and he rolled his golden eyes.

Lifting my right hand between us, I summoned a flame the size of a softball with my intent solely focused on Papi.

Communication by hellfire was some of the first magic I learned as a child. Jack and I would talk to each other this way from our separate rooms, well past our bedtime.

We were such rebels.

I called quietly into the hellfire floating above my palm, careful to keep my hand above chest level since I was still naked, "Papi, are you awake? Is this a bad time?"

His response took no more than twenty seconds.

"Of course not, My Sweet Little Devil," Papi answered as his face appeared in the fireball. "Is everything okay?"

His brows and forehead creased in concern. He waited patiently for me to speak, but I didn't know where to begin.

"I don't want to tell him about the letter yet." I sent the thought to Novak, and he squeezed my thigh in reply.

"There are a ton of things going on, sir." Novak leaned his head next to mine so Papi could see us both. "We were able to recover the druid and shut down the power farm he was being held at."

That was a good start for information.

"Papi, I need you and Dad to meet us at Father's house. I'm still waiting to hear from Simon, but we have enough evidence to suggest something big is about to happen with the vampires."

I kept my voice low. I had no idea who could overhear us from his end.

"Something big like what, Sloane? What's going on?" he demanded of me, using my name and not my nickname to show me he meant business.

"We've heard that the drugs are now in the hands of vampires and being distributed, specifically by one Kadence Moore. I don't know if that's true or not, but with Father gone I need to step in and investigate," I acknowledged.

"Kadence is on the council, sir. She's not a fan of Sloane, and we're worried it could get ugly. Having Nathaniel's co-mates there could ease the tension when Sloane steps up," Novak informed Papi.

"I suppose it could," Papi agreed. "But it may also make it worse," he contradicted himself in the next breath.

"Having both of us there would be the prime time to challenge you for your position, Little Devil. Are you ready for that?" he warned me as he worried with his bottom lip, rubbing his teeth across the surface.

"Yes, sir." I looked to Novak, and he nodded his head. He was ready too.

There would be no going back when we reached the

Sloane

council. We would seal our bond and go through with the ritualistic traditions.

A vampire wedding.

Not to be confused with a human wedding; a vampire wedding was all about sharing blood and speaking an ancient oath. Since I was next in line, behind Father, we'd need his equals present to witness our ceremony.

His co-mates and his second-in-command.

After Novak and I sealed our bond, I'd take over as High Coven Mistress of Vampyre.

We would take over.

Novak would become the High Coven Master, second only to me as the true heiress.

"I'll call Charles now, but, Sloane," he paused, making me anxious. "Be ready for a fight, My Sweet Devil, and give that bitch Hell. She's been after Nathaniel and his position since before Amelia went missing."

"Yes, Papi. I will," I answered truthfully, my determination seeping into my words.

If Kadence Moore was after my Father and his position, then she would not like my interference.

Too bad for her. I gave zero fucks about what she liked.

As soon as we stepped up, she'd be removed from the council.

"Your Mother would be so proud of you. See you soon, Devil. I love you." With those last parting words, the flames dispersed from my palm into a heart before disappearing completely.

The Devil was a showoff. I didn't miss the fact that he called me Devil. He'd never called me *just* Devil before.

"You didn't want to tell him about the letter," Novak pointed out.

"No," I concurred. "I'd rather show it to them in person."

That was not a "phone call" sort of conversation to be had with my parents. The thought of seeing them at the end of the week excited me.

The knowledge that Novak and I would seal our bond in a couple days had filthy images running through my head.

I wasn't sure if they were mine or his.

"*They are definitely yours.*" His voice entered my mind with ease, but he laughed out loud. "Stop. You're going to kill me before we make it that far."

"I can't just turn them off." I shrugged my naked shoulders. "But it may help to act them out."

I bit into my lower lip and winked at him. He groaned, but before he could follow up with any sort of comment, we heard my phone ringing from inside.

"Where is it?" he asked me as he stood.

"In the pile of clothes that I left by the door," I shouted when he zoomed away.

He was back before the ringing stopped, phone in one hand and a towel in the other.

"Trying to keep me pure for our wedding night?" I jested with a flirty grin.

Sloane

"Trying to keep my wits about me," he replied, dry and fighting a grin of his own.

I turned my attention away from Novak and to my phone.

"Hello?" I answered after seeing it was Simon.

I put the call on speaker so I could wrap the towel around my body. *Talking to Simon on the phone while I was naked felt kind of wrong.*

"I'm in Baton Rouge, and I have news." Simon sounded strained and out of breath.

"What's happening?" I asked, seriousness taking over the last of my good mood.

"Are you sitting down?" he countered.

"Tell me, Simon," I growled out.

"This place is a madhouse. The council is at each other's throats. Dominic and Kadence are running everything into the ground without Nathaniel here to put his foot down." He stopped, and I vaguely heard a crash in the background.

"And?" I pushed.

"No one can find Nathaniel, and the lower covens are outraged that they aren't getting straight answers about where he is. I know that we know his general location, but I'm not disclosing that to these fucking idiots. You have to come down here, Lo. You're the only one who can step in and control this shitshow," he vowed.

That wasn't all, though. I could tell by his voice that he was leaving something out.

"What aren't you telling me, Simon?"

He sighed loudly, clearly not liking whatever he was about to tell me.

"There's been seventeen cases of infected vampires since Thursday. Kadence is telling everyone that Nathaniel is behind it, and he ran when it backfired. He's been gone for two weeks. It doesn't look good, Sloane."

"Alright, I'll start planning a trip down today. We should arrive late Thursday or early Friday. Stay around if you're safe. Come back if you're not. I don't want you to risk yourself. Clear?"

"Got it," he affirmed.

"Call me if anything changes." I hung up after that and sighed just as loudly as Simon had.

It seemed that there was no rest for the wicked.

All the shit that had been stacked up for me to deal with was finally starting to chip at my resolve. I knew I had help. I knew the weight of the supernatural world wasn't on my shoulders alone, but it felt like it was.

The door beside the pool opened up, and York trudged out, looking worried.

Fuck. I'd forgotten he could feel my emotions now.

I tamped them down and took a deep, steadying breath before smiling slightly at him.

"Sorry," I remarked, "I didn't mean to wake you with my rollercoaster of bullshit."

"It's okay." He yawned.

"I was having trouble sleeping before your emotions hit me, so I went back to the greenhouse. I saw some movement in the woods, but it didn't look like the boys," he fretted, never taking his scanning eyes off the wooden line at the edge of my property.

"I haven't heard anything," Novak disclosed, "but I wasn't specifically listening either."

I closed my eyes and reached out to my hounds. "Cronus is patrolling around the gate right now. I can't reach Atlas or Helios." I snapped my eyes open and jumped to my feet.

"What's wrong, Trouble?" Novak questioned.

I looked from him to York. "I can't reach Atlas or Helios," I repeated frantically.

"I don't understand. Are they sleeping?" He peered down at me with confused eyes.

"No, mate," York whispered as his bare feet stepped onto the grass. "They're down. Atlas is on the west side of the property. Helios is near the garage on the east side."

"Do you feel anything else?" I asked, barely audible.

"Someone's here, Sweetheart. We need to move inside." He started to walk backwards to the door, tugging my hand in his.

Novak took two steps and stopped suddenly, eyes fiercely searching the trees across from us.

"Movement," he mouthed with no sound from beside me.

I mentally called Cronus to us, keeping the connection open so he could see what I was seeing.

I listened for any unusual sounds.

"There. ten o'clock." I slide into York and Novak's minds.

We all tilted or turned, trying to spot what, *or who*,

was out there. I angled my body to the right and twisted my head like I was talking to the guys.

I really wished one of my powers was heat sensitive vision right now.

A sudden pain struck my right thigh, followed closely by a stinging sensation in my left shoulder. I felt the blood oozing out before I saw it.

The sound of a silencer registered too late for me to move out of the next bullet's trajectory. I looked at York's blurry face, his fear and rage consuming me.

"Call... Jack," were the last words I said before something slammed into my skull with the force of a freight train, and everything went black.

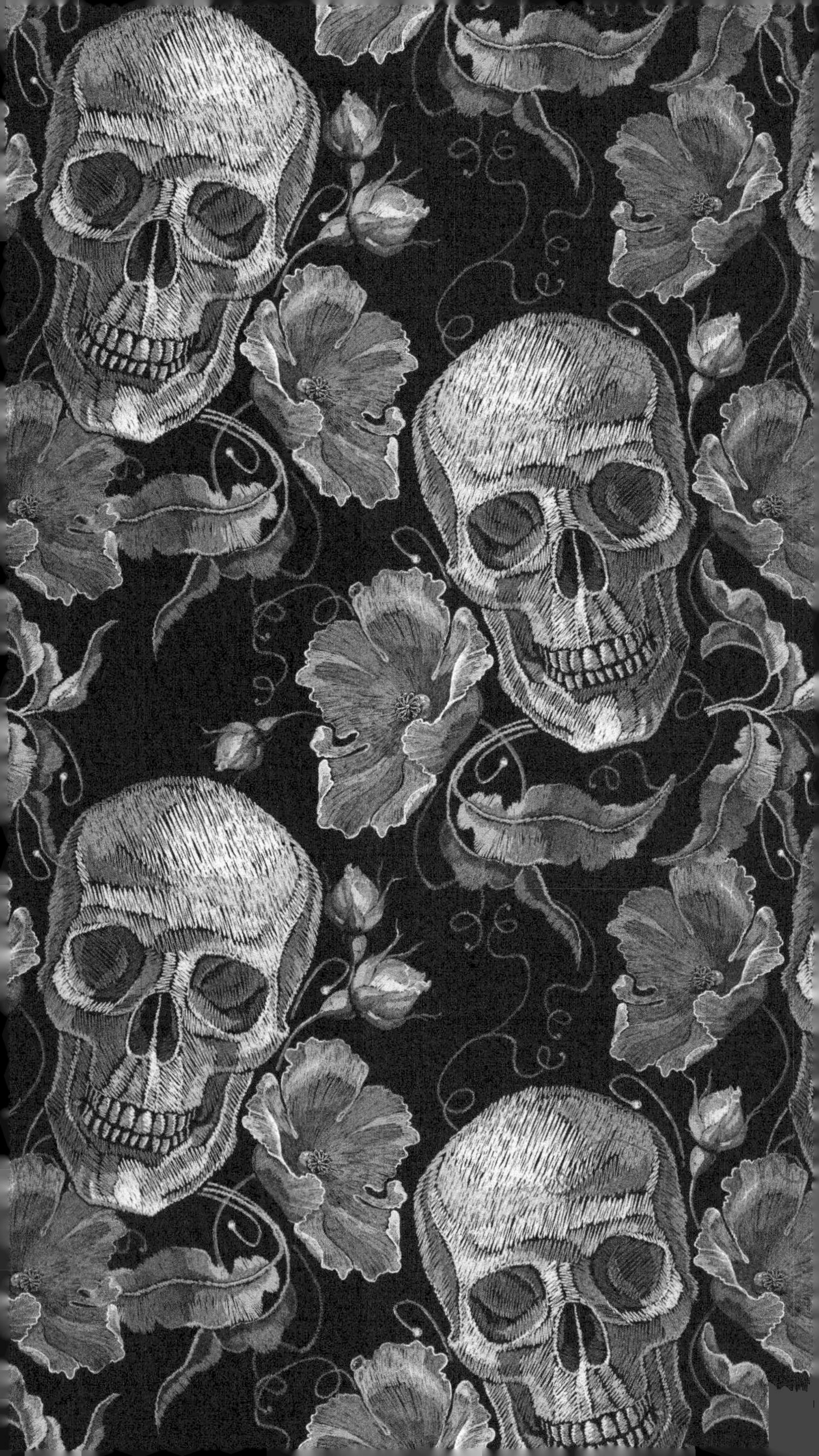

EPILOGUE

Kadence Moore
Tuesday, May 19th
Early Morning

Everything was going according to plan. Now all I had to do was sit back and wait for shit to really hit the fan so I could take over as High Coven Mistress.

A title I deserved much more than Nathaniel or his filthy daughter.

I'd been serving under Nate on the council for decades. No longer would I be willing to serve, though. I should *be* served.

The time to step up and forge a new path for the vampires was upon me. I'd made all the right alliances and planted the seeds of doubt in all the right minds.

As I sat on my throne, I picked dried blood from underneath my nails. I studied the lineup of poorly chosen, purebred vampires in front of me.

Old, young, weak, strong.

The weak ones never tasted good. They left a foul flavor lingering in my mouth when I fed on them. The old ones had a sour taste that always had me wishing I'd picked them a few years earlier.

Feeding from the young ones who weren't strong was like drinking liquid candy by the pint.

It was the strong ones that were addictive.

Strong *and* old could be compared to sipping an exquisitely aged bourbon, relaxing and intoxicating.

Strong *and* young blood was the cream of the crop. Draining one would have me flying high and brimming with magic. But draining two? I could run a week long marathon without growing fatigued.

The simply old and young were perfect specimens for my latest obsession. They could handle the side effects, allowing us to examine and research them properly.

The weak wouldn't last days before going mad. I pointed to each vampire that I wanted to dismiss.

My staff would take them away, promising them compensation for their time before injecting them with that brilliant fucking drug my brother created.

They would then be carried to my basement-turned-lab and quarantined for five days. If they made it that far then I would release them, after placing magic trackers under the skin on their necks.

Epilogue

The two vampires left standing in front of me were in for a treat. They were going to have the honor of being my meal.

I strode to the impeccably dressed female on the right. She'd be the perfect appetizer. I motioned with my hand for her to follow me to the soundproof chamber near my bedroom.

I didn't want to scare away my main course.

When I closed the metal door behind us, she started to shake. She would find no remorse from me, though. A Queen had to eat, and my subjects were scrumptious.

I attacked from behind without warning, giving her no time to defend her back. I wrapped my hand around her neck, squeezing just enough to hear her choked cry of surprise.

"Scream for your Queen," I commanded her.

The first shriek was music to my centuries old ears. I closed my eyes to revel in the echoing sadness that she felt.

She knew this was the end of the road for her. It would make her taste all the better.

I slowly pierced the flesh of her neck, holding my venom back. I wanted her to feel honor in her sacrifice. She was noble, even if she was unwilling.

Her blood held the flavor of sun-ripened strawberries picked fresh from the field. It reminded me of my childhood with my twin brother, Kelvin.

He'd love the taste of this one enough to not drain her. I didn't have that kind of control.

She went quiet and limp in my grasp. As I sucked away the last of her lifeblood, her skin chilled.

I dropped her to the ground when I was finished, wiping my mouth with my index finger and wearing a sultry smirk on my face. Someone would be along soon to clean up my mess.

She was a great choice, but the male would be better. I was already feeling tipsy and energized when I strutted out of the chamber.

No one else was in here, except me and the charming male before me. I'd make him watch in the mirror as I jerked him off, then drained him dry.

"Come with me," I encouraged in my drunken state. "Let your Queen pleasure you. Surrender to me," I whispered in a worship-filled voice.

I hooked my fingers in the waist of his pants and tugged gently to lead him to my favorite mirror.

It was a gleaming piece of etched artwork that was older than me. The fixture stood in the corner behind my throne like a frozen guardian, waiting to heat up and allow me passage to my father's location.

He owned one of the mirror's counterparts and had spelled the rest for fast travel to his children.

My main course didn't budge as I continued to tug at him. His curled upper lip twitched with distaste and rebellion.

"You are not *my* Queen. You're nothing but an unchaperoned advisor to the Master whose ego has outgrown her title," he growled out.

Epilogue

My manic laughter reverberated around the empty room.

"Oh, sweet boy," I acknowledged as I grabbed his jaw in an iron grip. "I am your new Master. I am your Queen. You *will* show me respect, or I will freeze your blood, stick a straw in your heart, and drink you like my favorite cocktail."

Now that I was thinking about it, that sounded like a grand idea.

He tried to pull his bottom jaw from my fingers, so I tightened my hold.

"You are nothing," he ground out, striking every nerve in my body with his blatant disrespect.

My left eye jumped as I forced myself to remain calm.

"Marge," I yelled, "bring me my vodka."

I dragged Mr. Rude to my mirror with my grip on his jaw alone. I heard a snap followed by his hiss of pain. I smiled viciously, feeling accomplished and a little less irritated.

When we reached the dais my throne and mirror sat upon, I snapped my fingers, thrilling in the sound of shackles dropping from the rafters above us.

I cuffed his hands and spun my right index finger in the air to shorten the length. By the time I was done, he was barely standing on his toes and Marge had appeared with a bottle of vodka and two stainless steel straws.

I waited for her to leave before I addressed the nuisance in the room.

"Scream for your Queen, and watch as I suck every drop of lifeblood from your body," I demanded of him.

I opened the top on my bottle of vodka and dropped one of the straws in, taking a big swig and enjoying the burn trailing through my chest.

I inspected my second straw as I confidently spoke the spell to drop his body temperature. It had to be precise. I wanted him to be conscious long enough to watch himself wither away at my touch.

I plunged the sharpened metal straw into his chest, careful not to pierce all the way through his heart. I capped the end of the straw with my thumb to keep his blood from spilling before I was ready.

With one more sip of vodka in my mouth, I removed my thumb and eased the straw passed my tightly sealed lips. He didn't taste as good as I'd hoped, but his disobedience made up for his lack of flavor.

I drank and drank until I felt my stomach swell. I was riddled with disappointment because he never made a sound.

By the time I had him sucked dry, my mind was so muddled I could only stumble to my plush throne and enjoy my inebriation.

High on the life of victims, I tried to coherently think about what was going to happen tonight. I hated relying on a human, but they were so easy to manipulate.

One of my informants filled me in about a man named Taylor Caplin who had been stalking Sloane King. That made him the best choice for the job I needed done.

Epilogue

I'd driven to Nashville last night in search of him. Once I'd found him, I'd had no trouble compelling the idiot to do my dirty work.

Now I was just waiting on his call to confirm the deed was done.

That had been my second trip to Nashville in less than three days.

I'd gone on Friday and spotted a very drunk woman outside of CBP. That *was* the company my brother was using to complete the manufacturing of the newest version of his drug.

Before the Kings bullied their way into a takeover.

She was the easiest target I'd ever compelled. I asked her to come back in the early morning hours on Saturday to let some of my guys in. They'd been canvassing the property long enough to catch on to the accountant's strange schedule.

He took Mondays and Tuesdays off. He went in at four in the morning and didn't return after lunch.

He was running errands for my brother when he wasn't at work, but he was expendable.

My team waited in his office with strict orders to tear him apart. From the video they sent back, I could tell they took those orders very seriously.

They broke into his safe and removed all the incriminating evidence he had against my brother.

Check stubs, original ledgers, the days he came into the building. All of it.

It was too much information for Sloane to get a hold of. We could not risk it, so we tied up the last loose end.

My brother gave me a letter for her, which I thought was incredibly stupid, but I did as he instructed. One of the males I sent placed the letter in the busted safe for her to find.

After that, I brushed my hands clean of the mess and started getting my own agenda under way.

I wouldn't be waiting around for Nathaniel to come back from his misadventures. The tips he was sent were false.

I'd sent them.

His actions would lead to angry Summer Fae threatening the covens.

That's when I'd swoop in and save the day.

I just had to bide my time for a little longer. I needed to have Dominic taken out of the picture soon too. Then I could win over the apprentices, and no one with a title would challenge my ascension.

"Your High Coven Queen, Kadence Moore," I whispered quietly to myself before mimicking the sounds of distant cheering.

I stared with unfocused eyes at my cell phone, excitement coursing through my veins as I waited for it to ring.

"The bitch is dead. Long live the new Coven Queen."

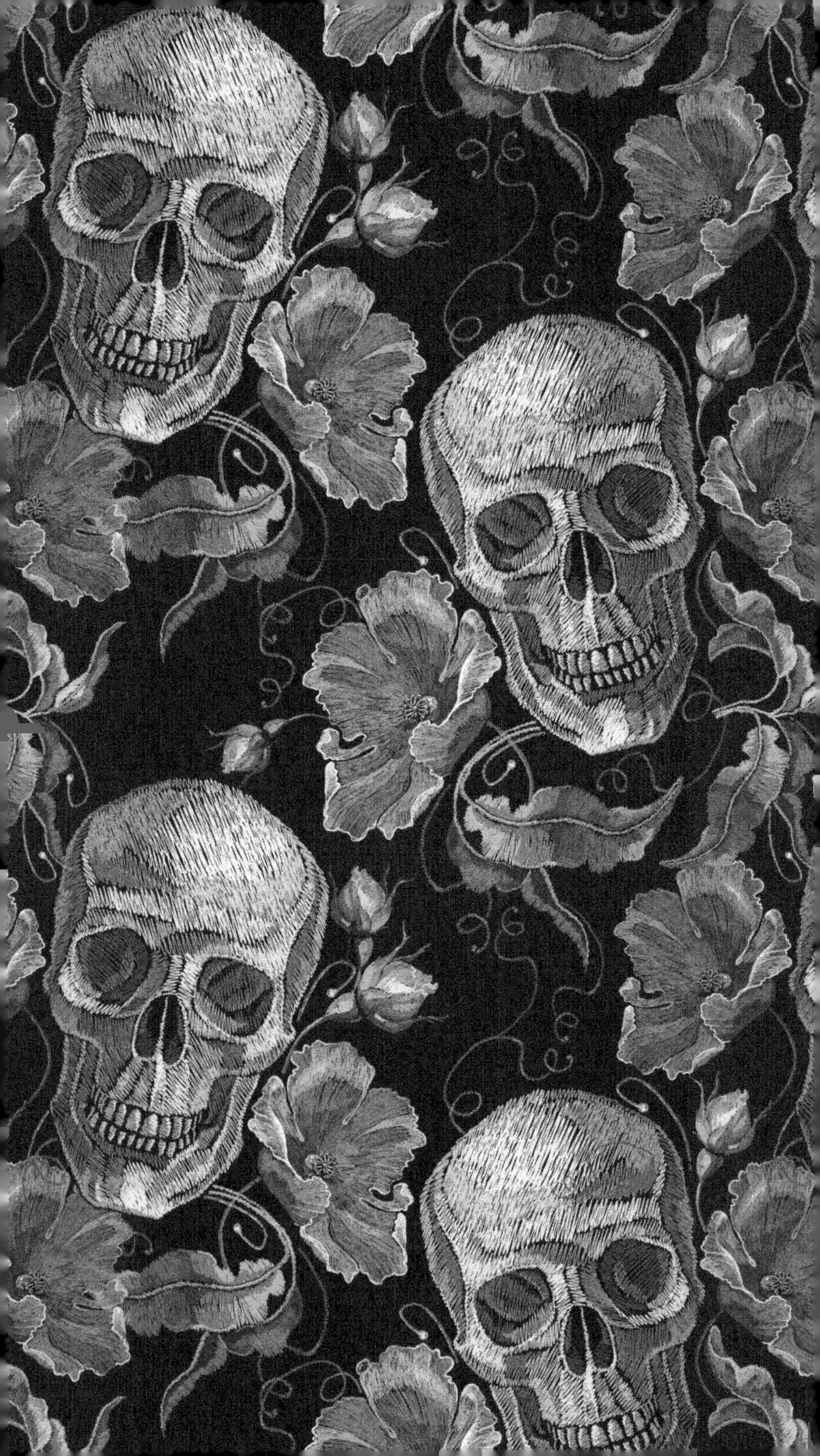

Character Information

Sloane King

    Hybrid - Druid Princess

York Briar

    Druid - Druid Prince

Novak Malin

    Vampire

Stone Embers

    Demon

Briggs Elliott

    Shifter

Palmer Lynch

    Mage

Vaughn Winterson

    Winter Fae - Winter Prince

Jack Steed-King

    Hellsteed - Sloane's best friend

Grim

    Grim Reaper - Jack's boyfriend

Character Information

Atlas, Cronus, & Helios

    Hellhounds - Sloane's pack

Franklin

    Vampire - Sloane's assistant - Weapons master

Samuel/Sam

    Demon - Second Devil of Hell - Sloane's papi

Charles/Charlie

    Shifter - Supreme Alpha - Sloane's dad

Nathaniel/Nate

    Vampire - High Coven Master - Sloane's father

Lucifer/Lucy

    Fallen Angel - First Devil of Hell - Sloane's grandfather

Lilith/Lil

    Demon - First Devil's Equal - Sloane's grandmother

Levi

    York's friend

Sarge

    Head of Club Security

Simon

    Vampire - Club Manager

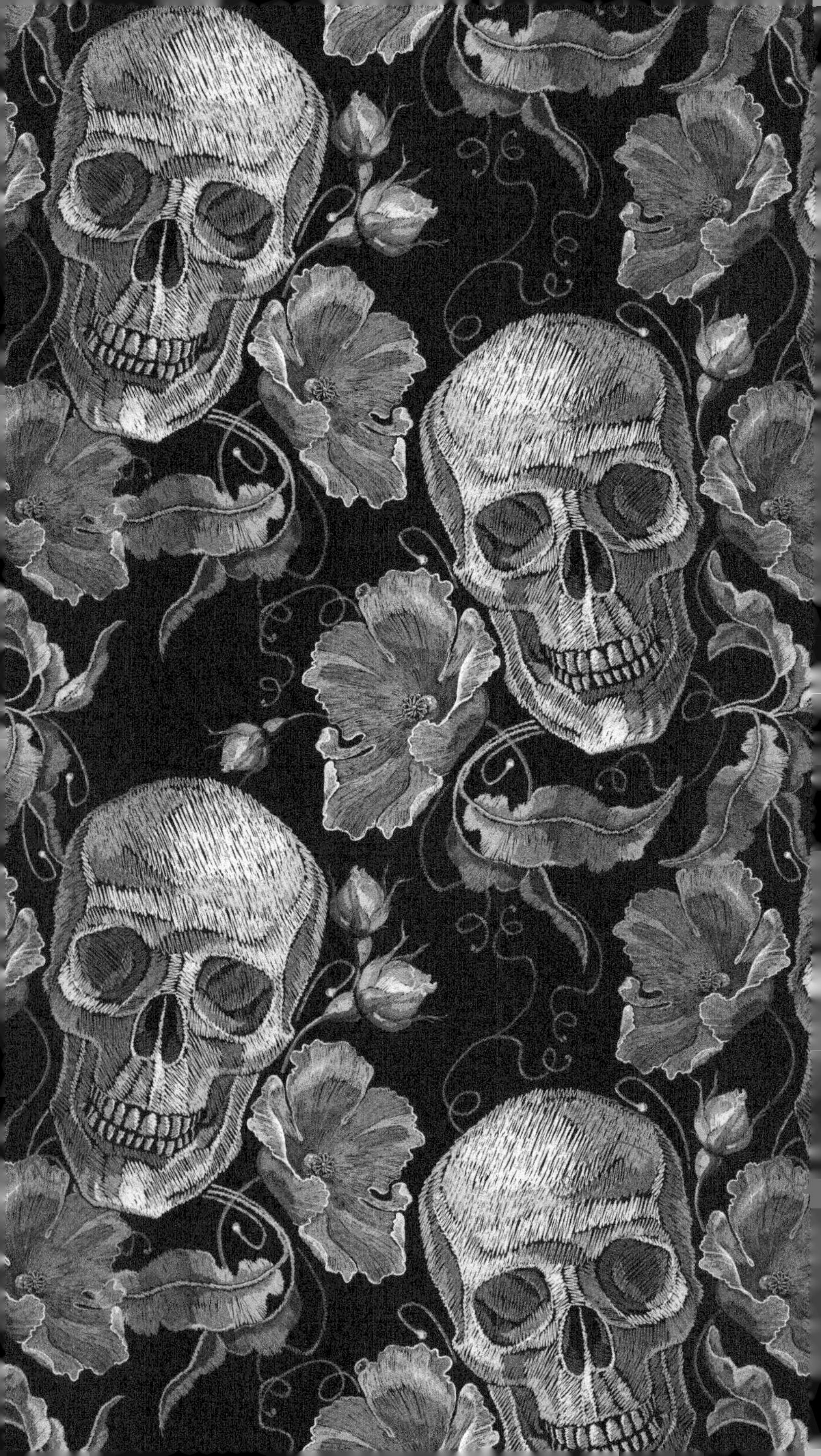

MORE PNR BY MF ADELE

The Chronicles of Sloane King
Druid Dreams - getbook.at/DruidDreams

Vampire Visions - getbook.at/VampireVisions

Demon Demands - getbook.at/DemonDemands

Shifter Situations - getbook.at/ShifterSituations

Mage Massacres - getbook.at/MageMassacres

Fae Farewells - getbook.at/FaeFarewells

Hybrid Heroics - getbook.at/HybridHeroics

King's Kismet - getbook.at/KingsKismet

Where They Are
Where the Mongrels Are

For the Strange and Surprising - getbook.at/StrangeSurprising

For the Ghastly and Beautiful - getbook.at/GhastlyBeautiful

For the Strong and Fragile

Armed & Venomous
Venomous as a Snake - getbook.at/VenomousSnake

CONTEMPORARY BY MF ADELE

Crimson Bay Cartel
The Rusted Heritage: Maldonado

No Name - getbook.at/NoName

TBA - July 2023

TBA - November 2023

TBA - January 2024

CO-WRITES WITH MF ADELE

Projects with TL Adele

The Chronicles of a Toy Monster

Onyx Sanctuary - getbook.at/OnyxSanctuary

Onyx Rebellion

Onyx Uprising

Projects with NV Roez

Dark Fairytale Retelling

Snow - July 14, 2023

Preorder coming soon

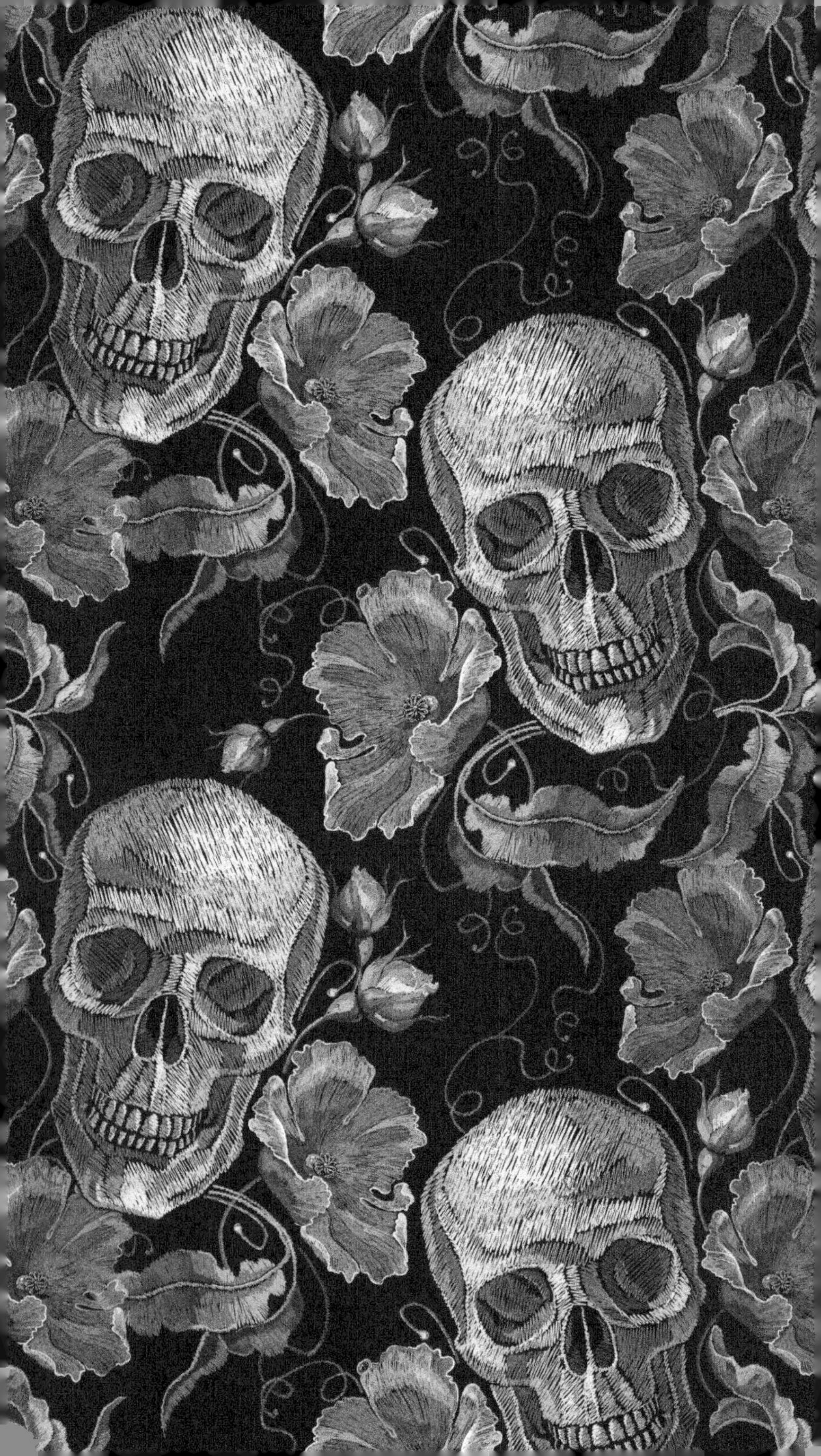

ABOUT THE AUTHOR

MF Adele resides on the outskirts of the Rocket City in Alabama. She lives in her overactive imagination, often fueled by caffeine and no sleep. When she isn't writing, MF is outdoors with her family or obsessing over spicy margaritas and cigars.

MF writes what she connects with. Her heroines are often emotionally challenged while remaining strong-willed. They're snarky, chaotic, and refuse to be damsels in distress. She has a flair for misdirection, keeping her readers guessing until the end. Within the complex worlds she builds, her stories feature epic battles, murders, and graying the lines of morality.

If you're looking for M.F. Adele, you can find her being consistently inconsistent in her group:

M.F. Adele's Hellacious Hybrids.

She likes to keep people on their toes... So you never know when she'll pop in with news.

For more consistent updates, join her newsletter.

Continue Sloane's story in ***Vampire Visions*** - The Chronicles of Sloane King 2.

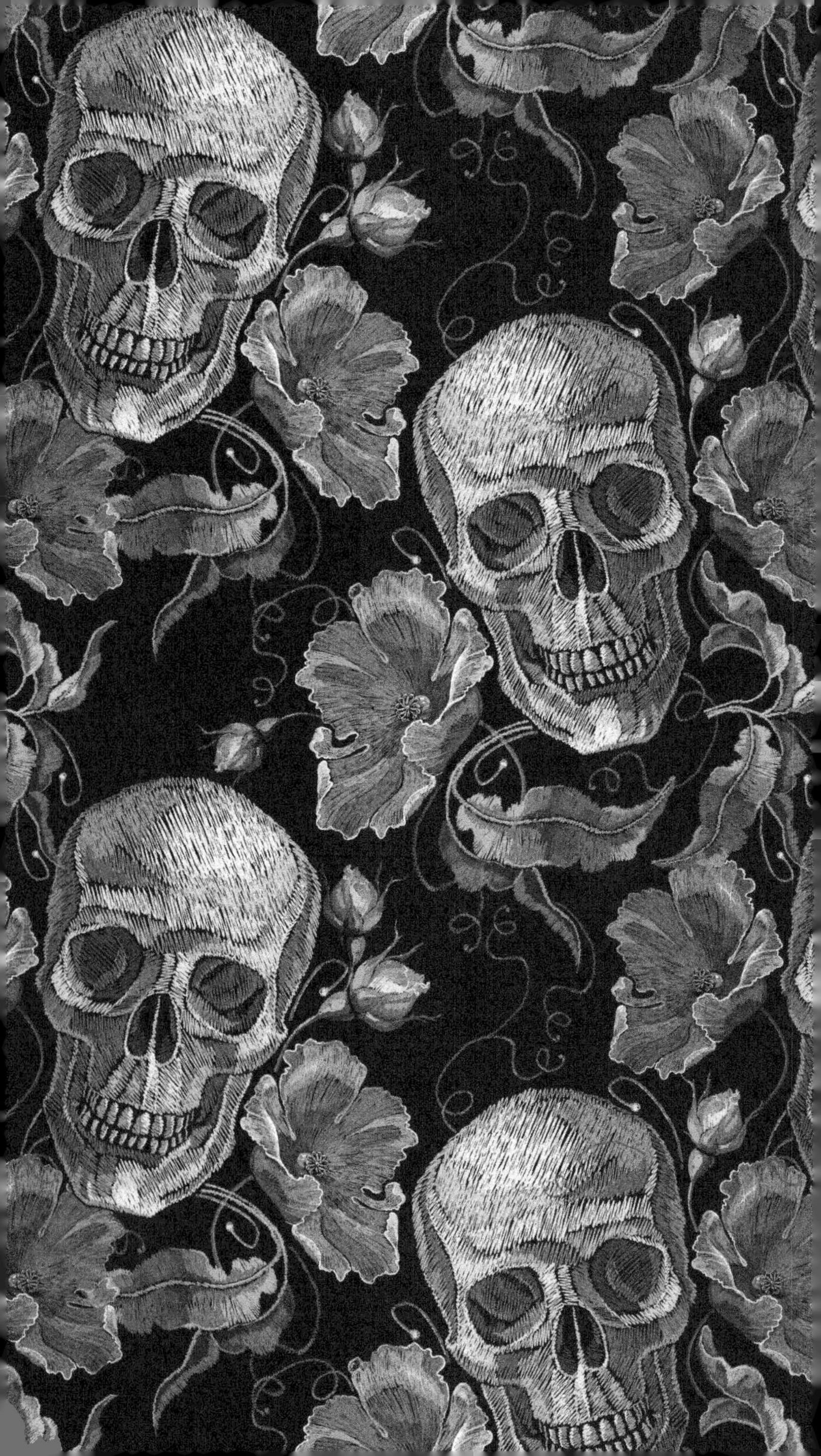

AUTHOR'S NOTE

I'd like to start this note off by thanking you for reading *Druid Dreams*. You are the bee's knees!

You're the fierce, badass main character of your own story, and I hope you never forget that shit.

If you ever need a reminder, come find me.

I got you, Boo.

Vampire Visions Blurb

I am not a good person.

I may have lied about the "occasional murder spree" bit, but I did say it was justified, right? It totally is, I swear.

Over the last week, countless heads have rolled—mine included. My life is becoming a roller coaster. Not the fun kind either. It's the kind that makes you sick when your feet finally hit the ground.

All of my mates are now living under one roof. My roof. And my ebony tower just got really f*****g crowded.

The trail to stop that drug just keeps getting more twisted. Now my guys and I are off to deal with the kind of psycho that makes me look like an innocent angel.

More bloodshed is coming, and it always comes at a price.

> *I'm Sloane f*****g King, Druid Princess.*
> *But don't let that title fool you…*
> *I'm no damsel in distress.*

M.F. ADELE

VAMPIRE VISIONS

THE CHRONICLES 2 OF SLOANE KING

Printed in Great Britain
by Amazon